EYE OF THE MOON

IVAN OBOLENSKY

ADVANCE PRAISE FOR *EYE OF THE MOON*

"Alice's complex character powerfully emerges as the plot's tonal center, a bewitching amalgam of moral strength, intellectual vitality, and a lust for life.... ingeniously constructed... an engrossing tale of mystery and magic."

-Kirkus Reviews

"*Eye of the Moon* throws you into the middle of the story, in a perfect way. It's gripping, intense, thorough. Everything I wanted in a thriller, and then some...."

-Nick Thacker, USA Today bestselling author, *The Enigma Strain*

"... A thrillingly eerie mystery novel with a Gothic ambiance and supernatural elements seeping through the storyline... a fabulously spine-chilling plot..."

- Susan Sewell for *Readers' Favorite*, 5 stars

"... The surprising revelations and apparent coincidences come fast and furiously as the novel approaches its climax, but the groundwork was carefully laid for this intricate plot structure."

-Bradley A. Scott of *Foreword Reviews*, 4 stars Clarion rating

"... The mysteries are finely woven together and readers must think fast on their feet..."

-IndieReader, 4.7 stars, IR approved

"… By the page 30, or so, I was well ensnared by Obolensky's captivating spiderweb. Richly nuanced, complex, highly readable, this yarn combines mystery, implied horror, the patrician class seen through a glass darkly, romance, and a wholly acerbic view of the inherent goodness (or evil) of man (and woman). *Eye of the Moon* is anything but an author's 'first work.'… A stellar, highly auspicious opening to a successful career."

-Hugo N. Gerstl, international bestselling author of *Scribe*

"As a reader, it felt as if this novel had been exclusively produced just for me… there's enough humour, mystery, suspense, romance and adventure to satisfy even the most jaded of appetites. … a gothic classic… a grand novel worthy of admiration and an extensive audience."

- Carl Delprat, *Compulsive Reader*

"*Eye of the Moon* is a rare and authentic glimpse inside the hidden world of America's upper class … Plan to stay up late. Once you get caught up in this extraordinary drama you'll find it hard to put it down. In ambiance it rivals *Downton Abbey*, but the plot tells a far more intense and shocking story."

-Tom Hyman, author of *Seven Days to Petrograd*

EYE OF THE MOON

A Novel

Ivan Obolensky

Published by Smith-Obolensky Media, DBA of Dynamic Doingness, Inc.

1146 N. Central Ave. #316, Glendale, California 91202

(818) 660-6852

www.smithobolenskymedia.com

ISBN: 978-1-947780-02-6

Publication date: February 6, 2018

Printed by IngramSpark in the United States of America

To Mary Jo, who started me writing.

NOTE TO THE READER:

This is a work of fiction. It is a product of my imagination. As with most stories, it is anchored in some form of reality. Rhinebeck existed. I visited only for a few vacations during my childhood, but its influence on my life was much greater than the time I spent there would seem to indicate.

The characters in this novel are not real, although some of the names are of people who lived. Most of them have passed away. None of them said or did the things I have written other than on the most conventional level.

The novel takes place in the period of the 1970s before there were cell phones and computers were in their infancy.

This work was written with only one purpose in mind: to delight the reader. If it does so, then I will have achieved what I set out to do. It is, after all, a story, and I like good stories. Most people do. I hope you will find it as delightful to read as it was to write.

Rain was threatening as I looked out my window on that Wednesday morning in the spring of 1977. I was anticipating breakfast in my room at the St. Regis in New York when there was a knock at the door. I answered in my bathrobe, expecting a waiter with a trolley, but in walked Johnny Dodge instead.

"Oh, no," I groaned.

Johnny was just over thirty. His blond hair was worn long, but he looked slim and fit in a dark pinstripe from whose breast pocket peeked a dark-blue handkerchief with small white polka dots that matched his tie. He wore a cream-colored shirt with french cuffs that were held in place by small gold Cartier cufflinks. I knew the cufflinks were from Cartier because I had given them to him several years ago.

He and I were practically brothers. We had grown up together. My parents were good friends with his parents, but mine were often traveling and out of the country. All concerned thought that such a nomadic lifestyle was ultimately not in my best interest and that I take up permanent residence at the Dodges'. There had been plenty of space in their Fifth Avenue apartment on the fourteenth floor overlooking Central Park. I slept in the same room as Johnny and went to the same schools. I was considered a semi-Dodge, which Johnny would often point out carried certain privileges but, just as importantly, carried certain asymmetric obligations that demanded my immediate involvement, even now, years later.

Now, I wanted to shut the door, but I didn't. I knew that he would only keep knocking or ambush me when I attempted to leave.

"And a nice hello to you, too, Percy," said Johnny. "Now, I know you're waiting for breakfast. Not to worry, it'll be up in a minute. I sent the order back and added some things because I'm joining you. We have a lot to discuss, and there's a car waiting downstairs, but we'll get to that in due course."

"We're going somewhere? Only to the airport to catch my afternoon flight back to California."

"Yes, yes, of course." He smiled at me, gave me a light slap on my shoulder by way of a hello, and then began rubbing his hands in anticipation as he looked around. "Nice room," he said, changing the subject.

Johnny could be so infuriating. He knew just what to say and what to do to get me to go along with his schemes. He always took advantage of my sense of obligation to him and his family, and I was sure this time was no exception.

"Johnny, I don't mean to pry, but how exactly did you manage to know I was here?"

"The concierge. He's on the Dodge family payroll, as if you didn't know, but I'm very glad he is, and you should be too."

"Glad?"

"Yes, very glad. I'm saving your bacon."

"Oh God."

I knew right then the situation was worse than usual. The

magnitude of the difficulty Johnny was involved in was in direct proportion to how much he thought someone else was at fault.

"None of this 'oh God.' You think that I have a big problem because I'm blaming you. Rest assured, you have a problem too. Think back to the last time you were up at Rhinebeck."

Rhinebeck was the name of the town in Dutchess County where the Dodge's hundred-acre estate was located, situated on a high bluff overlooking the Hudson River. Johnny and I called the estate Rhinebeck. We would often visit during school vacations, and in later years, it became a refuge on weekends.

Johnny took off his jacket and laid it on the bed before sitting down in one the chairs facing the window and waited for my response.

"The last time I was at Rhinebeck was with you quite a few years ago. Frankly, my memory's a bit hazy."

"Of course it's a bit hazy. You were in an alcoholic stupor for much of the time, and I must admit, so was I, but that's beside the point. Do you remember anything about you and me drinking a couple of bottles of Château Lafite?"

Rhinebeck did have an outstanding wine cellar into which Johnny and I often descended when no one was looking.

"Lafite, yes, they were very good, if memory serves. In fact, they were positively outstanding. I remember your delight when you discovered those two bottles hidden in the back of the cellar. We consumed both, one after the other, and you kept repeating that the wine was fit for the gods."

"Well, that may have been the case, but do you remember the vintage? Think carefully."

I thought for a moment and said, "Unfortunately not, but I do recall you saying that we'll cross that bridge when we come to it, should our pilfering be discovered."

"Too bad you don't remember the year because I don't either, and I'm afraid that the bridge may now be before us. Let me

3

explain. The parents have enjoyed quite a number of years of wedded bliss, as you know, and have an important anniversary coming up. They decided to celebrate the occasion with an intimate dinner for a select number of houseguests this weekend. You're invited, by the way. I managed to mention to them that you might feel slighted if you weren't, since you were in town and are family — or semi-family, at the least."

Johnny reached into his breast pocket and placed a small envelope made from thick cream-colored paper on a side table. I recognized the writing of Mrs. Dodge's secretary. "Your personal invite, as I know how you get when I simply say you're invited."

Before I could protest, the bell bonged, and Johnny jumped up to open the door. Two breakfast carts were wheeled in, and what looked like a veritable feast was set up in short order. The problem must be impressive. Johnny was pulling out all the stops.

Johnny thanked the waiters and passed them a couple of bills. "Keep the change," he said and hustled them out the door.

I grabbed a piece of toast and a cup of black coffee and looked over my eggs Benedict. "Okay, Johnny, you have me seriously worried. What gives?"

"Ah yes, I'll be getting to that. But first, let's dig in."

"Johnny!"

"Okay, okay, but I'm starving."

He poured himself a cup of coffee and grabbed a piece of toast with bacon, which he munched on between sentences. I ate and listened.

"A number of years ago the parents decided to lay away a couple of bottles of Château Lafite 1959 to be opened on a very special anniversary. Knowing how outstanding this wine was, they hid them in the back of the cellar at Rhinebeck. It was their secret, but last week I overheard them talking about their little stash. Well, imagine my horror when I found out that those bottles were not

4

kept under lock and key in New York, as they should have been, but hidden in plain sight where they could be discovered. They expect to drink what has been considered one of the finest vintages of Château Lafite ever created this Saturday night at dinner. I can barely conjure up in my mind the surprise and outrage they'll feel when they find out that those two bottles are missing — consumed some time ago by none other than you and me."

"I see. But did we really drink them? Perhaps we didn't, and they're still there."

"Too true, and therein lies the problem. We must be certain or come up with a plan to replace them."

"To replace them might not be too difficult," I said. "Correct me if I'm wrong, but aren't there cases of Lafite in that cellar?"

"Indeed, there are, but not '59s, or even '61s, I assure you. Bottles of those years are very rare. The parents even wrote little love notes to each other on the labels. I've been almost sick with worry thinking that we might have gotten our hands on them and that our theft is about to become very public knowledge — this week of all weeks."

"Bad week?"

"Horrendous." Johnny stood up and began to pace. He was definitely bothered. "I've been carrying the weight of the world on my shoulders for the last few days. The monthly trading report generates on Friday, and Father will be getting a copy for his review over the weekend. This will not make for a happy moment. Sometimes I hate that we have a family business."

"Bad report?"

"Awful. I really screwed up. A trade leg got unwound at the wrong time, really pumping up my losses for the month. He's aware of some of them, but not last night's attempted arbitrage, which really went south. He'll not be in a good mood after he gets the report. Add to that the missing wine, which they've been looking forward to for years, and my promising career could be flushed down the toilet."

Johnny made his way over to the window. He parted a curtain and looked out as if to distract himself. I knew from experience we were coming to the crux of the matter.

"And then there's the matter of Brunhilde," he whispered.

"Brunhilde?"

"Yes, Brunhilde. Bruni for short."

He turned away from the window and sat back down in his chair. He sighed and began to nibble nervously on more bacon. I let him take his time. At last, he stopped and looked at me.

"To add to my woes, Mother wants grandchildren and is eager to see me marry. She's put forward Brunhilde as a possible match. Not that she can force me. It's the twentieth century, after all, but she's starting to ratchet up the pressure as only mothers can. The whole subject is starting to get contentious between us. I know she'll lose patience completely if this latest gambit of hers should fall apart. To give you an idea of what's involved: Brunhilde's parents are Baron and Baroness von Hofmanstal. Very suitable and very rich. Mother has invited the three to Rhinebeck as houseguests for the special dinner and a look-around this weekend.

"Brunhilde, according to Mother, is extraordinary and able to stop traffic, which is the good news, and of which I have no doubt. The bad news is the mere thought of settling down with anyone makes me very nervous. I had a tarot card reading once, to say nothing of several other attempts at divining my marital future, and all have said the same thing with complete certainty: don't. One went so far as to say that a planetary disturbance of cataclysmic proportions might result and pleaded with me on hands and knees to never marry. I know you think that's a bit overly dramatic, but the incident affected me greatly, and I have, to date, avoided any such entanglements, with happy results.

"Besides, I fall in love far too easily, and that's always been my problem. I see no indication that my character has changed, or will any time soon, so I'd rather forego matrimony at all costs. My intention is to carry forward with my resolve, but I don't know if I can withstand a beautiful girl, my mother's machinations, and assured future great wealth for any extended period — hence, our conversation."

"Why, Johnny, that's quite a statement. I'm impressed with your astute self-observation. You never cease to amaze me."

I drank more coffee. The breakfast was having its effect, and the fact that Johnny was being so candid had softened my determination to resist at all costs accompanying him up the Hudson to Rhinebeck. The house's stately beauty cast a soft focus over much of my memory, but I knew that interspersed among the long interludes of tranquility and happiness were disturbing periods of disquiet, and more than one instance of terror that prevented me from simply acquiescing.

"Yes, even I can occasionally be aware of my own shortcomings. But there's once again more to it. I may have run into Brunhilde before, and meeting her again might prove to be extremely awkward."

"Oh yes?"

"Oh yes, indeed. I'm pretty sure I've met her. I mean, how many Brunhildes does one happen to run into who have black hair and electric-blue eyes and are called von-something? I never did get this woman's last name fully. I'd really like to forget that meeting. I place the blame squarely on that damn Robert the Bruce."

"The fourteenth-century Scottish king or your white bull terrier?"

"The dog."

"You told me that he was permanently banished to Rhinebeck. I take it this has something to do with that?"

"It does." Johnny got up, sat back down, and sighed deeply. "I've told this story to no one, and I impart it to you in strictest confidence only because if this is the same Brunhilde, you can understand my predicament."

"I'm listening."

"A few years back and very early one morning, I took Robert across the street to Central Park for a walk.

"I was going out with Laura Hutton at the time. She was very into dogs, so I purchased the young Robert the Bruce to impress her. I had no idea the breed was so damned pigheaded and ate anything that was not tied down. I mean, buying that dog was like jumping off a cliff and figuring that something would be worked out on the way down. I had no idea what I was doing.

"The creature was obsessed with tennis balls. I always carried a couple to throw and give him some exercise, along with one in reserve to help leash him when I wanted to return home. Of course, the little bastard would play coy and wait a few yards out, looking at me with those beady little eyes until I walked over and pried the damn thing out of his jaws. I'd utter a prayer that he wouldn't remove my hand in the process as he tried to get a better grip. I also had to be quick at firing the ball off again, or he would snap it out of my fingers with those teeth.

"That particular morning, we were playing fetch when up walks this absolute knockout with two yellow labs. She proceeded to let them off the leash and stood close to me. She asked if the bully was my dog and what its name was — that sort of thing. She looked my age, my height with black hair, wonderful clear pale skin, and the most electric-blue eyes I've ever seen. She was positively breathtaking, so much so that Robert went right out of my mind. He'd been waiting a few yards off, gnawing on the ball, expecting me to come get it. I'd normally respond rather quickly because left to his own devices, he'd pop the damn thing with his teeth and then rip it to shreds. This time, he flicked the ball in my direction, hoping to get my attention. But one of the other dogs intercepted and ran away with it.

"Well, this turned into a good-natured rumpus, with dogs bounding and sprinting here and there. We continued to talk and look up every now and again to see if everyone was behaving. I was facing the dogs, and she had her back to them when Robert decided that this amount of excitement had stimulated him to point that he needed to relieve himself. He hunkered down while the other two dogs swirled about with the ball. Everything seemed normal until I noted in the back of my mind that he was taking an inordinate amount of time. I wondered what he had been eating lately. He was some distance away, but the color of what he was producing appeared decidedly green, and that was odd.

"While I was watching, one of the dogs flicked the ball to Robert, who momentarily paused what he was doing and lunged for it, in spite of not having completed his business. He then proceeded to perform several 'run, stop, and hunkers' while the other two dogs tried to get the ball away from him. The more times he did this, the longer the greenish, brown log became. By now the length was such that even a Great Dane owner would have been astounded, and still it continued. I grew uneasy, but I was still captivated by the beautiful creature before me and spoke to her as if nothing was happening, while the more sensible part of my brain was beginning to register all this with some alarm. Her dogs started barking louder and louder as they became more and more impressed with Robert's Herculean performance. I, however, was hoping they would all just go away.

"I tried to keep the gorgeous lady looking in my direction, but the hue and cry proved too much. She turned to see what was going on.

"She gave a bit of a start and said in a breathless voice, 'Is there something wrong with your dog? He seems to be growing something out of his bum.'

9

"I actually said, 'Oh, that's quite normal,' or some such nonsense, to play the whole thing down, but truth be told, some perverted magician was performing some ghastly endless-handkerchief trick with my dog. The thing was now over three feet long, and to make matters worse, Robert had begun to bound and hunker in *our* direction. The ball now forgotten, the two labs followed, barking aggressively at the snakelike thing that flopped behind.

"I wanted nothing to do with him, but Robert had decided on this occasion to bring the ball to me.

"As he approached, the wonderful woman next to me suggested that I get a stick or something to help relieve the poor dog of whatever he was having trouble expelling.

"Her suggestion was not winning her any prizes, as my definition of complete mortification was being recalibrated upward by several orders of magnitude with each passing moment. I felt like I'd been thrown into some sort of horror movie, and I could not get my wits around what was happening — when I recognized what Robert was disgorging.

"Laura had been missing one of those expensive oversize scarves and was incensed over the loss. She said she was sure she had the scarf when she arrived for dinner the other night and that someone, probably one of the servants, had stolen it. Laura could jump to conclusions at the drop of a hat, but here before me was the answer.

"Robert had eaten it. Problem solved.

"I babbled some inane comment, but Robert the Bruce was now beside me. He banged the ball on my leg for me to take, when one of the woman's dogs managed to stand on the end of the thing while Robert jumped up. A foot more was expelled, and the whole mess fell to the ground. The stench was horrible, but the relief was immediate. Robert now jumped an additional two feet in the air with the ball in his mouth to get my attention.

"Instinctively I grabbed it out of his teeth and hurled it as far away as possible. All the dogs streaked away.

"I looked down and said, 'My God! Look at that. Hermes.' I gazed, fascinated, at what remained of Laura's scarf.

"Well, the person next to me interrupted my musings by saying, 'You're not going to just leave that on the ground? Aren't you going to pick it up and throw it in the trash?'

"Of course I was going to leave the bloody thing there. What else was I going to do with it? Only I didn't say that.

"She was beautiful, but she really was becoming a bit of a trial. All I wanted to do was flee. Under normal circumstances, I would've bolted and hoped that Robert would follow, but she stood in front of me, blocking the way, and continued to point out that I should somehow be responsible for the travesty that now lay before me. Whatever spark there was between us was rapidly disappearing. Giving in to her demands seemed the only course open to me.

"There were no trees nearby, so I stomped off to find some sort of stick to pick the thing up with and transport the remains to a trash can.

"Robert and the rest followed me with the ball. I took out my frustration by hurling it very far away indeed, and off they flew again.

"After several minutes of searching, I finally found a suitable pair of sticks and returned. I'd hoped that during that time she would have collected her dogs and gone. Instead, she had waited and then watched as I proceeded to gingerly pick up the gooey monstrosity, drop it, pick it up again, walk a few steps, and repeat the process. Eventually, I made it to the trash can and got rid of the mess once and for all. I almost threw up several times, but in the end, I succeeded. The damn thing was surprisingly heavy.

"Only after she had verified that I'd thrown the remains away did she whistle — quite impressively, I thought — leash her two dogs, and depart.

"I called out to Robert. I think I screamed rather loudly, 'You fucking bastard.' She was at a distance, but she turned around, looked at me now with disgust, and then continued to walk away."

Johnny paused and reached for some coffee.

"Good heavens!" I said. "That *is* embarrassing. Did she get your name?"

"I don't think I ever said it, but she might recognize me if we were to meet again. I'd certainly recognize her. Unfortunately, that's not the end of the story. There's this other part that sort of puts the icing on the cake."

"I doubt you could make it any worse."

"*Au contraire* — I had a chance to take a good look at the scarf while I was holding it at arm's length, gagging every few feet, when I noticed that the silk was still in pretty good shape. There were no teeth marks or rips that I could see, and since this was Laura's absolute favorite, and maybe because I felt a little guilty chatting up the blue-eyed vixen, I decided to rescue the remains from the trash and get it cleaned as penance. Complete insanity, to be sure, but I'd spied an empty paper bag in the same trash can that got me thinking that might be a good idea. Robert bounded over, so I put him on the lead and walked back to where I had chucked it. The bag was there, but the sticks were at the bottom of the trash can and out of reach. I contemplated what to do and concluded there was no way around it. I had to pick up the soiled scarf by one end with my bare fingers. I put Robert's leash on the ground and stood on it to free up my hands and then lifted the horror out of the bin. I tried to hold the bag underneath with the other hand, only the scarf was too long. I was forced to let go and take a grip somewhere in the middle. Imagine my surprise when whom do I see coming back again but that witch with her two dogs. She stopped short, gaped for a moment, and then turned around. The look on her face was one of such unmitigated revulsion and disgust that I hope never to experience anything like it in the future at any time, let alone by someone that good-looking. It was awful, just awful. Unbelievably bad."

"So you think she may be the same girl?"

"Exactly. Let's do the math, shall we? Let's state as given: she's the same woman, and meets the same man with the same dog again, but in a different location. What do you suppose is going to happen?"

"I'd hate to say," I offered, "but you definitely have my interest."

"Very funny. How much of a chance do you think he has of any sort of relationship, let alone a future marriage proposal?"

"Well, the odds of her being the same woman are pretty long, but I agree. If by some bizarre quirk of fate, the woman you are about to meet at Rhinebeck is the same one you subjected to that ordeal, I'd think you're pretty much a nonstarter. By the way, if you don't mind my asking, what happened to the scarf?"

"I eventually got the travesty into the bag, which I brought to a dry cleaner in a different part of town. I was forthcoming as to the fact that the article had been stained with some dog doo, which explained the bag tied with a string; however, I was perhaps remiss in that I didn't reveal the full extent of the soiling. I gave the man a hundred dollars in advance for his services after telling him quite firmly to open the bag away from public view. I could do no more. The result was worse than mediocre. The colors seemed faded, and by the time I got it back, Laura and I were no longer an item. I sent Robert to the country where he could run around and attached the scarf around his neck by way of farewell. He still has it, as far as I know."

"Well, if it's the same girl, you might want to bury the thing. But what are the odds, really?"

"What do you reckon they are?"

"Remote. Very remote. Billion to one?"

"Normally, I'd agree with you, but my belief is that life has peculiar ideas about probability that are quite different from our own, to the extent that I would wager Brunhilde von Hofmanstal and Brunhilde the dog woman are one and the same. Besides, there was a calculation I saw once that concluded that everyone who lives to be over seventy years old experiences at least two one-in-a-billion events during their existence."

"Actually, I do recall seeing that as well."

"You get my point. This may be my one in a billion, and I think you should accompany me to Rhinebeck to see with your own eyes whether she is the one or not. What do you say?"

"Let me consider that for moment. I admit that originally I was not about to accompany you, but the situation is intriguing. What about my flight?"

"Not to worry — I've already taken care of everything. I canceled your reservation and have you on the company Lear out of Teterboro on Monday that gets you into Van Nuys at around three."

"That's more than a bit presumptuous..." I said with some alarm.

"I know. I know," he said, raising his hands. "Look! I can't put it any plainer. Please!"

Johnny went over to the window again. He stood there looking out.

There had been a desperation in his voice that was unusual and that concerned me more than anything he could have said. Johnny was never one to offer up his true motivations to anyone, at least not on the first go-round, or even on the second. He wasn't telling me the whole story, this I knew, but I was concerned for him and found myself saying, much to my surprise, "Consider it done. I'm coming with you."

"You will?" He turned back to me obviously relieved.

"Yes."

"That's the best news I've had in a while. I mean it. You'll help me with the Lafite business?"

"Of course."

"And with Brunhilde?"

"I'm not sure how I can, but I'll try. What would you have me do?"

"I don't know. Talk to her?"

"I suppose I could manage that, but I doubt either of those are the real issue, are they?"

He looked at me carefully. "It's been so long that I've forgotten how well we know each other. You're right, of course, but for that answer you'll have to wait. Can you do that?"

"I can, if I must."

"Then that's settled. Best we get going. You'll need to pack, and the car is waiting downstairs. Chop-chop."

Whatever vulnerability he had shown was gone in an instant. He was always like that, but I knew he was troubled, and that was a rare day. He'd asked for my help, and that was rarer still.

2

Having decided to alter my plans and accompany Johnny to Rhinebeck, I quickly dressed, packed, and checked out of the St. Regis. True to form, a car was waiting downstairs to take us up the Hudson, just as rain began to fall.

Johnny and I sprawled in the back of a long black limousine for the two-hour drive. As our ride swished up Park, I asked him, "Has Rhinebeck changed much?"

Johnny took off his jacket and put his feet up on the jump seat before he answered. "It's still the same for the most part. A few improvements in the kitchen — upgraded stoves, fridges, countertops — but pretty much as you remember it. Stanley and Dagmar soldier on together. Stanley still wears a morning suit and is every inch a model of the English butler, but he now has a new helper, a young fellow named Simon, who looks after the more mundane tasks, like polishing silver. Simon also helps at table. The bell pulls have been replaced by electronic ringers.

"Dagmar rules the kitchen and cooks as well as ever. She looks forward to dinner parties, so she can order up a flock of help, but these have been less frequent. She has a permanent helper named Jane, who is also new. Oh, and Harry, the groundskeeper, is still there. He's as crusty as ever and drives a new faster fleet of lawnmowers. The grounds look immaculate; you'll see."

"You know, I still dream of toast at breakfast in those silver racks and Dagmar's famous Scotch broth for lunch. In my mind, Rhinebeck remains a mysterious and wonderful place."

"It's as mysterious as ever," said Johnny, turning toward me. "As you know, Great-Aunt Eleanor, who built it, was into fortune-telling, prognostications, witchcraft, that sort of thing. I think those qualities rubbed off on the estate itself. Besides, she snared my grandfather, old John B. Dodge, using those arts, according to some. Others have said it was because she was damn good-looking with a bosom unmatched in her generation. I'd be inclined to the latter, but you never know."

"Was Eleanor a fortune hunter?"

"Hardly. She came from a fine, upstanding banking family out of Philadelphia. Still, she was considered quite scandalous in her day. Churchmen were said to avoid her like the plague, either because she might tempt them down paths best left unexplored or because of her hankering for the occult. Which frightened them more was hard to say.

"After Alice was born and they endured several tumultuous years together, the two divorced, which did nothing to lessen Eleanor's reputation. Unfortunately, she passed shortly thereafter, and Alice took up in the scandal department, where Eleanor left off."

I nodded. "I'd say surpassed her, but I loved Alice growing up. She was always so glamorous."

"She was, but under the surface, her life was messy. Her marriages all bombed, mostly because she was either steeped in her research or gallivanting with someone else. I doubt there was a man alive who could have hung on to her. Stories about her death continue to circulate although years have passed."

"Ah yes. The famous 'socialite dies under mysterious circumstances' that sent everyone into a tizzy of speculation at the time."

"Precisely, and the parents are still silent about what happened."

"Do you think they know something?"

"I suspect they know more than they let on. I do try and get them to talk about it every now and again, but so far very little has been forthcoming. Mother changes the subject, and Father ignores the question entirely. He was quite close to Alice — maybe closer than anyone. I think her death is still a source of sorrow."

Johnny looked out the window at the rain while I looked back at that time and marveled at how skillfully we had been kept in the dark. Johnny and I did not attend the funeral because such things were considered inappropriate for children. Years passed before we learned how sensational her death had been. It was not that we didn't know her. We vacationed at her house and saw her regularly. We were in awe of her. In some ways, I was thankful we were left with only the happy memories of her alive.

Johnny stretched and said, "I don't blame the parents for not discussing her death. It was a dark time. The press had a field day. 'Plot thickens. Police called in' — that sort of thing. The headlines were enough to sour anyone on the subject. On top of that, there was no will. Although much was spelled out in the many trusts instruments that handled her finances, there was a significant bit not covered. I can hardly believe that her banking people didn't force her to write one up, but such lapses weren't particularly out of character. By the way, I hope I'm not boring you."

"Hardly — her life has always been a point of fascination for me. I only wish I had known her better and when I was older. I could have appreciated her more, but I remember her fondly as someone larger than life and always there in the background watching us."

"Yes, I know what you mean. She was something to be reckoned with. I have done a little digging. Not much, but some."

"And what did you come up with?"

"Unfortunately, not a whole lot, but some things you may not know. Her peers in the academic world considered her to be an exacting and brilliant researcher, but those who knew her socially thought she was careless in her personal affairs. The Mellon bank handled most of her money, but many things fell through the cracks.

"Father said that when he took over her finances after she died, there were huge clumps of pending bills, from parking tickets to demands for payment from Van Cleef's for diamond earrings. She had plenty of money. She just didn't have time for what she considered life's boring details. He ended up having to sort out the mess she left."

"I bet that took a while," I said.

"It did. She was always losing things. She misplaced a husband or two — left one in some remote location. He took years to return to civilization."

"I remember that. Arthur Blain?"

"Yes, that was the one. Alice married him after she divorced Lord Bromley. She cut loose from Blain just before the rainy season in some South American jungle. He was stuck for months along with his party. They ran out of food, drank bad water. There were rumors of murder and cannibalism. He contracted some tropical disease like dengue fever and almost died — took forever to recover. He came back a wreck, begging for forgiveness for something he had done on the trip, but nothing doing. Alice had moved on. She wouldn't even see him. He later told tales that she had wanted to kill him over something they found. She stole it and left him there to die."

"I had not heard that. Do you think that's true?"

"From what I understand, the guy was a real amateur in the jungle expedition game, so leaving him behind might be construed in some circles as a death sentence, but the reality was she left with only a single pack. He had most of the equipment and the crew. It was well timed. About what they found, I know nothing."

"I'm amazed that we knew so little about her. All that we were ever told was that she was 'away' for long stretches of time."

"Archeological expeditions were a major part of her life. She knew her way around a dig. She had the money to finance and support projects all over the world. I only found out about all this much later.

"As to what caused the break with Arthur, I discovered nothing concrete. There was a story going around at the time about him dallying with a native, gender unspecified, which could explain it. I can understand her leaving him, but she had plenty of partners of her own before and after, so I can't see her being all high and mighty and bugging out in a huff. She had a secretive side, so there was probably more to it."

"I thought she was supposed to be very overt. The papers painted her as one of those 'what you see is what you get' types, and often scantily clad at that."

"The papers portrayed her that way with good reason. After the Blain debacle, she became much less discreet in her personal life. Her many affairs drove Father around the bend because I think he admired her and hated that her appetite for sex and scandal overshadowed a monster intellect that few could see. Her antics reflected badly on her, according to him, although I think she used that as a cover."

"A cover for what?"

"Her private self, her collecting, and her research, I suppose. She was a noted Egyptologist with several works to her credit; however, she'd rather have people perceive her as a fool and a dilettante, when she was anything but. You knew her. She played on many levels."

"I remember that she could read us like a book. She was always one step ahead of us in the prank department."

"Exactly. Father tried to do his best by her in practical matters, but she was on a different channel than everyone else, tuned to what was happening in the outer cosmos as opposed to here on Earth."

"That was the problem, I think."

"Yes, and as a result, she left it to those around her to pick up the pieces. After her death, parts of her estate not covered by trusts had to be probated and became a matter of public record. The publicity frenzy started all over again. Father was the executor, and since he was the last surviving relative, most of the assets passed to him. I don't know all the details. The parents can be very tight-lipped on financial matters and still are, but Rhinebeck, another apartment in New York besides the current one, an extensive library worthy of a major university, as well as a large chunk of financial assets passed to him and helped turn Dodge Capital into a much larger player."

"I read about her in a magazine a while back. The article noted the suspicions surrounding her death, and how they keep persisting."

"There are rumors of foul play still around. Father benefitted the most from her death, but he was away with mother in Capri when she died. The fact that he had more than enough money of his own should have silenced them, but still the stories continue. Alice had many followers who refused to believe she simply died."

"Still, the circumstances were bizarre. She died at Rhinebeck in her bed reading an Egyptian Book of the Dead, according to one report."

"Yes, and that's true as far as I know. I remember one of the tabloids printing in big caps: 'Socialite died from pharaoh's curse.

Mystery deepens.' The facts must have seemed pretty weird at the time. I can tell you what I know and my own conclusions, if you like."

"Please."

"She was an academic as well as a socialite. Reading such a text was not out of character. I'm sure classics professors read Homer in the original Greek for fun all the time."

"What about all the rumors of murder? No one told us about those for years."

"The police found nothing suspicious. The book, according to the papers, was supposed to hold a clue, but few knew what an Egyptian Book of the Dead really was. The mere mention of the title created a sensation and sold papers." Said Johnny.

"I'm still not sure I know what one is."

"Most people don't. In truth, there's no single edition of the Egyptian Book of the Dead. The practice of using one started out as 'for pharaohs only' but proved so popular, high government officials began using them. Eventually anyone who could afford to have one drawn up got into the act. Each book was custom made, at least up until a certain point in time, when they became standardized and consisted of any number of spells, of which a couple of hundred are known.

"Some were to preserve parts of the body and aid a person to navigate through the underworld. Some allowed one to come forth by day, have power over one's enemies, and then return to the underworld at night like an ancient kind of vampire. There was even a spell to prevent one from consuming feces and urine."

"Splendid. Just what every mummy needs."

"The book was supposed to be placed in the sarcophagus of the deceased as a road map, survival guide, worst-case-scenario handbook, and travel diary all rolled into one so the dead could make their way successfully in the afterlife."

"Was Alice simply reading one?"

"I don't know. The book was taken in as evidence and then returned, but as to where it ended up, no one seems to know. We don't have a lot of information. Maybe she wasn't even reading it. Perhaps it was placed there by someone as a message, or a warning. The later books were all about being judged for one's transgressions."

"That sounds kind of sinister."

"It just depends on how you look at it. I could make a possible case for murder, or I could make a case for accidental death in that she was trying out a tricky spell and things went south. Regardless, it's all speculation. For now, the death certificate and the police investigation found nothing suspicious, and that's the only concrete opinion there is. That doesn't seem to stop the speculation. Even in death, she can't stay out of the papers," concluded Johnny.

I sighed. "It amazes me that mystery still surrounds her, but given the public's thirst for gossip and scandal, it's no wonder. She had quite a library. Maybe it might give us some hint as to what she was researching."

"The library has to be seen to be believed. Remember, that area was off limits to us growing up, and still is to some degree. There are parts that are kept locked, but where there's a will, there's a way, and we might have some time to do some research. I wouldn't mind getting into the locked parts. I overheard Mother and Father talking, and they said some insurance appraisal people had reported they hadn't come across anything like it ever. The library is still unexplored as an avenue as far as I know. I doubt it will give up its secrets on a quick once-over, but we should at least see the damn thing."

"Excellent. That'll help pass the time before everyone starts showing up."

"For sure. And speaking of things that are ancient and showing up like a mummy's curse, Maw is arriving on Friday. She'll be attended by her familiar, Bonnie."

"Good God. Your grandmother looked old when I first met her. I can't imagine what she looks like now."

"Trust me — she's very much alive, and more crone-like than ever. I suggest you gird your loins because dinners are going to be a source of entertainment not to be missed."

"She hasn't gone back to riding horses, has she?"

"Not lately. Since her last fall, several corporate boards have made giving up riding almost a condition for her continued participation. It was that or be faced with mass resignations. Healing apparently made her quite contentious."

"I should think so. Well, the house will have quite a collection: Maw, Bonnie, Brunhilde, her parents, your parents, you, and me. Are there any more coming?"

"I haven't a clue, but I'm hoping the mixture of guests will be so volatile that the trading report and the famous wine theft will be overshadowed by the fireworks that are bound to occur."

"Let's hope."

"I'm going to grab a nap. Wake me when we get there." Johnny closed his eyes while I thought about my spontaneous agreement to make this journey in the first place.

I felt nervous and unprepared for what lay ahead. The Dodge family had always tolerated, rather than welcomed, my presence — except for Johnny. He had fully accepted me into his life as a fellow conspirator from the start, and for that I owed him my unwavering support, and that explained my decision to some degree. But there were other considerations that gave me pause.

Rhinebeck embodied all that was precarious in my world as I grew up. The house was magnificent, but it had a dark side that would seep into my dreams and disturb my sleep, even now. Johnny, too, had sometimes been hard to bear. He was not always as forthcoming as he might have been, and often, I was unable to pierce the shell he used to shield his inner thoughts.

Right now, I knew he was troubled, but by what, I didn't know. He was much like the house itself, wonderfully engaging on the surface, but beneath roiled dark currents. His was the struggle to prove himself in a family that gave no sympathy for failure. I had felt a similar pressure. There was rest at Rhinebeck but no ease. Performance was continually demanded, and only the best was met with even limited approval. I suppose this was harder on Johnny than me, being the son, yet here we were, once again, under scrutiny.

The collection of guests added another troubling element. Putting all of them in the same room was like dumping several large solitary wolverines into a single pen and standing back to see what would happen.

There was Maw, Johnny's grandmother, the matriarch. She had been born wealthy and had married three times. The first marriage had been to John B. Dodge, out of which came John Senior. Divorce followed, along with a substantial settlement. Each of her next two husbands survived only a couple years of marriage before they expired, whether from being worn out or simply being beaten down was unknown. With each passing, her fortune increased several times over. The last marriage had been to a savings-and-loan pillar of the Southern states and had given her a daughter by the name of Bonnie.

To the family, she was known as Maw. I called her Mrs. Leland, after her last late husband. She caused me no end of nervousness. She lived for strife, and I did everything and anything to avoid it.

The competition and skirmishes between John Senior and his half-sister were legendary. Maw played one against the other. Although rich in his own right, John Senior could not resist one-upping his half-sister, and Bonnie was determined to see that Maw's fortune was left to her in its entirety as payback for the upset and inconveniences her half-brother had caused her. Part of Maw's estate included the apartment on Sixty-First and Fifth, where Mr. and Mrs. Dodge currently resided. Bonnie dreamed of the day she would be able to turn the Dodge faction out on the street once and for all.

Colossal amounts of money would change hands depending on who won the test of strength between the two siblings. Maw amused herself by coldly prodding whichever party slackened in their efforts to win the ultimate prize for being obedient and acquiescing to her every whim.

Although familial competitions and her wealth were of interest to her, they were not her passion. That fire had been reserved exclusively for her horses and her dogs. Those, she loved.

The woman I remembered was a formidable equestrian. Powerful horses with nasty dispositions that planned to toss their riders at the earliest opportunity would stand quiet, blowing with contentment, whenever she was in the saddle. I knew of only a handful of riders who could do that, and in that group, she had no equal.

To my mind, horses must have recognized her as their equine matriarch in another form. Not just horses but dogs too. At a command from her, a pack of yelping foxhounds would silence. Their tails would tuck between their legs as they milled about her in servile whimpering.

Animals obeyed her. Humans feared her and did the same.

She had once been an astonishing beauty, but a life of constant outdoor living had left her skin prematurely tanned and wrinkled, particularly her neck, like that of an old fur trapper of the American Northwest.

This aspect of her appearance had been my undoing when we were first introduced. Johnny and I had only just met and were getting to know each other. At that time, he was only too happy to take advantage of my prodigious gullibility. Johnny would tell me tales about her. He had me convinced that if I touched her, I would be infected by an affliction whose symptoms would leave me horribly wrinkled and my limbs deformed, to be followed by a long and painful death. Adults and blood relations were immune. I believed him and dreaded the day when Maw and I would meet.

We eventually did. My parents were there. I was told to go up and shake Maw's hand. I stood before her and froze. I was prodded and cajoled while Maw sat watching me. Finally, I burst into tears and screamed out, "I don't want to turn into a prune. I won't shake her hand. I won't!"

Time seemed to stand still after that outburst. My parents were horrified. The Dodges even more so. Maw, however, asked for an explanation. I knew the answer, but in my panic, I couldn't speak. I was removed from the room in short order like a puppy that had just peed on an eighteenth-century carpet. I was sent to bed at one in the afternoon.

Johnny joined me in my misery shortly thereafter, consigned to the same fate. He said, "I'm sorry. That was not a nice thing to do. It won't happen again. You didn't tell on me to Maw, and that's important. Friends?" He stuck out his hand.

I thought about his offer and decided to take it. "Friends," I said. "But you should know that it wasn't because I decided not to say anything. It was because I couldn't."

"Well, you didn't, and that's good enough for me. Anybody else would've told on me. No one can defy Maw when she wants to know something, and you did the next best thing. You were like a stone. I couldn't have done that."

That was the first time that Johnny admitted there was something that I could do better. We had made a start.

Later, he told me that Maw had pulled him aside after my removal and extracted the truth. Before he was sent off, she whispered in his ear that in time I would either stand with him or against him and that he would be better off to have me as a friend than an enemy. Enemies required constant vigilance, while friends needed none.

Then, and in the future, Johnny and I took such utterances that Maw delivered with the same respect given to oracles of earlier ages. Whether true or not, between us we thought she tapped into powers beyond those of mere mortals and that taking heed was the wisest course.

The relationship between Johnny and me changed permanently after that. He could and did ensnare me in many of his schemes, most of which caused me no end of trouble, but always as an equal and never again as the target.

Maw had treated us equally, and the entire household adopted this basis. Rewards and punishments were thereafter meted out in equal measure, regardless of who did what. We spent many an hour shoulder to shoulder, cleaning, mending, and generally helping the maids, butlers, and others who worked for the many Dodge households. We were no strangers to messy and tedious work, regardless of our sumptuous surroundings. We may have been born with silver spoons in our mouths, but unlike others of similar status, we sure learned to polish them, as Johnny would say.

Maw's presence was going to add fuel to an already incendiary mixture of personalities. One could only wonder what the von Hofmanstals would make of it, and whether they had any idea what they were getting into.

I hoped they had some spirit, or I was pretty sure they would be eaten alive.

3

———————

We reached the Dodge estate close to noon. The rain had stopped, but the sky was overcast and dark with the promise of more rain to come.

We turned onto a private road marked by two granite pillars. The wet asphalt ran west toward the Hudson beneath a leafy canopy of trees. Large drops dripped and splattered onto the windshield as we passed beneath the branches until the trees gave way to a close-cropped lawn covered with mist. The car slowed as the main driveway entrance appeared on the left. We turned onto a gravel road that sloped gently down to a large rectangular roundabout. The large, gray fieldstone house took shape out of the low-lying fog that swirled about the grounds.

A three-story part made up the center portion, and two wings stretched out right and left. The one on the left was two stories tall, while the one on the right was only a single floor. This last had been Alice's residence and contained her sitting room and bedroom. To the left were the kitchen and servants' quarters and, farther still, was another driveway that ran down to the garage. The main structure was capped with four chimneys.

"Johnny," I said, "it looks exactly the same."

"Yes, it does. Is it any wonder that Rip Van Winkle was supposed to have slept his way into history at the foot of the Catskills across the river?"

"No wonder at all. There is something timeless about this place, for sure."

The car pulled up in front of a door of dark, polished wood beneath an ornate white pediment. The doorknob was a large brass lion's head. As the car stopped, the door opened, and out stepped Stanley with a large umbrella, followed by a younger man whom I assumed was Simon, Stanley's helper, with another.

Stanley wore a morning suit consisting of a dark coat and gray trousers along with a light gray vest and dark tie. He was a tall man of indeterminate age — sprightly, knowledgeable, and extraordinarily silent on his feet. His hair had turned whiter from the frosty gray I remembered.

I got out and greeted him. "Stanley. It's a pleasure to see you again." I looked into his eyes. They were as coldly blue as I remembered.

"Welcome back. It's been some time."

"It has. Good to see you."

"Indeed."

I stood aside and watched Stanley as Johnny put on his jacket, walked around the car, and stood next to me. Stanley had been a background presence during our childhood. Despite knowing each other for years, he and I interacted only when necessary, and when we did, he was always formal, coldly distant, and unapproachable. Whatever feelings he had, he hid behind a mask of almost scientific detachment. We had tolerated each other, and judging from my current reception, that would continue to be the case. He rarely smiled, and we never shook hands, as was the custom at Rhinebeck.

Whatever Stanley's mood, Johnny was always pleasant and never seemed to mind. "Stanley, splendid to see you as always. How are you and Simon getting on?"

"Very well, sir. Very well, indeed."

"Excellent. Glad to hear it. Have you figured out where we're staying?"

"Both of you are at the top of the house, as usual. Simon will bring up the luggage. There will be some refreshments in the drawing room. We have been expecting you."

"Sounds perfect. Lead on."

We made our way up the front steps, while Simon put away the umbrellas and grabbed our bags. I didn't envy him carrying them up the two flights of stairs to our familiar rooms at the top.

We passed from dripping weather to the quiet interior of the house.

In my life, I have known few places where the immediate past was of no concern and the future did not seem to matter. Rhinebeck stood apart from the normal stream of time. How long it could continue to exist, I did not know, but I gave thanks to whatever luminal deity had preserved it until now.

I followed Johnny inside and looked to my left. There was the clock — an English longcase that was always the first thing I looked at when I arrived and the last thing I saw when I left. On its face, five ships of the line tilted back and forth, counting out the seconds on an angry ocean of blue-gray lacquer. Above the rocking ships were phases of the moon and constellations that moved slowly across the top dial. The loud click of the escapement and the moving ships would mesmerize me when I was younger. The clock chimed on the half of every hour.

We walked across the marble entrance to where a long table

stood with gladioluses in a vase and a marble bust of Alexander on a pedestal next to it.

Johnny and I walked over to him and patted his head. We thought the tradition gave us luck, a useful commodity that we often needed in copious amounts.

We passed through a set of double doors and into a large drawing room sumptuously decorated with Louis XV furniture. There were tapestries on the wall and carpets on the floor. To the right was a large Constable that transformed the room into that of an English country house. The french doors looked out on a lawn that stretched away into the fog.

Johnny walked over to a humidor that sat on a side table and took out a cigar just as a large white English bull terrier flung open the double doors with his head. They banged against the door stops.

"Ye gods, it's that creature!" said Johnny, turning and putting back the cigar.

Robert the Bruce was obviously glad to see him. He bounded over to Johnny and stood looking at him. His tail wagged back and forth like a metronome marking out the time in tenths of a second. He looked up expectantly at Johnny. Johnny stared back and unconsciously patted his pocket.

He caught himself and said forcefully, "No. I don't have a tennis ball. Forget it. Good heavens, I forgot about him."

"Obviously he didn't forget about you. By the way, where is that famous scarf?"

"I have no earthly idea. I'll ask Stanley just the same — can't have that thing turning up at the wrong moment."

Johnny gave him a pat and rubbed his ears.

Robert gazed at Johnny and then flopped into a sphinxlike position with his legs stretched out behind. He seemed quite content to simply look at him. He ignored me entirely. Johnny gave him another pat and said to me, "I was going to offer you an illicit Montecristo, but I doubt we'll have time to enjoy one at the moment. How about after dinner?"

"Absolutely, with some brandy."

"Of course."

We both sat down.

Johnny took out a cigarette as Stanley entered with two flutes of champagne on a silver tray. He offered one to each of us and announced, "Lunch will be served in half an hour. Scotch broth and Welsh rarebit."

Johnny said, "Splendid. We'll have a smoke, freshen up, and then we'll be ready for Dagmar's delights. By the way, we're the first to arrive, correct?"

"Yes, sir."

"Who else is expected?"

"Your parents are arriving tomorrow, Thursday, along with Baron, Baroness, and Miss von Hofmanstal. Mrs. Leland and Miss Leland arrive the day after. Mr. Malcolm Ault is expected, but his itinerary is uncertain as to his arrival time, but I would expect him tomorrow late."

"A full house then. It's been a while."

"A while indeed — we are all looking forward to it."

"Excellent, and before I forget, we would like to peruse the wine cellar after lunch."

"Very good, sir. The key will be on the side table."

"One last thing. Do you happen to know where Robert's greenish Hermes scarf might be?"

"He sleeps with it. One doesn't dare touch it, as he seems quite attached to it. I have taken the liberty of moving his bedding up to the top floor, so he can be with you, which I believe is where he wants to be."

We all looked at Robert, who remained suitably inscrutable, gazing at Johnny with the rapture that only a dog can muster.

"I see," said Johnny. "Thank you, Stanley."

33

Stanley glided away and closed the double doors.

"Scotch broth and Dagmar's Welsh rarebit. My favorites!" I exclaimed.

We sipped our champagne.

"I told Dagmar you were coming, and she remembered what you liked. Plus, tonight is roast beef with Yorkshire pudding. I figured we could explore the cellar, see what's what, and then take a look at that library while no one else is around."

"Good plan. Although it's rather wet, I wouldn't mind taking a look around the grounds as well."

"Absolutely. I doubt we'll see that much in the fog, but I like the place when it's like this. We could be in England. We'll take young Robert along."

"By the way, who is Malcolm Ault? Have I met him?"

"Probably not. You would know if you had. Malcolm lives in England and has something to do with films. I don't know exactly what he does, and I don't think anyone else does either. He is tall. That's his main claim to fame. Apparently, he can see over the top of everyone, and that has proved useful at horse races and directing. I have no idea what he's doing here, but Father and Mother like him, so there you go. He's quite well off, lives in Shropshire, and pops by whenever he's in the States. He knew Alice, but how well I don't know."

"I never met him, then. Shall we head up?"

We drained our glasses and walked out of the drawing room, across the entrance past the clock, and up a broad staircase. Robert the Bruce brought up the rear. He wasn't going to let Johnny out of his sight if he could help it.

The second-floor hallway led to the master bedroom and several guest rooms. The dark red carpet was thick and soundless as we walked to the far end, where on the right was a special door that was set flush with the wall. The door opened outward by means of a small, recessed handle. Before us was a narrow flight of stairs that led steeply upward and ultimately to another door that opened onto a large common area. This was the top of the house. Light streamed down into the center of the room from a large skylight of frosted glass.

The common area was set down two steps and contained two comfortable armchairs with standing reading lights, along with a sofa and table. Set in each wall was a door. The one to the east led to the stairs we came in from. The one to the north led to Johnny's room, which overlooked the driveway. The one to the south led to mine and overlooked the back lawn. Each of our rooms had a distinctive circular window. Opposite the entrance were two doors: one to a large modern bathroom, the other to the governess room, if there was one in service. Along each of the walls were bookcases that stretched from floor to ceiling and were packed with books. There were the entire Tom Swift series, the Hardy boys, Nancy Drew, Edgar Rice Burroughs, encyclopedias, textbooks, an outstanding collection of fairy tales and myths from around the world, works on military history from Xenophon to Liddell Hart as well as novels of all sorts.

Johnny and I had spent hours and hours in this room simply reading. The space was set up exactly for that purpose.

I opened the door to my room. Simon had placed my bags on a rack at the foot of my bed. I looked at the desk with my ship models and then at the window. The room seemed smaller than I remembered but still marvelous in its sameness to when I was growing up.

I stepped out into the common room, and there was Johnny in his chair, looking at a large book on English landscape artists. Robert lay beside him on the floor. Just outside Johnny's door was Robert's bed, and sure enough, in it was a green, blue, and white Hermes scarf. It looked a little faded.

"Good heavens," I said. "There's the scarf."

"Yes, that's the beastly thing. Care to touch it?"

I shuddered. "Absolutely not." I went over to a book shelf, grabbed an old book on World War II airplanes, and sat down. "Nothing's changed. I can't get over it."

"Yes. At least that's the appearance. It has stayed in its own time while we've moved on. Still, it's great to be here and grab a few moments of peace and reflection before the coming fray. Which reminds me, the earlier we get into that cellar, the better. At least we might be able to put to rest *one* of my nightmares. Let's wash our hands and have some lunch."

The three of us were descending the main staircase when a gong sounded to announce that lunch was served. The dining room was accessed through the drawing room. The long, polished table was set for two. We sat down opposite each other, and Stanley entered with the soup.

I tasted some and said to Johnny, "This is heaven. It's as good as ever." At that moment, a smallish, bright-eyed woman in an apron appeared. I sprang up and gave her a big hug. She laughed and said, "You've grown a bit, and is that some gray hair I see?"

"Well, maybe. Dagmar, you look the same. I'm so happy to be here. You've no idea how much I've missed your cooking."

Johnny said, "He tells me that so often, he's like a broken record."

"Well, I'm glad you do, and it's such a pleasure to see you two together again."

She and Stanley went back to her kitchen.

We finished lunch, drank coffee, and smoked in complete contentment.

I asked Johnny, "Well, how about the cellar? Dare we find out?"

"Time we did."

"Then lead on. I'm ready for almost anything."

4

The cellar was entered by a concealed door underneath the main staircase. The three of us — Johnny, followed by Robert and me — descended the narrow stairs.

The light was dim, but what could be made out immediately was a series of wine racks that stretched for a distance to our left. To our right was shelving that held banker boxes as well as bundled and not-so-bundled objects.

"Johnny," I asked. "I don't remember all these shelves. Are they new?"

"Relatively new. Harry, the ever-resourceful handyman, built them to accommodate what continued to arrive after Alice's death as well as make a storage space for things that nobody knows what to do with or dares chuck out. Take that antique lamp, for instance. Hideous. That being said, we should check out Alice's section once we find those bottles. I doubt anyone has really gone through everything except on a cursory basis."

"Really? How is that even possible?"

"Alice subscribed to many journals, magazines, maps, societies, you name it. There are boxes of the stuff. Besides, who's going to go through all this junk? Father? Stanley? I don't think so."

"I could start going through it right now."

"Not on your life. First, the wine; then, the treasure hunt."

"Okay," I said. "Lead on."

We turned left and headed down the dimly-lit aisle. Racks of wine bottles extended from floor to ceiling.

Robert was leading the way when he froze. His tail quivered and stood straight up. He growled low in his throat. His lips curled up to reveal a set of truly frightening teeth.

"Rats or ghosts? What do you think?" Johnny wondered.

"I've no idea, but he seems a bit put out."

"Go get 'em, Robert," commanded Johnny, but just as suddenly Robert stopped his growling, and his teeth seemed to recede into his mouth. He wagged his tail and continued down the aisle, as if nothing had happened.

I looked at Robert. "I tell you, that's one dog I wouldn't want to meet in a back alley. I'm glad we have him around, but is he temperamental, or am I imagining things?"

"He's quirky," said Johnny, "and he scares the hell out of me when he does that growling-teeth thing. I just hope he frightens anything else, living or dead, that might be wandering around these parts. This house can be seriously creepy."

"Tell me about it."

The creepy aspect of our surroundings was a topic Johnny and I had long discussed as we grew older within its walls. Rhinebeck had a sinister side that we both loved and hated. The dark shadows by the cypress trees or the brooding marble statues could harbor all sorts of spirits, both friendly and unfriendly. The dark, silent emptiness could be a scary place to grow up in, and I was easily frightened.

Still, I had to acknowledge that this element had made me feel deliciously alive. I suppose Johnny felt the same way, although he had hidden it better than me. We had nonetheless played on each other's fears. Our games of hide-and-seek were just as scary for the seeker as the hider. The setting was too perfect, the possibilities too numerous. If ghosts existed, there was no better place for them to inhabit than Rhinebeck.

While scaring each other was exciting, frightening the daylights out of others was even more so.

As per usual, Johnny and I often went too far.

Nannies were a regular part of our upbringing but never a permanent fixture. We went through them on a continual basis. Often they left after spending only a single vacation at Rhinebeck, as was the case of a particular one of Russian extraction named Miss Ponchikov. She was a youngish woman. Mrs. Dodge liked her because she spoke several languages, including French, and hoped that her ease with foreign tongues would somehow rub off on Johnny and me. It didn't, but she seemed like a nice quiet creature, having passed a month's trial at the Fifth Avenue apartment and gained Mrs. Dodge's approval in the process.

Alice was still alive at that time and in residence at Rhinebeck. Johnny and I were nine.

The Miss Ponchikov incident started on the second morning of a school vacation. We had settled in on the top floor the day before.

Children were served breakfast at seven each morning in the dining room. Adults were served at nine.

That particular morning, we were alone with Miss Ponchikov. Mr. and Mrs. Dodge, as well as Alice, were in New York and would not be back until Friday night. We had finished eating our oatmeal when Miss Ponchikov asked if we had heard anything during the night.

Johnny and I looked at each other. The question was unusual simply because we were never asked anything as a rule. Johnny recovered and said, "No, Miss Ponchikov. Did you hear something?"

"Yes, I did. I thought I heard someone crying."

"It wasn't me," I said.

"It was the sound of a woman weeping late in the night. When I got up to find out, the crying stopped."

"Ah yes," said Johnny. "The parents told us not to talk about that very thing."

"Talk about what very thing?" asked Miss Ponchikov.

I wasn't sure where Johnny was going with this, but I followed his lead and hissed, "You're going to get us in trouble, if she finds out."

"Finds out what?"

"I'm sorry, Miss Ponchikov," said Johnny. "I shouldn't have said anything. It's about a previous nanny. We were told specifically not to mention it. It's not suitable for children."

While fishing for sailfish or marlin, we had been taught to release the drag on the big Penn Senator reels and let the bait drop after an initial strike. A big fish would turn back and swallow the bait if it appeared incapacitated, allowing the angler to set the hook in earnest. One had to be patient.

We waited to see if she took the bait. Miss Ponchikov looked like she was about to say something. Her spoon paused halfway to her mouth before she continued eating, and the moment passed. We finished our breakfast and moved on to our homework.

Johnny and I always had homework to do over vacations that usually required a fair amount of reading. Miss Ponchikov insisted that we study every morning. We set up our materials underneath the skylight at the top of the house, while Miss Ponchikov leafed through magazines or read her romance novel.

An hour later that particular morning, she asked how we liked our previous nannies. Our Russian fish was back.

Johnny sighed, got up, went to his room, and closed the door.

"What happened? What did I do?" she asked me.

"It's nothing," I said. "He'll recover."

"Was it something I said?"

"Miss Ponchikov, I'm really not supposed to talk about the previous nanny. Please don't make me." I looked at her imploringly.

Johnny opened his door. He carried a handkerchief and sat back down. He looked like he had been crying.

"Are you all right?" Miss Ponchikov asked him.

"Yes, I'm fine."

"What's the matter?"

Johnny turned to her and told her, "I can only talk about her if you promise me from the bottom of your heart not to mention this to anyone. Do you promise me, Miss Ponchikov?"

He looked her in the eye, a little blond boy with blue eyes and a sincere expression.

Miss Ponchikov put her hand over her heart and said, "I promise."

The hook was set.

Johnny sighed. "She was a nice woman. Her name was Tabetha Tinsley..."

I wondered just how he could possibly get away with a name like Tabetha Tinsley. The name was just too preposterous, but Johnny always said that if you are going to tell a tall tale, be outrageous, because the bigger the lie, the more ornamentation it will hold. He was only being true to form.

Johnny proceeded to spin Miss Ponchikov a story of a well-bred woman betrayed by fate. Her lover had disappeared under mysterious circumstances. She was forced to take care of children to make ends meet.

Miss Ponchikov sat and listened in enraptured amazement, her society magazines and romance novel forgotten.

I wasn't sure which plot line Johnny was following, but I knew that few could withstand the sight and words of an angelic little person telling a story far too grown-up for him to imagine, with an innocence and sincerity that would set any heart aflutter.

Little did others know of the masses of books of all types we had consumed within these very walls. We may have been small, but we were quite well read.

Miss Ponchikov, however, was Russian. She came from a culture that lionized wealth and power, believed strongly in the supernatural, and was superstitious by nature. At Rhinebeck, she was surrounded by riches and status in abundance, along with something mystical that was peculiar both to the location and the house. I never doubted its existence. I just never knew what to call the presence I felt. Although not necessarily malevolent, I thought that whatever it was could change its mood quite easily.

My mind returned just as Johnny was wrapping up with a bit about the luckless nanny having received a mysterious letter. She learned the fate of her former lover. He was dead. She was undone. Johnny told her how he, little Johnny, had tried desperately to comfort her, but in the end, the heartbreak proved too much. She took her own life by hanging herself in this very room from the iron ring that hung from the skylight. The tragedy had broken his little heart and seared his soul. Tears streamed down his cheeks. Miss Ponchikov held him and rocked him in her arms. Her eyes were wet.

I thought the whole charade was a little thick, but I had to give him credit. Johnny was always gifted. How else could he get people to fork over millions of dollars today and thank him for the privilege?

Once his tears had dried, Johnny quietly explained that the

sobbing of her ghost was what she had heard. He had heard the weeping too but didn't want to say anything.

Into this pregnant silence, I injected, "Johnny, if the folks find out that you told Miss Ponchikov about her, we'll be roasted."

Miss Ponchikov said, "No, this will be our secret. I will tell no one." She smiled but appeared a little pensive.

I had no idea what was going through the woman's head, but I could tell the tale had affected her. She stared at the ring in the center of the skylight. She got up and went to her room for several minutes.

My experience even then was that people, including myself, did irrational things when they were afraid. The seed had been planted, and I started to form the opinion that we had once again gone too far, and that this might all end rather badly. She believed what Johnny said. I had no doubt. Her ready acceptance and subsequent unease cast light upon her mental state, which I thought was more fragile than she let on. Although she was an intelligent woman, historically, the display of innocence has fooled far more souls than the appearance of guile, and Johnny looked like an angel. Besides, she was in the presence of a master, even if he was only nine years old. She had been thoroughly taken in.

Later, when Johnny and I were alone, I scolded him. "Johnny, tell me we are not doing the hanging maiden trick on her."

"Precisely! We just need a wet and stormy night. I looked at the forecast, and something suitable is coming up in a couple of days. She bought the whole thing — hook, line, and sinker."

Johnny was thrilled with his performance. There was just no talking to him. He chortled and cackled, the very picture of self-satisfaction. I shook my head.

The days leading up to that memorable night were filled with eager anticipation. I too got caught up in the excitement. Alice and Mr. and Mrs. Dodge were due to arrive on Friday. We had the run of the house.

In a previous vacation, we had discovered a mannequin tucked away in an upstairs closet that now found itself in Johnny's closet. It looked quite lifelike if one squinted one's eyes and used a bit of imagination. To this we added a purloined wig of long black hair, compliments of Alice.

The item had been left out one day in the laundry room. Alice's reputation of being only slightly less powerful than Morgan le Fey in the intuitive sorceress department meant that anything belonging to her was pretty much out of bounds. The wig was an exception simply because it was left in an area of the house she did not frequent.

We collected other materials, including a serviceable hangman's noose that both Johnny and I learned to tie one summer, as well as some old sheets.

To keep the presence of ghostly spirits firmly in mind, the next couple of mornings, Johnny asked Miss Ponchikov if she had heard anything the night before. Miss Ponchikov replied each time that she was not sure. She appeared to be sleeping badly. Johnny told me that he had thumped about in the wee hours and even went so far as to do some chain-rattling. He almost got caught when she flung open the door to her room and called out.

I suppose I contributed to her unease shortly thereafter, when I knocked over a lamp on my way to the bathroom in the middle of the night. I saw the light go on underneath her door and fled to my room. I leaped into bed and feigned sleep. A few moments later, my door quietly opened. I slit my eyes and made out the drawn face of Miss Ponchikov looking in on me, illuminated by the moonlight streaming through my window. I breathed regularly, and the door quietly closed.

The next morning, I mentioned to Johnny about the fact that Miss Ponchikov appeared to be a little unstable, but Johnny had a full head of steam and said her precarious state would make the whole trick even more memorable, which proved remarkably accurate.

During our study time, Johnny would occasionally sit up straight and appear to be listening intently.

"Vut, vut is it?" Miss Ponchikov would ask, her Russian accent more pronounced as her unease grew under both the steady pressure of Johnny's ministrations and the house itself, which could take on a sinister aspect starting in the late afternoon. This attribute increased in strength as darkness fell and mist formed outside the windows and obscured the grounds. We were, after all, completely alone, except for Stanley and Dagmar, who slept in a different part of the house, along with the rest of the staff. Harry had a room over the garage. The isolation could unsettle even the most stalwart soul.

Friday morning, the air hung close and unmoving. Miss Ponchikov complained about the weather, while we prepared ourselves for that night's festivities.

Mr. and Mrs. Dodge arrived at three.

We waited out front along with Stanley, Harry, and Miss Ponchikov. Johnny and I both gave them a big hello, said we were enjoying ourselves, and that Miss Ponchikov was very pleasant.

Alice arrived at four. She loved to drive, so she rarely used a chauffeur.

All of us, including Mr. and Mrs. Dodge, were outside to greet her. Her dark-green Jaguar convertible with the top down crunched toward us and rolled to a stop. She shut down the car and stepped out.

She was a striking woman in black slacks and a white shirt. Her hair was jet black and cut short. It contrasted with her pale skin, which set off eyes so dark they could be mistaken for black as well. She exuded energy, command, and sexuality that drove both men and women mad. All of them were either in love with her or hated her. Johnny and I were simply in awe.

She gave us kisses, hugged Mr. and Mrs. Dodge, flung the keys to Harry to get the bags and put away the car, gave a warm hello to Stanley, and proceeded to skip up the stairs, when she stopped in her tracks. She turned toward Johnny and me and asked, "What have you little men been up to?"

Johnny gurgled, while I gawked. She had that sort of effect on us. We were saved by a low rumble in the distance. She looked up at the sky and said, "There is a delicious storm coming. You boys aren't afraid of a little thunder, are you?"

We said, "Oh no," in unison.

She laughed and disappeared into the house in a flash.

Johnny and I breathed a sigh of relief. We were seconds away from telling her everything.

By dinnertime, which for Johnny, Miss Ponchikov, and me meant six, the threatened storm was still hanging in the distance with furious rumbling that often went on for minutes at a time. The sound was like distant artillery, not loud but unmistakably present and ominous. Miss Ponchikov was nervous, whether because of the approaching storm or the presence of her employers, I did not know. Her Russian accent was even more in evidence, and she clutched a rosary of pale amethysts as a constant companion. We would hear the mutter of her prayers as they slipped out between her lips at odd moments.

Rain was falling when we went to bed at nine. By ten, it was pouring, and by eleven, Johnny was at my door. The storm was approaching in earnest, and the electricity was out. We dragged our maiden into the common room as lightning flashed above our heads and illuminated us through the skylight. Thunder followed four to five seconds later. A big cell was about a mile away. Normally I would have been a frightened wreck, but our preparations kept me focused. By the time we had finished, it was close to midnight, and the storm was on us. Rain drummed on the skylight with a roar as lightning coruscated across the sky. The plan was simple: to wait for a huge flash of lightning and for me to scream as loudly as I could and then to cut it off abruptly.

I was wondering when to begin when there was a simultaneous flash and peal of thunder that was so loud I was scared in earnest. Miss Ponchikov's door flew open, and I screamed. In the flickering light, Miss Ponchikov looked positively awful. She was in a long white nightgown tied at her neck. Her hair was sticking out in all directions. Her eyes were so wide I thought they would fall out at any moment. I heard a quick intake of breath as Johnny let loose a scream that put mine to shame. Her eyes looked upward in her appeal to the heavens and noticed the hanging lady swinging from the skylight. She grabbed her face with her hands and, in that moment, lost her mind completely. She gave out a shrill, keening sound like an animal and then bolted down the stairs. She was in the grip of a panic so profound that she was discovered at the end of the driveway by Harry, whom Mr. Dodge had ordered out after her. Apparently, she had almost knocked over Johnny's parents as she flew down the stairs, before she flung open the front door and disappeared into the night. They admitted they felt terrible because they too had screamed in fright when they saw her ghastly appearance in the light of a candle they were holding as they climbed the stairs.

After Miss Ponchikov's abrupt departure, Johnny and I decided that prudence dictated we hide away our creation before we were visited by parental authorities. The storm raged but was forgotten in our haste. We were not sure how much we were responsible for what had happened, but the less evidence on hand seemed the wisest course.

Mr. Dodge came up shortly with a flashlight. We ran to him and made our way downstairs. The family gathered in the drawing room, which was lit by candles, as Dagmar put on a kettle in the kitchen. Alice and the parents were still dressed, having not yet gone to bed, while we were in our pajamas. Alice wrapped us in blankets on the couch. Miss Ponchikov was discussed in hushed voices. Before long we were fast asleep.

The next morning broke wonderfully sunny and clear.

Dagmar took care of us at breakfast. Alice, the parents, and Miss Ponchikov were nowhere to be seen. Dagmar informed us they were dealing with the authorities. We had no idea what that meant exactly, but the implications sounded bad. We were good as gold, knowing that our doom was approaching with each passing minute.

The adults arrived, and we were summoned to appear before them. We had discussed our likely fate thoroughly before this, with no consensus reached, since we had sailed into uncharted waters.

It was Mrs. Dodge who told us that Miss Ponchikov would not be back. She apparently had a history of nervous breakdowns and should not have been looking after us in the first place. She apologized. We relaxed until Alice asked pointblank about what we knew of a previous nanny committing suicide. How she knew this, I don't know. She must have questioned Miss Ponchikov and gotten the story from her. She looked at us steadily. We cried. We howled. All to no avail. We confessed everything.

The matter was argued, discussed, and decided by the adults present, not for the first time regarding Johnny and me, that idle hands do the devil's work, and that we should occupy our hours with more constructive activity. We were turned over to Harry to work with him on the grounds. Further, our guardians decreed that henceforth Teutonic nannies should be the order of the day — the Russians being too mystical, the French too mercurial, and the English too dull.

That summer we were introduced to camp in the great state of Maine. By Christmas that year, Alice was dead.

My mind came back to the present. "I just flashed on the Miss Ponchikov incident. Do you remember it?"

"Oh, don't remind me. That was a bad one." Johnny stopped

and looked at me. "We really traumatized that woman. I think we even stopped all pranks for a year. No, probably only a few days. We were such little shits. That was also the last time we saw Alice."

"Yeah, I was thinking the same thing."

"Time has certainly moved on, yet here we are, and we're *still* in trouble. Some things never seem to change. Let's continue. Perhaps we can avoid some sort of karmic retribution now that you mentioned her. At least poor Miss Ponchikov didn't die of fright."

"Barely."

"Yes, barely."

Robert judged the coast clear and trotted on ahead. We followed and arrived at the back of the cellar where there was a table, a candle, an ashtray, and two chairs.

"We return to the scene of the crime."

Johnny and I had sat in those chairs many times. We had consumed some excellent spirits and had gotten seriously blasted in the process.

"We had some good times down here."

"That we did. Let's get busy. Those '59s were somewhere in the far rack, if I recall," said Johnny.

I went back to the far rack, which must have held over a hundred bottles. They were Château Lafites of various vintages. We spent a good fifteen minutes looking at bottle after bottle of Château Lafite, but the 1959s we wanted were not among them.

"Crap," said Johnny. "I was afraid of that. Looks like we'll have to consult Stanley on this one after all. I was hoping to simply verify they were there, and that would be the end of it. No rest for the wicked, I'm afraid."

"Okay, so let's start exploring the shelves while we have the chance."

We retraced our steps until we saw the shelves that Harry had built.

There were several banker's boxes in Alice's section as well as several stacks of magazines, periodicals, and auction house brochures. Robert had moved on down the line but stopped and rose on his hind legs to sniff and peer more closely at one box on the second row.

"Johnny, why don't you start with that one, while I take this one."

"Might as well. Robert likes this one."

I took down my box and lifted the lid. It was full of envelopes, mostly of museum and auction brochures, invitations, and correspondence to Alice.

"You really think nobody's gone through this stuff?"

"I should think not, but I don't know for sure. We could take the boxes upstairs and go through a few of them to see if we need to really tear the place apart. Hey, look what I have here."

Johnny's box contained a smaller square package wrapped in brown paper and tied with string. He took out a penknife, cut the twine, and began to unwrap it.

Robert was interested as well. He stuck his nose in the box and began to whine.

"Back off, you mangy mutt. Let me see this thing."

Inside the package was a cardboard box in which lay a lumpy object wrapped in cotton cloth. Johnny unwound the cotton to reveal a worn figure of dark stone while Robert took hold of the cotton wrapping and began to shake the strip back and forth like he was killing a rat.

"I have no idea what this is — odd that it's down here," said Johnny. "There might be more things tucked away, so why don't you grab a box? I'll take one as well, and let's go upstairs." He put the figurine back. "I'll ask Stanley to bring the rest up to the top floor where we'll have some room to go through this stuff."

The three of us tramped up the stairs with Robert the Bruce bringing up the rear, the wrapping still in his jaws.

We arrived in the foyer, and Johnny put down his box.

"Take this upstairs if you can, while I go and talk to Stanley."

I took the extra box. That was typical of our relationship, but I didn't mind. We had all afternoon, and there was nothing like a mystery to stir the imagination.

5

I managed to carry both banker boxes up the stairs without dropping them. Pausing for breath, I decided I might as well go down and get a few more rather than wait to have them brought up. After several solitary trips from the bottom to the top of the house, I had gathered six boxes. They lay in a row against the back wall, like I was doing a forensic analysis or trial preparation for a big case. I was glad I was having a chance to organize the search at the outset. If ever there was an example of the difference between Johnny and me, it was in what I was doing now.

I believed in results based on meticulous preparation, while Johnny was inclined to avoid what he considered unnecessary work. Johnny did put in the required effort when needed, but his greatness lay elsewhere. His strengths were in the performance, the presentation, his passion, and his ability to get others to do what they would consider either beneath them or beyond them. He was a master of persuasion. Growing up, I had admired him, but I had been jealous too.

Life for him had seemed so easy, while I stumbled a lot. When things got unbearable, I had fled. Of course, life is never easy for anyone, even Johnny Dodge, but it had taken me years to understand that.

I sat down heavily. My thoughts had drifted down into what I considered to be my dark place. Months had passed since I had last wallowed in self-pity and depression. As usual, the reason was the crash.

Johnny and I had been so close growing up, only to go our separate ways. The split had happened years ago and had been completely my fault.

We had both graduated from college and then grad school — he in economics and me in financial analysis. Over a round of drinks, Johnny and I had decided to create a partnership. Our rise had been spectacular. I did the analysis. Johnny executed the trades and handled investors. We leveraged everything and anything, and after five years we were on easy street. We had made a fortune — not a large one, but impressive nonetheless.

That next summer, I traveled to Europe on a whim, while Johnny held the fort.

I was in France when I saw a chateau by a lake, complete with gardens and a small vineyard. It was for sale, cheap, and I wanted it. I realized then that I had the chance to own something comparable to the splendors that surrounded me growing up. I flew back the next day determined to make that dream a reality.

In truth, I had the money to buy the property right then and there in my portion of the partnership, but Johnny and I had made a rule: don't take money out of the business. If we needed cash, we made it. I was just a few good trades away from my dream. I got to work and came up with a foolproof plan. Soybeans were the commodity that was poised for greatness, and we would be too.

I convinced Johnny that beans would rise dramatically. He agreed, and he executed the trades, but just after our buy orders filled, soybeans started to collapse. I told Johnny that something was wrong, and that we should get out of the position immediately. Johnny entered the sell orders, but before they could process, soybeans had reached a price so low that the commodity could no longer trade per the rules of the exchange.

Soybeans did not trade the next day, or the next, or the next. Each day the price dropped to the limit, and our sell orders remained unfilled.

Each day, 15 percent of our net worth disappeared. I was at fault. I knew this. I was paying the price for wanting something just for me.

By the fourth day, I found myself drunk in a bar. I told my tale of woe to anyone who would listen. I was eventually asked to leave. On the way back to my apartment that afternoon, I made a deal with God that if soybeans traded that day, I would quit the business. But beans did not trade that day.

On the fifth day, I decided that I was getting out of the business, God or no God. The moment I announced my decision to Johnny in his office, soybeans traded. All our sell orders filled in an instant, and we were out of soybeans altogether. We had experienced a catastrophic decrease in our equity.

Perversely, soybeans reversed like a scalded dog shortly thereafter, only we were no longer in the market. The train to riches left without us on board. Our trades had marked the top of the market and the very bottom. To me, the timing was a sign. All that was left for me to do was pack up my office.

Johnny tried to console me. He said I just needed to get back on the horse. He said these things, but I could tell his confidence in me was shaken. I told him I didn't have any fight left and that our business was over for me. I had dropped ten pounds in five days.

In my mind, I had had my chance, and I had blown my opportunity utterly.

There was a clause in our partnership agreement that if we

experienced a decrease of over 50 percent in a single quarter, we would return all funds to investors and dissolve the partnership. Luckily, the investors were just Johnny, a few clients, and me. I used the remaining part of my equity to return them the value per their last statement, avoiding any possibility of legal entanglements. I had a little left over but not that much.

I shook Johnny's hand, mumbled my sincerest apologies, and took the first flight I could get out of New York, which happened to be to Los Angeles.

Months passed before I pulled myself together. My money, what was left of it, was disappearing fast. I decided to resurrect myself in a new field: forensic accounting. I started from my rented apartment. Little by little, I began to make ends meet, and within a few years, I had several clients in the form of legal firms that needed my services. I leased a proper office. I kept raising prices to get rid of the few clients who were bothersome, but they kept offering to pay me what I asked and more. I stuck with it.

I would read about Johnny in the papers from time to time. He had joined with his dad at Dodge Capital.

Johnny and I had not met since the disaster until a year ago. I had flown to New York to see a client and ran into him at the King Cole Bar at the St. Regis. Nothing had changed. He was the same — flamboyant, brilliant, and persuasive.

Any jealousy or resentment I had harbored toward him had evaporated by that time. I had grown to accept my own limitations, but more importantly, I had accepted that others struggled similarly, albeit on different issues. He still considered me his friend, and that was a relief. He never blamed me for what happened, and for that I would forever hold him in high esteem.

I sighed and looked around the common room. I was back on the top floor, sitting on the couch. The dark clouds in my mind had moved off, and the sun appeared to be shining again. I was filled with wonder to be here at Rhinebeck. I had been so certain that I would never see this place again, but here I was. Johnny and I had started a new chapter, and that was a good thing.

I looked at all the boxes in front of me. I needed to do some work. My dark thoughts could return just as quickly as they had dissipated unless I kept my mind busy on other matters.

I grabbed a legal pad out of my briefcase and began to catalogue and separate the hundreds of pieces of correspondence from periodicals, auction house brochures, and what looked like manuscripts from colleagues that had been forwarded to Alice to be checked.

I had gone through three boxes when I found something that I thought might be of use — a manila envelope addressed to an M. Thoreau, care of the Carlyle Hotel, from Alice in her personal hand. The envelope had been returned marked unable to forward and postmarked close to the date of her death. I debated opening it but thought Johnny should be present. Johnny was taking a long time with Stanley, and in this house, I knew from experience that to remain alone for long was not a good idea.

Much of this feeling was probably the result of an overactive imagination growing up. Just the same, Johnny and I often felt there was more going on around us than we could see. I would often have nightmares sleeping here.

My nameless fears and troubled sleep followed me to the West Coast. I decided to master fear in general by swimming alone in the ocean after dark. In deep water off the coast of California, I would occasionally feel myself lifted by the displaced mass of something large passing beneath me in the darkness. It would take all my self-control and effort to continue to count my strokes and keep a measured pace, lest my imagination take over and I scream and flail in panic at the thought of what hunted below.

Such attempts at mental toughness had proved only partially successful. Darkness and the same nameless fears remained and were still my foes that stalked me just outside my vision, like the unknown predators of the deep that made their presence known, even if indirectly. Routine and a measured pace were my only anchors and salvation as I tried to quell my unruly imagination. I endured each day through discipline and effort rather than simply vanquishing my terrors to the nameless abyss from which they issued.

I shuddered. The envelope I held in my hand was definitely from Alice. It could mean something or nothing. I couldn't tell.

Alice and I had shared a bond, but that was long ago. In my attempt to put my life back together, I had put on hold many memories and debts owed to those who had helped me in the past, not the least of which was to Alice. Without her sixth sense, I would be dead. It had slipped my mind completely.

Alice had been a watchful presence while we were growing up, but in spite of her vigilance, strange things had a way of happening.

The game of hide-and-seek was a house favorite in which adults as well as Johnny and I participated. Alice would play when she was there, along with Johnny's parents. It was mandatory entertainment for houseguests.

The rules were simple. There was one seeker, and all the rest were hiders. The seeker was chosen by lot.

After one hour, announced by the striking of the hall clock, the game was over. Any hiders not found were declared winners. The field of play was the entire house other than the servants' quarters. Adult winners were awarded the beverage of their choice, while Johnny and I received cups of hot cocoa. The game was held after our dinner and before the adult cocktail hour.

The seeker was to remain in the drawing room until the clock in the reception area chimed, at which point he, or she, was free to hunt. I remember Alice always cautioning the field that no hider was to remain hidden for over sixty minutes and had to report back to the drawing room shortly thereafter or be disqualified.

As we grew older, the game devolved to only Johnny and myself with no set starting time, although after dark was preferred because the house was creepiest at night. We added rules and subtracted them, but the one-hour rule we always retained.

In one round that occurred shortly before the arrival of Miss Ponchikov, I was the hider and had managed to get into the trunk room that was located at the top of the servants' wing. Although not exactly off limits, it was not precisely inside the established rules of the game either. Usually the room was locked. The rules stated unequivocally that the servants' quarters were out of bounds, but the trunk room, although in the servants' wing, was not technically part of the servants' quarters, since no servant lived there. At least that was my logic at the time.

Was I cheating? No, I had thought. Besides, I wanted to get one over on Johnny, and this hiding place I felt pretty certain would do just that. In addition, I could scare the pants off him if I opened a trunk from inside and screamed as he approached.

The trunk room contained more luggage than a luggage store. There were dozens of suitcases and dozens of trunks in all shapes and sizes. Lighting was by means of two bulbs in metal cages suspended from the ceiling.

One large trunk, set apart from the others, looked particularly promising. It was almost six feet long, three to four feet wide, and two to three feet deep. The sides were of black leather over a hard wood of some sort. There were brass fittings on all the corners, but they had grown dark with age. There were dull brass strips along each edge and brass bands that circled the trunk both lengthwise and crosswise.

The locking mechanism was made of a metal other than brass, perhaps hardened steel, and looked particularly robust.

The lock was made up of two parts. A hinged portion that lay flat when closed but connected to a bottom part that contained the lock. The key was in it and attached by a chain to an eyelet. The key could be removed and the chain clipped to a ring for safekeeping when traveling. The key, too, was unusual. I unclipped the chain and examined the key closely. It was a work of art, complicated, finely cut, and intricate. One would not be able to pick this lock easily. This trunk would keep out all but the most determined thief, even if he had all the time in the world to open it.

After I inserted the key again and turned it, the lid opened smoothly on hinges hidden from view. The top and sides were lined with cushioned white satin held in place by hundreds of small brass studs in a regular pattern. The bottom was of the same white satin but with no cushioning.

Stepping inside, I felt like I was climbing into a coffin. I hesitated as I sat down before lowering the lid. What if the lid somehow locked? I decided to be very careful in how I lowered the lid, and just before I did, I remembered I still held the key in my hand and that the lights were on — a dead giveaway. I was pondering this when I heard a sound that might have come from the hallway outside. Quickly I got out of the trunk, tiptoed to the light switch, and turned off the lights. I felt my way back in the darkness and got back in.

I reached up and pulled the lid down. It shut faster than I expected and closed with a mild thump followed by a click, the sound of which was quickly absorbed by the trunk's lining. Was that the lock clicking into place? I was astounded at how truly dark it was. I opened my eyes and closed them. I could not tell the difference. What about the key? I tried to remember whether I had left the key in the lock before I got in. I pushed the lid. It did not budge. I searched for the key in what little room I had. In spite of my rising panic, I was able to think clearly enough that not having the key was more promising than if I had found it. Just the same, I had moved in a fraction of a second from experiencing a childish game to deadly peril.

I would like to think that I behaved admirably, but I did not. It was when it seemed hard to breathe that I started to become truly frightened; then I panicked in earnest. I screamed. I screamed over and over, but my cries were muffled in the confined space and only seemed to make my predicament worse. In time, I knew I would run out of oxygen and suffocate to death — my mummified corpse to be found years later, or maybe never. All I could do after that realization was whimper.

What started then was a peculiar dialogue inside my mind of cold logic on one side and panic on the other. I would observe myself crying and screaming. In a calm voice, I would think, *This is what it's like to die. I thought death was supposed to be extremely painful and awful. It doesn't seem that way. I'm too young to die, but that's what's going to happen — such a waste.*

While part of my mind remained calm, the other part went through endless loops of hope, fear, tears, and angry desperation at my approaching death. I don't know how long I had been in the trunk, when suddenly the lid was flung open, and there were Alice and Johnny looking at me. I wasn't sure how they had found me, or even if they were real, but there they were.

I was led away barely alive, given some brandy, and put to bed.

Later, I had to explain exactly how I managed to get into such a dangerous position. I told them I really had no idea, but I promised not to be so stupid in the future. I had never seen Alice upset, but she was then. She said she should have locked that trunk and taken the key. Johnny's parents as well as the entire household were beside themselves. My escape had been a close call.

Afterward, I lay in my bed and Johnny came into the room and sat down next to me. He looked a little pale.

"That was close. I had no idea where you were." He breathed out heavily.

"Leave it to me to both win and lose at the same time. I locked myself in a trunk. How stupid can you get?"

"Pretty damn stupid," he said and laughed. I did too.

"How did you know I was in there?"

"It was Alice. I was searching upstairs when I turned around, and there she was. She asked me what I was doing. I told her we were playing hide-and-seek. It was pretty weird. She looked upset and proceeded to go through the house room by room really fast and then headed for the servant's quarters. I followed her as she zeroed in on the trunk room. She opened the door and saw the trunk. She actually said the F word, as well as a few more. The key was in the lock, so she opened it, and there you were. You looked rather awful."

"Yeah, I felt rather awful, and I was pretty sure that was the end for me. I really thought I was going to die. I mean, really."

"You had that look that said your rescue was a near thing. I would've been so pissed at you. You've no idea. By the way, Aunt Alice said something else under her breath. She said that wasn't the first time that trunk had locked someone inside, whatever that means. The moment was very creepy. I had no idea what to say, so I just shut up."

"You didn't ask her what she meant?"

"Are you kidding?"

"No, no. You did the right thing. Better to have let that slide."

We sat there happy to be in each other's company. Finally, I said, "I guess we won't be playing a lot of hide-and-seek for a while."

"Looks that way."

After I recovered the next day, our hide-and-seek activities were severely curtailed and replaced by a great deal more household chores for the duration of that vacation.

That was a long time ago, but the incident could have been yesterday. I remembered what happened so clearly after having forgotten all about it for so long. I got up and went downstairs.

6

I wandered into the kitchen where Dagmar was making tea for herself.

"They're in Stan's office, last door on your right."

"Thank you, Dagmar."

I walked down the corridor to an open door. Inside were Johnny and Stanley, along with Robert the Bruce. Johnny and Stanley were drinking and chatting amiably. Straight whiskey, from where I stood, and they must have had more than one, because Stanley's Scottish roots were much in evidence and Johnny had a grin on his face that seemed to be more or less permanent. Robert was lying down with his head on his paws with a peaceful expression.

"Ah, there you are," Johnny said. "Join us. I was going to get you, but I couldn't seem to make it out of the chair."

"Yes, please," said Stanley and offered me a seat. He whirled around with his back to me as he splashed two inches of amber liquid into a cut-crystal glass. "Try this on for size," he said, handing me the glass.

I took the glass and sniffed. The smell was heavenly, if heaven had a slightly smoky aroma.

"Ninety-proof from his family's brewery," chirped Johnny. "Bloody marvelous."

I sat down and took a swallow. My discovery and my questions evaporated in blissful satisfaction.

I raised my glass. "Marvelous indeed, Stanley."

I had another swig, and as if by magic, I was grinning too.

"We're celebrating?"

"Oh yes, we are," said Johnny. "Stanley has saved our backsides once again. In fact, he saved them years ago; only we never knew it. Tell him, Stanley."

"Well, you see, you left the bottles on the table in the cellar. I was telling Johnny here how I discovered you both had managed to drink the two '59s. Naughty boys," he said shaking his finger at us, "although I had to admire your taste.

"I also told your partner-in-crime that I had not fallen off the turnip cart yesterday. We in service know how things stand. Some young idiots grab an expensive bottle, and then the head butler has to replace it somehow, some way."

He looked significantly in our direction.

"I saw the state of affairs and figured I would do everyone a good turn. To my mind, the '61 Lafite is by far the better choice, better than the '59, although some would tend to disagree, and more power to 'em, I say. Few have had the opportunity to choose between the two like I have.

"To steam the labels off the empties and apply them to two '61s, which we happened to have at the time, was but the work of a moment.

"You see, the '59 was what everyone drank, waiting for the 1961 to come into its own. That is why they became so rare. They were very good but definitely a runner-up when compared to the

'61. The '61 has aged delightfully well and can probably improve more, but I digress."

"He samples them. Can you believe it?" bubbled Johnny. "Every now and again he has a go to see how the wine is getting on. No wonder he loves this place. He's sitting on a wine lover's treasure trove."

"Well, 'tis true. I could not forgive myself if a spectacular wine was needed to impress a guest, and the reality wasn't that spectacular. The only way to know is to taste occasionally. Dagmar, bless her, pulls out all the stops on a roast beef Sunday dinner, and we have a taste of an Haut Brion or a Latour. Some vintages we've had to consume in full because they passed their peak. Most people nowadays have not had the chance to drink an aged Bordeaux of the quality found in this cellar. Such precious moments are rare. The dinner will be a great success, I'm sure."

"Well, Stanley, we thank you. You're a saint," said Johnny.

"It's my pleasure. Now, you mentioned you wanted some boxes moved."

"No need," I said. "I wanted some exercise, so I moved them up to our floor. Johnny, perhaps you should explain."

Stanley looked at Johnny expectantly.

"Ah yes. We thought we'd go through some of the boxes of correspondence and magazines and either chuck what does not seem worth keeping or archive it."

"I see, and you are doing this because…?"

Johnny paused. "I think curiosity is as good a reason as any. We didn't know Aunt Alice that well. We were too young. After she passed, her life and the circumstances of her death became subjects the parents didn't want to talk about. We knew her, of course, but not really. We weren't old enough to understand her life, particularly its context and complexity. Now that we're older, we would like to know more. We want to hear her story."

"I see. Allow me to think on this for a few moments, if you please."

"Of course," Johnny answered.

Stanley swiveled his chair away from us and looked out the window. We waited. The window overlooked the lawn that stretched down to the woods, hidden from view by the fog. He seemed to be making up his mind about something, and after a minute he turned back.

"I apologize, but I had to make a decision that took some time. I have worked for this house for many years. Your aunt originally employed me. During that time, I've been privy to many things, not all of them savory. We all have acted in ways that question our good opinions of ourselves. That being said, she was a marvelous woman, who led an extraordinary life. I saw some of it but not all.

"I asked myself, what would she have me do? Would she want me to tell you her story or not?

"The truth is she never really cared what people thought of her. She marched to the beat of her own drum and tended to shun convention. That being said, my decision is difficult. I must reveal much that is dark in order for you both to appreciate how truly dazzling and rare an individual she was. Nobody, other than me, knows her story, and that is a shame."

"So, you agree?" Johnny asked.

"Yes. What I would like, with your permission, is to sit down after dinner and tell you what I know. In addition, I would rather this remain between ourselves for reasons that will become obvious."

Johnny stood up and put down his glass. "Stanley, that sounds excellent. In the meantime, we'll leave you to get on, with our thanks."

I said my thanks as well and accompanied Johnny up the back stairs to the bedroom hallway rather than passing through the kitchen and bothering Dagmar. We arrived at the top of the house, where I had laid out all the boxes.

Johnny eyed them. "Just like old times."

"Yes, I was thinking much the same thing."

"Percy, I didn't mean to remind you…"

"Have no fear. I'm certainly not broken, and I can talk about my leaving and all that, so feel free to say whatever is on your mind. Fragile, I'm not, in spite of any appearances to the contrary."

"I'm so glad to hear it," said Johnny, looking at me closely. "For my part, I would like to say that you and I working together was the happiest of times. You have no idea how glad I am to see you and how much I've missed it. I mean, who am I really going to talk to? There's been no one."

Johnny turned away. I could see him make an effort to quell his emotions. He then asked, "So, what do you have going on here?"

"I'll show you, but first, thanks for saying that. I feel the same, but let's pick that topic up later, when we have more time. Perhaps you will also give me your other reason for my being here?"

"We'll get to that, but for now I'd rather forget my troubles until tomorrow."

"Fair enough; back to the boxes," I said, changing the subject. "I carried them up here and went through them on a cursory basis, pulling out the correspondence and seeing what was there."

I picked up my legal pad and consulted it.

"After her death, there were several requests from colleagues to look over research papers, a few invites, with the rest being printed stuff such as catalogues, periodicals, and the like. There were no bills or financial information. I assumed these were pulled by Mr. Dodge. The two things of interest were the figurine, which Robert keyed on, and this."

I handed him the envelope.

"You see it's postmarked just before her death and returned

unable to forward. It's handwritten. I thought you might be the one to open it."

"Interesting," said Johnny, examining the envelope. "I've never heard of an M. Thoreau. Shall we read it? I'll pass you each page as I finish, and then we'll see where we are."

Johnny sat on the couch and opened the letter. I waited for him to finish the first page. He handed it to me.

7

Dearest —

I am sorry we fought and that I upset you. Please understand it is not easy for me to write about these matters. I would rather not even now, but I seem to have no choice if we are to continue together.

You are so jealous. That green-eyed monster lives inside you like a beast. You need to lock that away. Promise me you will? Please?

I have the figurine en route to me. It does not look like much. Such things never do, but I am relieved to know it is safe.

"So, how did all this happen?" you wish to know. "Do I still love him?" you ask. How could you?

I am sickened to think that you would even consider the thought. But what can I do? I can only repeat over and over that you needn't worry yourself. You will anyway, but I suppose that is my cross to bear.

What follows will ease your mind, but then again, it may not, for reasons that will become apparent.

When last I saw Bromley, he was with Freddy and Arthur. They were drinking, laughing, and carrying on about how rich they would become. He referred to me as "that bitch" and told them how he was looking forward to my comeuppance again after a few more drinks. I forced myself to not pull out the Webley I had hidden and see what size hole a .455 bullet would make in him, but I was only one, and they were three. They would find out soon enough. I was finished with them.

Thankfully, they were busy drinking what I had taken such care to provide. They had sent away all the guides and hired hands to safeguard the find.

We had discovered the tolas *only a week before. It had been one discovery after another, but the most exciting was the figurine. Arthur found it. Typical—but lucky he was the one who did. He had seen enough raw stones to know exactly what he held in his hands. He said he had never come across one that size. The gem was held in the arms of a female figure.*

Arthur realized that the discovery changed everything, and I did, too. I had become unnecessary, and I was alone.

I watched them whisper amongst themselves. I saw the looks on their faces, and they frightened me. I had to do something, and fast.

I had noticed quite a number of Brugmansia *nearby. Whether B. versicolor or another species, I did not know. If you are not familiar with it, this is a large plant with many yellow, or in this case pinkish, trumpet-shaped flowers that droop down. The flower is particularly fragrant at night as it tries to attract certain pollinating moths.*

I had encountered this plant and its seeds some time ago when examining various South American burial sites and tolas. *It was used to drug wives and slaves, so they might be buried alive with their dead lords, but I found out from the indigenous peoples that in less concentrated forms, the plant can be used as a soporific, an anti-inflammatory, or a gateway to the spirit world. All parts of the plant contain powerful alkaloids that affect the mind and the body.*

Since it was found at several digs, I had spoken about the plant with nearby shamans, who had cautioned me. Brugmansia *was occasionally given to unruly adolescents so that their dead ancestors in the spirit* world could berate them for their behavior and make them more compliant. It was not to be used lightly.

One shaman in particular smiled and laughed when he saw me. He told me through an interpreter that he had heard from his father that I would be arriving soon and that he was to give me some seeds. Further, he was to teach me how to take the flowers and turn them into a tincture using the local alcoholic beverage. He even spoke my name.

When I demanded to know how this was possible, the shaman didn't answer but kept smiling and nodding. The interpreter said, "Learn what you can. Muy importante."

On the way back, my guide told me that the father had been a powerful shaman. He continued to be honored in the village even though he died years ago.

I still have those seeds.

The difficulty was the dosage and the taste. The amount of alkaloid present varies from plant to plant, leaf to leaf, and flower to flower. It is even affected by the time of day it is picked.

I found out much later one must harvest many leaves and flowers at the same time and experiment, creating stronger concentrations. Too much would send me into a delirium that can be truly terrifying. The drug can even affect the muscles of the eyes that control focusing, adding to its already hallucinogenic effects, which I can tell you are fierce.

Shamans use this plant combined with other ingredients to talk to those who are dead, to command those who are living, and to speak with those of the future to learn what the gods are planning.

Too concentrated, and the results can be horrific beyond any imagining. I am neither sorry nor afraid to tell you that the mixture they drank was so concentrated that whether they lived or died would be in the hands of the gods that guarded the tolas we had discovered. I trusted those guardians would at least welcome a little sport. Sitting around a tomb for years without end can be so boring.

I almost fell victim to my own plan.

I had wanted to see the results of my work. I strayed too close. They grabbed me. Bromley was on top of me when sweat began to bead on his forehead and chest. His jugular vein and the veins on his forehead started to swell to the size of fingers and pulse in throbs that became faster and faster. His eye misted over and began to tear, while his respiration increased and his arms began to twitch. I threw him off. The others looked at me in a strange way and then not at me at all. Thick white foam began to form on Freddy's half-open lips while Arthur's eyes turned bright red. Both were covered in sweat that seemed to pour from their bodies. Their limbs began to contort, and that is when the screaming began. They started as murmurs and then rose to ear-splitting shrieks. The gods were busy.

I grabbed my clothes and began to search for the figurine. I went through each of their belongings, but I couldn't find it. I returned to where they lay, sprawled about. I grabbed Bromley by the hair and struck him violently across the face several times. I yelled to get his attention.

"Where is it? Tell me!"

He looked at me with vacant eyes, his mouth stretched impossibly wide. No sound came out. I dropped him and reached for Arthur, when I saw a bag underneath a chair. I knew the jewel was there. They wouldn't let it out of their sight. I grabbed the bag and started to walk away when I noticed Freddy. He was staring at his bleeding arm out of which he had bitten a meaty chunk. I wished him a merry feast, grabbed my pack, and left. I didn't look back. I was filled with terrible rage. I had wreaked a horrible vengeance. I was barely satisfied, but it would have to do.

They took months to get back to civilization. I heard that Bromley returned to his estate. Freddy I never heard from. Arthur contracted dengue fever and tried to visit me when he was recovered. I refused and had him thrown out instead. The divorce had already gone through by the time he showed up. His skin color, I am happy to say, had changed to gray.

So, my darling, you got your wish. I told you everything. Did you get more than you bargained for? Do you still love me?

Tell me, soon.

— ALICE

I finished reading, put the pages in order, and passed them back to Johnny.

"Wow," I said, shaking my head. "Extraordinary. The letter answers several questions while generating a host of others."

Johnny placed the sheets back in the envelope. "That it does. I can't say I'm surprised by what she wrote, given the circumstances, although I am completely, if you know what I mean. It makes me angry."

"Me too. She was a woman isolated and alone in a jungle, on top of that she was Alice, and we knew her."

"Precisely. Just the same, she bided her time and got her revenge. I admire her for that. Her plan was well conceived and executed. I would have used the Webley, I think."

"Three against one. Not the best odds. At least we know the story behind Arthur Blain and where that little statue came from," I said.

"That we do. I suggest we keep our discovery of that little item between ourselves for now. I'll have Simon take these boxes back down. For now, let's dress for dinner. What do you say?"

"Good plan."

8

Johnny and I changed into blazers and ties, the minimum attire for dinner. We went back downstairs with Robert close behind as the clock struck six. The drawing-room drapes were shut and a fire lit in the grate. Johnny went over to the bar to make us vodka tonics, while I gazed at the Constable. He came up beside me and handed me my drink.

"Cheers," he said.

I clinked his glass.

We stood silently before the painting until Johnny commented, "He transports me into a place of peace and tranquility, although the clouds in the distance always seem to portend an approaching storm."

"Rain, at the least, I think."

"When I stare at it, I wonder which is more real: Rhinebeck or Constable's nineteenth-century England?"

"You mean, both don't represent reality."

Johnny chuckled. "That's why I like having you around." He

slapped my shoulder. "You understand me. Remember the story of *Brigadoon?*"

"Yes, your mother took us to the Broadway musical when we were small."

"I loved the idea of escaping into another world," said Johnny. "Rhinebeck has been that mythical place for me. It's always been far from the realities and struggles of life. At least I used to think so."

"Not anymore?"

"I can feel something stirring. This house used to be quiet and restful, like the painting. Now the water looks a lot deeper than I thought, and there are things moving beneath the surface. My world is changing. Look at the picture on the table. Do you see the same person?"

I looked at the silver-framed photograph of Alice. "I admit our past image of her may have been naïve."

"Tell me about it," said Johnny. "And I have a feeling we'll know far more than we bargained for by the time all is said and done. I am more than a little nervous. I really liked how I used to think of her. I loved her glamour and the security she represented."

"Yes. Obviously the image of her that we believed growing up was just that — an image. Now that we're seeing the real Alice, our notions of her are being shaken up a bit."

"More than a bit — my entire perception of her has changed, and there's no going back. It's more than a little distressing."

"Yes, but Alice is still the same Alice she always was," I said. "She's there in our memories, just as alive, caring, and vibrant. We can keep her that way if we want. We don't have to judge her or her actions. After all, you never seemed to have judged mine, and if you want to know why I'm here, I think it's because of that."

He looked at me. "Oh, I judged you all right. I was so upset with you — you have no idea. But underneath all my upset, I had faith, faith that somehow you would recover and life would all work out.

That belief was unshakeable. It's kept me going, and here we are today talking to each other."

"Well, I'm certainly glad someone believed in me. Personally, what little faith I had in myself evaporated when I left. I held myself responsible. It took a long time to recover. I appreciate and thank you for your unabated confidence in me."

"You're welcome." Johnny looked back at the painting. There was just the sound of the fire.

"I propose a toast," I said, interrupting the quiet.

"A toast?"

"To faith, the universal solvent of all logic and rational thought." I raised my glass.

"To faith, the unending source of relentless persistence," replied Johnny, raising his.

Our glasses clinked again.

At that moment, Stanley opened the doors to the dining room. The long table was set for us and lit by two gigantic silver candelabras.

"Dinner is served. You may bring your drinks, or leave them. I have decanted a very nice Pétrus, should you choose to start afresh."

Johnny looked at me, swallowed the rest of his drink in one gulp, and said, "I'm for the Pétrus."

I did the same but placed my glass with a sip left on the table next to the picture of Alice as a token of my esteem and an offering for her continued protection. In this house, I felt better covering all the bases. I followed Johnny into the dining room and seated myself opposite him.

Robert's black eyes followed us, but he remained by the fire.

Simon entered with two bowls of consommé from behind a Chinese screen that hid the passage to the kitchen. Stanley busied himself with the wine, while Johnny and I sampled the soup.

Dinner moved from course to course as Johnny and I chatted.

After finishing, and gaining at least five pounds in the process, we thanked Dagmar, Stanley, Simon, and Jane for their efforts. The dinner had been superb.

Stanley said, "Gentlemen, I have laid out some port and brandy on the side table in the library. I will join you in twenty minutes."

Johnny and I, with Robert following, passed down the hall to the library. It was only slightly smaller than the drawing room. Three of the four walls were covered by floor-to-ceiling shelving, filled with books of all sorts. The wall facing the door had drapes that were closed for the night. Behind them, french windows looked out toward the sweep of lawn at the back of the house. We poured ourselves some port and lit up two Montecristos while we waited for Stanley.

About twenty minutes later, Stanley slipped in. He held a leather case in his hand, the size of a diary.

"I hate to disturb you now that you are sitting down, but I would rather we move to her ladyship's sitting room. It is rarely used, but I would feel more comfortable sitting there than here, where I often serve. It is hard for me to stop being a butler, you understand. The story I have to tell is long. If you both will follow me…Bring the port if you will, as well as the humidor. I will sample both to make sure the house is living up to its standards of excellence," he said with a thin smile.

Johnny and I got up and carried our glasses and cigars. I brought the decanter and an extra glass while Johnny took the humidor. We passed out of the library to the west wing, where Alice had resided. Robert's toenails clicked on the marble floor as we entered. The apartment consisted of a large, well-lit sitting room and a separate bedroom with a bath and walk-in closet that was entered through a connecting door. As we seated ourselves, Stanley lit the fire. There was a low black-lacquer table, a couch, and two comfortable chairs at either end. The theme of the room was gray, done up in subdued elegance. Alice's long Louis XIV desk in dark mahogany and ebony was set in front of the window whose drapes had been drawn for the night. The carpet was unusually thick. Johnny sat in one of the chairs while I relaxed on the couch. Once the fire was burning brightly, Stanley turned off the lights, so only the glow of the fire lit the room. I handed him a glass while Johnny opened the humidor. The case he placed on the table. Robert stretched out by the fire and closed his eyes.

"Gentlemen, now that we are settled, I am sure you have questions, but before I answer them, I thought I would tell you the story of her ladyship from the time I first met her. I have always referred to her as 'her ladyship' because of her first marriage to Lord Bromley. What I will tell you should satisfy your curiosity and give you some of the context you seek.

"In addition, I have chosen to put aside my butler duties for the night and sit down as a normal soul. Starting tomorrow, the rest of the family will be arriving, along with guests, and I will have neither the time nor the inclination to discuss what I am about to relate. Tonight is all we have.

"Lastly, whatever I say is between us. What you do with the information is up to you, but as far as I am concerned, we never talked. Agreed?"

Johnny and I voiced our assent. Stanley cleared his throat and began.

"I first met her ladyship in England just after she had married Lord Bromley. We met in London at her suite at the Connaught Hotel where she and her new husband were staying before journeying to North America. She offered me a position as head butler. His lordship was not in attendance, a point that troubled me, but which was happily eclipsed by the warmth with which I was received.

"She informed me that she and Lord Bromley would be moving

to New York and that part of my duties would include opening up and maintaining this estate and her ladyship's apartment in the city. Both had been closed since the death of her mother.

"I asked whether in addition they would be keeping Lord Bromley's estate in Shropshire. She told me no. She had hired an independent accounting firm to do an analysis of Lord Bromley's situation. The firm had deemed it not only prudent but necessary to liquidate the property in its entirety to cover the various taxes and legal entanglements that had dogged Lord Bromley for some time. Unfortunately for him, his estate was too small to be profitable and too expensive to be run continuously at a loss. They would move to the United States instead.

"I then inquired when I would be interviewing with Lord Bromley so that I might meet with his approval. At this suggestion, there was a pause. She said quite carefully that *all* financial matters, including the hiring of staff, were in her hands. The trustees that handled and oversaw her assets were confident in her dealings, and if need be, she could be as frugal as any Scotsman.

"Here she poked fun at my Scottish accent, which was more pronounced at the time. She smiled at me and by doing so, vanquished any hesitation I had in making my decision to accept her employment.

"In those days, I must admit, I was a bit more impetuous than I am now. I considered that my favorable impression of her ladyship was sufficient grounds for taking the position and told her so. She shook my hand in the American way to seal the bargain.

"At another time, I might have had serious reservations.

"England in those days was a country whose government, heavy industries, and large estates were controlled almost exclusively by men. Not so in this case. Here, a woman signed the checks, hired the staff, and decided how to allocate resources. I also felt that she did not entirely trust her husband in financial matters. I could explain her behavior and his absence in no other way.

"Even more alarming was the conclusion that she must have been the one to insist that his lordship give up a patrimony that must have been in his family for generations. This may have been sound financial maneuvering, but as a foundation for a tranquil marriage, it was a risky venture.

"At best, the arrangement might make for a rocky start. At worst, the loss of the property might be such a wound to his lordship's pride that no amount of time could heal it. Violence and hatred might become his only means to restore his dignity.

"Although I did consider these things in a vague sort of way, there was nothing to be done. She had won me over completely, and that was that. On looking back, I think a little more thought at the time might have prepared me for what was to follow."

At this juncture, he paused and took a drag of his cigar and a sip of port. He then got up to stir the fire and sat back down, as if he was debating how best to continue.

"I was to start immediately. My employer at the time had agreed to let me go if I should be accepted in the position, so I found myself awaiting my first meeting with Lord Bromley with both curiosity and trepidation. In service, at that time, there were whole networks of butlers, coachmen, chauffeurs, maids, cooks, and staff who were devoted to collecting the latest information regarding the leading families.

"My sources told me to expect a man of prickly disposition and accustomed to getting his way. He had attended Eton and then Oxford, where he excelled at sports, particularly rugby, but little else. He loved fast cars and airplanes, considered himself to be devilishly handsome, and thought himself the smartest person in the room. He enjoyed gambling at cards and was known as a lady's man. There were also rumblings of a dark and sinister side, but as to what exactly, no one could say with any precision, other than they had heard rumors.

"We met the following day again at the Connaught. Her ladyship was not present. The information I had did not prepare me for the overpowering charisma and charm of the man. I was no longer surprised that her ladyship had fallen for him. I doubted anyone would be safe once he had made up his mind that he wanted them, be they male or female. I don't know why or how I got that impression, but I did. There was a sexual magnetism about him that was almost palpable. He balanced this with a grace and ease of communication that was so masterful that I wondered if I had misread him. We got along famously, and I ended up speaking far more about myself than I had expected.

"It was at the end of the interview that he received a note from the concierge delivered by a bellman. He apologized, took out a platinum fountain pen as he read it, and began to write something on the note. I caught my breath in this interlude and observed him more closely.

"He was a tall man and extremely fit. His hair was black as jet, the same color as her ladyship's, and longer than was the fashion. His eyes, like her ladyship's, were so dark as to appear completely black. His skin was white and somewhat translucent. He was dressed immaculately in a charcoal-gray suit, white shirt, and club tie. He was the epitome of the English lord in manners, speech, and behavior.

"As I sat there, I became aware of the more carnivorous nature of the man. It was not my imagination. I was sitting down in front of a black panther who glanced at me every so often in relaxed disinterest while the tip of his tail in the form of a pen traveled this way and that as if of its own accord. He was a predator, and I knew it. I felt at once at ease yet filled with a nameless dread. There would be no bars separating us.

"I knew then and there that if he decided I was prey, I would be eaten. It would not be personal. Such lethality was both spellbinding and hypnotic.

"At that moment, her ladyship slipped into the room and perched herself on the arm of his chair. She encircled his shoulders with her arms as they chatted about the note his lordship had received. I relaxed as I watched. They were supremely well matched. Their beauty together and their palpable and obvious love for each other was something to behold. I was their head butler, and I decided that I was well pleased.

"Unfortunately, that equanimity was not to last."

Stanley paused again in the narrative as he drank his port and smoked his cigar. Johnny and I sat back and waited for him to continue. I shivered, thinking that this was just the type of tale to be told on a rainy night in a dark room lit only by a fire. Stanley's voice started again.

"We traveled to America aboard the Queen Mary and arrived in New York. From there I traveled to Rhinebeck to survey what would be required to open the house. After I made my report, I was given approval to make the extensive changes and repairs.

"It was not until the couple returned after about half a year to take up residence permanently that I felt something was amiss.

"There were two points that troubled me. The first was that her ladyship was unusually quiet. I thought that this might be the result of their not producing an heir, but this did not seem to answer why she seemed almost cowed. I observed that his lordship would ask her to do something and that she would immediately hop to it. The smile that had so captivated me had disappeared.

"The second was the trunk. It was an extraordinarily heavy and well-made affair that his lordship insisted be kept at the foot of their bed. I did not know what to make of it."

Stanley poured some more port and continued.

"They were rarely alone. They either had houseguests or they traveled to New York during the week. One night in particular, there was just the two of them. They had dined and had moved to the library, where they began to argue.

"The servants had been sent to bed. I was the only one in attendance and remained in the hallway. The argument must have begun civilly enough, because I could hear nothing from outside the door. But by the end, the disagreement had escalated into a notable altercation. They screamed and yelled at each other for at least an hour, eventually devolving into cursing each other in various languages. The things they said to each other were violent and cruel. I could do nothing.

"Eventually, his lordship yelled that he'd had enough and that her ladyship was to be taught another lesson. I heard her ladyship scream, 'No!' when the door to the library burst open and slammed against the stop. I quickly ducked into a doorway.

"I heard him drag her down the hall, across the foyer, and up the stairs. She struggled, but it was no use against such a powerful man. I heard their bedroom door slam and then silence. I went into the library to collect the glasses and coffee cups, muttering to myself that my place was not to interfere. Such words did nothing to erase the shame I felt for having done nothing. Later, I soothed my conscience by deciding to speak to her ladyship, even if what I had to say cost me my position.

"I did not see her the next morning and asked her maid how her ladyship was feeling. She said she would be staying in her room for now. His lordship came down for breakfast in high spirits, announcing with his dazzling smile that he would be staying at his club in the city for a few days and returning on Friday.

"After he had left for town, I climbed the stairs to confront my employer. I knocked on the door and asked if I might have a word. I was refused, but I persisted until I was let in. I would not be denied.

"The room was darkened, and her ladyship was sitting on the

floor with her legs outstretched, leaning back against the far side of the bed.

"I could see the top of her head. She asked what was so important, not even bothering to look at me. I answered that if she wished to dismiss me after what I was about to say, that was her prerogative, but I was not about to stand by and see her ladyship manhandled by anyone, even his lordship, ever again.

"She said softly that there was nothing I could do. I disagreed. We went back and forth. But I can be quite forceful and persistent when I have made up my mind. I told her that she needed someone in her corner. I was that person, but we would not discuss the matter in her bedroom. She needed to get dressed and meet me in the study where there would be coffee waiting, as well as something stronger. To this, she agreed and promised to meet me in thirty minutes.

"She arrived looking pale but presentable. I served her coffee. She added a splash of brandy and sat down. She told me that she had made a decision but was uncertain exactly how to proceed. She understood my feelings but thought it best that I hear what led up to the current disturbance in full, before going any further. According to her, she had no one to blame but herself. She would not look at me as she spoke of the events leading to the night in question but stared steadily out the window as she spoke.

"Their life together had started out wonderfully. They were so in love. Life could not have been better; at least, that was her impression. She had known his lordship needed money. He had been upfront about this from the beginning. Nonetheless, her finance people were alarmed. She thought the state of affairs was fairly simple. She wanted a title, and if he needed money, that was the cost of doing business. Titles were paid for all the time. The trustees understood this easily enough and were quite content to go ahead with an arrangement if that was all that was required, but there were other troubling indications as well. They had done some checking.

"Lord Bromley had recently been asked not to visit Brook's in London due to concerns about his card-playing. Although he had not been asked to resign his membership, various private sources had confirmed that there had been a peculiar string of good luck in his favor and a corresponding string of bad luck against a member of the Court of Directors of the Bank of England. There was insufficient evidence to accuse him of cheating, but the laws of probability had been stretched far enough to warrant a prohibition.

"Additionally, there were stories that he dabbled in what could only be characterized as mesmerism or hypnotism of some sort. He appeared to have some power over women whereby they did whatever he asked.

"If there was any truth to these allegations, the trustees felt the match should not go forward. If for some reason she still thought she should, then their duty was to place a limit on the total amount of expenditure that would be authorized for a period of at least two years. The trustees advised her that this was to remain between her ladyship and themselves as a fail-safe, should she be coerced into authorizing expenses that, although she could well afford them, were deemed unsuitable.

"Her ladyship confronted him with these issues.

"His lordship admitted that he saw the member mentioned in the card incident as a pigeon ripe for the plucking. He needed funds. Cheating had not been necessary — the man had been that inept. And as to his supposed supernatural powers over women, he claimed the story was a complete fabrication. He had heard the rumors and had done nothing to discredit them, as they served him. Such supernatural tales had done wonders in backing off his creditors, of which he had more than a few.

"Gradually, she allowed herself to be persuaded that the reports were the result of misunderstanding rather than fact and that the source of all of Lord Bromley's difficulties was the financial morass he had inherited when his father died.

"She went back to the trustees and wrangled an agreement to allow one of her many trusts to cover the balance of his debts, but only after his estate was sold. Everyone was in agreement.

"They married.

"The wedding was a success, and all seemed well.

"She told me they were in Tuscany when his behavior took a peculiar turn.

"One morning, a large trunk arrived for him at the villa where they were staying. His lordship had two men place it in a corner of their bedroom. When she asked why it was there rather than in a storeroom, he said that it was a work of art made for him in Germany to his specifications. He found it beautiful, and other than its aesthetic value, it served no purpose at this time. Such behavior seemed to her eccentric, bordering on the bizarre. Not wanting to disturb their harmony, she agreed.

"One morning, her ladyship was called to the telephone by the majordomo. His lordship was out riding and couldn't be reached. On the line was the accountant of the owner of the villa they were vacationing at. He wanted to know the name and address of her bank, so he could present the bill for their stay.

"Her ladyship said she was confused. Her husband had extolled the owner's generosity on allowing them to stay at his estate for a month for free. It had been a wedding present.

"To clear the matter up, she asked for and received the owner's telephone number in Rome. She reached him, and after a great deal of histrionics on both sides, the truth was finally revealed.

"The accountant had been ordered to speak only with his lordship and no one else. He was to have gotten the address of her ladyship's bank in New York so that he could submit a bill for the stay. She was not to know anything about it. In addition, the owner and his lordship had struck a deal whereby the accountant would bill triple the cost and remit half to his lordship's bank in London upon receipt. Since this was their honeymoon, the bill would be mistaken for that of a hotel and be paid without a second thought.

"By the time his lordship returned, her ladyship was outraged. Why do this when if he needed money, all he had to do was ask? She met him coming up the stairs and confronted him with the deception. His lordship smiled at her, and everything changed in an instant.

"He struck her across the mouth with the flat of his hand. Her ladyship fell back on the stairs, stunned. He said to her softly, 'Do *not* defy me. You are mistaken.' She shook her head and attempted to reply, when he reached back and struck her again. Once more he said, 'You are mistaken, aren't you?'

"She shook her head, only this time he grabbed her wrist and dragged her up the stairs to their room. He whispered to her as he pulled her along, 'I was hoping I would not have to resort to this, but I see you need to be taught a lesson.' He unlocked the trunk that lay in the corner of the room and proceeded to strip her naked. She struggled to get away, but he was the stronger. He dumped her in and closed the lid. The trunk had been for her.

"How long he left her there, she did not know. A simple routine was repeated over and over. He would open the trunk and let her out in the darkened room, so there was no way to judge the time. He gave her water and a small amount of food. He let her relieve herself, and then he would lock her back inside. She tried to escape, but that was impossible. He was always there to ensure she didn't. Time ceased to have any meaning. There was only the trunk, the darkness, and her isolation.

"Inside, there was no sound. Her thoughts would fly wildly one way and then the other. She was sure she was going insane. She wept often. She called out, but nothing ever came of it. Her imprisonment continued. She slept. She woke. All she saw was black. She stank. She was alone. The ordeal continued with no respite."

Stanley paused once again to let the magnitude of what he had said sink in. Johnny and I were speechless. Stanley took another drink to wet his throat and went on with the tale.

"At this point in her narrative, her ladyship stopped and turned to face me directly. She looked so anguished. I asked if she might wish to take a break, but she insisted we continue and that I listen carefully because what she was about to relate was likely to make me doubt her sanity and mental competence. After I agreed to listen and make no prejudgment, she went on. She smiled bravely, and as she spoke, she looked me in the eye from time to time to see whether my regard for her had been replaced by something less. I kept my face impassive until she finished.

"She had been in the trunk for what seemed like days and days when she began to see strange lights. She knew she was beginning to hallucinate. The lights did not necessarily bother her, but when the people appeared, she felt she was poised on the edge of madness.

"By any measure, she thought her mind had broken, only it hadn't. Her thoughts were clear. She knew who she was, where she was, and how she had gotten there. But she also knew she was no longer alone. She would catch glimpses of pale figures at the edges of her vision. They spoke to her and kept her company in the dark. Sometimes, what they said was unintelligible, as if in a foreign language, but at other times, she understood every word. They told her not to worry. She would survive. They said there would come a time when she could change her fate, but not now, not for a while. The first thing she must do was learn to breathe.

"To breathe in and out slowly and evenly. If she did this, they would stay with her for a time. They told her a little about themselves. They were ancient. Earlier cultures knew of them and spoke with them. Present-day cultures had no such pathways, except in the case of indigenous people, who retained their old ways. They said she didn't have to believe in them. She simply needed to trust. They told her that she would be released, but she was to agree to whatever she was told to do. Fighting back would come later. They asked her to think of herself as a raft being carried by a current and floating down a river.

"At this point, she was barely alive and beyond caring. Whoever, or whatever, they were, real or imagined, she was, at the least, not alone. They had provided her a support she needed most desperately. She agreed to do what they said and thanked them. As suddenly as they had appeared, they were gone. Where they went, what they were, she couldn't say.

"Shortly after, her husband let her out. Weak as she was, she felt relaxed and better than she had in a very long time, as if she had awoken from a deep sleep. When his lordship asked her if she had made a mistake, she readily agreed. He asked that she write him a check for their stay. She said yes. Life went on. They visited places. They saw friends. She went with the flow. She stuck to her agreement, but on the night of the quarrel that I had observed, she defied him once again, and with good reason.

"He had demanded that she sell Rhinebeck, and she had refused. They fought. He had told her in no uncertain terms that he wanted her to experience what she had made him do — sell that which was most dear to her. Because of her recalcitrance, he had locked her in the trunk to break her once again.

"This time, the people did not come. She was alone but not afraid. She was able to breathe and to think. She realized she did not need them to keep her company. The time had come for her to do something about her situation. In the dark, she made a plan.

"In the morning, he let her out and once again asked if she would sell Rhinebeck. She told him she would if he wanted. She acted subdued, and he believed her. He was so pleased, he immediately left for New York to draw up the papers.

"'So, here I am,' she told me. 'What are we to do? Even though I said I would do what he demanded, I have absolutely no intention of selling a thing. I am finished with him, with his trunk, with his abuse, with everything. I feel like murdering somebody, and I will give you three guesses as to who that might be.'"

The fire gave a loud pop, and sparks flew up the chimney.

9

The room was silent for a few minutes as Stanley gazed into the fire and said nothing.

Johnny and I looked at each other again. We'd agreed to ask no questions until the end of Stanley's narrative, but as the silence dragged on, Johnny could contain himself no longer and blurted out, "Jesus, Stanley, what did you do?"

Stanley looked at him. "I did what I always do whenever there's a crisis on. I rang for a cup of tea."

He chuckled and smoked his cigar. He looked at us for another minute. I watched his eyes. They did not blink. He looked back at us steadily in a detached way.

He reminded me of an attorney Johnny and I once met when we were in business together. We had been asked to meet the man in his office on Wall Street. He had a corner suite from which he could see the exchange. His gray hair was brushed straight back like Stanley's, and he had similar cold blue eyes. He didn't rise when we entered his office but simply motioned for us to have a seat. He didn't introduce himself.

With no preamble, he said, "I have a client who wants to invest a great deal of money with you. He is taking a risk and is willing to pay for that privilege. What valuable consideration will you be delivering to my client, and how will you be doing that exactly? Performance will be an issue, and my time is valuable. Be succinct."

I remember looking into that man's eyes and thinking: *They are very cold eyes. Be careful here; be very careful.* They looked like Stanley's eyes now. Concerned, I sat up straighter, alert. I could tell Johnny had also subtly changed his position. He had his game face on. Even Robert raised his head. Something was up.

"I am afraid I am going to make you uncomfortable," said Stanley. "I won't keep you in suspense, but we have reached the point in this narrative where we have to make a decision, the three of us. I think you have some of the context you desired, but from here on, I require something more than just your silence.

"We must make a bargain, and then we need to seal it. You are both familiar with contracts, I'm sure. There must be an offer and acceptance by competent parties. There must also be the exchange of valuable consideration to create what might be called a 'mutuality of obligation,' and here, I emphasize the latter phrase.

"Understand this: you have me at a disadvantage. I am this house's butler. I am not a member of the family. The valuable consideration I am giving you is this story. One that needs to be told, to be sure, but it contains information that many would consider harmful, even dangerous, if known. For a bargain or a contract to be actual, there must be something of value exchanged between the parties. So far, the movement has been in only one direction. Reciprocation is required. Let me say that it is not monetary consideration I want. Her ladyship took care of all my needs on that score. Rather, I want a promise, a pledge, from both of you, individually and together."

Here he paused and looked at us as he smoked. He had our attention. This was a side of Stanley I knew only in glimpses. He was cold, unsympathetic, and implacable, just like the Lord Bromley he had described.

He interrupted my thoughts and said, "Here is my offer. In exchange for the rest of the story and the contents of this case, you must promise to honor the following: I will come to you at some point in the future, and I will ask you to do a service for me. You will agree to do what I ask without question or hesitation, no matter how strange, no matter how insignificant or significant. I will call upon each of you separately, or together, to honor your promise. I will tell you specifically that I am invoking the pledge you made this night, so there will be no mistake. You will be obligated to do what I ask, if we have an agreement.

"Once I have your promise, we will seal the bargain, and only then will I continue. How do you wish to respond?"

He looked at Johnny and then at me.

Johnny answered first. "May we ask you some questions and then confer in private before we give you our answer?"

"Of course."

"First question," asked Johnny. "What's in the case?"

"Her ladyship's diary. I took possession of it after her death. I thought doing so appropriate at the time."

"I see," said Johnny. "Have you read it?"

"Yes, I have, and I think you will find its contents engrossing."

"What if we refuse?" I interrupted.

"Then our conversation ends here. The diary will be destroyed, and sleep follows."

"Assuming we agree," said Johnny. "Can you give us an idea of what you'll expect us to do?"

"I can't because I don't know at this time."

"Will it be legal?" I asked.

"Perhaps, perhaps not. Let me elaborate. First, I may choose never to redeem your pledge, but then again, I might. It is my choice. Second, I have looked after the members of this house for many years, always with its best interest in mind. I do not intend to change that policy. Lastly, in some relationships and circumstances, there can only be trust or no trust. This is one of those times when you must decide. I will leave you for a few minutes to confer."

At this, Stanley rose and silently left the room.

Johnny eyed the case that still lay on the table.

"Don't even think about it," I said. "He did that deliberately. He needs to know he can trust us just as much as we need to know we can trust him."

"Just a thought…Well, this certainly has added some zing to an already remarkable evening."

"We seem to be prone to that sort of thing. So, what do you want to do?" I asked.

"What do you want to do?"

"I asked you first."

Johnny smiled and said, "I think we should go with it."

"I think we shouldn't. Remember that devilish attorney we met down at Broad and Wall, the one that even looked like Stanley? Recall how that worked out?"

"Ah yes," said Johnny. "I was thinking much the same thing, but we survived, and it was a tidy piece of business, if you remember. We made a chunk and so did the client, but…"

Johnny held up his hand as I opened my mouth to protest. "I know what you're going to say. There was that performance clause, and we went through hell when we were down 20 percent the first month. Too true, but we made it back, and we did manage to avoid a massive penalty by the skin of our teeth."

"Oh, how quickly you forget. Do you even remember the number of sleepless nights we went through — the endless stress? Somehow, I was always the one who had to talk to that nasty little man and explain how we were only down a little bit more. The experience was positively awful."

"You thought we'd made a deal with the devil. The pressure was a bit wearing, I agree, but everything did work out, didn't it?"

"It did," I said reluctantly.

"Besides," said Johnny, leaning forward and looking at the case, "don't you want to know what's in the damn thing? I do. More to the point, as Stanley said, it's all about trust. Do you trust Stanley, yes or no? That, right there, is the crux of the matter and is really all that counts."

"Well, yes, I..."

"It's settled then. We're in agreement."

Before I could voice any more protests, Johnny was up and at the door, calling for Stanley.

Stanley walked in as quietly as he had left and sat down. He looked down at the diary on the table and then asked, "You've made your decision?"

Johnny answered for both of us, just like in the old days.

"We have. Trust is a commodity that seems to defy what others might consider to be good sense, but that is the basis of our decision. We trust you, and that's the truth of it. We agree to your terms."

Stanley looked at us and said nothing for a time.

"Sometimes I am surprised by what others decide — not that I had much doubt as to the outcome. Just the same, I thank you for your agreement."

Johnny and I nodded. I realized as I did so that we had crossed into territory that would once again change our lives forever. I did trust Stanley for the most part, but I knew that few victims of unspeakable crimes were ever dragged down into a cellar kicking and screaming — rather, they walked in of their own volition.

"So, gentlemen, we need to seal this bargain properly. Allow me a few minutes to prepare."

Stanley got up and left, leaving Johnny and me alone once again.

"Well," said Johnny, "I don't know what he has in mind, but this evening has been extraordinarily entertaining at the very least."

I put aside my negative thoughts but couldn't help saying, "It is all a bit peculiar, you must admit."

"*Peculiar*, I think, might be too strong a word. *Mysterious* would be more appropriate."

"Okay, mysterious then, but, Johnny, I really think we're in over our heads. I swore I wasn't going to go off the deep end anytime soon, and yet here I am again. I can hardly believe it."

"I wouldn't beat yourself up too badly," said Johnny. "It's the nature of this place, so you might as well enjoy it. Besides, I'll be right there with you. Just like old times."

I sighed heavily as Stanley entered with a tray on which were placed three tiny crystal glasses and a small emerald-green bottle caged in silver. He placed the tray on the table and removed a small black book from under his arm.

He laid the volume next to the leather case and poured out three thimble-size measures of a dark liquid.

"Gentlemen, it is time to seal our bargain. We will do it the old way. First, you must place both of your hands on this book and swear to follow without question, and to completion, my instructions or suffer the consequences. Do you so agree?"

Johnny and I looked at each other. *Consequences? What consequences?* my thoughts screamed, but there was no backing out.

We stretched out our hands and placed them on the book. I looked at it carefully as I did so. The volume had wooden boards covered with black leather and certainly was no Bible.

"Repeat after me: I so swear."

"I so swear," Johnny and I repeated in unison.

"Very good," said Stanley briskly. "Now we seal the bargain this way." He held up one of the glasses. "Drink in one gulp, but only after you hear what I have to say."

Johnny and I reached for the two glasses and raised them up. Robert the Bruce sat up and watched us, his eyes inscrutable.

Stanley spoke: "We have made an oath. May faith rule our fears, may trust overcome adversity, and may we be guided by the gods that now stand silent around us, watching."

Stanley drank it off and put down his glass. Johnny and I did the same. The liquid burned hot down my throat and tasted of meadow grasses and flowers but with a strong metallic aftertaste.

I managed to say, "Was there blood in that drink?"

"I will answer all your questions, but only when the tale is done. Shall we adjourn for a quick break, or are you both ready to continue?"

10

I opted for the quick break. Not only did I want to drink something to get rid of the aftertaste of whatever we had just consumed, but I also wanted to get a look at Alice's bathroom, since I had never seen it.

We agreed to a ten-minute recess, while Stanley made coffee. Johnny and I walked down to the library to grab some cognac. Robert clicked along behind.

Johnny poured us both a generous measure from the bar, which we both drank immediately, swilling the liquor around in our mouths before swallowing to get rid of the aftertaste.

We looked at each other.

"Well?" I asked.

"Well, indeed. Let's wander back," said Johnny, carrying the bottle. "Thank God for this cognac. I wouldn't consume that little draft on a regular basis, but you must admit it was a nice touch and strangely appropriate."

"Humph" was all I could say to that but finally I added, "I'll give thanks if we simply remain in human form. Stanley drank some too, which raised my hopes, but I'm a little concerned about that 'suffer the consequences' clause that appeared out of nowhere at the very end."

"Yes, we were a bit sideswiped there. We should get that spelled out. It could be important."

"Damn right it could be important. I must admit old Stanley has been full of surprises. He sure had me fooled. So much for the gentle family retainer, all smiles and simpers — that idea has gone by the boards completely."

"Well, he's a member of the Dodge household and was Alice's factotum for years. It's no surprise when you think about it. Our retainers tend to be tough as nails and good at their jobs."

"Yes, I should have known…Still, Stanley of all people…Just make sure you have all those questions he's managed to duck at hand, so we can get them answered before we're done here. It's like old times, Johnny. I can hardly believe it. We're in it for sure."

Johnny laughed.

We were back in Alice's apartment. I went off to investigate the plumbing, while Johnny lounged about, looking into the fire. When I returned, nothing had changed other than Robert was now sitting directly in front of Johnny, gazing up at him. He turned as Stanley entered with a coffee tray.

"Gentlemen, please help yourselves. There are a couple of small sandwiches as well."

I had to hand it to the man. He knew how to do things right.

We were soon settled, and Stanley started up his tale again.

"As you will recall, her ladyship had confided in me her experiences at the hands of his lordship.

"I thanked her for being so candid, but I was nonetheless resolved to help in any way I could. Her confession about being visited by the people while she was locked in the trunk and in peril did nothing to dispel that intention. I had heard of such visitations while under duress. The fells and moorlands of Scotland are strange places and have spawned tales and legends aplenty.

"As to his lordship, I thought we should stop short of cold-blooded murder, not because I was squeamish or felt the action undeserved but because the potential legal and criminal repercussions to her ladyship were too great to risk.

"It was my opinion that the man was a complete bounder and needed a good thrashing. Barring murder, I suggested that we send him packing in his own trunk to his club in New York. He would then experience the same ordeal as her ladyship. To this she heartily agreed and clapped her hands in approval. We just had to work out the details, particularly as to how to prevent his coming back and either charging us with criminal conduct or taking revenge by some other means — an action I was certain he would attempt.

"Her ladyship thought the matter over and said she might have a way. She stated that she had no qualms about taking out a full-page advertisement in both the *London Times* and the *New York Times* simultaneously, spelling out in detail Lord Bromley's actions. She added that he must have practiced his ways on others before her and that a substantial monetary incentive for successful prosecution would have his former victims clamoring for his head on both sides of the Atlantic.

"The more she thought about it, the more she liked it. His life would become an open book, unless he agreed to all her terms. In addition, she pointed out she had more than enough money to weather any storm, while he had far fewer resources. Exposed for what he was, he would be branded forever in the eyes of the public as a depraved sadist, making any kind of future in a civilized country impossible.

"As a final touch, she would have a letter of instructions kept on file at her lawyers' to immediately launch the campaign if she were to die in the next several years for whatever reason. She asserted that he'd better hope and pray she remained in good health and that not a hint of him should cross her path or he'd wish he'd never been born.

"She liked where she was going with this. She would make the arrangements with her legal people and have them draft a letter to be given to him at his club. She decided that I should be the one to present it. Further, to make sure he understood his position, I was to inform him that he would be arrested if he was seen anywhere near her properties.

"Their relationship was over, and she would divorce him as soon as possible. His only recourse to prevent all this coming out was to leave the country immediately. There were to be no negotiations. She had very good attorneys in New York and London who would be given extremely lucrative incentives to ensure he ended up penniless and behind bars, if she unleashed them. By the time she finished, she had convinced herself that life for her would begin again with a fresh start in a new direction.

"I was happy with her decision and told her so.

"I also informed her ladyship that the club should not be a problem. I knew the headman, Cedric, and he owed me several favors. I would arrange for a Saturday delivery and store the trunk in the basement of the club until I opened it. The only question that remained was how to get his lordship in it. To this we turned as our next order of business.

"His lordship was expected to return on Friday afternoon, which gave us just a few days to prepare. His usual behavior when he arrived was to ask for a whiskey with no ice. I would give him his drink, but with the addition of a powerful soporific, such as a combination of chloral hydrate and phenobarbital. I would also contact a veterinary friend of mine to get some kind of tranquilizing cocktail, such as ketamine and atropine, that could be injected if all else failed.

"I'd had a fair amount of experience with horses and had to sedate many of them when there was a hunt and the rider's skill was questionable. My former employer did not want to take the chance of having some luckless peer of the realm hurtling across the English countryside on an out-of-control mount. The proper dosage for a human would be critical, and this was an area where I would have to guess and have plans in place to handle any eventuality, including what I would do if I administered a dose that proved lethal.

"With our plans made, it was just a question of making adequate preparations. Her ladyship arranged to meet with her attorneys, being careful to avoid any contact with his lordship while she was in New York, and would return on Thursday with everything in place.

"For my part, I arranged the pickup of the trunk for Saturday morning. I saw my veterinary friend and came away well supplied.

"I thought about this extensively. Lord Bromley was not a man to be trifled with. If he got wind of what we were up to, there was no telling what he might do. I had to be prepared for every contingency. I rehearsed my actions in my mind, including what would happen if the drink proved ineffective.

"Friday arrived, and her ladyship and I went over our plans again to make sure we had missed nothing. In anticipation, I had arranged for the other servants to have a day off. Her ladyship and myself were the only ones present in the house. We were as prepared as we could be.

"Lord Bromley arrived that evening in high spirits. The front door was flung open, and he yelled immediately for his wife, holding a sheaf of papers in his hand for her to sign. Her ladyship informed him that she would sign them after dinner, but this was not soon enough for him. He wanted her signatures now. Her ladyship sized up his mood and acquiesced, anticipating that he might calm down after that was done. She was correct, and after he watched her sign in several places, he was all smiles again and asked for a whiskey. I added more than enough drugs to knock out a large man, but to no avail. He was still standing with not even a slur after forty minutes. He asked for another, which I also doctored and gave to him with no small amount of trepidation. If anything, he seemed even more animated. I decided then that he needed to be injected. I announced that dinner was served, and that I would be taking care of both of them as several of the servants had flu-like symptoms.

"The syringe was in my pocket. I put the bowl before him with one hand and struck with the other. Unfortunately, he turned at the last second and the needle caught his shoulder blade, bending the point sideways. He cried out and started to rise from his chair when I hit him full in the face with my fist, still clutching the syringe. He went down with a crash, falling onto the table before rolling onto the floor, out cold. I doubt my skill as a pugilist knocked him out but rather the delayed effects of the drugs. Now I was worried that I might have given him too much. Her ladyship was beside me in a flash as we looked down at the man. He looked very pale.

"'Is he dead?' she asked.

"'I don't think so,' I replied. 'He's breathing, but we should hurry in case he should come around.'

"I knew it would take time for both of us to carry the trunk down the stairs, strip him, and put him in it. I had the horrible thought of his lordship recovering and wandering off when we weren't looking. I grabbed a lamp from the drawing room and tied the electric chord around his feet. We would hear him if he started to get away.

"We climbed the stairs to bring down the trunk. Carrying it was heavy work, and both of us were panting and shaking by the time we got the monstrosity down to the foyer. We both sat on the lid to rest. Eventually, her ladyship got up and said in a tone of voice I will never forget: 'Let's send this man packing. Whaddya say?'"

"He was still stretched out on the floor, so we dragged him over to the trunk, stripped off his clothes, and dropped him in. His head hit the bottom with a thud. I flipped the lid closed, locked it, and pocketed the key.

"Her ladyship and I went upstairs to pack up his things. We decided that it would be best if he had something to change into rather than let the club deal with him when he was released, so I put aside a bag to take with me.

"I listened to the trunk before I went to bed. I could hear nothing. I didn't dare open it.

"Early the next morning, the trunk was picked up. That afternoon, I heard from the club that it had arrived and been put in the club's storage room in the basement.

"I had a distracted couple of days. Red wine was even served in white wineglasses. I was out of sorts. Even her ladyship acted preoccupied. All I could think of was appearing at the club and finding I had a corpse on my hands.

"Monday dawned, and I arrived as planned, having driven into the city. I spoke with Cedric immediately, who directed me to the basement. I was alone, and there was the trunk. I had the letter.

"What I was not prepared for was the condition of the man when I opened it. He was alive, I will say that much, but barely. I had to think fast. I closed the lid and went upstairs to the headman and informed him I needed a room and a doctor who was discreet. Cedric looked at me and asked if we had a situation. I said we did and that he would be compensated accordingly for his help in dealing with it. He said he had just the man and went off to make a call.

"He was back in a minute and said a doctor would arrive in a quarter of an hour. In the meanwhile, he showed me a suitable room on the top floor. The trunk was carried up with the help of two men from the kitchen. I phoned her ladyship, told her the state of affairs, and advised she make plans to go to Europe immediately, in case things took a dark turn. She agreed and told me she would be in touch.

"It was now time to deal with his lordship. I placed several towels on the bed and opened the lid of the trunk. He scrunched up his eyes with the light. I reached in and took hold of his arm. He grabbed my wrist. His mouth worked, but what came out was a mewling sound that I interpreted as the word *water*, only an octave higher than I had ever heard him speak. I removed his hand and filled a glass with water, which I helped him drink. I got him up and out of the trunk somehow and into the bathroom, where I ran a shower. He was a mess and stank to high heaven. I washed him off and more or less carried him to the bed, when there was a knock on the door. It was Cedric and the doctor. I covered his lordship with a blanket, closed the trunk, and tried to air out the room.

"The doctor examined him and then turned to me. He said with some asperity, 'The man looks to be in shock and is severely dehydrated. That he's alive is a miracle.' He looked at me, expecting an explanation. I shook my head and whispered to the doctor, 'Not only that, he failed the physical part of the club's admission process most horribly. The poor chap will be so disappointed.' I can be amusing when I want to be. The doctor gave a start at my flippant attitude. I told him rather severely, 'How this man got into the condition you see before you is no concern of yours. His recovery, however, is. How long until he is well enough to travel?' He gave me a long look and then nodded. 'I will give him an injection immediately and start a drip to help him rehydrate. He should have oxygen and round-the-clock nursing. I make no guarantees. We will see once he's stabilized.' Cedric chimed in that there was a full nurses' station on the second floor with oxygen. The doctor said, 'Show me,' and went out with him.

"I was left with his lordship, who looked half-dead. If he lived or died made no difference to me. I would nurse him back to health because duty demanded it. Looking back on that decision, I should have smothered him with a pillow while I had the chance."

11

The fire popped again, giving Johnny and me a start. Stanley got up and put on another log. He poked at it until the fire was burning to his satisfaction and sat back down. He continued.

"I won't bore you with the details of nursing Lord Bromley back to health. As he grew stronger, he became surly. Rage would dance in his eyes whenever he looked at me. I felt now was the time to take steps for my own safety and peace of mind. This man was a bully, and bullies need to be handled forcefully.

"It was in the morning perhaps a week later. He was sitting up in bed. I had just brought him breakfast and put the tray on the side table. I thought I would start right in. 'Your lordship, I see you are making a recovery. Now is the time for you to consider your position. I have a letter from her ladyship's attorneys.' I gave it to him. His hand shook as he read it. He threw the correspondence aside when he had finished and looked out the window. He put his fist to his mouth and bit down. When he took it away, I could see the puncture marks from his teeth. He glared at me and said, 'You have all the cards. I surrender...for now. But know this and mark it well: you have not heard the last of me. I will have my revenge on that slut of a wife of mine...and on you. She has wrapped you around her little finger — I see that. You will not be able to protect her, I promise you. I will win in the end. You think you have taken everything from me, but I'm not without means. I have time. It's my greatest weapon. How quickly you'll forget, but I won't. Every day I'll remember. Now get out. I don't want to see you. You're beneath me.' He turned away and would look at me no more.

"It was vital that I did something then. He was too smug. This would only give him confidence, and I needed to unbalance him. I snatched the knife from the breakfast tray, grabbed him by the throat, and stuck the blade right up his nose. I did not draw blood, at least not much. I waited until his eyes began to water, and then I said, 'I have let you live. Remember that, when you get too high and mighty. I might just forget myself next time.' I removed the knife, gave his nose a playful twist that caused him to cry out, and walked out the door. I saw Cedric and told him that his lordship was on his own. Her ladyship would cover all expenses up to this moment and to send a bill for all costs including a cash bonus for his discretion and loyalty.

"His lordship was gone the next day. Where he went, I do not know, but in the end, he was right. We forgot about him. Her ladyship decided to take a completely new tack. Spurred, I suppose, by the unexpected spiritual experience with 'the people' whom she encountered during her husband's abuses, she decided to learn all she could about this type of phenomena. She took up psychology, anthropology, archaeology, Egyptology, as well as the occult. She gave liberally to the finest university departments that specialized in antiquities, who were only too happy to accept her as a student and, eventually, as a colleague. She consulted everyone from professors to fortune-tellers, gurus, and shamans all around the globe in her zeal for learning.

"Her pursuits caused her to spend less and less time at Rhinebeck. Partly, this was due to her studies at university and other places, but later, she joined in expeditions throughout the world. Her only stipulation for funding many of them was that she was allowed to take part.

"From here on, I can give you only snippets of her life, because the times I saw her grew fewer and farther between. I was never sure whether this was because she would rather not be reminded of Lord Bromley or because of something else. Once again, I must relate some personal details.

"I knew from the start that I was completely captivated by my employer, perhaps even besotted. I also knew that this was a potential disaster in the making. There've been numerous instances of those in service creating liaisons with their employers. These have either ended badly, or when the relationships have come to light, they've been at great cost to the reputations of those involved.

"In addition to this peril, being in service in a large house where the employer visits only occasionally can be a lonely and forbidding occupation. I would receive telegrams now and again: *IN LIMA STOP HOME MAR 11 LA*. The *LA* stood for 'Lady Alice,' or so I thought. She would stay for a week or two and then be off to somewhere else. She would remain in residence for perhaps eight weeks of the year. I pined and suffered in silence, until I determined to do two things.

"First, I resolved to read every book in the massive library, including the volumes accumulated by her ladyship's mother, of which I will have more to say in a minute.

"Second, I needed to find myself a wife. Although her ladyship had the final say, I could put forward for consideration of employment whomever I wished. I had my eye on one such lady. She was in the employ of a banker in New York and had a reputation as an outstanding cook. This, of course, was my Dagmar.

"I will never forget when I informed her ladyship that I had asked for Dagmar's hand in marriage and that she had accepted. We were in this very room when I told her. She said simply, 'Oh, Stanley.' She paled and sat staring out the window. I realized that *LA* had always meant 'Love, Alice' and that she must have felt for me what I had only imagined. I was speechless. Eventually, she blurted out, 'What am I doing? Of course you have my permission. Have you set a date?' I managed to tell her when, and she said she would take care of all expenses. At the end of our conversation, she said, 'Now, if you'll excuse me, I have some letters to write.' She did not appear from her apartment until the next day, when she announced she was off to Paris. She didn't attend our wedding, and we did not see her again for an entire year. We did, however, receive a congratulatory telegram.

"It was shortly after that time that rumors of her participation in a very fast set began to hit the papers and magazines even in New York. In spite of my concerns for my employer, life with Dagmar proved beyond my expectations. I was, for the first time, happy beyond all imagining. We saw her ladyship for only brief periods over the next several years and had the house pretty much to ourselves. When her ladyship did appear, she often looked different from when we last saw her. Sometimes she would come back tanned almost black, when she had been in Egypt or in South America. Other times, she would arrive white as porcelain, when she returned from stints at the British museum or other establishments where she examined ancient texts. Boxes filled with books and manuscripts would arrive from time to time, many to be cataloged and preserved in the special library, which I will show you now."

Stanley got up and walked to the wall to the left of the entrance to the sitting room. He flicked what looked like a light switch.

There was a click, a hiss, and the edge of a door appeared where before had been a blank wall. Light streamed from the opening. Johnny and I followed into a chilly space that was filled floor-to-ceiling with wooden shelving holding books of all shapes and sizes in no apparent order other than a series of numbers and letters.

The repository was larger than expected, some ten by fifteen feet, but the striking part was its height. The ceiling was higher than that of the sitting room. There was a sliding ladder to get to the upper reaches. Almost every shelf was filled to capacity.

There was a background hum of air-conditioning. Otherwise, the room was singularly quiet.

Stanley pointed to a pair of boxes.

"There is a filing system based upon subject matter, with a large section under *Miscellaneous*. The room is hermetically sealed, with temperature and humidity controlled automatically. Her ladyship was an avid collector of many books on the occult. Some of those that are stored here are hundreds of years old. You are looking at probably one of the most extensive libraries on witchcraft and black magic in the world."

Johnny and I were speechless.

Johnny eventually said, "This has been here all along?"

"Yes. It was built before you were born and was her ladyship's private repository. Her most valuable books, including some of her mother's, are kept in here. Her ladyship was quite adamant that their existence and the location of the repository be limited to a few. Mr. and Mrs. Dodge know about the library, of course, but have chosen to let me remain the caretaker."

I couldn't help asking, "Stanley, were you the one who cataloged them?"

"Oh yes. Most of them I have read — at least those that can be. Many are in foreign languages and not of any modern variety. Some of those are beyond my skill, but I have looked at all of them at the very least."

Johnny looked about, touching the bindings. "To think there was a whole room that we never knew about. We were only told that there was a locked section. By the way, is this a lending library? I mean could we borrow the odd volume now that we know about it?" asked Johnny.

"I see no reason you can't, provided they are returned. Most can be removed, except those kept in these cases over here. These must remain in this room because of the potential damage due to contact with untreated atmosphere. Each of the books in this library has been put through a freezing cycle to kill pests, but still, some are very ancient, particularly those made from papyrus, and must be especially protected."

"How about the one you had us swear on this evening?" The words came out before I could catch them.

Stanley smiled. "That was a personal copy, but there is another charming volume on summoning demons and other spirits that you might find amusing over here in this section."

He pointed to an oddly shaped book that could have been rectangular when bound, but was now bent out of shape.

"I don't know how much you believe in that sort of thing. We live in a modern world, after all, but let us go back to the other room. Such discussions are best done outside of this particular place."

We filed out. Stanley shut the door and toggled the switch on the wall. There was a hiss and a click. We took our places before the fire. Robert had not moved.

"Where were we?" he asked.

I was quite sure he knew exactly where we were, but said nothing. It was not that I now disliked Stanley. He had numerous outstanding qualities, but he was also a hard man, a cruel man, a man of many secrets, and we were being given only those he wished us to have, and for what purpose, I was unsure.

Johnny answered, "We were talking about spirits...and speaking of which, please pass the decanter."

It was by my elbow, so I handed it across. Johnny poured another round for all of us and sat back down.

"Spirits..." said Stanley. "I have always been practical by nature; after all, Hume was Scottish, and so was Adam Smith. Prior to my current employment, I had no place for superstition in my life. When I arrived, I had a house to run, so practicality was always foremost. But as a rule, we humans see only what we want to see, and that is not so much. If you've lived in this house consecutively day after day for as long as I have, you will have observed things that cannot be easily explained, which we will be getting to. Are we ready to continue?"

Johnny and I nodded. Robert continued to doze. Stanley started up again.

"One freezing night in winter, her ladyship arrived unexpectedly. She asked for a large vodka and a conference in her sitting room, while handing me her coat. We always assumed that she could show up at any time, so all was ready for her, including flowers in her room. I entered her quarters with her drink and served her. She gulped the vodka down in one go, put the glass on the table, and sat down in this chair. Her shoulders began to shake. Her tears turned to sobs. She held her head in her hands and whispered, 'Oh, Stanley, what have I done?'

"I said to her, 'My lady, you are home again. All will be well.' She seemed on the verge of collapse. She sat up and fell back in the chair, curling herself up in a ball.

"I went to her and lifted her up. She was light as a feather. I carried her to her bedroom, laid her on the bed, and covered her with a blanket. I whispered, 'Sleep is what you need. Everything will be better in the morning.' She was snoring by the time I closed the door.

"The next day, she asked to see me. She apologized for her

behavior the night before. She said she was exhausted by travel and that she should have held herself together a bit better. She asked how I was keeping and then blurted out that she had remarried. This surprised me, but I congratulated her. How could I have done otherwise?

"Her new husband was the mining magnate Arthur Blaine. He had made a fortune diamond mining in Africa. She thought that he was at least as rich as she was. The wedding had taken place in a thirteenth-century church near the fortified manor house that was now the Blaine residence in Shropshire. The ceremony had been small and discreet. There had been no news in the American press and hardly any in the British papers. I asked her why. She said that both of them preferred it that way. I had no problem with that, but then I asked how come she was here and not with her husband, to which she replied that after the wedding they had attended a party in London. Someone had snuck up behind her and put their hands over her eyes and whispered, 'Guess who?' Alice had whirled around and been struck speechless as she looked into the black eyes of Lord Bromley. 'Surprised, Alice? I thought you'd be. I told your man we would meet again, and so we have. Arthur and I have known each other for years. What? Arthur never told you? I made sure of it. Poor, poor Alice.' He had left her there with her mouth open. The surprise had been complete. She just made it to the bathroom before she got sick. As soon as she was able to, she fled and did not stop until she arrived at Rhinebeck.

"I had heard of Arthur Blaine, of course. In my circles, he was considered a bit of a lightweight, but to have amassed his considerable fortune spoke otherwise. I decided to suspend judgment until I saw him.

"I met him later that week. He arrived by car, knocked at the door, and asked politely to speak to his wife. She invited him in. He looked half-frozen, and they were married, after all. He begged her forgiveness. He explained most earnestly that he had seen her at a shooting party long before she had wed Lord Bromley and had been in love with her ever since. After the divorce, he had informed Lord Bromley of his intentions to woo his former spouse. Lord Bromley had warned him that if he was to have any chance of success, not to mention their friendship. Her ladyship then acknowledged that had she known that the two were friends, rather than acquaintances, their wedding would never have taken place. Blaine appeared sincere and genuine. Her ladyship relented, and a new chapter started in her life. They moved into the upstairs bedroom. Her ladyship used this area of the house as her study and informed me that under no circumstances was the existence of the secret library to be revealed to him or to anyone.

"In spite of the rocky start, I think she was happy with Arthur. He was the opposite of Lord Bromley in almost every way.

"For a couple of years, all was peace and harmony, until they went off to Ecuador. They were lured there by a rumor of lost treasure that came in the form of a map and a letter sent by one of Arthur's cronies, Fredrick Deprizio, known to all simply as Freddy. I think the excitement of a new find unknown to the modern world captivated them, rather than any monetary gain, although that may have been on Arthur's mind. His fortunes had by this time suffered a steep decline due to the simple fact that he was not in South Africa looking after his business affairs.

"After doing some research, her ladyship announced they would embark on an expedition to discover the truth of the matter. I did not hear from them for half a year. Out of the blue, her ladyship appeared, without her husband and angry as a hornet. She filed for divorce immediately. I must say, I was not altogether surprised, but after she related what happened, I agreed with her in every way."

At this point Johnny interjected, "I hate to interrupt, but we found a letter in our search of the basement that was written by

Aunt Alice to an M. Thoreau, care of the Carlyle. It was returned shortly after her death, unable to forward. I have the letter here."

Johnny handed the letter to Stanley, who read it carefully. He showed no indication of surprise at its contents, however.

"I suggest this be kept in the repository" was all he said as he handed it back to Johnny. He then added, "It confirms what I have learned about the incident, but more importantly, what she writes hints at a change in her ladyship's habits and concentrations. After her return from that expedition, she became much more obsessed with the world of the spiritual and the occult. I will have more to say about that shortly, but what is interesting is that she mentions the figurine, an object that I believe may be responsible for more than one death."

12

―――――――

"More than one death? What do you mean?" asked Johnny.

"That figurine her ladyship mentioned has been a source of trouble and intrigue for some time, but I will get to that in due course. Perhaps, more importantly, at least to me, is that the letter suggests her ladyship's state of mind, which is what troubled me most after her return. She became a study in contradictions. She was at times filled with anger and rage. I would find her staring off into space with a look that surprised me. Lines of hatred that I'd never seen would crease her face. One day when I saw that expression, I asked if I could be of help. She said, 'Stanley, I feel so violated. I'm so angry all the time! I wish I could find out what happened to them. I want to *know* how much they suffered. Maybe then I can let go of the rage that I feel almost constantly.'

"She got her wish. Arthur showed back up again, but a year after her return from the jungle, and much had happened during that time. She had rammed through a divorce and removed any evidence of the man by dumping all his things in the garbage. Her periods of anger had thankfully become fewer, but these were replaced by what I now considered a mystic daze.

"As to the source of her changed personality, I think the drugs her ladyship experimented with had much to do with it. She had begun to collect seeds and plants from many locations. In this, I think she found escape, enlightenment, and relief. I noted her behavioral changes and asked her about the long-term effects of her investigations on both her physical self and her mind. She told me that the majority of her experimental efforts were interesting but of little utility, with one or two exceptions. Those exceptions were what mattered and allowed her to access areas she was keen to explore, which were inaccessible in any other way. Over time, she became thoroughly convinced of two things. First, that she was reincarnated and, second, that the use of certain drugs, particularly those she had learned to prepare under the guidance of various indigenous priests and shamans, were essential to create the states of mind she required to achieve greater awareness. I was less than sanguine at this development. To me, she was charting a course between death on one side and madness on the other. I was frightened for her, but what could I do? She was a grown woman, a keen researcher, and a force in her own right. There was nothing to be done.

"The evening Arthur Blaine returned, her ladyship was at home. We found out that the gruesome revenge she had called down on Arthur, Freddy, and Lord Bromley was not just speculation but real horror visited on real people.

"As with his first appearance, Arthur arrived unexpectedly, this time in the spring rather than the dead of winter. He knocked on the door, which I opened, and there he was. Her ladyship had come out of the drawing room. She recognized him and began screaming. The man cringed. I took him by the arm and hustled him outside. He looked about as if he was going to make a run for it, but I held onto him. He must have arrived on foot, because I saw no car. To me, he looked a bit out of his mind, and I felt pity for him. Harry had heard the ruckus and came running. I told him to take the man and put him up in one of the rooms above the garage and that I would be there shortly. I had two concerns. The first was to calm her ladyship. The second was to find out the full extent of her ladyship's revenge from one who knew.

"I opened the front door. She was still standing there, her hand to her mouth. I said, 'That was Arthur Blaine, of course. I put him up in one of the rooms above the garage. We must know what happened. I will arrange for some food to be prepared and then go see him. Harry is looking after him for now.'

"She snapped out of her trance. 'Very well' was all she said and glided back into the drawing room. I went to the kitchen to get a tray made up and prepared myself to hear his story.

"I grabbed a bottle of scotch along with the food. I made my way outside to the garage and up the stairs that led to the rooms above. Arthur was sitting at a small table looking at his hands. He brightened with the sight of food and drink. He was ravenous and told me his story between bites. Here is what I remember him saying. He spoke in bursts of lucidity and tears.

"'It was Bromley, that bastard. The trap was all his idea. He put Freddy up to it, of course. He just wanted to get Alice and me; well, Alice, actually, in the middle of nowhere, and his plan succeeded admirably. He knew she couldn't resist the bait of a lost city in the jungle. He had to be clever, though. She wasn't stupid, but Freddy's account stood up to a great deal of scrutiny, because he enclosed a real letter from a sixteenth-century Ecuadorian version of Father Junipero Serra that had been buried in the Vatican stacks for ages. God knows how Bromley had gotten the document out of there, but in the end, Alice decided it was genuine and worth a gamble based on the contents. The problem, we later discovered, was that the city we searched for was nowhere near the location the priest had indicated.

"'Instead, we found Bromley. Alice didn't have a chance, and I could do nothing. He had hired a bunch of thugs, and we were in the middle of a jungle far from civilization. Tropics are not my forte, I can tell you — give me desert any day. We were trapped. Alice had driven him to display such cunning. He must have been consumed with paying her back, and he did so. He took her to his bed that night and every night. She screamed a lot at first, then not so much. Eventually, I figured, when in Rome, and so did Freddy. I'm not proud of what I did, but we paid the price. Did we ever pay!'

"Blaine broke into tears now. They stopped once he had a shot of whiskey, which I made sure he had aplenty. He gave his nose a blow and carried on.

"'That Bromley, he was a careful file. He had Alice watched, so she couldn't escape, but he underestimated her. In the midst of her captivity, she had found something we overlooked. Not too far from our base camp, which was set up near a river, was a series of mounds. She called them *tolas*. They were burial spots, and since they were untouched, she convinced us to do some excavating. That woman wasn't going to waste an archeological opportunity, regardless of the circumstances. She sure loved a dig. She made her case to us all and convinced us that gold was the least of the treasures buried right next door, if we had a mind. I was the one who found it. Lucky that — anyone else would have missed it: a raw emerald as big as your fist, buried in the dirt. The gem was held by a carved figurine. Alice insisted the figure and the stone not be separated. I could understand that, so I convinced Bromley to leave the thing as it was. It didn't really matter one way or the other until we got back to civilization. How the stone got to that place, I don't know, but there it was. There were gold pieces and smaller emeralds, but the big one held my interest. Most have impurities. This one looked highly transparent. The stone might yield two or three very special pieces. Cut right and marketed well, they were worth a small fortune. Bromley, I think, had it in mind from the beginning that the find belonged to him. That idea didn't sit well with Freddy and me. We began to argue about what should be done. There was discord in the camp. Even the hired men started getting uppity. Riches from the earth scramble the minds of men. Bromley had to order them off at gunpoint — all except two to help us. We moved our camp closer to the dig, which was a more defensible position. In our excitement, we forgot about Alice, and that was our undoing. She seemed so subdued, but she must have been plotting all the time. She saw her chance and took it. She served us drinks each night, which thrilled his lordship no end. He loved to have her ladyship do the work of a servant. She did not protest and was grand. Then one night, she slipped us something. The drug she used launched us on an express elevator to hell that lasted for days.'

"Here he broke down and blubbered some more until I shook him and gave him another drink. He got back on track.

"'I lost my mind. I couldn't say for how long. I just remember that I experienced such pain and fear that it's a wonder I'm not insane. Well, maybe I am…a little. I must have been out for days. What woke me was pain. Ants were stinging and biting me all over. I scrambled to the river and dove in to get them off. I hurt so bad, all I could do was weep. I got out after the stinging stopped and started to look about. The tents were gone. Little remained of the camp other than garbage strewn about. Off to one side, I saw Freddy. Something had eaten him. I have no idea what, but whatever it was had gnawed great chunks out of his arms and legs. Bugs were feeding on what remained.'

"He began to weep some more. I shook him until he stopped.

"'Freddy was dead. He had no eyes, just empty sockets. I looked around for Bromley…anyone, really. I found him staring at a tree trunk. I touched his shoulder, and he launched himself at me, throwing us to the ground. His face was a contorted mask of pain and rage. I screamed, and he seemed to recognize me. He stopped and got off. I knew we needed to get to a place to recover and take stock. I spoke with him and soothed him, but he was still in a bad place. He would stand in front of the odd tree and rub his hands together, over and over, like a field mouse or squirrel. I let him be and rummaged about until I found some leftover food. I'm not sure if that had been left deliberately or was simply overlooked in the scattered remains of our camp. I buried Freddy as best I could, but the river got him in the end. I spent several days nursing Bromley back into some semblance of health, when the rain began — not just any rain, but a deluge. The river rose, and we had to move to escape the flood. We became trapped on the wrong side of the river. Our situation became desperate. I cobbled together what I could, and we made our way downstream until we stumbled into a village. We collapsed there. They were humans, at least. They must have pitied us, because they gave us food and water. I caught some sickness and could go no farther. I started to waste away in a fever-driven delirium that was almost as bad as what I experienced back at the camp. I recovered, but only after months. Bromley must have regained his strength and decided to press on rather than wait for me. When I finally came to, he was gone.'

"Arthur then passed out on the table with head in his arms. Before he did so, he gave me one last fact. Lord Bromley had made his way back to civilization, because he had left a note for Blaine at the American Express office in Quito. He wrote that he owed Arthur his life and that he was off to Europe. The postscript said that she would be paid back in kind, even if it took him all of eternity.

"I left Arthur asleep and went to tell her ladyship. I had been hoping that Lord Bromley had died in the jungle, but no such luck.

"When Arthur Blaine awoke the next morning, I informed him

of the divorce. He nodded to himself. He said he expected that and would be on his way. He mumbled that he had money, so not to worry. Harry drove him to the train station, and that was the last I saw of him.

"Her ladyship's comment was: 'So, he's still alive. Shit. We had best watch ourselves.' I agreed, of course, but the question was how..."

13

S tanley paused in his narrative and lit another cigar.

Once it was smoking well, he said, "With this next part of the tale, the occult, or otherworldly elements of her ladyship's life, begin to figure prominently, and we must digress. I have held off discussing these matters until now so that the facts of her life were not eclipsed by the mere sensational. From this point on, that is not possible. To understand her ladyship, it is necessary to go down paths that are electrifying to some, incredible to others, and preposterous to most. I will say this by way of preamble that for myself, her ladyship was always an extremely intelligent woman endowed with extraordinary character and determination. Yet at the same time, it isn't easy to encompass in that noble image a person who also felt that she carried with her a curse from a prior incarnation.

"How such a level-headed woman could believe in and pursue the stuff of hoaxers and frauds, while holding advanced degrees, is, likewise, difficult to understand. The sums she spent on artifacts and books alone, if known, would give even the most generous and affluent pause for concern and open the door for many to question her sanity. Yet, I assure you, she was a remarkably sane woman. Most people are motivated by dreams, visions, or goals. Her ladyship was driven by nightmares.

"She told me about her affliction one morning shortly after the Bromley affair. We were coordinating an upcoming house party when she asked, out of the blue, if I had ever had a recurring dream. I answered that I had not. She said she had, and the nightmare was always the same:

"She is in ancient Egypt. Her father is a high priest, and she has stolen a golden necklace and an amulet from his temple. Her theft is discovered, but before she is captured, she hides what she took. Because she refuses to reveal the location and has desecrated the temple by her theft, she is cursed to be held in the dark forever. She is taken and placed, suspended between life and death, on a slab of stone inside a tomb beneath the ground and left there. It is utterly black. When she tries to rise, an arm reaches out from behind her and drags her back down. After numerous attempts to sit up, she would awake, shaking, and covered in perspiration.

"She told me that she had experienced this same dream off and on since she was a little girl. The nightmare played on that which she feared most and was relentless in its repetition.

"Some men have an uncanny ability to peer into our souls and divine our most secret terrors. Lord Bromley is such a man. Whether through intuition or some evil clairvoyance, his lordship had hit upon the one thing that would terrorize her more than any other: he locked her up in a box. To her ladyship, her nightmare, which had always been troubling, but never to be taken with complete seriousness, was now proved incontrovertibly real, frighteningly active in the present and had crept out of its nightly lair and into broad daylight.

"She told me that it wasn't the darkness that frightened her but rather the dawning realization that she was factually cursed. She knew there was nothing she wouldn't do to escape it, and that terrified her.

"To us, bad dreams, even recurring ones, are not life-and-death matters, but rather preoccupations of our imagination that can be shrugged off with a morning coffee. To her ladyship, it was a deadly business. How else could the years of dreams and her recent imprisonment be explained? With her final acceptance of the reality of her situation, a desire to change her fate and release the curse began to burn within her. From this time forward, an intensity and a passion for extremes permeated everything she did. After all, she had nothing to lose, and how else was she to convince herself she had tried everything in her power with the attention and focus it deserved? She believed in her doom, and thus her sentence to be held in the dark forever was made real.

"No possible avenue for commuting the curse was left unexamined.

"The 'people,' as she called them, the spirits she encountered in the trunk, seemed to offer a possible lifeline. She reached for them, but to do so meant her journey had to be an internal as well as external one. One discovered them either through experiencing prolonged periods of extreme physical hardship or through the use of drugs that unlocked the mind. She chose the latter path. She had met shamans who had explained to her in detail how to prepare and consume various mixtures of plants to be able to contact them, but there was danger. One's spirit could get sucked out of this world and into another, from which there was no return. At least, this was how she explained it to me. In addition, contacting them was not the end of her task, but merely the beginning. She needed to convince them to intercede on her behalf, to lift what assailed her when she slept.

"In her quest for expiation, she traveled many roads. She crisscrossed the world in search of mystics, mind-altering drugs, mountaineers, tomb raiders, shamans, spiritualists, and explorers, because these were the demographic that understood and experienced something of what she had. The possibility of success was remote. She told me several times that she thought his lordship might have unhinged her mind, but she really had no choice but to persist. It was either carry on or check herself into an institution.

"She mentioned she had thought about institutionalization quite seriously. She even went so far as to visit several facilities under the pretext of making a donation. In the end, she thought her best course was to gamble on making her own way. The thought of his lordship discovering that she was alone in a padded cell in a straightjacket, put there through her own decision, was an affront too great to be born. She would rather have killed herself, which she told me she had seriously considered more than once.

"Contemplating suicide and staring death in the face eventually hardened her resolve to survive and solve her problem. She put her dilemma this way: If indeed she was cursed, the dreams and the manifestations would only transfer to her future lives. If science was correct, and we simply cease to exist after death, relief would be immense, but what if science was wrong? To her mind, the possibility of a heaven or a hell seemed unlikely; reincarnation a distinct possibility; and the infinite sleep of the cadaver, although welcomed, too uncertain. In her current life, she had resources far beyond those of ordinary people, so she thought it best to take advantage of them.

"The first step on her path became clear. She needed knowledge. She launched her career as an Egyptologist.

"From my point of view, she wanted to know if what she was experiencing was a re-experience of something that actually happened. She knew two facts: the location of her dream and that her father had been the high priest of Amon. From this beginning, she began her research.

"Her specialty became the Atenist heresy in which the

fourteenth-century pharaoh Amenhotep IV threw off the religion of the day and made his own. He took the name Akhenaten and founded the city of Amarna in the desert. Its discovery led to finding the Valley of the Kings and the tomb of Akhenaten's son, Tutankhamen — an event that electrified the early twentieth century.

"Using her vast wealth, her ladyship was able to acquire certain artifacts of the period, one of which was a peculiar necklace that she would wear on fancy occasions. I doubt anyone knew of its significance.

"That she was able to make such acquisitions should not be surprising. Her ladyship moved easily throughout the world of Egyptian antiquities as a collector, researcher, and monetary supporter. That she should wear such items as often as she did may have been foolhardy because it is possible that someone recognized them for what they were.

"On another tack, I don't mean to give the impression her ladyship during this time simply retired from society to further her research. She did not. She maintained an active social life. She needed contacts to seek out artifacts and human interaction to relax her. Parties lightened her spirits. She would travel far, even to Europe, to attend a particularly large and important one.

"At other times, she would turn inward.

"One evening, I entered her quarters having knocked and received no reply. I found her sitting in front of the fire just as we are but dressed in Egyptian clothing and wearing the necklace. This was not long before she died. She had a dazed look and was speaking in a language that I didn't understand. I gave a start.

"She turned to me and said, 'He comes, Stanley.' She went back to looking at the coals. I did not know what to say. I asked if there was anything she needed, and she shook her head. I left her.

"The next day I requested an interview. This she granted, and we spoke at length. She told me that she'd been experimenting with the *Brugmansia* plant and hoped that I had not been alarmed. I told her that I was becoming so. I begged her to tell me how I might be of help.

"I was becoming truly concerned. To my mind, her behavior had turned erratic. She would oscillate between having weekend parties that were marked by a forced gaiety, where numerous lights from all walks of life would attend: famous artists, musicians, authors, actors, and socialites would participate. Your parents would make their appearance on numerous occasions. During the week, she would travel to New York.

"At other times, she would close herself off in this part of the house and ask not to be disturbed. Food would be brought on a tray only to be picked up later untouched. She lost weight.

"Still, there were moments of extraordinary lucidity and serenity. She would shine with an inner light that was almost holy. I have no other word for it.

"She told me during that particular interview that she had finally reached some sort of culmination of her research.

"She took the necklace from its hiding place in her repository and handed it to me. It was gold in color and made of a number of half-inch ram's heads. The weight was unusual. I learned that the heads were made of bitumen dipped in solid gold. What struck me initially was the design. It was either very modern or extremely ancient. I must admit that I have rarely felt something that seemed to exude so much energy — whether for good or evil, I could not say. It leaked a force that was both electrifying and powerful. I gave it back and was happy to do so.

"She told me that the necklace had been hers. She had recognized it immediately and had moved heaven and earth to obtain it. She said that, wearing it, she had managed to make a breakthrough in her research and that she thought she had a way to lift the curse. She had to purify herself and atone, but to do this, she needed access to several ancient manuscripts known as Books of the Dead, but not just any would do. There were many, and most were worthless, other than for their historical significance. Her ladyship explained that to the ancient Egyptians, it was necessary to have a map when entering the underworld, and that without one, it was possible to remain lost in the darkness, which she felt described her situation very well. There was one book in particular that she had to follow to the letter. She thought she knew where a copy might exist. She was filled with hope.

"On revealing this, she glowed happily. It had been so long since I had seen her do so with the artless innocence that I remembered from so long ago that I almost wept. There was more. She had met a special person but was not ready to reveal any more than that. Overall, life for her had taken a marked turn for the better. She asked that I be patient. The change in her was so apparent that I acquiesced and, once again, offered my services to aid her in any way I could. Before I left, I asked who 'he' was. I told her that she had turned to me last night and said quite distinctly, 'He comes, Stanley.'

"At this, her smile faded. She turned away and then faced me. She said, 'He is the one who cursed me. We are locked together in some fashion. I learned last night that he is aware of my efforts as I am aware of his. It is a race, and I am uncertain as to the outcome. Our collision is only a matter of time. I saw that last night. I have to move quickly. I am off later today. I will return soon.'"

14

"Her ladyship arrived back at Rhinebeck a month later. I was setting out some flowers when I heard the crunch of gravel on the driveway. As I moved toward the front door, it burst open, and there she was. She saw me and giggled like a schoolgirl. 'I have it, Stanley. I have it. Come. Come. Let's talk. I'm so excited.'

"She handed me her coat and hat and clicked rapidly toward her rooms, carrying a valise. She smiled at me over her shoulder and cried, 'Bring me some champagne! And hurry!'

"I moved rapidly to the kitchen, picked out a nice bottle of Dom Perignon, and had Dagmar make up some smoked salmon and slices of toast, while getting one of the footmen to take the bags to her ladyship's rooms.

"I carried in the champagne in an ice bucket, along with a single flute on a silver tray. She was lying back on the couch relaxing, happy as could be. She sat up and waited impatiently while I opened the bottle and poured. Once I had done so, she began to tell me how she had managed to find records of the scroll she sought in the Ägyptisches Museum und Papyrussammlung in Berlin, and from there, she went to the British Museum and on to the Petrie to confirm it was the one. She was able to trace a copy to that of a colleague in London. The scroll was not the original, as she had hoped. That had gone missing, perhaps misfiled. The museum had thousands of papyrus scrolls, but a single filing error, and the scroll could be lost among thousands of others. Such mistakes often took months to correct. She could not wait. Still, the copy was by all accounts faithful to the original. The colleague had been most reluctant to part with such a unique document. She had paid a high price, and only for a copy, but such is life. She had examined her treasure minutely. The text was older and rather different from the typical Book of the Dead in both format and content. This intrigued her. She was certain she was on the right track.

"After the champagne, she was in a jubilant mood, flush with success, and told me that she would have a party this weekend to celebrate. In the meanwhile, she would study her treasure and work out how to implement the complicated spells the text called for.

"I asked, of course, if I could help her in anyway. She laughed and told me to make the party a success, and that would be enough. 'Death comes to us all,' she said. The ancient Egyptians took comfort in their rituals, and so would she. There was nothing I could do.

"The party that weekend was a delight. The affair included several celebrities, including one of the guests we are expecting in the next day or so: Malcolm Ault. He was much younger then, of course. Your parents were in Capri and could not attend.

"Two days later she was dead.

"The breakfast tray was by her door, left there by one of the maids, as was the custom. I was called when there was no response. I have keys to every lock and entered her room, after having knocked repeatedly. It was dark and completely still. She was in bed, dressed in white satin pajamas. A manuscript lay across her stomach. I called out to her but knew in my heart she had passed on. I checked for a pulse, and there was none. Although I was upset beyond all measure, I sat down in one of the chairs in her bedroom and looked over the scene. I had to discover for myself whether her death looked the result of natural causes or something more sinister. Her face was calm and composed. Her skin was cold. There was no visible sign of trauma or agitation. She had been dead for several hours. The appearance was that she had put herself to bed and died. I checked the windows behind the drapes, and these were locked from the inside. I carefully examined the floor around her. There was nothing out of place — everything from her hairbrushes to the toothbrush in the bathroom was as it should be. I was left with no alternative but to examine her body.

"I undressed her and examined her carefully. I was mortified, but I had no choice — I had to know. I can steel myself when necessary to do whatever must be done regardless of the circumstances. Her body was unmarked. There were no puncture marks, no bruising other than the pooling of blood at her back — nothing to indicate that she had been killed rather than died in her sleep.

"I sat down again and looked over the scene one more time. I could find nothing untoward. The police, who had yet to be called, would soon take over, and the tabloids would have a field day. The only thing out of place was the valise, which I moved to the repository. I left the scroll on the bed since the maids had seen it when I had opened the door. I had done all I could to protect her reputation.

"When I finished, I apologized to her lifeless form for having failed her. She had deserved a good and happy life. I felt she had been taken prematurely. My duty had been to guard her, and I had failed. I remembered her words to me that 'he comes.' Perhaps 'he,' whomever 'he' was, had won the day after all; only I had no idea whether that was so. In my heart, I felt only sorrow.

"My eyes filled with tears then. She was so very beautiful. But there was no time.

"I pulled myself together, locked the room, and went to my office. I phoned the law firm that handled many of her trusts, the banks that managed the others, Mr. Dodge in Europe, and lastly the police. I knew that the house would become a circus and I the ringmaster, to ensure its continuation. I had to soldier on.

"The police arrived and took charge. There was no indication of foul play, but just the same, an autopsy was ordered. After a time, the findings came back. Cause of death was heart failure. The Book of the Dead was taken and duly reported, which sent the press into a frenzy of speculation, but eventually, the scroll was returned. I had it locked away.

"Your father took over the house, as was his right. Once the commotion had settled to a tolerable level, I sat down with him and related how I found her. He told me to pursue whatever avenues I saw fit in investigating her death, but since the authorities had returned a finding of death by natural causes, we should make every appearance of agreeing with them, at least on the surface. I was instructed to keep him informed.

"Time passed. The press found other pursuits. Her ladyship ceased to be front-page news, and the house settled down to its usual routine but with a new owner. Everything was kept as it had been. From all indications, we have at last come to the end of our story and, thus, our evening together, but life often takes strange and unpredictable twists. Contrary to expectation, the tale continues, but for that part of my narrative, you will have to wait. I must take a quick break."

15

After Stanley left the room, Johnny looked at me and said, "This has been an eye-opener, I must say. I had no idea my aunt was so far out there. I knew she was eccentric and all, but this is beyond anything I imagined."

"Indeed. She was in a league of her own."

"She was. I'm grateful that Stanley did this. Still, we missed out on an extraordinary amount of drama, which is just too bad. I would have loved it. Could you imagine if we had known about all this at the time?"

"What could we have done? A wise move by the parents, given our ages, don't you think?"

"Yes, but I should have gotten the scoop a lot earlier than tonight. To have had only a few hints for years, when Stanley had the story the whole time, is galling. I should have asked him sooner, but in truth, I didn't have the nerve. He was always so imposing and reserved. Before tonight, I rarely saw him smile, let alone display any emotion at all. I may have thought I knew him, but not really. In fact, not at all."

"So, why now?"

"Simple. We asked."

"You and Occam would have been fast friends, but I have my reservations just the same. It's out of character, and I don't know why. I think Stanley is being candid regarding Alice, but I sense an ulterior motive."

"You still don't trust him, do you?"

"Completely? No. He has managed to hook us into agreeing to do who knows what, with unspecified consequences if we fail to deliver. We were tricked, pure and simple, and I'm not happy about that."

"Well, don't get your knickers in a twist. Not only have we hit the mother lode of information but I think there's more to follow. Besides, how else were we to find out? Should we have waited until someone sat us down and told us? I don't think so. It was never going to happen."

"You're right, of course."

"And here's something else: he said the tale continues. What does that mean? We did hear some rumblings about ghosts when we were growing up, although not recently. Remember that governess, Mrs. Ballway, who got so upset? She told anyone who would listen that she had seen the spectral form of Alice one night. She went sort of bonkers and then refused to ever return to Rhinebeck."

"Oh yes, the famous Mrs. Ballway. There was a lot of commotion over that. Everyone clammed up after she was sent packing. I often wondered where your mother ever got some of those governesses. I mean, the psychological profiles of the majority of them would have been worthy of serious professional scrutiny and oversight."

"Yes, they were a strange lot, and mother would always sigh after they left and exclaim, 'But she had such good references!'"

Stanley reentered silently and sat back down. "How are we doing? Fine?"

We both answered in the affirmative.

"The night is still young…Well, not really, but we'll just have to ignore the time for now. We should wrap up before too long. So, where were we?"

"You said the tale continues," Johnny answered.

"Yes, I did. Before we end, I'm going to relate an incident that involved a guest who was a theater producer and scriptwriter from London. I will give you my perspective when I'm finished. What happened has troubled me for some time and would be a good point to end on. You still have the diary to peruse, but probably not tonight. Shall I continue?"

We both nodded.

"One morning not long after her ladyship had passed, we had a full house. Breakfast was served at nine sharp. If you were late, it was very likely you would not be invited back. This held true then and holds true in the present.

"Earlier that evening, a distinguished gentleman called from town to speak to Mr. Dodge. It was so rare for him to be in the city, your parents felt that to invite him for the weekend was the only option. The problem was that we were full up — except for one bedroom: the one right next to where we're sitting. We felt we couldn't very well put him up in the servants' quarters or over the garage, so a hasty conference was called, and we decided by mutual agreement to allow him to sleep in this wing. This was a decision that was not arrived at without some trepidation. No one had slept in that room since her ladyship's death. Everything had been left exactly as if she were alive. In some ways, this was done out of respect, and in others, because nobody wished to risk disturbing whatever resided in this part of the house.

"There has always been a presence of sorts here. We have all felt it."

Johnny and I voiced our agreement.

"It is not something one can put one's finger on exactly. As her ladyship ventured further into the more surreal, the house seemed to resonate in a strange way, as if it welcomed it. Since that time, the presence has not abated but continued like a chord that sustains itself just below our consciousness.

"I'm from Scotland. I am hardheaded, and I don't put up with a great deal of shenanigans. I tend to be scientific. In her ladyship's case, and in regards this property, our mutual perceptions and conclusions — independently arrived at by yourselves, your parents, myself, as well as those who knew her and stayed here for any length of time — all underscore our acknowledgment of an unknown yet potent force, that even if we cared not to believe in it, at the very least, instills a sense of caution. Call it superstition, but there it is.

"Your parents and I decided to put aside our vague misgivings and allow our guest to sleep in her room.

"He arrived at one in the morning. His hosts and the other guests had already made their way to bed, so it was only myself and a footman who greeted him. He wanted nothing other than a brandy, which he wished to have placed beside his bed. He also mentioned he wanted to read for a while to unwind from his journey. I saw him to his room. He commented that he had never been put up in this part of the house before. I replied that since he was a highly esteemed guest and good friend of his hosts, an exception to the usual was in order. I made sure his case was unpacked and left him, alerting him to the fact that breakfast was at nine and to be prompt.

"Later that morning, I rang the gong as usual at ten minutes to. By nine, your parents and all the other guests were seated, but not our late-night visitor. Your father instructed me to wake him and bring him to breakfast. He knew our habits and should have been present. I went to the bedroom and knocked. There was no answer. When I entered, he cried out. I asked if there was anything amiss. He seemed disoriented, so I opened the drapes to let in some light. The covers were all thrown about, and he looked like he had had a rough night. He croaked that he had experienced a nightmare like no other. I apologized on behalf of his host. In short order, I had him presentable.

"I gave a sign to your father that there was something wrong and nodded in his guest's direction. Your mother, being the more curious, asked if he had slept soundly. To this, he responded rather emphatically that he had not, and if possible, he would like a word with his hosts in the library at their earliest convenience. They agreed to see him immediately. Mr. Dodge asked if I might be present, to which the guest assented. The others resumed their meal, while the three of them excused themselves. I followed.

"Your parents took him to the library, where they all sat down, and your father asked what the trouble was. He informed them that he was off to the city as soon as he could arrange a lift to the train station. He was sorry, but he wouldn't spend another minute in this house. It was haunted. He would not go back to his room and asked that I pack up his things. He would not explain or elaborate what prompted him to make that decision. He had some final words for his hosts before he left. He said, 'I will now beat a hasty retreat. Why you let me sleep in her bed, I cannot fathom. What were you thinking? Over the garage would have been better. I will have nothing more to do with this place.' With that, he parked himself outside the front door and waited for me to collect his things while Harry brought the car around.

"No amount of persuasion would alter his decision, and off he went without another word.

"Your father and mother discussed what to do next, but there was nothing to be done. They were extremely upset, of course. No other guest had ever complained about their time spent at Rhinebeck. He was the first. They asked if I might use my connections to discover what had occurred specifically, and if there was any way to repair the damage. That I did.

"The gentleman had a manservant who cared for his house in London. I contacted him and asked if he might find out in detail what had happened to cause such a break between our respective employers. He wrote me a letter, which I will retrieve from the repository."

While Stanley went off to get it, I whispered to Johnny, "Have you ever heard about this incident?"

"It's news to me. Once again, I'm surprised by the number of goings-on in this place that I have been completely unaware of. It's as if I've been living in some sort of parallel universe. Where have I been all this time?"

"Right here. Remember, the family only doles out information on a 'need to know' basis. You should know that better than me."

"But, Percy, I *am* family."

"You are, but there's family and then there is *family*. We were never part of the inner circle."

"I suppose. It's almost humiliating."

Johnny had stumbled upon exactly how I had felt for much of my life.

"Yes. Yes, it is," I said.

He looked at me, but before he could comment, Stanley returned with a letter attached to several typewritten sheets of paper.

"I suppose," said Stanley, "I could read the letter to you, but it might be best if you both read it over yourselves, while I put some of the things we have collected back in the kitchen."

Johnny passed me the covering letter and then the sheets as he read them.

Stanley,

Thank you for yours of the 23rd. I trust you and Dagmar are well.

You asked if I could find out what happened that night. I can do better than that. Sir Henry returned quite agitated and called me in to discuss the matter. I told him that I had just received your correspondence the day before, inquiring as to the specifics of what had occurred and if there was any remedy that might heal the breach. He told me that he would be writing to the Dodges straightaway to apologize. In addition, he told me that he had written up an account, while his memory was fresh, to make a record of the incident and to possibly use in a later project. He asked that I send you his recollection of that night in answer to your query. See the enclosed. In addition, he told me he regretted his abrupt departure and wanted me to express to you his gratitude for both your care and your service, which he greatly appreciated.

Best,

— GEORGE

PS Are they paying you enough?
PPS That was a joke, but then, maybe not.

An Incident in the Night

I arrived after 1:00 in the morning and fell asleep almost immediately after reading only a page of a script I was trying to finish. I awoke at 2:50. I always wear my wristwatch and noted the time. I was not sure what had awakened me. I felt chilled to the bone and disoriented, so I sat up. I saw a hazy gibbous moon above me that gave a diffused light to my surroundings. I recalled that the drapes had been closed before I turned in, so how could I see the moon? I felt a severe sense of dislocation, as I put together slowly in my mind that I was not under the covers at all. I was, in fact, outside, sitting with my legs outstretched on a lawn. I looked about frantically, trying to grasp what was happening. There was thick fog at ground level, so my surroundings were hazy and indistinct. I was frightened, but the situation was so bizarre, I was more paralyzed in bewilderment. *My mind simply could not process what I was seeing. I turned my head. Slowly, in spite of the gloom, I recognized the wing of the house behind me as that of Rhinebeck. I dimly saw one of the large stone urns off to the side. That further confirmed my location. I also realized that I was freezing. My pajamas were soaked from the damp grass and the fog. How I got there, I don't know. I still don't know.*

I'm usually a sound sleeper. I suppose I dream like we all do, but I rarely remember them. Not like this. I tried to stand, but I couldn't. My limbs just wouldn't respond. I tried to call out, but my voice was more a husky whisper. I began to shake from the cold. I don't think I was truly frightened. I was more puzzled, which probably kept me from panicking.

I began to hear a grinding sound, like something very heavy rolling toward me. The fog obscured the source, so I couldn't tell the direction the rumbling was coming from or what it was. Bit by bit, I perceived a dark-gray box making its way slowly toward me out of the gloom. I saw dim figures taking rollers from the back and carrying them to the front. Who was doing this, and where did they come from? I waited transfixed as the box inched toward me. The deep grumble of the rollers was all I heard.

I have no idea how long this took, but I was fascinated as I stared at its approach until the object was directly in front of me. The terrible sound of its movement stopped. I could make out the shape of a box clearly, but for only brief periods when the moon broke free. The object was rectangular, maybe ten feet long, four feet wide, and four feet deep. There were vague markings along the edges, but I couldn't make them out.

I'm not prone to hallucinations — at least, I didn't think so. Now, I'm not so sure.

The box I recognized as a sarcophagus, and I became very frightened. Was it for me?

I thought of Alice then. I had met her several times and recalled she had died suddenly and mysteriously. I'd been put up in her room, and I had slept in her bed. This so galvanized me that I was able to stand, but that was as far as I went, because something was happening with the box.

A number of the dark shapes grabbed hold of the lid and removed it. I heard them straining with the effort. The lid gave a tremendous thud as it fell next to the sarcophagus onto the grass. I felt the impact in my feet in spite of their numbness. My attention was drawn to the container inside. This had a more familiar form. It was shiny in a dull way, as if covered in metal. It was curved at the top, and the cover was of the distinctive headdress of buried royalty, Egyptian, for sure, although I am no expert. The dark figures lifted this out as well and laid it down carefully. There was a form beneath, certainly that of a woman. She was wrapped in gauze except for her head and her hands.

The fog above me parted for a few seconds, and what light there was grew brighter. Whoever was in the coffin was alive and awake. I saw her eyes move. They flicked from side to side, back and forth, back and forth. She seemed frightened, which made me lean forward. She noticed me and tried to sit up. Her eyes met mine. The light flared and then grew dim as the mist dissipated and closed in again.

In that brief moment of illumination, I saw that her hair was black and set in fine braids. She wore a simple necklace of gold fashioned to look like the curled horns of some animal. Her lips moved. I leaned forward to try and catch what she was saying, but no sound came from her mouth. She became agitated when she saw I could not hear her. Her body began to thrash about. The wrappings kept her arms pinned. I started to reach out for her as her mouth opened, and she started screaming something, but I could hear nothing. I thought for a moment she called out, "Help me!" — but that may have been my imagination. With a valiant effort, she lifted her shoulders above the rim, but then from behind her, an arm with a large forearm bracelet of gold set with a dark-red stone in the center snaked out, grabbed her mouth, and pulled her back down. She fought against the hand but could do nothing. Her eyes opened wide, and she thrashed about frantically. I reached out to her again, and for a second, I think I touched the rim, when I fell over.

One moment the sarcophagus was there, the next it wasn't, and I was under the covers. The curtains were closed. The table between the windows was like it was when I went to sleep. The script was across my chest, and when I turned, my drink was still there. Everything was the same. I was now fully awake. I looked at my watch again and read 3:20 in the morning. I was soaked and still frozen. I sat up, happy that I now had control of my limbs, and downed the rest of the brandy. I decided I needed a hot shower and a change of clothing. I thought vaguely, I was probably suffering from hypothermia. I felt much better after my shower, but I was still troubled by what I had experienced.

There was a picture of Alice on the dressing table that I picked up and examined closely. I will not swear to it, but the similarity between the woman in my dream and the photograph was striking. It was still too early to get dressed, and I knew I was fatigued from travel and my recent ordeal. If I had bad dreams, good dreams, or no dreams, I was exhausted beyond caring and slept through the rest of the night without incident.

1 6

Stanley returned and seated himself as I finished reading. Johnny turned to him and said, "Extraordinary. I have a few questions. Do you think it's true?"

"I have no reason to doubt it. Although he is a scriptwriter, Sir Henry is not one to simply tell a lie. Of that, I am quite certain. It would be completely out of character."

"Did Sir Henry ever get back in touch?"

"He did, and the breach was mended; however, he has never set foot here again. Rather, he sees your parents at the Fifth Avenue apartment or in London."

"Lastly, was it a message?" asked Johnny.

"I don't know the answer to that. Thankfully, nothing like it has happened since. When I received this account, I was alarmed. I sensed that her ladyship was trying to communicate something from whatever dark place she had fallen into, and that was deeply troubling. I was also concerned for another reason — the forearm bracelet with the blood-red stone. No one other than her ladyship and I knew of its existence. I repeat, no one. That he accurately described it has forced me to reassess my views on many things. The fact is, I cannot explain his account, nor can I dismiss it, and that has bothered me ever since. Allow me to elaborate.

"All humans wish to give meaning to inexplicable occurrences. I am no exception. To put this in perspective, Rhinebeck has experienced a recent influx of crows. Is that significant? Crows are intelligent and resourceful. They're also considered to be mediators between life and death. The crow was the symbol for the Egyptian goddess Nepthys, or Nebt-het, which means 'lady of the house.' Are we to suppose that this inundation is a manifestation of her ladyship, wishing to make her presence known? I think such things can be taken too far, yet the crows are real."

"Stanley, there's something that troubles me," I said.

"And what is that?"

"You've obviously studied a great many of the books from Alice's private collection. You give the impression that you don't believe a word, yet your actions speak otherwise. For instance, you have Johnny and me swear on a black book, seal a bargain with an oath I've never heard before, and drink a liquor that tasted of blood. Perhaps you can help me understand what appears to be a contradiction."

Stanley chuckled. "Thank you for your candor. I'm aware of your skepticism. In truth, I am conflicted. I tend to disbelieve, yet I've seen things that are hard to credit and for which I have no explanation. I've studied and tested many of the darker methods that are detailed in some of the books found in the special library, and I can say unreservedly that only occasionally have I encountered results that have given me pause. Every bit should be hogwash and a sham. And it is, until one comes across that small, yet ultimately significant, part that isn't. Sir Henry's account is such an example. There are others, but I won't go into them.

"For myself, I think we've been led to expect too much from

what is commonly thought of as magic. Our concepts are based on myths and legends that are mere fantasies. The laws that govern how the universe works cannot be changed by appealing to some deity, demon, or spirit — at least I've found that to be the case. Real magic is quite surprising and unexpected."

"How so?" I asked.

"We humans have a limited sensory knowledge of the world, but we are compensated for this lack by minds that create, supplement, and often substitute their own information for that of the senses. We perceive the world through our beliefs. Alter our beliefs, and we change how we see the world. Powerful magicians have the ability to change, suspend, or accentuate certain of our beliefs for their own purposes. The will and the way are simply that."

"Mass hypnosis," said Johnny.

"Yes, which would seem to make the subject easy to dismiss, but as I said, there is this tiny other bit that throws everything on its head. Put in another context, there are saints and then there are *saints*. When one meets the real thing, there is the recognition one is in contact with a person who has reached places that are quite beyond the norm. There is the story of a young scientist from France who saw only a film of several Tibetan monks and was so struck by their spiritual presence that he visited them and became a monk himself. He recognized that they were gifted in some way, and he had to know more. I count her ladyship among those extraordinary individuals. They're rare — extremely so — but they exist nonetheless.

"A similar thread of the extraordinary runs through many of the texts in her ladyship's repository. Imagine reading a book of random letters and spaces. There is gibberish for thousands of pages, but all of a sudden one comes across whole sentences and paragraphs that make perfect sense. Coincidence? Perhaps, but that doesn't make it any less disturbing. Real magic is like that — disturbing.

"I would like to make one last point before we end this discussion. For myself, magic has everything to do with the connections that we make. Life has little regard for our supposed accomplishments. How many lives are taken at their apex or even at their lowest point? Hardly any. Chances are, we die when we are old and unexceptional. Such is a bleak view when seen through human eyes, but life has different standards. It seems to value our connecting. We connect with others from the moment of our birth to the second of our death. It is worth considering.

"The overall patterns our connections form, only those with the gift of sight can make out, and even they cannot always see clearly. Real magic lives in the emergent surprises that result.

"I will say no more. For the rest, you are on your own."

There was a silence when he finished. It was a lot to take in. This was a man of quite some depth and complexity. He had skillfully dodged the question about the book and the drink, but I understood the contradiction better. I was certain he would give me no direct answer. I looked to Johnny to begin his questions.

"Stanley, I'd like to thank you for taking the time and for being so forthcoming. It's been an extraordinary and revealing night. My first question is who is M. Thoreau? Alice wrote to him or her in the letter I showed you."

"I don't know. Her ladyship had started a relationship that she was very pleased with before she died. That is all the information I have."

"Was Alice murdered?" I asked.

"The available information is inconclusive. If I suspect she was, I am speculating. Lord Bromley was intent on seeing that she paid for what she did to him, so there is motive, but the how is elusive. That he indirectly played a part is closer to the truth. Conclusions are easy to jump to. The press has certainly done that."

"You mentioned the figurine," Johnny said. "Can you tell us something about it?"

"Her ladyship described the piece as a female figure holding a raw gem of some size and was quite significant. Its existence was known among the indigenous peoples of the area and, according to their oral tradition, was a source of great power that had been used for ill. They buried it for that reason. That Freddy died soon after it was unearthed and that Lord Bromley was so keen to possess it are reasons enough to think the locals were onto something. Her ladyship also told me that it was too difficult for her to carry into this country because not only would the authorities confiscate it but she might be liable for charges. The risks were too great, so she sent it to herself another way. She never said how, and the figurine was never received."

Johnny continued. "I suppose we have other questions, but I, for one, am too tired to think of them. Just the same, I'd love to see the Egyptian pieces — the necklace and the bracelet. Can we?"

"I think that would be appropriate, but after that, we must part and get some sleep."

Johnny and I agreed while Stanley opened the repository and disappeared inside. Robert got up, stretched, and then shook himself. He wandered over to the door and stood looking at it.

"I think he wants to go," said Johnny.

"I think so too."

Stanley returned with a black velvet box on which lay a gold necklace of tiny ram's heads and a hinged gold bracelet several inches wide with clasps that allowed it to be attached to the forearm. On one of the halves was set a large reddish stone that was almost black. The gem picked up the light of the dying fire as Stanley put down the case before us. Johnny reached for the necklace and examined it before passing the piece over to me. The bitumen dipped in gold gave the necklace a heft I found unusual — lighter than expected but not so. As Stanley had observed, it was either very old or very modern. I carefully laid it back down on the velvet. Johnny handed me the forearm bracelet. This was heavier than the necklace and was also made of gold. The stone in the center I could just make out as red. The clarity I found interesting and unusual. Perhaps it was the lateness of the hour, but at first, the bracelet seemed quite plain and ordinary. My perception of it changed when I noticed I had to use conscious effort to put it back on the velvet and drag my eyes away. I felt strangely tired afterward, like it had sucked something out of me.

Johnny ended our discussion. "Thank you, Stanley, for your time and information. Really extraordinary. I think that does it for now. I'll let Robert out the front to relieve himself, and then we're off to bed. Need we do anything here?"

Stanley said no. He would take care of whatever was left and wished us a good night. He had enjoyed our conversation and thanked us for the promise. Breakfast was at nine.

Johnny and I let Robert the Bruce out the front door and into the night. When he returned, we made our way upstairs.

"We have much to discuss," Johnny said as we parted in the common room, "but I am way too tired to make much sense. Good night."

I got undressed and lay down on the bed in the room I had grown up in long ago. Nothing had changed, but everything had. My image of Alice as a glamorous divine protector, who streaked through my early life like a sizzling comet, lay in pieces. In its place, I saw a woman who struggled with the dark corners of her mind like I did, but whose ultimate end was both tragic and disturbing. What lessons could be learned, and how I might salvage some of the luster and hope her life had given me in the past, I didn't know. For now, I felt the loss most keenly. I set the alarm for eight and concluded that if tonight was any indication of events to come, I might have to rethink many of my assumptions.

17

I awoke to light streaming through the window of my room. I got up and looked out. There was hardly a cloud in the sky and only a few wisps of lingering fog — the beginning of a glorious and beautiful day. I felt good in spite of only a few hours of sleep. I went out to the common room to get to the shower, but Johnny was already there, and Robert was standing with his nose against the bathroom door waiting for it to open. I stood in line.

By 8:40, we were dressed and trooping down the stairs to the drawing room to wait until breakfast was ready. Stanley, immaculately attired as always, came in, wished us good morning, and hoped we had slept well in spite of the lateness of the night before. We answered that we felt just fine. Stanley looked spry and energetic. There was not a hint of tiredness. He reminded us that the parents, accompanied by the von Hofmanstals, would be arriving in the early afternoon, with Malcolm Ault sometime in the night.

Johnny and I had a leisurely breakfast and decided to explore the grounds with Robert. I hoped we might use the walk to discuss what was really on Johnny's mind. I also wanted to get his take on Stanley's narrative.

As we walked, admiring the day, I wondered about Stanley taking the time to tell us about Alice. There was no reason he shouldn't have, but other than as a means to extract our promise, I could discern no concrete motive for doing so. Altruism was not something that came quickly to my mind when I thought of Stanley.

In addition, all thoughts of today's upcoming arrivals had been forgotten. The dog-lady confrontation would be upon us shortly, and although minor compared to Alice's tale, and everything else, we needed some sort of a plan, even if it was as simple as keeping Robert the Bruce out of the way during the initial meet-and-greet, while Johnny determined if she was the one. After that, all was up in the air.

Still, the day was gorgeous, and I felt wonderfully alive. The fog had now burned off completely and the south lawn stretched before us. Robert, off the leash, frolicked about, racing this way and that as Johnny and I strolled toward the woods.

"Which would you like to tackle first: the real reason for getting me up here, dog-lady, or Stanley's tale?" I asked.

"Oh God, you would remind me, but I suppose we must discuss them. Easiest first: dog-lady."

"Okay, here's my suggestion: keep Robert the Bruce out of the way, at least until you confirm whether she is the dog-lady or not."

Johnny grunted.

"There are three scenarios: If she is and she recognizes you, there is no point in continuing to keep him sequestered. If she is and she doesn't recognize you, you will have to keep him hidden away. Robert will not take kindly to being kept out of sight of you for any length of time, but that will just have to be endured. If she is someone completely different, no problem."

I felt I had elaborated all the options succinctly. Johnny sighed and looked up at the sky as if seeking guidance.

"I suppose I'll just have to confront being matchmade, but maybe not." Johnny stopped as if his request for divine intervention had been answered. "Of course! Why didn't I think of that before? If she recognizes me and Robert, so much the better. In fact, I'm going to tie the damn scarf around his neck. It will be like breaking out a battle ensign and steering directly for the enemy. I like it! No more skirting the issue, and if our meeting all falls apart, I can hardly be blamed. 'She didn't like me' is what I can tell Mother. Brilliant!"

I could tell Johnny had grabbed onto this lifeline with gusto. He looked positively relieved. "Are you sure that's wise?"

"Of course it is," said Johnny, thrilled with his decision. "I know in my bones it's her. You'll see. Next?"

"You mentioned there might be another reason for inviting me this weekend."

"Ah yes. I suppose I did mention something along those lines. I hesitate because I have nothing concrete to confirm what I think. With the sun shining and a new day before us, my fears seem unfounded and without substance."

"Tell me anyway."

We walked along in silence. Finally, he said, "I'll put it to you this way — I think we're in trouble. By we, I mean Dodge Capital, my parents, Rhinebeck, everything. The economic environment has changed, and our little neck of the woods is under pressure. Costs have risen. Competition is fierce. It's not the same anymore. I feel our days are numbered. The parents feel it, and I know they're worried. They won't talk about money — at least not *their* money, and that bothers me. I need a fresh pair of eyes to confirm my fears or dispose of them. I need to know how bad the situation really is."

"You think it's bad and they're not saying."

"That's pretty much how I see it." He stopped and looked at me. "You were quite the analyst, Percy. You did get one wrong, but overall, we did quite well together."

"Until we didn't."

"Until we didn't. But one mistake does not negate the validity of the process."

"The results say otherwise."

"If the results were as bad as you think, then answer me this: why do I feel so rudderless and without purpose, and why do you feel the same? You know I'm right. Admit it."

I looked away. "Perhaps."

Johnny had struck far too close to home. I didn't want to think about that.

Johnny continued. "I've been lost ever since our partnership went into the toilet, if you must know."

We started walking again. He had more to say. I could tell.

"My trading has been lousy as well. Father will not tolerate much more incompetence in that department. He's made that quite clear. I'm on thin ice, and I'm worried sick. I'm afraid that my future, along with everything that I know and love, will disappear, and there'll be nothing left."

Johnny shook himself.

"You see? I can get positively morbid even on a beautiful day like today. It's criminal. We'll go over all that in more detail later. I also thought I'd float the idea of reassessing our prospects together. I don't wish to discuss it now. I just want you to think about it. What's next on the list?"

Johnny would often leave what was most on his mind to the very end and then say it in an offhand way to downplay the significance. I sometimes did the same. Knowing him as well as I did, I knew his vision of the future filled him with dread, but I also knew he was a lot tougher than he let on, even if he didn't think so. He would survive. He always would. He was a Dodge.

I continued. "Next on the list is your thoughts on Alice and Stanley's narrative, but before we go there, I would like to say that you're not wrong. Okay? Like you, I'm getting by day-by-day, but that's all. I put one foot in front of the other. That's the best I can manage. What you suggest has merit, but we should table all that for a later discussion. Agreed?"

"Agreed."

"Thoughts on Stanley's narrative?" I asked.

"That's a tough one. I think I'm still processing the information from last night, and I'm sure you are too."

"I am, but you were right about what you said about Alice just before dinner last night. My image of her is now hopelessly shattered. There's no way I can cement her back together the way she was in my mind, and that saddens me."

"I thought about that as well and have made a reassessment. Remember that time we managed to get lost in the woods in the middle of winter? Snow started falling so heavily our tracks were wiped out, and we couldn't see more than few feet in front of us."

"Our Artic adventure."

"Exactly. As darkness fell, the household went into an uproar. The next morning, when we finally returned home, everyone treated us as trauma victims, when in fact we thought our bivouac was great fun and said so. That didn't go over very well, if you'll recall. The truth was the parents were the ones traumatized, not us. All I'm saying is don't assume Aunt Alice had a miserable existence. She had a purpose and a reason to live. You saw her. She enjoyed life to the fullest. You can make a tragedy out of her all you want, but can you recall even one time she looked miserable?"

"No, I can't."

"Precisely. So, snap out of it. No more dark thoughts from you, Percy. The day is full of promise."

"Nicely put." I said, thinking it over. "You're right, of course. Stupid of me. You changed my mind."

"Excellent. She lived her life with gusto, burdened but unbowed, and we should too. I will follow in her footsteps to hell and back. To mark the moment, I'm resolved to do one thing."

"And what is that?"

"I'm going to check out a few of those books from the secret library, now that we have lending privileges, and see what happens. I'm in the mood for a good demon summoning. We'll know for sure whether this magic stuff is all hocus-pocus. What do you think of them apples?"

I shook my head and had to smile. "Very brave. Foolhardy, of course, but brave."

"You think it's all a crock anyway. Tell me the truth."

"Well, yes, but ..." I knew I was often too grim in my outlook. I needed to get into the spirit of things, and Johnny's insouciance was infectious. I continued. "The very thought of you and I, by some remote miracle, unleashing a relation to Moloch or Belial on our little family get-together in this house of all places could really create some drama and excitement. I suppose we could always say that Stanley did it, but, no one will believe us. My money's on Maw, if there's a showdown. Maw would probably eat it poached for breakfast."

Johnny laughed. "I'm with you there, but what has come over you? Has Mr. Skeptic turned into Mr. Semi-skeptic?"

"I wouldn't say that, Johnny, but the day is bright with portent, and as you are well aware, in this place, anything is possible. I feel better, and I might fancy a little experimentation, just to confirm, mind you. In this instance, a negative is as good as a positive."

I had no idea what I was thinking, but it seemed a good idea at the time. It must have been lack of sleep, my lightened mood, and Johnny's influence. I have tended to get a little reckless when we're together.

"We're on then. Now, where's that dog?" asked Johnny, looking about. "I bet he's in the woods. Damn. I have a tennis ball, but that's not going to do a thing until he sees it. Robert! Robert the Bruce! Get back here this instant!"

Johnny and I headed into the woods. It was darker in here underneath the leaves, and the ground was sloppy from yesterday's rain.

After several minutes of calling and searching, we spotted Robert, wet and covered in mud, trotting through some shrubs with an ancient tennis ball in his mouth. He was happily chewing away until he was five feet from Johnny, at which point he dropped the ball and looked up expectantly.

"Damn that dog. How does he find them? I know what he's going to do. He's just going to snap it up when I get close and run away. I'll fox him. You watch."

Johnny pulled out his reserve ball and presented it to Robert, who eyed this new treasure with his beady black eyes. Still watching intently, he lay down on the wet ground and began to gnaw on the one he had. Johnny stepped closer with the ball in his outstretched hand. Robert stood up but continued to chew, his eyes never leaving the proffered ball. Johnny moved closer, but quicker than I would have thought possible, Robert spat out the one in his mouth, leaped, and snatched the ball out of Johnny's fingers. Johnny roared his displeasure. Robert, his theft complete, spun and bolted for the undergrowth. We could hear him streaking away through the brush as Johnny, screaming like a madman, plunged into the bushes in hot pursuit. I reluctantly followed but soon was bounding after Johnny.

Two hours of excruciating negotiations, mad sprinting lunges, attempted tackles, threats, pleadings, and screamed curses followed before Robert was finally captured and put back on the leash.

Wet, splattered with mud, exhausted, and hoarse from shouting, Johnny and I made our way back to the house. Robert, fresh as ever, strained against the leather. As we made our way around to the front, Johnny summed up our hike by saying, "It's good to get him out, but he can be so frustrating. He led us on a merry chase, but I got him in the end, so I suppose that's something."

I croaked something unintelligible.

"Not to worry. He and I are going to have a talk."

I was too spent to comment. As we walked past Alice's wing, I became sufficiently recovered to ask Johnny about the figurine.

"Ah yes. I was wondering about that myself," said Johnny. "Let's keep that between ourselves. I'm not sure why, but I have a feeling that'd be best for now."

I thought for a moment and said somewhat hoarsely, "Strangely, I agree. The less others know, the better. By the way, I'm in need of strong drink and then a nap, in that order, so let's keep moving."

"Absolutely."

We were only a few feet from the door when Robert's ears perked up as a long black limousine turned left to make its way down the sloping driveway to the roundabout at the front of the house.

"Looks like they're early," said Johnny. "Damn."

18

The limo, with Raymond, Mr. Dodge's personal chauffeur, at the wheel, cruised sedately down the drive toward the roundabout. As if on cue, the front door of the house opened in front of us, and out came Stanley, followed by Simon and Jane, as they assembled to greet their employer and guests. Harry appeared around the far corner to help with the luggage. Johnny and I, looking disheveled and muddy, had no option but to turn and be part of the welcoming committee.

The car crunched to a halt and Raymond opened the rear door. Mr. Dodge stepped out. He greeted Stanley and the staff and then passed down the line to Johnny and me. He looked at Johnny closely and said, "You might want to get cleaned up once you meet our guests. I'm afraid they'll just have to meet you the way you are. No way around it, I'm sorry to say, without appearing rude."

Mr. Dodge then smiled at me and shook my hand. He seemed genuinely pleased. Johnny handed me the leash and followed his father to meet the rest of the party.

Mrs. Dodge disembarked and after giving Johnny a kiss,

whispered something to him. Probably that his sense of timing could be better. She moved down the line and stopped in front of Robert and me. She gave me a kiss and said she was thrilled I had made it. No hugs, which I thought was understandable, given our appearance.

After a brief pause, out popped the baron.

Baron von Hofmanstal was short, slightly round, and very pale. He looked like a reincarnated version of Napoleon. He wore his black hair brushed forward in the same fashion as the former emperor's and wore a countenance that boded ill to any who crossed him. Like most men of smaller stature, what he lacked in height, he made up for in subtle — and not so subtle — forms of intimidation.

His dress was immaculate from the tiny hand-made, dark-brown shoes that glistened with polish to his tailored three-piece gray suit. He blinked like a malevolent toad as he surveyed the house and the assembled servants without any change in expression, other than to take the camel hair coat that he was holding and flick it disdainfully about his shoulders, like an Italian movie director, as he reached in to hand out the baroness. She was a tall blond who favored a tan Chanel ensemble with matching leather purse in creamy beige. She looked like she could model for *Vogue*, and probably did on occasion. As she stood next to her husband, the difference in height was more pronounced. In heels, she towered over him by several inches.

I had just finished gawking at the incongruity when out stepped the final member of the party. Striking was perhaps an understatement. Her hair was black like her father's. It cascaded to her shoulders in silky waves. She wore a gray dress that fit her perfectly and accentuated her figure. Her eyes captured my attention even from several feet away. They were so blue they sparkled like gems. She was not as tall as her mother but not as short as her father. She gave one and all a dazzling smile.

They stood in a row in front of the assembled household and waited. Mr. Dodge beckoned to Johnny and proceeded to introduce him. I was so caught up in the proceedings that I failed to remember Robert's strength. One moment I had hold of the leash, the next it was ripped from my grasp as Robert bounded forward to be with his master, just as he was shaking hands with the baron.

I must admit the baron was quick. Perhaps it was his alacrity in stepping out of the way that caused the coat to slip off his shoulders and hit the driveway just as Robert arrived. The baron tried to snatch it up, but too late. Robert had planted his rear and then lay down in the middle of its creamy smoothness as he gazed fondly up at Johnny.

The baron cursed and tugged at the coat to no avail. He gave Robert a vicious kick in frustration. Outside of making a muffled thud that was heard by one and all, it did absolutely nothing. His daughter rescued the moment. She stepped forward, picked up the lead, and gave a strong jerk while yelling "Heel!" Robert, whether because this word harkened back to some long-forgotten obedience training or because he appreciated her commanding tone, complied by getting up off the coat and moving to her left. She promptly handed him over to Johnny and stepped over to her father to console him. She knew dogs. There was no question about that.

The baron had by now retrieved the soiled garment and held it out at arm's length, not only to survey the damage but to avoid it making the slightest contact with his suit. Stanley approached discreetly and took the coat from the baron's shaking hands. Still holding it out front like a matador's muleta, Stanley turned and announced that champagne would be served in the drawing room and to follow him.

While everyone started to move inside, I heard Stanley tell the baron that his staff were expert at cleaning anything and everything, and that the coat would be good as new by the following morning. The baron grunted his disbelief and stomped toward the door. I stepped aside to get out of the way.

I waved at Raymond. I had not seen him in years. He looked the same, and true to form, he merely nodded back in acknowledgment. Johnny and I had known him all our lives. He was a permanent yet menacing fixture of the Dodge household. Crude, of sullen disposition, and immensely strong, he looked like a pirate and merely tolerated Johnny's and my existence when he would drive us to school and back. He worshipped the very ground Mr. Dodge walked on. Why he restricted his adoration to only Mr. Dodge, and what Mr. Dodge had done to command such unreserved loyalty and respect, was a constant source of speculation between us. Mr. Dodge would simply ignore us when asked, and to query Raymond for the reason demanded more courage than we could possibly muster. He had a nasty streak that was best left unprovoked.

I brought up the rear of the procession and noted the baron was limping just a little. Score one for Robert. The baron might as well have drop-kicked a rock when he tried to shift him off the coat. Johnny stepped to the side and let his parents and their guests go first. He fell in beside me and whispered, "Well, that was a memorable meeting."

Johnny cocked his head toward the stairs. We needed to change, so the two of us, with Robert firmly in hand, mounted the stairs to our rooms. When we got there, we cleaned and dried Robert as best we could and quickly showered. We changed into the more presentable attire of sport coats, dark flannel pants, and ties. We met in the common room to discuss what to do next.

"Well? Is she?" I asked.

"Dog-lady? Oh yes. Without a doubt."

"Did she recognize you?"

"She gave no indication, but Robert's antics should have clued her fairly quickly."

"Sorry about that. He got away from me."

"Not to worry. It's his nature, I'm afraid. By the way, we'll have to consult with Stanley on our way downstairs. I think it best that young Robert not be part of our little gathering. If he knows he's being separated from me, he gets really annoyed and eats things."

"Like scarves?"

"Much worse. He'll chew entire chairs and couches into kindling. He gnaws the legs off. Filthy habit, and expensive if they're antiques."

"Well, I hope Stanley can think of something because I have no ideas. On a different subject: dog-lady. What should be our plan?"

"I think we will have to play things by ear for now. It's just about lunchtime anyway. What do you think of the baron?"

"He's a complete jerk. He even kicked Robert."

"He did. How about the daughter?"

"What about the daughter?"

"You're smitten already. I can tell."

"Nonsense. Absolute nonsense."

I said this with a little too much emphasis, because Johnny looked at me in that way of his and said, "Of course. Of course. Do you think it's getting a little warm in here, Percy? Or are you naturally flushed as a rule?"

"Not funny, Johnny. Not funny at all."

"I feel your pain, but duty calls. Are you ready to meet our guests?"

"I suppose so." I resigned myself to at least being civil to the baron regardless of my first impressions. Then again, he was probably not too impressed with us either. I figured the score was even.

We went down the back stairs to the kitchen. Stanley was preparing to carry out some hors d'oeuvres of caviar. Johnny asked where he should put Robert, and Stanley told him to put him in the office. He had a special blanket in there underneath Stanley's desk. It would hold him for a while.

We led him into the suggested space, and Robert seemed to accept his fate. He curled up underneath the desk and went to sleep. Johnny carefully shut the door and said, "Well, that's something. Things are looking up."

I wasn't so sure, but duty called. Off we went to meet the guests in what I hoped were better circumstances. At least we looked the part.

19

Johnny and I passed through to the drawing room by way of the kitchen and the dining room. Mr. and Mrs. Dodge and the von Hofmanstals were standing in front of the Constable, admiring it and chatting among themselves. Mrs. Dodge spotted us as we entered and announced, "Here they are."

We were both welcomed as if the previous encounter in the driveway had never happened. I followed Johnny and was introduced to the baron by Mr. Dodge as a longtime friend of the family. He gave me a polite smile, which meant the corners of his mouth moved upward by a fraction as he offered his hand, which I took. His grip was shockingly firm, and if I had not moved my hand forward sufficiently against his when I took it — an old habit from childhood when Johnny and I would try to force the other to submit by gripping the other's hand at the knuckles — I would have been in for a painful surprise. He looked up at me with pale-blue eyes that gave nothing away, but I knew he'd done it deliberately. As to why he should pull such a stunt, other than to assert himself, I had no idea. I decided to ignore the provocation and make conversation instead. I noticed when we shook hands that he had a scar that split his left eyebrow. Mr. Dodge turned toward the baroness to answer a question about the Constable when I asked the baron in German if he had fenced in his youth. I had taken up both at university and then spent a year abroad studying economics at the University of Freiburg.

The baron muttered, also in German, that he fenced, and that saber was his weapon of choice, although he was skilled in both épée and foil. I told him I had fenced saber as well and wondered if that was the cause of the scar above his left eye. He reached forward like a striking snake, grabbed my arm in a vice-like grip, and pulled me forward and down, so his mouth was inches from my ear. He hissed with unrestrained venom that although the assumption was logical, I was mistaken. Saber scars were longer, deeper, and uglier. He had fought several duels. More than one of his opponents had lost an eye due to his skill with a blade. I had no idea what I was talking about. He then released me by shoving my arm away with undisguised contempt just as Mr. Dodge turned back. Sensing some tension, Mr. Dodge asked, "Is anything the matter?"

At this, the baron laughed and said in English, "I was simply making a point to your young friend here regarding assumptions. It is all too common, yes?" He looked up at Mr. Dodge, smiling sweetly.

Mr. Dodge answered in the affirmative and asked politely if he would like to make the introduction to his wife and daughter.

He scrunched up his mouth as if deciding and then answered, "You do it."

I reeled in shock from the baron's surprising hostility. I was introduced to the baroness and their daughter, but all I remember babbling was "It's a pleasure. It's a pleasure," as I shook their hands. I barely looked up. Finished, I stood to the side, perplexed and disheartened. I felt like an animal that had been whipped for reasons it didn't comprehend. A feeling of humiliation washed over me as I sank into my dark place, even as I appeared to be present to those conversing around me. I had obviously hit a nerve trying to ingratiate myself with the baron and erred badly in mentioning the scar.

Wanting to be liked and to make a good impression were poor habits of mine that I thought I had left behind, but obviously not. I analyzed the encounter and concluded there was more to his animosity than my bungled attempt at conversation. The man had displayed antagonism toward me even before I opened my mouth. Whether this was directed against me personally, the Dodge family, or people in general, I didn't know. If the baron's target was the Dodge family, how could he possibly consider marrying off his daughter to Johnny? But how could it be me he had such contempt for, as I had never met him, or even heard of him, until yesterday. If he hated people in general, then why did he act civilly to everyone else? My mind buzzed with calculations and potential scenarios to explain the outcome, but underneath I felt wounded and immensely hurt. My emotions lay just beneath the surface, barely in check as dark feelings bubbled inside me.

I have never done well with physical confrontation and open hostility. I was not a coward, but my instinct was always to flee and only afterward regroup. I remembered being blindsided by an older boy at school. His name was Peter Lewis. Johnny was nowhere around. I was small, even at twelve, and the other was a year older than me. We were alone in the stairwell when he turned and punched me in the face with no warning. He screamed at me, "You think you're so great with your chauffer and your money? There's no one here to protect you now! How does that feel?"

I saw stars as he stomped off. I burst into tears. I sat through my classes in a daze, hearing nothing, seeing nothing. I was certain I had done nothing personally to provoke him. It was my first experience of hatred for which there was no rational explanation.

At the time, I felt compelled to respond even if only to repair my damaged image of myself in my own eyes. I made a simple plan: find Lewis and attack, regardless of the consequences. I found him later in the day coming out of the locker room. I whipped him around and said, "I owe you one." I punched him and a melee ensued. We were pulled apart by scrambling teachers. Afterward, I was no longer so afraid, but I was dismayed by the unprovoked attack just the same. The incident bothered me long after, and I resolved to become better at defending myself. At my insistence, Johnny and I took up martial arts, fencing, shooting, boxing — we did them all. My plan had worked somewhat, until now, when once again I found myself defenseless and unable to respond.

In truth, I concluded I had an enemy. I silently asked Alice for some help.

While I was lost in my musing, Johnny slipped up beside me, holding two glasses of champagne and gave me one. "That baron is a bastard. I saw the whole thing."

I had forgotten how very little escaped Johnny even though he sometimes gave the opposite impression. I grunted, still in a dark cloud.

Johnny added, "Drink up and put a smile on your face, or else he'll have won completely. Our time will come, you'll see. Nobody shits on us in this house and gets away unscathed, that I can assure you, so brace up. Remember, we have access to higher authorities."

"Strangely," I said, "I was thinking that very thing." I drank half the glass and felt better.

"That's the spirit. Besides, there's always Maw, and she arrives tomorrow."

I drank the other half of the glass and actually smiled at the thought. It was the first time I ever looked on meeting Maw with something less than dread. She scared me more than the baron, although in a different way.

As I finished my glass, Stanley was at my elbow and said, "If you both could spare a moment after lunch, I would like a word." He took my empty glass and glided off.

Johnny and I looked at each other. He shrugged, and I did the same. It was nearly time for lunch. Stanley announced the fact at the dining room door. The party filed in with Johnny and me bringing up the rear.

20

The long dining room table was set with a white, embroidered tablecloth and thin, white china with gold edges. Seating was assigned by small cards with our names on them. The setting was more formal than usual, in honor of our guests. Mrs. Dodge was at the end of the table closest to the kitchen entrance while Mr. Dodge was at the opposite. The baron and baroness were seated on one side of the table, with the baron next to Mr. Dodge, while Johnny and I sat opposite, with the daughter in between. I sat at Mr. Dodge's right, facing the baron.

Stanley and Simon served the first course of smoked salmon flown in from Scotland, with small points of white toast, along with a cold Sancerre. It was delicious. Mr. Dodge and the baron were discussing some business ventures in Europe. I simply looked on until the lady on my right leaned over and whispered in my ear, "I'm pregnant." I wasn't sure I heard her right, so I turned and looked at her in surprise.

She laughed. She had a nice laugh. "Oh, I'm not, by the way…just in case you were wondering. I said that to get your attention. My name is Brunhilde. My friends call me Bruni. You seemed elsewhere when we met a few minutes ago, so I wasn't sure it registered. Did it?"

"No, not really. I was distracted. Thank you for the reintroduction."

"You're very welcome."

"I'm Percy. In case you missed it."

"I know."

I glanced over at Johnny, who was in a discussion with the baroness and his mother. "I'm glad that's settled," I said to Bruni. "Do you often accompany your parents on visits?" I had no idea what to say to her, so that seemed fairly safe. Up close, she was frighteningly beautiful.

She looked at me with brilliant eyes that seemed amused at my awkwardness. "If I had said yes and left it at that, what would you have done?"

"I suppose I would have continued with 'Did you grow up in this country or in Europe?'"

"I would have said, 'Both.' But you didn't ask. How about I make an observation, and you comment on it?"

"Okay."

"I noticed my father doesn't seem to like you very much."

"I'm aware of that. I'm not sure he likes very many people, least of all a friend of the family."

"You see? This is much more fun than small talk. We've moved from the merely social to the more relevant. It's much better, don't you agree?"

"Perhaps, but you didn't answer my question."

"Was it a question?"

"It was a comment, but the question was implied, as I think you know."

"It was, but I prefer the direct approach by saying what you mean. It saves time."

We were interrupted by the next course, which was Scotch broth. I put my attention on the soup. Dagmar was a master and I a faithful follower. I finished before Bruni, and on a whim, I leaned over as she was lifting her spoon and whispered, "Will you marry me?"

The spoon dropped with a sharp clatter, interrupting the other conversations at the table. All eyes turned toward her as she picked the utensil out of her soup and apologized to the table. Conversations resumed, but I noted that the baron's gaze seemed to linger a bit longer on both of us before he returned to Mr. Dodge. Bruni turned toward me with a look that did not bode well for our future happiness.

I headed off the explosion by whispering, "You did say you preferred the direct approach, and marriage usually precedes pregnancy, does it not?"

She continued to look at me directly, as I watched her mind weighing possible responses. Finally, she laughed. I could learn to like that laugh. She leaned closer and said, "You're very bad. I suppose I deserved that. Shall we call it even?"

"Even it is. So, back to my implied question: does your father dislike most people or only select ones?"

She looked at me again for a long moment and replied with one word: "Both."

She turned away to converse with Johnny.

The honeymoon was over. It was just as well. I needed time to think. Her presence was only slightly south of overwhelming, and she knew that. I reckoned she had broken more hearts than most people had had ordinary conversations. I had definitely gotten a reaction on the marriage proposal, although what it meant I couldn't say at this point. She was extraordinarily good-looking, obviously intelligent, and an unknown factor in a host of unknowns. I resolved to be very careful. Falling in love with her would be all too easy and very dangerous. If only I could convince my racing heart.

The baron interrupted my thoughts. "You find my daughter attractive?"

"Yes, she favors her mother."

The baron laughed. "I see you've recovered. That's good. Resilience is always an important aspect of trading. You were a trader, yes?"

Mr. Dodge looked like he was about to interrupt but held back.

"Yes, Johnny and I partnered a while back."

"Not now?"

"No, we ended our partnership. I now do forensic accounting out of Los Angeles."

"Too many losses, I suppose. It's a hard business."

"Yes, it can be — and it was."

"Perhaps you can give me your card. I could always use another person to count my money." He laughed at his joke, if it was a joke.

"I'm not an accountant or bookkeeper, per se. I investigate where money goes and where it comes from, particularly as it applies to legal matters. My clients are attorneys."

"I see. Like an office detective."

"More like an analyst. People who wish to hide either the sources of funds or where they stash them can be extremely sophisticated and creative. I discover what they have done, how they did it, and when."

Bruni had leaned closer to me, even though she was still talking to Johnny.

"You're right. Criminals are some of the smartest people I've ever met. Good luck with that."

The baron asked Mr. Dodge a question, but as he did so, Mr. Dodge gave me a wink before turning back to the baron.

The next course was served — a series of pâtés with different sauces that were a delight to taste. This was followed by sorbet.

The baron ate with pleasure and complimented Mr. Dodge on having a cook of such outstanding competence and sophistication. He was enjoying himself, if only because he was no longer frowning. I looked about the room. Mr. Dodge was his usual unruffled self, attentive and completely present. Mrs. Dodge and the baroness were engrossed in conversation on some subject that only they were interested in, while Johnny looked to be in oscillating states of excitement and reservation, both of which were evident in his body language as he moved closer to Bruni one moment and then shifted away the next. Judging from the amount of wine he had consumed, the battle was heavy-going. I knew how he felt.

I turned to my left and listened to Mr. Dodge and the baron discuss yield curves and economic situations around the world, while another part of my mind tried to sort out what was happening here. I felt that we, myself included, were under scrutiny, but for what ultimate purpose, I hadn't a clue. Bruni handled herself with a sophistication and ease that was inconsistent with a young woman in need of a match. I was willing to bet that she had already fielded several offers of marriage from some very qualified applicants. There was no ring on her finger, and one hadn't been removed recently either. There was no telltale indentation or change in color. I tended toward paranoia. I drank more wine to shake the mood and noted Stanley's presence. He stood like a statue in front of the passage to the kitchen. When a glass became half-full, he moved ghostlike to refill the glass. He never looked at the company directly but at a point in the distance.

I had once studied black widow spiders because they fascinated me. With many dangerous creatures, one gets a sixth sense of their existence before they make themselves known. Black widows, however, are a psychic black hole. They have an ability to mask themselves completely. Stanley on duty was the same. One never noticed he was there, but he was all the same, listening and observing.

The meal drew to a close. The ladies went to the drawing room, while the men moved to the library. Bruni, I noted, looked miffed at being segregated, but that was the rule of the house, and for once, I was only too pleased that it existed. Johnny looked relieved as well. He and I followed the older men.

"Well, what do you think?" I asked, unable to contain myself.

"Yikes. Conversing with that girl is like wrestling with a man-eating shark — an awfully attractive one, mind you."

"Tell me about it."

"She definitely gets the heart racing. I kept remembering that fortune-teller predicting the end of the world if I should marry. That was all that kept me and all living things from certain death."

"Well, I beat you there. I already asked her."

"No!"

"Yes."

Johnny stopped in his tracks and asked, "What did she say?"

"She dropped her spoon, and after a brief honeymoon, we ended up divorced."

"Well, you do move quickly, I must say. I think that was the fastest romance on record."

We had reached the library door.

"Too true. But something bothers me — only I can't put my finger on it."

Johnny slapped me on the shoulder and said, "Something *always* bothers you, Percy, but I thank God for paranoid friends! They stimulate the mind. Let's grab some good spirits, smoke a fine cigar, and sing the praises of male company. After that, we'll look up Stan the man, and have a chat. Perhaps he has some information that will help. But first, we need to refresh ourselves from our brush with Circe personified. What say you?"

With my wholehearted agreement, we entered the library.

21

The baron and Johnny's father were seated next to each other in front of the fireplace. The baron was speaking to him in a low voice. He looked like a goblin king sitting on a leather throne with a cigar for a scepter and a snifter of brandy for an orb. Both of them looked up as we entered, but the baron merely noted us before turning back to Mr. Dodge to resume his conversation.

Johnny and I helped ourselves to cognac and cigars from the bar and sat down in the two empty leather chairs placed on either side of a small table. We relaxed, enjoying the cigars and the drink, until one of the baron's comments floated into our thoughts.

"This is a beautiful property," the baron said in his soft voice.

The baron's eyes flicked in our direction. They glittered briefly before he turned back.

"It is," replied John Senior. "I suppose you are now a major collector…among other things?"

"Among other things, as you say, but I am only a small player.

As you know, my businesses keep me occupied, but nonetheless, I have acquired some exquisite pieces."

I was willing to bet he was understating himself to a large degree. I glanced at Johnny, who was staring off into space. He was listening.

The baron paused and looked at the tip of his cigar and said, "I would be most interested in viewing anything you might be willing to show me. Of course, everything would be held in strictest confidence. It is a delicate matter, and I do not wish to presume."

Mr. Dodge said nothing.

The baron glanced about the room before asking, "Shall we join the ladies?"

Mr. Dodge agreed, but whether he referred to the request to view Alice's collection or simply to rejoin the ladies, he left up in the air.

I took up the rear as we filed back to the drawing room. Mr. Dodge held the door for the baron and Johnny, but before I could enter, he said, "Walk with me."

He closed the door and proceeded to take me out the front of the house. The air was cool and breezy. Clouds had sprung up during lunch, and the sun played hide-and-seek behind them, casting us in alternating bright afternoon sunshine and shadow. We stood for a moment and then began to make our way up the driveway.

Mr. Dodge spoke after we had stepped away from the house, "It's good to see you. How've you been?"

"Quite well, sir."

"I'm glad to hear it. I'm happy that you and Johnny are friends again."

"Yes, I am too. Now it's like old times."

We continued to walk at a leisurely pace.

Mr. Dodge interrupted the silence. "Friends are important. In the end, they mean everything, but I didn't pull you out here to lecture you on the value of friendship but rather to impart something that might explain a few things. Did your parents ever tell you the story of their marriage?"

"Just that they ran into each other in Europe and fell in love. Eventually, they married and moved back to the United States, where I was born."

"That's true enough, but like many simple stories, there's more to it. What I wish to tell you is quite relevant, as you'll hear. Your mother and my wife grew up together. They went to the same boarding school in Lausanne. Often, they would travel throughout Austria, Bavaria, and Italy without a chaperone — quite unusual in those days. I met Anne during one of their vacations and proposed soon after. She made an impact on me then and does to this day. I think we are one of a few genuinely happy couples. Every day, I thank all the powers that be for her coming into my life."

He paused for a moment and continued. "During one of their travels, and before I met either of them, both were introduced to a young Austrian aristocrat by the name of Hugo. He liked Anne but was completely smitten by your mother. He courted her and was successful, in the sense that they became engaged."

"Hugo von Hofmanstal, I take it?"

"The very same."

"So, we do have a history."

"Oh yes, and quite a history, as you shall hear. It's not the most flattering of tales, but necessary that you know it, even if it has a darker side. Your parents are some of our best friends. After all, that friendship allowed you to become part of our lives, and we are truly grateful for it." He paused and looked at me.

"And I am too. Really."

We continued in silence for a bit before he said, "Hugo was a serious fellow, even then. He was small but a scrapper. He developed a formidable reputation as a fighter and a duelist. At that time, dueling was illegal, but nonetheless an accepted practice in his culture and level of society.

"Your parents met after your mother was already engaged to Hugo. How that happened exactly I don't know. Anne said that Mary needed some assistance with her luggage. She asked your father for a hand, and he was only too happy to help. The two girls were traveling from Switzerland to Austria to visit Hugo's family for the third time. For your future parents, it was love at first sight. They acted on their feelings. By the time they arrived at Hugo's castle, they were committed to each other, and there was no turning back. To compound the issue, both had decided that Mary should break off the engagement with Hugo as soon as possible by announcing what had happened between them. This, they decided, must occur during the coming visit. To make sure there would be no mistake, she was to make the announcement in front of witnesses. Meanwhile, your father was to await the outcome at a hotel in a nearby village.

"Love can be so grand, but it's a difficult emotion to deal with for many. It's easy to throw caution aside, believing that love, if true, will conquer all. I knew your father from school. Thomas and I were good friends. It was just like him to downplay the consequences of his actions. We were constantly getting into difficulties from this facet of his personality. I was not there to counsel him, because I was visiting Paris with my father. I would have advised both of them to handle the matter in a completely different way, but I wasn't there. They decided on the bold approach.

"You father waited at the hotel for two days while events at the castle took their course. He was a bit far gone and called me at the start of the first day. He had to tell somebody of his joy and his agony from being parted from Mary. When I managed to finally extract the story from him, I explained to my father what was going on, and he rightly concluded that I had best get there in a hurry, before events spun completely out of control.

"I traveled as fast as I could and arrived at the hotel by the end of the second day. We had barely greeted each other when the door of the hotel was thrown open, and Hugo, accompanied by two friends, stormed into the lobby. He went up to your father, seething with emotion, but the rules of etiquette forbade him from using physical violence then and there. He demanded satisfaction. He had been wronged in his own house, in front of his father, his friends, his guests.

Hugo told me later that he had had to argue the case for a duel to the old baron before he could proceed. In his argument, he stated clearly that even if the man who had wronged him was an American and ignorant of the standards of behavior expected in their level of society, he should be held accountable for his actions. He was in their country and on their turf. Mary was not to blame. After much arguing, the old baron relented, provided proper form was carried out.

"Hugo was surprised when he saw me. He had no idea I was involved. He asked, 'John, is that really you?' I said, 'Hugo, it's me.' Hugo took hold of himself. Briefly, he explained the events leading up to the current meeting. He asked if I was to act as second. I delayed my answer. I told your father to go to his room, do nothing, and say nothing, while I talked with Hugo, and not to expect me until late.

"I left for the castle. Hugo and I had known each other since childhood. Our families were very close, and my father respected the old baron immensely. In Paris, when I explained what had happened, my father was very upset and urged me to try and rescue the situation before it escalated to this level. He told me to

179

do whatever I thought necessary but with one restriction: if there was a duel, which he felt was highly likely, given the magnitude of the offense in the eyes of Hugo, I was not to act as your father's second. The ties between our families were such that if I was forced to participate, the relationship with the von Hofmanstals would be forfeit, one way or the other. Whichever friend won, or lost, and I was forced to participate, there would be blood. Looking back, it was wise council. I was in an untenable situation nonetheless.

"When we arrived at the castle, I was met by the old baron, who invited us both into his study. He was as surprised to see me as Hugo. We spoke. I told him I was your father's friend, but I had been instructed by my family that I was not to be his second. I made my case for calm. Your father had no friends available who might be called on. Further, he had never fenced — a duel with swords was out of the question. Lastly, there must be some way to achieve satisfaction other than by a duel, which was illegal.

"I hoped that these arguments would put a stop to the proceedings, but I could tell from their attitudes that there would be no backing down, and no apology in whatever manner given would be acceptable. Hugo and Mary's engagement had been publicly announced. The way your mother had rescinded it left no doubt as to the nature of the relationship and the reason why. Further, this had been done before Hugo's friends and guests in their own home. The best I could do was negotiate for a more even match. The terms agreed upon were that Anne and Mary were to remain in their rooms at the castle until the duel was finished. Second, pistols would have to be the weapon used, and not just any pistols, but proper black powder dueling pistols. There was no way I would sanction Walther .380 semiautomatics or similar modern weapons. The probability of death of one, or both, was too certain. This was agreed. The old baron suggested that a disinterested party would have to be the second. A professional man, a doctor who lived nearby, would have to do. Further, he was an amateur gunsmith and collector, who owned a splendid set of Gastinne-Renette percussion dueling pistols. The baron himself made the call and confirmed the arrangement.

"With a heavy heart, I returned to the hotel. The duel had been set for seven in the morning on a green patch below the castle walls. Death of one them was a likely outcome, but there was nothing to be done. When I arrived, I explained the situation. Your father was aghast. He had no idea what he had unleashed. He shook. He wept. He said he would run away, but I explained the consequences if he should do so. There was Mary's potential shame to consider as well as the repercussions his flight would have on his family. In the end, Thomas decided to go ahead. He vowed that his love for Mary would see him through. I left him in the bar as I went up to bed to try and sleep.

"That morning, a car met us at the hotel, along with the doctor. The doctor protested the stupidity of the affair, but he had acquiesced because with a medical man present, perhaps lives might be saved. The parties met as agreed. There was no backing down. No apology was offered, and no reconciliation was possible. The pistols were loaded by each of the seconds and then assigned by a coin toss. I explained to your father that to fire the pistol, it had to be double-cocked. When released by the trigger, the hammer would hit a percussion cap that would explode, igniting the primer, which in turn, would set off the powder in the chamber, thus discharging the pistol. There was a lag between both events, and if he was to have a chance, he had to hold the weapon rock-steady for several seconds once he pulled the trigger. Deliberately shooting into the ground or into the air would require a repeat. Both would fire simultaneously once the signal was given. The old baron had decided that I was to be the one who gave the signal by dropping my raised arm once the two were in position, as he looked on from the rampart above.

"When I lowered my arm, both fired, but Hugo's pistol exploded, such that a piece blew back and struck him above the left eye, while the other ball went who knows where."

"The scar!" I exclaimed.

"Exactly. Fortunately, the doctor was there. Hugo was unconscious. At first, we thought he had been shot, but the doctor confirmed that he had received the wound from the pistol's fragments, and his life was not in any danger. Blood had been spilled and honor satisfied. Both men had acquitted themselves well.

"After making sure that Hugo would recover, and expressing my regrets to the baron, who assured me I was not at fault whatsoever, the girls, your father, and myself were driven to the hotel, where we had a jolly breakfast. I was relieved beyond anything you could imagine that the outcome had not been fatal to either party. Anne and I got quite drunk, and our relationship started right there at the hotel. Mary was also in good spirits, but your father was more reserved and even a bit pensive.

"It was not until we were back in the States that I was able to pull out of him the cause of his mental turmoil. He told me that after I had gone up to bed the night before the duel, the doctor paid a visit to the hotel bar. He needed a drink and did not wish to drink alone. They got to talking and discovered their mutual dilemma. The doctor detested the idea of being party to a duel. It was against the law. But because the baron had asked him, and because his income depended on being in the baron's good graces, the request was interpreted as a command. Long after closing time, they brooded and commiserated over their respective situations, sharing a bottle of local spirits between them. They concocted a plan. Both reckoned the probability of surviving without injury were at best one third, and more likely half that, given Hugo's proficiency at all types of weapons. But there was a way to adjust the odds. If one of the pistols were altered so that it misfired, or even exploded, the chance of his surviving unscathed would rise from 16 percent to a much better 50 percent. The outcome depended on who received the altered pistol. Rather than trying to ensure he got the right one, they decided to leave that to chance. They had changed fate as much as they dared. The doctor left to make the arrangements.

"So, he cheated," I said.

"In an absolute sense, he did indeed, but I tend to a more lenient view. He was facing a man who, in comparison, was a professional killer. The winner was an almost forgone conclusion. He did not change the game to such an extent that he would win outright or that Hugo would be killed. He set up the duel so that each of them had an equal chance. Had your father received the exploding pistol, he would have most certainly been killed because Hugo was a crack shot. After he told me this, he explained that he felt immense shame for what he had done. He felt like a cheat and a liar. His view of himself was irrevocably destroyed. In fact, he did not think he even deserved to marry Mary, the woman he had fought for. After trying to console him and seeing that he would not let go of his self-obsession, I went to my father's study and pulled out a revolver. No one was in the house other than us. I loaded five of the six chambers and slammed it on the desk in front of him. Thomas stopped his sniveling. I had his attention. I made him examine the pistol and tell me what he saw. He told me that one chamber was empty. I ordered him to close the wheel and spin it. He did so. I fired into the book case. The sound was immense. We were deaf for an hour. I actually had to pull out a pen and paper and write, *Those were the odds you faced, and that is what would have happened to you. How dare you squander such an extraordinary opportunity to lead a better existence, when the gods decided in your favor!* The demonstration snapped him right out of it. After we could hear again, we broke out the best champagne and celebrated for the rest of the night. He never looked back. Few men can do that. He did."

"I never knew any of this. Good God! I see your point, of course, and you are correct. I can be a bit judgmental, particularly when it comes to my father. It was a very good solution, given the circumstances. He survived, and no one was killed. It's unbelievable that the practice existed even then."

"It still does today."

"I get the feeling that there is more."

We headed back to the house.

"Yes. Yes, there is. Hugo, now Baron von Hofmanstal, suspects that all was not quite right with the duel. What makes him suspect, I have no idea, and I'm not going to question him about it either."

"I certainly won't," I said. "He was remarkably frosty when we met. I suppose this must be the reason."

"I'm sure of it. I think he was quite surprised to see you. Hugo and I have enjoyed a friendship that is over half a century long. He has many outstanding qualities, but I'm afraid you saw only the worst. He can be vindictive and a real pain in the ass, but then, can't we all."

"How do you suggest I handle this?"

"With grace. I'm afraid the sins of the father are visited on the children, and I'm sorry for that. I doubt you're in any danger, but getting close to him will surely be an uphill battle. Courting his daughter might be difficult as well." He looked at me again.

"I think that ship has sailed. She is lovely, exceedingly so, but to my mind, disturbing in the extreme."

"For what it's worth, I found Anne to be the same at first."

"Oh boy."

Mr. Dodge laughed and slapped me on the back, just like Johnny. We had reached the front door.

"Mr. Dodge..."

"We've known each other way too long for that. Call me John. Anne and I are so proud of you both."

We entered the door and I wondered if he had seen Johnny's latest trading report, but knowing him, he knew days ago.

22

Mr. Dodge and I walked into the drawing room. The baron and Johnny were standing by the french doors overlooking the lawn, while the ladies were clustered together on the couch at the other side of the room. The baroness and Mrs. Dodge got up when we entered. Anne asked John if he could relate a story about a mutual friend of theirs from Italy.

I wandered over to sit with Bruni. She didn't move but watched me as I approached. I noticed the indentation at the base of her neck and the fair skin below, which disappeared beneath the front of her gray dress. Her long legs were crossed as she relaxed into the sofa with one arm stretched across its back. On her left wrist, she wore a gold bracelet of large rectangular links. I sat down.

"Secret conference?" she asked.

"Family matters."

"That covers a broad area. Did it include my family as well?"

"The subject may have come up."

"I bet it did. Our family has known the Dodges for a long time. We're thick as thieves."

"For generations, if I'm not mistaken."

"We have an interlinked history and a long memory. Light me a cigarette."

I opened a silver box that lay on the side table and took one out. They were fresh, probably put there this morning. I lit one for her with a lighter in the shape of a silver bird that stood beside the box. I passed her the lit cigarette but not before I took a drag. I was slightly on edge. As she took it from me, our fingers touched. Electricity coursed upward from my fingers.

To cover my reaction, I asked, "A long memory...What does that mean?"

"We have many shared stories. They help define who we are."

"I see. Maybe you'd like to tell me one?"

"Perhaps, a little later. You seem very familiar to me. Do you know why that might be?"

"I don't know. I doubt we've ever met. I think I would've remembered."

"Why is that?"

"Well," I answered tentatively, "I don't think you are a person who is easily forgotten."

"I'll take that as a compliment. You grew up in this house with Johnny?"

Happy to change the subject, I answered more eagerly, "Yes, I did."

"It's a fascinating place, and I want to see it. Will you give me a tour?"

"Of course. When would you like one?"

"Now, unless you've something else you must to attend to."

I hesitated. The idea of being alone with Bruni was both appealing and intimidating. I was becoming aware that I really would like to spend more time with her, but I would be swimming into dangerous waters. Further, if we simply got up and left, we would be noticed, and being conspicuous was not my forte. I decided to pass, but before I could voice my decision, I heard myself say, "Now is fine."

So much for free will.

If she had expected me to equivocate, she showed no indication. Her bracelet clinked as she smoothly unfolded herself from the couch. She walked over to her mother, spoke a few words, and rejoined me. I looked over at the baron, but he was talking animatedly to Johnny. His eyes glanced in our direction, but only for a moment.

"Let's go," she said.

I opened the door to the hallway, allowing her to go first. I closed it quickly behind us. I had expected some sort of objection, but there was none. We were alone.

I sighed.

"Nervous being alone with me? Many men are," she said, looking around the reception area and then walking over to the clock by the front door to have a closer look.

"Why do you think that might be?" I asked, joining her.

"I intimidate them. I'm smarter, more attractive than most women, and I have a mind of my own."

"Works for me."

"I don't intimidate you?" she said, turning to face me.

"Not in the way you think." I looked steadily back at her. She had the most marvelous mouth. Her lips were perfect.

I turned away and asked, "Where would you like to start?"

"Anywhere. How about down that hallway."

"Very well — it leads past the library and a larger reading area before entering the west wing where Lady Bromley resided when she was alive."

We walked down the hall. I opened the library door, showed her the room, and continued until we were in front of the door to Alice's apartment. We stopped for a moment.

She turned to me. "I've heard that she still lives here in spirit form, waiting to avenge her murder."

"Yes, there are many rumors. What have you heard specifically?"

"Nothing concrete, just tales from friends of my father. One man in particular won't set foot in this house ever again. Many in the group of collectors my father has dealings with say similar things." We stood quite close together. "What do you think?"

"That she was murdered? It's always been a possibility, but there's been nothing concrete, as you said. For what it's worth, I don't think the house is haunted. I never saw a ghost in all the time I lived here. That's not to say there isn't a presence. It seems to permeate the entire property, but it's strongest in this part of the house. We all feel it, at least those who have stayed here for a while. One treads carefully. Some things are best left sleeping."

"So you *are* a believer."

"I think there are things I can't explain. You would have to have known Alice to get a sense of why I think that way. She was a force to be reckoned with in her own right. She was a noted Egyptologist — a woman in a man's world. She held her own. She had a presence like no one else, other than perhaps Mrs. Leland, Johnny's grandmother, whom you will meet."

"I look forward to that. In the meantime, I'd like to see where Lady Bromley lived. Perhaps I'll *feel* something."

"Do I detect a note of sarcasm?"

She smiled. "Perhaps a little. I'm sorry. I tend to stick with facts rather than beliefs."

"By habit or by training?"

"Both. I engineer corporate and financial structures for my father, and I tend to be skeptical of the less material. Perhaps I'll tell you about it some time."

"I'd like that, but before we continue, a note of caution. We rarely enter this part of the house. Touch nothing and be as quiet as possible."

I had just put my hand on the doorknob when she said, "You think we'll disturb her?"

I paused, my hand still on the door, and looked back at her.

"If you like. Just the same, the less we intrude, the better."

"I'll respect your beliefs, although I think they're in error."

"Fair enough. Just have a care. Here we go."

I had cautioned her as best I could. I was not certain that showing her this part of the house was a good idea, but I could hardly refuse now that we had come this far. I opened the door, allowed her to pass, and followed inside. Her closeness sent my heart racing again.

The room was the same. Only a few hours ago, Johnny and I had listened to Stanley for half the night. One of the staff must have come in and cleaned. The room was spotless.

Bruni wandered about, looking over the furniture and the fireplace, saying nothing. I showed her the bedroom. She moved throughout the room, looking. I turned away for a few seconds. When I turned back again, I saw her put down the picture of Alice in fancy dress that had stood at the side of the dressing table.

"Sorry" was all she said and wandered about again. I went over to the picture but did not touch it. Alice was wearing an Egyptian costume with the necklace. I wasn't sure what that meant, but I felt it was time to end the tour of Alice's rooms.

I walked to the door of the bedroom and motioned her out. We walked through the sitting room and out of Alice's apartment. I looked around as I closed the door. Everything seemed the same, but somehow it wasn't. Some people hear but never really listen when they should. They insist on finding out for themselves.

23

"What's next?" she asked.

"What would you like to see?"

"Where did you and Johnny hang out?"

"At the top of the house. Would you mind climbing some stairs to get there?"

"Not at all."

I took her up the main staircase, showed her the guest rooms, and then opened the recessed door. "Please allow me to go first. There's a door at the top."

I opened the second door. "Here we are."

A hint of perfume hung in the air and tantalized me as she brushed past. She was impressed by the shelves of books and the comfortable-looking couch and chairs.

"I love this!" she exclaimed as she circled the common room, gazed at the rows of books, and touched several with her fingertips before settling herself in one of the chairs. I sat on the couch. "I'm glad you brought me here. I had a room like this growing up. It reminds me of home." She looked more relaxed and comfortable surrounded by the books. Her smile was dazzling as she continued to look about.

"Tell me," I said.

"It was close to the top floor, like this one, in our castle in Austria. I was an only child at first. I have a brother, but he came much later. I think I disappointed both my parents. I was a girl, and they didn't quite know what to do with me. At the very least, they decided that I should have a nanny and be well-read. A library was built just for me. My first languages were German and Austro-Bavarian, followed by English and French. I would read all day. I was quite happy. I'm not sure I understood all that I read at first. Many were too advanced for me, but I reread most of them again as I grew older. I loved encyclopedias. Books were the window through which I saw the world. They opened my mind."

"That happened to me as well. Do you think they helped you in the long run?"

"Undoubtedly. Books were also an effective antidote to loneliness. My parents were away a great deal. My nanny raised me, but she died suddenly. Afterward, I was sent away to an American boarding school for a change of scenery. It was probably for the best. I was thirteen. I recovered, but I was quite different from the rest of the girls, more mature in some ways and intellectually more precocious — not so in others, such as in relationships. I loved mathematics and the sciences. At university, I studied economics and finance and eventually international law. I practice here and in Austria."

"I noticed you don't have an accent."

"I do when I get angry."

"Let's hope it doesn't come to that. Johnny and I had a nanny as well—several, in fact."

"I had only one: Nana. Her death affected me deeply. I took years to get over it. I suppose that's why I have such a low opinion of God, religion, and spirituality in general. One moment, Nana was my constant companion. The next, she was gone. She slipped and fell head first from the top of the main stairway. My parents were away. I ran to her and tried to revive her, but she didn't respond. Finally, in desperation, I fell to my knees. I prayed to God for help. I promised anything and everything I could think of in exchange for a miracle. It was quite impossible, of course. A broken neck tends to be quite final. It broke my heart. I became skeptical, if not cynical, about all things religious and spiritual. I have no patience with the occult. I don't believe in ghosts, or in a divine presence. I learned then that nothing is permanent in this life — not even the gods. I see several familiar titles about them on your shelves. Surely you must know that too."

"I am sorry to hear about your nanny. What happened explains what you said downstairs. No doubt, I would feel the same, and I do, for the most part. As to the gods, our respective paths no longer intersect the way they once did. The world has moved on, but I'm not so sure they simply died. Our modern world simply has different ways to account for their participation. They may never have existed in the first place, but a world with no magic is just a world. I'm not entirely convinced that is the case. I don't think I would want one like that either."

She frowned. "You've gone native."

I laughed. "That's one way of putting it."

"But you're a certified analyst."

"I am, but I no longer practice. I do forensic accounting now. You're well informed."

"I am. But both professions require similar skills. Your thinking puzzles me."

"It shouldn't. We've each experienced different things in different ways. We've reached different conclusions. I'd like to continue this discussion, but we have to be getting back. Before we go, though, I have a question to ask."

"What is it?"

"Who takes care of your dogs when you're away?"

"How do you know I have dogs, and why do you want to know?"

"You handled Robert the Bruce quite well, and he's tough."

"The bull terrier? They are a stubborn breed and very attached. I have two labs. They're much more malleable. You want to know, because…?"

"Because you are the dog-lady, after all."

"What do you mean by that!" she said sharply.

"I apologize. Johnny was wondering if he and Robert had run into you before in Central Park. It appears that's true. I mean no disrespect, but we did refer to you as the dog-lady because we had no other name for you. Johnny felt that you were one and the same. I thought it unlikely, but I was wrong. You and Johnny have met."

Bruni laughed. "You're thinking of the scarf. That was the most bizarre experience and, in truth, quite disgusting."

"I'm sure it was. Well, I'm glad that's been cleared up. You've been the subject of quite a bit of speculation on our part."

"I trust I will not be referred to as the 'dog-lady from this time forward. It sounds quite derogatory and rude."

"It won't happen again. Can you forgive us?"

"I suppose. You should tell Johnny that based on first impressions, he has some serious catching up to do, but I'm willing to give him a second chance. He's quite charming, but you're right, we should be going." she said, standing up.

"Yes, we should. I enjoyed our conversation. I look forward to another."

"Me too."

As we made our way down the main staircase, I couldn't refrain from asking another question. "One last thing. Can you tell me why you were invited this weekend?"

Bruni stopped halfway down the stairs. "Why do you want to know?"

"I'm curious. I'd heard there was an interest in seeing whether you and Johnny might be a suitable match."

"You do have a tendency to beat around the bush, don't you?"

"Well, I suppose that's true, although I thought my question fairly straightforward."

"Yes, but I don't think that was your real question. Perhaps you should rephrase it."

"Are you looking at marrying Johnny?"

"That's better. I have the right to marry whomever I choose. It's also customary to have a proposal. I have received none. Does that answer your question?"

"I suppose it does."

There was not much to be said after that. We continued on down the stairs and past the clock. I felt I knew her better, but I wondered if I had upset her. She hadn't answered the question as to her purpose for being here, but I had failed to ask that question directly. She was an attorney, after all. Should I have expected anything different?

We slipped into the drawing room. Johnny and his father were now talking to the baron while the two ladies were back on the couch. We had been gone maybe thirty minutes.

The baroness asked, "Did you enjoy the house, Brunhilde?"

"Yes, very much."

"I would like to see the house also. Anne, would you care to show me?"

"Of course," said Mrs. Dodge.

The baroness added, "Brunhilde, please join us."

Bruni looked like she was about to object but acquiesced. They left, and I wandered over to join the men.

Mr. Dodge said to me, "Hugo wishes to walk the grounds. Perhaps you and Johnny would like to collect Robert and join us?"

The baron held up his hands. "If it's all the same, I'd rather they walk the dog in an area that excludes myself."

"Not to worry. We'll make sure our paths don't cross," said Johnny cheerfully. He winked at me as the two older men walked out the french doors to the south lawn.

Once they were well out of earshot, Johnny turned to me. "While we have a chance, tell me your news, and I'll tell you mine."

"Very well. She is indeed the dog-lady. I promised not to refer to her in that way, but there's no doubt. She confirmed it."

"You see? I was right. A billion to one. I should have bet on it. I take it I made a rather poor first impression."

"She said it wasn't exactly favorable, but she's willing to give you a second chance. She said you were charming."

"I am indeed. I'll have to think about that. She's quite something to look at, I must admit, but she strikes me as the overly controlling sort. All she needs is a riding crop to complete the picture. Better you than me, if you're into that sort of thing. Are you?"

"Well, I hardly know that's true. You dislike her?"

"First impressions again. They can be wrong. We'll see. Drink?"

"Good idea. You fix them while I tell you what I learned." We walked over to the bar that had been set up in a corner with a white linen tablecloth, glasses, decanters of liquor, mixers, and a silver bowl containing ice cubes. As Johnny poured, I continued. "Bruni is an attorney by trade and works for her father structuring deals and corporate shells. As to why she's here, I couldn't find out. During the tour, I showed her Alice's apartment, which may have been a mistake. I told her to touch nothing, but she picked up the picture of Alice in fancy dress wearing the necklace. There was no reaction on her end, but I sensed—and I admit this might be my imagination—this act did not go over well with the powers that be. She'd say I'm imagining things, since she believes solely in facts, not spirits. Her father is definitely a collector and has heard quite a bit about Alice. Lastly, in spite of her bossy nature and my tendency to be somewhat negative, I like her."

"Interesting, an attorney. That fits. I'll tell you why shortly, but first, a toast to good times," said Johnny, handing me a glass of scotch over ice. "And second, to your budding romance. Cheers."

I refused to take the bait that Johnny dangled before me. If I reacted in any way, I'd never hear the end of it. That being said, I was pleased that Johnny had little interest in her. We drank for a moment in silence.

Reading my thoughts, Johnny added, "Now, I know what you're going to say. There is absolutely nothing between you two, but what if she's playing for the other team?"

As evenly as I could, I answered, "That's a factor, but there's more. Your father took me aside and spoke with me at some length. It was quite enlightening." I told Johnny the story that Mr. Dodge had related in full.

Johnny whistled. "That explains a few things, but before I comment, here's what I've gleaned so far: The baron is into all types of financial shenanigans, in my opinion. Nothing illegal, but borderline, in that he has a network of people who gather information for him in ways that are definitely suspect. He buys this and sells that, taking advantage of price discrepancies and such in the currency and other markets. His family always had money, but he has set up an information network that allows him to not only profit from central bank maneuvers, but other situations as well. Lucky for him he has a full-time in-house attorney. He needs one. She would also have to be extremely good to have kept him out of serious trouble this far, so don't underestimate her. He's crafty and ruthless as a pirate. What surprises me most from your tale is that my father and he are really quite close and have been for years. There's a level of trust between them that I would not have expected at all. Still, I think the baron has designs on the stuff in Alice's secret room in spite of the relationship. It's simply a question of how far he thinks he can stretch it, which I think is just short of outright theft."

"I'd have to agree with you. The trust factor surprised me too. I may be reading too much into this, but if Bruni already knew who you were, it seems odd she never mentioned that she did. With her father's businesses to look after, I doubt she has the time to even think about marriage, which, of course, begs the question: why is she here? Grant you, it all makes sense on the surface, but the pieces don't quite fit."

"You always look at the more twisted and devious side of things. The truth is we don't know. Personally, I think you may have upset some plans. Your presence was a random event that I don't think anyone was expecting, which plays in our favor, and if you turn on that charm, you might upset them further. In any event, I doubt the baron will resort to reprisals in this house, but I would not put it past him to try something. So, let's tread carefully in spite of what Father thinks. I think it's time to talk to Stanley."

24

We found Stanley in his office and immediately heard the thumping of Robert's tail against the inner sides of the desk. Stanley rolled his chair back and let him escape. He scrambled out to look at Johnny, slid down into his sphinx position, and silently watched Johnny's every move.

Johnny reached down and gave him a pat. "Stanley, you wished to have a word?"

"Yes, I did." He got up and shut the door. "Please sit down."

We made ourselves comfortable.

Stanley sat back down and began, "I will make this brief, as I have a great deal to do.

"I have done some checking. Besides his financial dealings, the baron is a collector of antiquities, particularly those with occult properties. He has recently been in contact with Lord Bromley, who told him all about the small figurine, the jewel, and other artifacts. The baron is eager to acquire any of Lady Bromley's treasures, whether openly in a purchase or covertly through other means. It's become an obsession of his.

"Of course, whether a person can possibly harness any of the supposed powers inherent in such objects is questionable, but in the minds of those who are conversant and knowledgeable, the fact that one is known to possess such items has a dual result. It gives others pause if they should plan to make a move against the owner, and second, it makes them want to be on the same side. It's good insurance, and a few choice stories circulated here and there enhance the effect. We're on the list of those who possess more than a few. The baron finds owning such things to be beneficial, and he's here, in part, to get a feel for how easy it might be to obtain as many as possible.

"The influence of the von Hofmanstals has grown significantly over the last few years in no small way due to his daughter's ability to engineer faster access to capital, structure entities that mask their real ownership, and move funds secretly and easily wherever they are needed. In addition, he has developed his own private intelligence network.

"There are ties between this house and theirs going back several generations, but the possibility of a move against Dodge Capital is greater now than a year ago, when such a move would have been out of the question. There are no outward signs of this, of course, but it's always best to be aware of the potential. If you see or hear something that does not seem right or is relevant, let me know as soon as you can.

"I also found out that the baron has also been in contact with Bonnie Leland. She and Mr. Dodge have a profound animosity between them that spans many years. I can hardly imagine what she's planning, but put her, the baron, and Lord Bromley in the same camp, and no good can come of it.

"Therefore, I would like to say the following: Have a care with the daughter. She is extremely clever. Do not underestimate her. Also, the baroness may appear like window dressing, but she's not. He consults with her regularly. I advise as well that you be very circumspect about entering the secret library, unless you are certain of not being observed. Lastly, watch what you say and don't allow any of our guests to slip away and roam around unobserved. Now, I must get back to work. Any questions?"

"What about during the night?" asked Johnny.

"I have made arrangements. Anything else?"

"Yes," I said. "I showed the daughter the west wing apartment. She picked up the picture of Alice with the necklace. Other than that, she simply looked around."

"I doubt there was any harm done. They're aware that Alice was in the possession of many items, including the necklace, but I would rather that area remain off-limits to our guests. Besides, they may get more than they bargained for if the past is any indication of the future." Stanley smiled at the thought.

We all departed the office, Johnny and me to take Robert for a walk and Stanley to see to the dinner service.

25

Knowing that the baron and John Senior were to the south, Johnny and I went out the front door with Robert in tow and turned left, past Alice's wing. To the west, cut grass stretched unbroken to an embankment at the bottom of which was a tennis court. The embankment was designed to create the illusion of an uninterrupted vista of green stretching to a line of distant woods, when viewed from Alice's sitting room. The three of us walked in its general direction across a moving tapestry of light and shadow as low-lying cumulus raced across the afternoon sky at supernatural speeds.

Even Robert was sufficiently intimidated by the strangeness of the afternoon to seem quite happy to be on the leash. Although he trotted jauntily out in front, he paused every now and then to look over his shoulder, to make sure we were either keeping up or that we were still there. I noted that he was nonetheless subtly angling us toward the tennis court, no doubt drawn by his addiction.

Before we walked down the steps to the sunken court, I looked back at the house. I had rarely seen it from this angle. I was just thinking that Alice would have had a fine view, when I saw a curtain move in one of the windows of the sitting room. It was just a flutter and happened so fast I wondered if I had imagined it.

"Someone's in Alice's apartment. I just saw a curtain move."

Johnny turned around and looked back at the house. The breeze whipped his hair, and he brushed it back with his hand. "That's not good. Could be one of the help tidying up, but that isn't likely at this time of the day. Perhaps we should head back and check it out."

Robert was not pleased with this decision and made his point by straining against the leash in the direction of the undiscovered treasures that he knew dotted the undergrowth beyond the tennis court fence.

"Heel, you mangy mutt," grunted Johnny as he attempted to drag Robert in the opposite direction. Eventually, with both of us pulling, we managed a slow resistive backward march toward the house. Robert realized he was outmatched. He suddenly relented, causing Johnny and me to barely keep our balance on the slippery grass. Meekly, he about-faced and retraced the way we had come. Johnny was pleased with this display of canine mastery and smiled the whole way back, allowing Robert once again to lead the way.

He commented as I opened the front door, "You see, he's learning. Such a good dog."

He reached down and gave Robert a pat as he unlatched the leash. Too late, Johnny realized his mistake. Always one to take advantage of life's unexpected opportunities, Robert whipped around and bolted for freedom. Johnny attempted to stop the near one hundred pounds of compact muscle in motion by the simple expedient of jumping on him, only to miss completely and land heavily on the stone. Robert flew down the steps and skidded left, out of sight.

"After him, quick," said Johnny in a peculiarly strained voice as he lay on the floor. "I don't think I can move. I may have broken something. God, how I hate that dog. I hate him! I'm going to kill him!" Rage can often lead to feats of superhuman strength. Fully consumed, Johnny managed to raise himself up and grab on to the doorjamb. "Bastard!" he said as he grimaced in pain, rose to full height, and then staggered down the front steps. He began to limp bravely in pursuit. I watched him slowly gaining speed as he turned left. "Come on!" he yelled at me, waving as he went.

All thought of investigating the moving curtain pushed aside, I picked up the leash and headed back out the door. By the time I rounded the west wing, Johnny had made a remarkable recovery, because he was sprinting gamely after Robert, who was so far ahead, he was a white speck in the dappled distance.

I picked up my pace. "Damn that dog," I gasped out loud as I ran after them.

Several minutes later, I reached the edge of the embankment as Johnny came up the stairs, followed by Robert.

Johnny, still breathing heavily, grabbed my arm for support. "Damn that dog. He has succeeded in wearing me out. I have to catch my breath. On top of that, an odd thing happened. The side gate into the court area was open, and as I ran down the steps to the tennis court, I came across Robert lying like a sphinx in the middle of the court before at least a dozen very large crows. Robert was staring at them, and they were staring at him. They didn't move a feather even when Robert got up, turned around, and walked back to me. Damned strange, if you ask me."

"A murder of crows," I said.

"Makes you wonder. Let's get back."

We had returned to the house before we realized that Robert was not only off the leash but acting extraordinarily well-behaved. I draped the unnecessary leash over the banister before following Johnny to Alice's wing.

Johnny and Robert were inside when I entered. The sitting

room looked undisturbed. The bedroom also looked the same other than the picture of Alice that Bruni had picked up.

"The picture's been moved. At least I think so. I seem to remember it was on the other side of the table."

"Are you sure?" asked Johnny.

"Not completely."

"Let's check the secret room."

Johnny made sure the door to the apartment was shut before he flicked the fake light switch that unlocked the repository door.

We went inside and looked around. Everything seemed in order.

"Johnny, now that we know how to open it, the room seems insecure, doesn't it?

"Not really. We never knew it even existed until last night. Unless you know where to look and how to open it, I would venture, it's quite safe."

"I'm not convinced. I wouldn't put it past Bruni to do some off-the-cuff calculations to see if a secret room exists; then it would be just a matter of time before she figured it out."

"You have a point," Johnny said, still looking around. "Ah, here it is." He picked up the brown book with the peculiar shape and slipped it under his jacket. "For later," he whispered.

We secured the secret room and were just opening the door when we literally ran into Stanley.

"Ah…It's only you two. What were you doing in the vault?"

I answered for both of us. "We went outside for a walk, when I saw one of the curtains move in this room. We came to investigate and see if anything was disturbed. I might ask you the same question."

"Yes, you might. To answer it, there are other security measures in play than simple camouflage. You activated several."

I felt relieved. "Well, I am certainly glad to hear that. I was beginning to get a little worried. Once you know the room is there, it's hard to miss, and I would not put it past someone figuring out the square footage doesn't match."

Stanley smiled. "Just so. I'm glad you have a devious mind and that we think alike. Alertness is good, but now I must get back. Drinks will be served in an hour."

With that, he moved to go, but after just a few steps, he stopped and turned. Looking back at Johnny, he said softly, "Be careful with that particular book. It has the reputation of having driven more than one user permanently insane. Good luck, and it's most effective when used in the dead of night." He chuckled as he walked away to resume his duties.

26

Johnny and Robert went upstairs to put away the borrowed book while I stopped by the drawing room. Mrs. Dodge was sitting on the couch reading a magazine. She informed me that Bruni and the baroness had decided to rest before dinner. John Senior and the baron had still not returned from their walk.

I mixed myself a small drink and sat down by her on the couch.

"How was the tour?" I asked.

"They liked the house very much, of course."

"What did they think of Alice's area?"

"We just looked in. The ladies had heard the rumors, so I am sure it was a little electrifying. They didn't say much about it, though."

"I wondered, because there may have been someone looking about in there while Johnny and I were outside walking Robert."

"Really? That's disturbing. I only opened the door and let them peek inside. You must tell Stanley."

"Already taken care of. Also, Johnny came face-to-face with a rather large number of crows down by the tennis court."

"I see," she said slowly. "I have heard and seen them about. They seem to have adopted Rhinebeck as their home. Their presence is one of several strange occurrences. There's also a peculiar sort of tension in the house that I've not felt before."

"You're concerned?"

"I am. I have no idea what it's all leading up to, but I expect we'll find out before too long. How about you?"

"I'm a little apprehensive as well, what with the baron and all. John Senior told me all about my parents and the von Hofmanstals. He said not to worry, of course, but it concerns me."

"Understandably so. I'm sorry you only just found out, but then, it has all been rather sudden, with no time to really sit down and tell you. Hugo can be a bit of a bully. You just have to give him a good kick."

She laughed at the thought, while I inwardly cringed. It seemed I would just have to deal with my intense dislike of confrontations.

"How are you getting on with Bruni?" she asked.

"That obvious?"

"You and I have known each other for some time, so, yes."

"I do like her more than I expected, but some things have to simply take their course. I barely know her. Besides, I thought she was invited as a potential partner for Johnny."

"Well, that may be, but Johnny and marriage are not compatible at this time. I know this, but that doesn't mean I stop trying."

"Yes, I suppose so. What do you think of Bruni?"

"Sometimes those who shine the brightest do so because they are compensating for something else. She's charming, intelligent, and perceptive; however, I feel she's not happy with herself the way she is, at least in her own estimation. To the question of is she a good match for you, which is what I think you're trying to ask, I will say this: if she has strengths where you are weak, and weaknesses where you are strong, that is a good start. I think that may be the case, but that is something you must discover for yourself. True?"

"Yes, only I'm not sure she and I are on the same team."

"Oh, I think you are. I know Hugo would love to get his hands on Alice's treasures. That's the essence of Hugo, but there is much about him that is worthy of admiration and respect. We hold him in high esteem. He's one of the good people."

"In spite of his machinations?" I asked.

"Real friendship involves acceptance of the good and the bad. Are you and Johnny not the same?"

"Yes, I must admit that he can drive me crazy, but when all is said and done, he is who he is, and I can't help but be his friend."

"Exactly. Trust is developed over time. Real trust is to trust in spite of all indications to the contrary. After all, isn't that the definition of trust?"

"I think I would find that very hard."

"It is, but anything else is not really trust, is it?"

I thought about what she said before I answered. "You are correct, but I think I have a lot to learn in that area. Thank you for being so frank. I also wish to thank you for inviting me this weekend."

"Darling, you know we love seeing you, and we are thrilled that you and Johnny are back in each other's good graces. Friendships can ebb and flow like anything else. Real ones are rare and should be nurtured."

"Yes, Mr. Dodge said the same thing, and if there is anything positive to be gained from this weekend, it's that realization. Seeing you and John Senior again is also a great comfort. On another subject, Malcolm Ault is expected. I don't think I've ever met him. Who is he?"

"A friend of the family who drops in from time to time. We've known him for years. He was very fond of Alice. They were quite close."

"Very close?"

"Not that close." She laughed. "You have a wicked mind. She had several lovers, but I don't think he was one of them."

"I see. Coincidence that he happens to be in town this weekend?"

"I think both you and Johnny read far more into things than they might warrant. Perhaps you are seeing a reflection of your own deviousness." She smiled at me with a raised eyebrow.

"No doubt, but doing so keeps us amused and on our toes. I apologize for peppering you with questions, but we rarely get to talk alone. Is there anything you can tell me regarding the baron and my parents?"

"I can tell you what I can. I assume you know the details. Hugo and Mary met when she spilled coffee all over him at a ball we attended in Vienna. She was so mortified that she promised him whatever he wished if he would forgive her. They negotiated and agreed to meet the next day for lunch. Mary can be enchanting, and she really wanted to enchant Hugo, so you can well imagine that Hugo stood little chance. I was thrilled for her, but I was a bit put out because I knew our relationship would change. In spite of this apprehension, I was genuinely happy for her. She had found a man who adored her, who was rich and titled as well. He was constantly in attendance and treated her like a princess. I will say this much for him — he never let me feel like a third wheel in spite of the fact that his world revolved around Mary. Mary, however, was more in love with the idea of Hugo than with Hugo himself. I think this became clear to her over time, particularly when your father entered the picture. It was a bolt from the blue that has caused ripples to this day. Hugo was devastated and still feels that pain. Seeing you brought the memory back, and Hugo hates to be reminded of any past failures.

"To continue, throughout that time, I was simply an observer. I tried to counsel all sides as best I could, but emotions ran high. It was a difficult time, but I met John in the midst of it all. After the duel, I think I was so relieved that no one was killed that I drank an entire bottle of champagne on my own. John and I got completely smashed. That was wonderfully transformative. Somehow we all remained friends, although Hugo will avoid your parents like the plague. I must say, he does tend to hold a grudge, but to his credit, he did not let the incident define him. Hugo moved on and eventually married Elsa. Misfortunes can be blessings in disguise. Elsa is very much Hugo's equal and a much better match for him than Mary would ever have been. Although she may appear to be a vacuous blond, she is educated, uncannily shrewd, with an excellent head for business. She prefers to remain in the background and let Hugo take the spotlight, but she calls the shots. Behind many successful men are women of rare talent, and she is one of them. Much of Hugo's success can be attributed to her ability to point him in the right direction. Between Elsa and Bruni, Hugo has an excellent support network, and he's smart enough to utilize them. Anything else?"

"To backtrack a bit, how exactly did my father enter the picture?"

"It's funny how the past sometimes catches one by surprise. I've never told anyone this. I had met your father sometime before he met Mary. He had seen her from afar and was fascinated by her. I mentioned that we would be traveling to Austria. I gave him the date and the time we would depart. Much to my surprise, he showed up, so I suppose I am at fault for what happened. I can be a little manipulative." At this she laughed again.

"So, it was no accident that my father and mother met."

"Not in the usual sense."

"I suppose I ought to thank you."

"Not really. I outsmarted myself. Somehow, in spite of everything, all turned out for the best, but I learned a good lesson.

I like to think I'm now more restrained in my meddling, but maybe not. It's a bad habit but exciting nonetheless."

We chatted about other things until Anne suggested we change for dinner. She gave me a big hug when we parted, and I thanked her for her meddling. Johnny and I knew she loved to do it and expected her continued forays. Nonetheless, her kindness and love for me as I grew up was something I would always appreciate and remember.

I made my way up the stairs as Bruni was coming down. She had changed into a simple black dress that emphasized her figure and the whiteness of her skin. Around her neck she wore a string of large black pearls.

"You look stunning," I managed to say.

"I aim to. Don't be long."

With that, she continued to walk down the stairs, leaving me more uncertain than ever. She could be most unsettling, which was her intention, of course. I retreated to the safety of the aerie at the top of the house.

Johnny had the book open on the table along with several other volumes, while Robert lay next to him on the couch with his head on his paws.

"Research?"

"Oh yes, oh yes. You took your time."

"Chatting with your mom."

"How is she?"

"In rare form, as usual."

"I suppose she said we must change for dinner."

"That was her message."

Johnny put the volumes back on the shelves and took the oddly shaped book to his room.

After we dressed, I mentioned a few points that troubled me.

"Johnny, we seem to have our own little repository going on up here, what with the figurine and now the book. Are they secure?"

"Have no fear. You remember that hidden bottom in my set of drawers?"

"The one where we used to hide cigarettes?"

"The very same. They are safely tucked away in there. Feel better?"

"A bit, but I'm still somewhat concerned. We now have two rather powerful objects, if such things can be called that, sitting in the same location. Do you think they could interact, hypothetically speaking, of course?"

"I kind of doubt it, but we're in unknown territory with no idea how to proceed, other than to begin a little experimentation. In keeping with that, let me tell you my plan for tonight."

"Okay, let's hear it."

"We come up here at a reasonable hour, without getting too blasted, mind you, bolt the door, and examine each of the pieces more closely. I have always wanted to summon a demon, and tonight I think we'll have an opportunity to do so."

"I seem to recall something by Goethe regarding that sort of thing." I commented.

"You refer to that creepy little apprentice. Well, we don't exactly have to fetch a ton of water, do we? Still, I see your point. My thought was to proceed slowly, step-by-step."

"That implies we have a set of directions, which I doubt comes with the volume you borrowed. We are also assuming we can read the damn thing, which judging from its age, is highly unlikely."

"Getting a bit on edge, are we? I bet you saw Bruni coming up the stairs."

I grunted as neutrally as I could. I hated when he did that. It was extremely annoying to be so transparent, when I thought I was the opposite.

"Of course you did. Back on point, let me remind you: first, you don't believe in this sort of thing, so why worry about it, and second, if all else fails, we'll roust old Stanley out of bed and say there's a demon loose on the top floor and ask what ought to be done. What could be simpler?"

"You see, that's exactly what I mean. You have this 'devil may care; let's see what happens' attitude. It drives me crazy—"

"Which is precisely why we work so well together," interrupted Johnny. "For your information, I did examine a bit of the aforementioned volume, and I have news. Firstly, the language is definitely Germanic in origin. It is written in a combination of Old High German and High German with some Old Norse thrown in for good measure. We may have to crack a few more volumes, but it shouldn't be that difficult to understand. Secondly, I came across a section on demons that looks fairly straightforward. I know how you feel about all of this, so think of our little summoning as an experiment and as an exercise in scientific curiosity."

"I'm more than a little apprehensive."

"Frankly, I'm a little as well, but I'm determined to discover whether there is some truth to all this, and my summoning is a good way to find out."

"The crows?"

"Yes, well…I don't know what to make of that either. We should set all that aside and look on the bright side," said Johnny as he put the final touches to his tie. "There's always Dagmar's cooking."

"Yes, there are compensations." I put aside my paranoia with that thought, even though I still felt like I was dressing for dinner on the Titanic.

27

While Johnny was putting Robert in Stanley's office, I made my way to the drawing room.

Bruni stood by the french doors, smoking. It was dark outside, and I could see her reflection in the glass. She was lost in thought. She heard me open the door behind her and turned.

"You took your time," she said, stubbing out her cigarette.

"I'm a slow dresser."

"You may have missed your opportunity."

"I'm here now."

"Come closer."

I did as she asked. We were the same height, and I looked into the blueness of her eyes. She placed one hand behind my neck and drew me to her. Her body felt soft. She kissed me gently on the lips. After a few seconds, she stepped back.

Still looking at me, she said, "I suggest you be more prompt. Pour me some champagne?"

I turned away, my world having swapped poles. I managed to

uncork the bottle of Cristal that was cooling in a silver ice bucket without spilling it. I poured slowly to reduce the bubbles and to allow time to get myself together. It was distinctly uncommon for beautiful women to decide to kiss me. If she wanted me unsettled, she had succeeded.

I turned back and handed her a flute, keeping one for myself. "Cheers," I managed.

We clinked glasses.

"Why?" I asked.

"Why what?"

"Why did you kiss me?"

"I trust you don't look for ulterior motives in everything."

"Not in everything, but in some."

"Most things."

I was about to respond, when the french doors opened, and there were the baron and Mr. Dodge.

I immediately started calculating the relative light and darkness inside and outside the drawing room, angle of approach, and the elapsed time to gauge whether the baron would have seen what had just occurred, but that was unnecessary. His attention was on something else entirely. He held on to John's arm with one hand as Mr. Dodge guided him to a chair. His hair was disheveled and his face unusually pale.

John Senior went to the bar and poured him a large measure of whiskey, while Bruni went down on one knee beside him. "Papa, what's happened?" She took his hand.

The baron took a sip of the proffered drink and told her, "We were walking by the edge of the trees. It was getting dark, and we were about to head back, when an animal screamed close by. It startled me. I stepped back and twisted my ankle."

"What type of animal was it?" asked Bruni.

"A rabbit, I think. They're paying me back for hunting them." He chuckled.

"Did you hurt yourself?"

"No. I'm fine. Not to worry. I think I'll head upstairs to change for dinner." He patted her hand and rose out of the chair.

Mr. Dodge added, "I must do the same. Shall we?" He opened the door for the baron, and they both went off to change.

"Do you know anything about such things?" asked Bruni, looking at me accusingly.

"Well, Johnny and…"

"Talking about me behind my back, are we?" interrupted Johnny as he entered silently from the dining room and made his way to the champagne. Johnny's hearing was remarkably sharp when his name was mentioned. "To top things off, Stan put out the good stuff. I do love it when we have guests."

"The baron apparently encountered a creature in the dark," I told him as he poured.

"Not mine. I'm responsible for only one, and that is Robert the Bruce. For once, I can safely say that neither of us played a part. What happened?"

I told him what the baron had said.

Looking at me mischievously, he said, "Perhaps it was that bad bunny that's been prowling around?"

"What are you talking about?" asked Bruni in a voice likely reserved for opposing counsel.

Johnny was obviously winding her up.

"Johnny's pulling your leg. Although rabbits can scream surprisingly loud when they're threatened. Right, Johnny?"

"Indeed, they can."

Bruni wasn't sure if we were being serious, but the fact that her father had said it was a rabbit gave some credence to what we said.

"Does that type of thing happen around here often?" she asked doubtfully.

"In this house, almost anything is possible. It's part of the charm of the place." He gave her a little smile.

"What does that mean exactly?"

Unintimidated, Johnny said, "The unexpected is expected. Strange things happen here. I cannot be plainer."

Bruni looked at Johnny coldly for several seconds. She was about to say something, when once again, we were interrupted — this time by the entrance of a very tall man. He was dressed in a slightly rumpled business suit. He saw Bruni, and his eyes lit up in recognition.

"Brunhilde? Is that you? I heard you might be here. It's wonderful to see you again."

He stepped toward her with studied deliberation, as if he might step on something he shouldn't, but he covered the distance from the door with surprising speed. He bent down and gave her a kiss on each cheek.

Bruni smiled and said, "Malcolm, so nice to see you again. May I…"

"Hello, hello." He waved vaguely in Johnny's and my direction. "No time. No time," he said, holding up his hand. "Just stopped to say hello. Must rush and change. Stanley's already seen to my things. By the way," he said, looking back at Bruni, "saw your husband in Cannes but didn't have a chance to say hello. See you in a few!"

With that, he turned away and in several long strides was gone the way he had come in. An awkward silence reverberated around the room like a shockwave. Brunhilde turned very pale, put down her drink, and walked out.

Johnny, rising to the situation, commented, "Well, I must say one thing is certain: something stronger is most definitely in order."

He proceeded to pour a large whiskey and a smaller one. He handed me the larger. "Expect the unexpected. I must remember that." He looked at me over the lip of his glass to see how I was doing. "Drink up. Drink up," he commanded.

2 8

The large glass of whiskey tasted fine and on an empty stomach felt even better. I concluded, after examining the bottom of my glass, that I was definitely out of sorts. Malcolm Ault's offhanded remark, and what preceded it, had precipitated a cascade of turbulent thoughts and feelings over which I had little hope of asserting any measure of control. Stanley would announce that dinner was served at some point in the next hour. Before that, I would have to make conversation with whoever might decide to talk to me, and I was not in the mood — with Bruni in particular.

She had simply walked out. She had never said she was married. She never said she wasn't, merely that she had the right to marry whomever she pleased, an answer vague enough to take on any number of meanings. One might even infer that she was free to do so in the present and that she was divorced. A happy thought, but I knew I was grasping at straws. There was something there. What, exactly, was an unknown.

I was feeling anger bordering on rage. I was angry for being so easily led, angry at Bruni for being opaque from the start, and angry for being here in the first place.

Sensing my mood, Johnny said, "Breath of fresh air?"

I grunted.

Johnny led me gently out the door into the night. "Deep breaths, deep breaths. How are you feeling?"

"Grim."

"Yes, you look it. In fact, I don't think I've seen you this upset since that time when you found out Tiny Edwards took five points on that bond swap and you stormed into his office to make him eat his monitor."

"It was criminal."

"It was, and how did that work out?"

"Not good. Not good at all. How was I to know that Tiny was actually a giant and had turned down a chance to play pro football to work on that trading desk?"

"My point exactly. It may be hard, but you must get a grip. We have an exciting and event-filled evening ahead; we just have to get through the dinner bit."

Johnny was obviously eager to get on with our late-night research. He was almost jumping up and down in frustration, seeing his great plan in jeopardy.

"You must let it go," he said. "Really, great things are afoot. Hard as it is, you must."

"I don't want to. I'm enjoying my sullen mood."

"I should have given you vodka. Those dark drinks can bring out the worst. Look at me. Just try. Deep breath in, and let it out."

Johnny could be like a mother hen.

In a flash of insight, he said, "Vengeance. You want revenge! Oh, I have just the thing, but only if you calm yourself. Remember that old saying about it best being served cold? Trust me, I know what I'm talking about. Come on, look at me."

I looked at him.

"Brother, I promise you will not regret it. Now, take a deep breath."

I breathed. I began to relax. We had acted out this same scene many times over. Sometimes I would be the one saying what Johnny was saying. Other times, like now, he was the one taking control, smoothing the ruffled feathers, and jollying the other into a semblance of good humor and calm.

"That's better. Firstly, only light-colored drinks tonight and only in moderation. No red wine. No whiskey."

"What if it's an Haut-Brion?"

"One glass only."

"Okay," I said. "I'm better. Well, somewhat. I reserve the right to be verbally combative but not physical."

"Fair enough, but verbally combative in moderation. Secondly, I want to get upstairs at a reasonable hour, and arguments can take forever. Agreed?"

"Agreed."

"No yelling."

"Okay, but I still feel testy."

"No worries — I'll be right beside you. Now, how 'bout a happy face?"

"You're pushing it," I said, feeling my temper rise again.

"Well, neutral then."

"Fine."

"Excellent. Neutral is good. See, that wasn't so bad. Let's go in and get through this. Excitement waits in the wee hours. I can hardly contain myself." He actually started to wring his hands.

"Oh, come on," I said, opening the door. He could be so exasperating.

"There you are, boys."

It was Mrs. Dodge, of course. I suppose she still thought of us as youngsters. They were all there, standing around sipping champagne, except for Bruni and Malcolm, the men in dark business suits and the ladies in black cocktail dresses with flashes of large diamonds at ears, necks, and fingers.

The baron said, "I am so looking forward to dinner."

"You are, are you?" I interjected. I was feeling wonderfully reckless.

"I am."

"More champagne is in order," Johnny said. He managed to kick my ankle and steer me toward the small table all at the same time.

"Steady," he said under his breath. "I think I'm going to have to chaperone you throughout this entire dinner, and it is only the beginning. Just sip it. No gulps." He handed me a flute. "Behave."

Johnny and I returned to the melee. I smiled — at least I thought I smiled. It might have been a sneer for all I knew. I was a little blasted, but the feeling suited me. I sipped my champagne like a good person and nodded at intervals. I had no idea what anyone was talking about. I drank more champagne. It went down like water, and I was thirsty. I moved myself nearer the champagne table. Johnny remained talking to his father. I busied myself with the glasses and looked over the scene. My vision was not as sharp as it had been just a few minutes ago. Time seemed to be keeping its own pace, independent of my own. I was content to watch from a distance until Stanley rang the bell and the lot of them jockeyed for dinner. I wondered who would be first through the door. Dagmar was that good.

Bruni appeared in front of me and interrupted my musings. She was wearing the same thing she had been wearing before. It seemed like a long time ago.

"What d'you want?" I said.

"There's no reason to be surly."

"I wasn't being surely, ah…surly. Or should I say surly, surely. I was asking a simple question." I smiled. I can be clever when I want to.

She paused and said, "And I have answers, but now is not the time."

"When, pray tell?"

"Perhaps later." She squinted her eyes and looked at me. "Are you drunk?"

"Drunk, no. Mad, yes."

"You're drunk," she said with some frustration and turned away.

"Can't wait to meet your pal, Malcolm, and find out all about your husband," I hissed at her back. It was a nice back. I must have hissed louder than I thought, because I heard a voice from on high.

"You mentioned my name?"

I turned to my left and noted that I was staring at the middle of a man's chest or maybe his stomach. From my vantage point, I couldn't tell. He had on what I guessed was an old Etonian tie.

"My, but you're tall." I looked way up to see his face. "Were you that tall when you went to Eton?"

"A bit shorter."

"Champagne?" I asked and grabbed a flute, but I think he thought the better of it.

Malcolm picked one up and said, "Allow me."

"Question. Is it Mrs. or Miss?"

"Who, me?"

"No, Brunhilde."

"Well, that is a question that I am not prepared to answer."

"How come, big guy? Let me guess. She told you not to tell me, and that she would explain everything to me later."

"Precisely. By the way, this is excellent champagne but probably should be taken in moderation. Cristal is delightfully sweet for a champagne. It's the chardonnay that does it. Did you know that Cristal is the only champagne made in a clear bottle with no punt, the pointy thing at the bottom, so the golden color can be appreciated more? It was served originally to the czar in 1867, who made it his beverage of choice."

"Fascinating. You are a veritable fount of information. How come I've never seen you before?"

"Perhaps because we've never met?"

"Good point. You mind if I ask you some other questions?"

"If you wish."

"I don't mean to be rude, but how did you get to be so tall? You must have had a very big mother."

"Actually, she was rather small. My family came from Scotland, Ayrshire, and moved to Perthshire in the fourteenth century, and they tend to run very tall. It's genetic."

"Shire, I mean sure, that makes sense. What should I call you?"

"Malcolm."

"Okay, Malcolm, here's one for you: what do you call a very large Ault carrying a battle-axe?"

"I have no idea."

"Sir."

He laughed. "Well, here's one for you: you can call me that anytime."

He thought his joke was pretty funny too.

We laughed some more. To me, they were good jokes, but my neck hurt from looking up. I decided to look at his chest. The view was better than looking into his nostrils. He had a big nose. I couldn't say he was handsome. I mean, who could from that angle. All I knew was that I couldn't look up anymore without feeling slightly disoriented. I wondered what it was like to look down on everybody's head; perhaps that wasn't exactly pleasant either.

"Well, I am glad to have met you, Malcolm," I said.

At that moment, Bruni slipped up beside me and took my arm. "Malcolm, I hope this man is behaving himself."

"Oh yes."

"Allow me to borrow him."

"Of course. Cheers," he said, raising his glass as she guided me over to the sofa.

"Sit down here and behave."

"Hey, I'm being good. Have no fear."

Johnny sat down in the nearby chair.

"How is he?"

"What do you think?"

"Only moderately intoxicated. If you take one arm and I take the other, I'm sure we can discretely put him in his chair at the dinner table. Some food will settle him down."

It's funny how people talk about you and think you're not listening just because they think you're drunk. "I'm right here, you know."

At that moment, Stanley announced that dinner was served. The throng moved to the dining room. The baron won by a nose across the threshold. I should have put money on him.

29

***

Seating was assigned as usual, and I found myself between the baroness and the newest addition to the party, Malcolm Ault. Bruni, Johnny, and the baron were seated opposite, with John Senior and Anne at either end. I managed to do pretty well with my partners by saying little. Dagmar's culinary skills left little room for conversation, allowing my mind's higher faculties to slowly reengage. I noticed Johnny and Bruni inspecting me surreptitiously on several occasions as they talked to each other. Perhaps they expected me to topple over. They had moved to the opposite side of the table with reluctance and only after carefully seating me in my chair and, by their expressions, willing me to stay put and not slide beneath the table. I appreciated their concern, but they need not have worried. I have always stood by the assertion that Dagmar's cooking could cure just about anything, and my faith was confirmed once again. There was magic in her food.

Perhaps to titillate the baron's penchant for fois gras, Dagmar had created a small pâté ball surrounded by watercress. Chicken soup with egg-lemon sauce followed and then a delightful cube of salmon surrounded by a lemon jelly and blackened leeks. By the time I had consumed the first few dishes, the room had stabilized on its axis, and I could feel my lips and the tip of my nose. The main course was beef tenderloin served rare. I weighed continued sobriety against the deep ruby color of a French Bordeaux. Stanley allowed me to peek at the label as he offered to fill my glass, and my decision was instantaneous. The wine was a Château la Mission Haut-Brion. Johnny and Bruni looked like they would have leaped across the table had propriety not prevented them. They shook their heads with a determined ferocity, but they should have known that resistance was futile against the jewels tucked away in the cellar down below. It may have been the beef, the dreamy mashed potatoes, the brussels sprouts in browned butter with garlic pecans, or the combination of the three, but I was feeling lucky. I thought I'd start to know more about the creator of my distress by going to the source.

There is a saying that if you want to know what a woman will look like given time, observe her mother. If there was any truth in this, then anyone who managed to live with Bruni for any length would be amply rewarded. The baroness was of indeterminate age, but by whatever measure, she was the real deal. Her blond hair was styled somewhat short, cut and colored by someone who had exquisite skill. Her daughter had inherited the same luminescent blue eyes, but her mother's were set in a slightly darker face of such intelligent elfin perfection, I almost asked her what face cream she used, but managed to check myself. Up close, I think the two women were evenly matched. The baroness's diamonds were larger and finer. I am drawn to those of FL and IF clarity with a D on the color scale like a moth to a flame, particularly if they are larger than three carats. The baroness was sporting several that flashed in the candlelight and stood out against her flawless skin and her black designer evening dress. I was putty in her hands.

"Baroness, how are you enjoying your visit?"

"Wonderful, I love this house. The ambiance…" She had a slight German accent, but what was most intriguing was the quality of her voice when she spoke, and the extraordinary focus of her attention when she listened. She managed to effortlessly instill in the speaker the sensation that whatever was said was important and required her earnest and wholehearted consideration. She had a gift and was far more formidable in every way than I had thought. As if to emphasize that realization, she reached over, took my hand, and said, "Call me, Elsa…please."

Nervously, I glanced about to see what the baron was up to, but he and John Senior were deep in conversation as usual. Bruni, observing her mother's touch, gave me a frosty glance and looked away, while Johnny savored the wine like it was a gift from the gods, which indeed it was. I took another sip to fortify myself and moved my hand.

I said in German, "Elsa, I know little about you other than that you are married to the baron and have a beautiful daughter."

Switching to German, she replied, "I acknowledge your indirect compliment. Daughters often reflect their mother's charm…"

Elsa complimented me on my language skill, and gradually my nervousness passed. We talked like old friends. I was intrigued. The wine added to the richness of the setting, the register of her voice, and the sparkle of her character. I sipped and listened to her story. She had grown up in Germany. Her parents were wealthy and had presciently parked the majority of their assets in Switzerland, where she had been educated. Afterward, they had invested heavily in the construction business. Her beauty had been renowned even from an early age and had caught the attention of the baron's family. After the disaster with my parents, they were eager to get Hugo's attention on someone of good lineage whose looks alone would attract him, whose mind might keep him enthralled, but regardless, who would ensure the continuation of the family by producing an heir. Hugo's foray into matrimony proved a glorious success. There was a son still in Europe, who had the same steely resolve and overbearing personality of the father, refined by the gentility of the mother. These traits were also passed to the daughter, who had acquired in addition her mother's brilliance and communication skills. Elsa was wonderfully frank. She told me that whoever would win her daughter would have to be supremely skilled to not only handle Brunhilde's prickly personality, her intricate mind, and her tendency to dominate those around her but have the sexual appetite to satisfy her physically — a point mentioned only in passing by Elsa, but which caused me to choke on my dessert, a wonderful puree of berries, whipped cream, meringue, and handmade vanilla ice cream. Elsa rose to the occasion by smacking me firmly on the back.

"Did I surprise you, *Liebchen?*"

By now we were on a *liebchen*, or sweetheart, familiarity. "Yes."

"Sexual appetite is a family trait on both sides, so it's natural to discuss it. You are familiar with the *Freikörperkultur?*"

"The German naturism movement. I believe that had to do with nudity as opposed to sexuality."

"Just so. You are remarkably well informed. I trust I'm not being too frank when I say that nudity, sexuality, and deviancy are not the same, although naturism can lead to an exploration of sexuality that might not occur otherwise, yes?"

"Indeed," I said tentatively, wondering how I might steer the conversation away from where it was headed.

Luckily, Mr. and Mrs. Dodge stood to inform us that coffee would be served in the drawing room, while brandy and cigars would be available in the library. Relieved, I stood as well.

The baroness looked up at me, amused. "Saved by our hosts. I so enjoyed our conversation. You are an excellent listener. I hope we'll have a chance to talk again soon."

I pulled out her chair. She stood and moved smoothly into my arms and hugged me with a sensual pleasure that left nothing to my imagination. She did it so artfully and in such a relaxed manner, I decided to not allow myself to push her away. Still in her embrace, I thanked her with what I hoped was the spirit with which the embrace was given, but I couldn't be sure. Such things can be remarkably delicate. We moved apart and wandered out of the dining room following the others. I left her in the drawing room.

Pausing in the front hallway on the way to the library, I congratulated myself. I thought I had handled her rather well. To reject a gift is to accept its opposite. The baroness, I was certain, would make a terrible and frightening enemy. The females of many species are far more dangerous than the males, and I felt in this case that I had made a friend. She was a remarkable woman. I wondered if her daughter had received, perhaps, too much of her father's domineering personality. Living with her would be a perilous business. Had the balance come out more like her mother, I could have cared less if Bruni was married or not.

"Smitten?"

I turned and looked into the same crystal-blue eyes I had gazed into during dinner, only they belonged to Bruni. "Completely."

"Many are. She can be quite the troublemaker. Have a care."

She turned and walked into the drawing room. I wondered why she had said that, only to realize that I'd been so captivated by Elsa that I'd forgotten to ask her whether Bruni was really married or not. It had completely slipped my mind. Bruni was probably correct in her assessment. I made my way to the library.

30

The men were gathered by the bar. I joined them. Johnny looked up after pouring himself a brandy and asked how I was feeling.

"Good, actually."

He gave me a careful look-over. "Well, you definitely had me worried. Our little experiment could have been blown out of the water, but no harm done. You look back to normal. I was a little concerned when you opted for the wine, but I could hardly blame you. It was exquisite, and I would not have heard the end of it had you missed it. Welcome back to the land of the living."

He put a hand on my shoulder and gave it a squeeze.

Another time I would have been upset at his preoccupation with his plans, but not tonight. Without his ministrations, events could have taken a disastrous turn. I might even have to thank Bruni as well. Whether it was Elsa, the food, or the wine, I couldn't say. I just felt good.

"Thank you. The wine was amazing."

"Amen to that. How was your dinner partner?"

"The baroness? Enchanting."

"Tell me." One of Johnny's eyebrows arched up. He expected complications.

"Imagine a more refined Brunhilde with communication skills that are terrifyingly good. Whether because of them or due to something else entirely, she also has a physical attraction that I had not anticipated. In a group, she probably dulls it down, but one-on-one, it comes on like a heat lamp. She had me so turned around I even forgot to ask her about the whole Bruni thing."

"That's bad. I'll make sure to stand clear of her in the future. How you've managed to get both of those ladies going, I have no idea. You do remember that 'hell hath no fury' thing?"

"I would hardly go to that extreme, but the thought did cross my mind. Mother and daughter seem a bit competitive, but I shouldn't be too concerned. They're probably just bored, like two cats with a limited number of playthings. How did you get on with the younger version?"

"Well, careful you don't get shredded. Sitting next to Bruni all night went much better than I expected. She does have an allure that is quite captivating. I probably misjudged her. To me, it's whether her sexuality trumps her tendency to micromanage. The jury's still out on that, but I'm willing to reconsider. We should be saying our good nights."

"A little early, isn't it?" asked the baron. He was right behind us, and for how long I had no idea. The little man had a nasty habit of popping up at awkward moments.

"Country life does that," answered Johnny. He yawned and stretched to emphasize the point. I managed to get out of the way of the brandy snifter he was holding.

"Who were you talking about earlier?" inquired the baron.

I answered, "I was describing the baroness. You're a lucky man."

He laughed. His eyes crinkled in what I hoped was genuine good humor. He looked at me for a long moment and then said,

"Yes, lucky to find her, but to keep her—that is not so easy. That takes real skill on many levels. Some of them require those of a young man. Perhaps yours…" He gave an evil chuckle.

Before I could gather my wits, he had turned and walked toward the door, waving with his back to us as he left. I quickly looked around to see if we had been overheard, but John Senior and Malcolm were chatting away, oblivious.

"Did he just say what I think he said?" asked Johnny.

"God only knows."

"You'd best lock your door tonight if you expect to have any sleep. Good heavens, you've really done it this time." Johnny looked at me in wonder.

"Don't look at me that way. I had nothing to do with it," I snapped. Johnny and Bruni getting together made me a little nervous, although I had nothing concrete to justify my feelings.

"If you say so," said Johnny, smiling. "You seem a tad jumpy."

"Not at all. It's been a long day with more to come."

"Oh yes, indeedy."

With that, we said good night to John Senior and Malcolm, who smiled and wished us the same.

We left the library and paused at the door to the drawing room. "Dare we say good night to the ladies?" I asked.

"We could skip it, I suppose," said Johnny. "In fact, that might be the better course. We have work to do. Onward and upward."

31

It was getting late, and we had reached an impasse. Robert the Bruce was asleep in his basket, while Johnny and I struggled with the verbiage of the strangely shaped book.

I had often complained about Johnny's tendency to gloss over specifics, but when he wanted, he could be just as detail-oriented as me. The couch and the table were piled with volumes and notepads as Johnny and I worked through the text word-by-word and line-by-line to get some idea of the meaning of the passages and the correct pronunciation.

The text presumed we were familiar with the elementary setup to summon spirits, something perhaps obvious at the time of writing but today unknown. The book told us what to recite, but other than a few lines about the need for containment and using an object to aid in the summoning, there was nothing. Even those brief instructions were a stretch, given our limited abilities to decipher the source language and wrestle with the ancient grammar.

Johnny closed another reference with a thud and sat back

among the notes, dictionaries, papers, and other paraphernalia of a research project turned overly complex. I could tell from his expression that he was determined to continue, even if we were missing some vital details. In his current state of mind, he was impossible to talk to simply because in the midst of tedious work, he had a habit of lecturing to anyone within earshot. Explaining things to lesser souls helped his mind grasp and make better sense of complex issues. I figured one was about due.

"We have decisions to make, so let's review, shall we?" commanded Johnny.

He stood up. I sighed as he picked up his yellow legal pad and a sharp number two pencil to tick off the relevant points.

He looked down at me sharply. "Let's focus, shall we?"

Anything other than studious attention during one of Johnny's summations tended to annoy him and extend their length. I settled down and waited for him to begin. It was better that way. Robert, too, made an effort. He opened one eye and cocked an ear in Johnny's direction.

Johnny cleared his throat and began. "From everything I'm reading, procedure is important but not the deciding factor to materialization. It is the will of the participant that is paramount. It takes reciting the full thirty-one verses to summon and to handle something suitably epic, and I say we go all the way on this. In for a penny, in for a pound."

He looked at me, but I noted he did not ask for any concurrence. I held my peace.

"More specifically, the first part, of which there are some ten verses, seems to me to be all about offering an invitation. From that, I infer that demons don't simply appear but have to be invited.

"The next chunk of text appears to spell out a contract, in the sense that there are specific things we don't want the demon to do, such as kill us, drive us mad, or trash the place. That part seems straightforward, but it is the next couple of sections that concern me. They involve the freedoms that we specifically prescribe, such as what we wish the demon to do. There are several words and phrases in this section that are beyond me. They could mean anything. Lastly, as outlined in verses twenty-one through twenty-seven, in order to have a contract, we must exchange one valuable for another. The demon is asked strongly to appear, not kill us, and consider our request, but we will have to ante up in some way, which again is couched in phrases that are not exactly clear."

Pausing to consider what he just said, he began to tap his pencil on the pad.

Stabbing at it this time, he said, "This whole part reads like something out of contract law, which I seem to recall is not dissimilar to a conversation we had the other night with Stanley. There is also a sealing section, a small set of verses where all parties are in agreement, and perhaps a toast is made, again strangely familiar. Next, there is a long part on breaking the contract and the consequences thereof. Lastly, there is an exit plan where the parties agree to dissolve the relationship on friendly terms and go their separate ways.

"In truth, this all sounds like a mishmash of a prospectus from some obscure fund that has had an overfamiliarity with lawsuits and a master agreement for a partnership, with particular emphasis on a prestructured exit plan. Who would have known such ghastly stuff existed back then. But hang on…"

At this point Johnny paused and began to admire his ability to put things together. He waved his pencil around like a baton and jabbed it in the air as if he wanted a bit more volume from the string section.

"Get this: if it is extremely similar to a prospectus and master agreement, then it *is* a prospectus and master agreement. We treat it just the same."

Johnny sat back down, basking in self-admiration. "I must say, that is sheer brilliance on my part. Now, I know what you are going to say, and I will listen, but you see, that solves our little problem. The language probably does not matter, but the intention surely does, so we set this up like one of our old contracts, and we're good to go."

Johnny's mood had lightened substantially with this realization. I saw the logic but thought I might play a bit of the devil's advocate.

"How do we translate such a thing into Old High German, or whatever?"

"We don't. It's the intention that matters. The language is secondary. We simply add a few choice bits of our own and skip the rest. I mean, who knows what we might be saying? We keep the parts we think we understand and do the rest in English. Simple and efficient. I like it, so let's get cracking."

An hour later, we had hammered out a contract that looked airtight. We had expanded several of the sections to considerable length. I asked Johnny in jest if we might invite Bruni to review it. This type of thing was her forte, after all, but I dropped the idea midsentence, given Johnny's look.

Our next task, according to Johnny, was to outline the procedures we would follow now that the language elements had been resolved to his satisfaction. This took another half an hour. Once we had come up with them, Johnny went to his room and came back with the figurine that held the jewel. He placed it on the table. It looked like a gnome holding a dirty piece of quartz, looking at us with unseeing eyes. Robert sat up in his bed and looked at it intently. His black eyes were eerily similar.

"Okay," said Johnny. "Are we ready to begin?"

"Not quite," I said. "First, do we have an emergency plan, if things get out of hand?"

"What would you suggest?"

"Even if it's as simple as run downstairs screaming and find

Stanley, I would feel a bit better, but we should consider something more substantial before we start."

"Excellent. That's it then. We run and get Stanley." Johnny was itching to begin.

"Really? Is that all? We definitely need something more. Second, let's suppose we do manage to get the demon to appear — what *exactly* do we want it to do? Verse fourteen calls for it to simply make its presence known."

"Correct. Right now, I just want to see one, but now that you mention it, how about we have it scare the crap out of the baron? Payback can be such a bitch."

"Absolutely not! Seriously, we have no idea how that will be interpreted. Let us define specifically what we want it to do. The 'make its presence known' is vague and open to interpretation. What would you like it to do, precisely?"

"Okay, you have a point. Let's think. Perhaps the demon could tell us something important that we need to know. Like, was Alice murdered?"

"Fair enough. Okay, let's have it answer one question. Is that what you want to know?"

"Sure."

"Lastly, what about Robert? Surely, we need to afford him the same protections as ourselves."

"Excellent idea. We'll add it in."

We were close to a final rendering, and with Johnny eager to begin, I could have asked for almost anything and he would have agreed.

We made several changes. Our emergency procedure, other than running away as fast as possible (still an option), was to immediately proceed to the section regarding exiting and get through it as quickly as possible. Robert was added to the protection clause, and we had spelled out clearly that we wanted one question answered and that was all.

I, too, had a question, but for Johnny rather than for what we were about to meet. I hesitated but went ahead: "This question may seem pointless after having gone through all this work, but should we really be doing this?"

Rather than dismissing my query out of hand, Johnny looked at me and said, "I understand your trepidation. Frankly, I feel the same, but I also feel there is something calling me in this direction. We both know strange things happen in this house. We've heard from Stanley that Alice was caught up in this type of thing far more than we ever thought possible. But regardless, the question remains: Is this all just BS, or something else? I, for one, would like to know firsthand. Wouldn't you?"

I nodded. He had hit the nail squarely on the head. We had to know.

"I tell you what," Johnny said quietly. "Let's sit Robert between us. He, at least, has some serious teeth."

I realized that in spite of his bravado, Johnny was as nervous as I was. As if to confirm my observation, Johnny got up and went to his room. He came back with two full shots of liquor.

"I think we are in need of some liquid courage before we begin. In spite of your earlier excesses this evening, I counsel you to drink up."

I nodded, and he passed me one of the shot glasses.

"Are you ready?" Johnny asked.

We looked at each other, clinked glasses, and drank. I needed all the fortification I could get.

"Now I am," I replied.

Johnny took the book in his hands and gave me a handwritten copy of what we had to say. We set up the space according to the procedures Johnny thought best and sat down again. I looked at him, and he looked at me. Robert swung his head from one to the other. With a nod, we began to chant the peculiar words the book called for, interspersed with odd bits of modern English.

32

———

My alarm sent out a muted bray. I reached over and shut it off. The sun was up and streaming obliquely through my circular window. I stretched. I felt wonderfully alive and refreshed. I was luxuriating in this sense of well-being, when Johnny poked his head around the door and said rather forcefully, "Get up. Get dressed. We're going to be late for breakfast. Come on — there's no time to lose!"

He seemed harassed and agitated. When Johnny started ordering me around, one of his plans had unhinged in some way, and badly at that.

I got up and made for the bathroom.

Dress was casual for breakfast. By the time I was ready, Johnny was pacing back and forth. Robert sat waiting to the side, his eyes locked onto his master's every move. His head swung back and forth like he was watching a tennis match.

When Johnny saw I was presentable, he said, "Remember. Say nothing. Absolutely nothing!"

I had no idea what he was talking about and said so.

"Please don't tell me you don't remember last night!"

"Not really," I answered. "Not really at all. I feel terrific, by the way. I really do."

"Oh God, as if I didn't have enough problems."

He looked up at the skylight for a moment beseechingly and quickened his pace. He said half to himself, "I can't believe it...and there's no time to go over the details...What a mess." Stopping midstride, he said, "Remember, just say nothing. That's all I ask."

He turned to go and then spun back again.

"One other thing...If by some chance you have a sudden flash of memory, don't react. Simply continue eating. We'll discuss all this later. I am pretty sure everything will work out okay. At least I think so. Just keep calm and carry on. Got it?"

Johnny, followed by Robert, dashed down the stairs before I was able to formulate a reply. I felt a little slow on the uptake, like I was stuck in one of my childhood nightmares in which the teacher handed out an exam on complex mathematical operations I didn't know, using notation I'd never seen. In the dream, I sat there in stunned disbelief as the students around me eagerly started writing.

Looking back on last night, I could remember most everything up until Johnny and I went upstairs. I did get a bit drunk. But other than that, my memory held no clue. I decided to take things one step at a time. I was hungry — therefore, food.

When there were guests at Rhinebeck, the first meal of the day did not have assigned seats other than John Senior and Anne, who manned the ends of the table. Both of them looked rested and refreshed as they read their separate copies of the *Times*, their usual morning routine. I found an empty chair next to Bruni and sat down. I said hello, and she murmured something unintelligible back. She appeared subdued and a little pale. I was promptly served a plate of scrambled eggs and bacon, which I ate ravenously. After a time, I noted something peculiar. No one had spoken for the entire meal. Elsa, to my left, was drinking her coffee with her gaze leveled at something in the far distance. Whatever she was seeing was well beyond the walls of the dining room. Bruni, to my right, stared at her plate and picked at her food, while the baron, sitting opposite Elsa, had his attention in the *Financial Times*. Malcolm simply ate slowly and carefully. Johnny, opposite me, looked about, covertly shielding his glances behind his coffee cup as he leaned one arm on the table. He needn't have bothered. No one was looking anyway.

In the meanwhile, Stanley and company kept the food flowing and the coffee coming, but it was a lost cause. No one other than Malcolm and me were really eating.

I buttered some toast. Johnny peeked at me a little wide-eyed and then furtively glanced around the table. He was growing more nervous by the second. After a few minutes of this, Bruni slammed down her knife and fork with a clatter. We all jumped with the sudden noise, but other than Johnny and me, everyone else went back to whatever they were doing. With just a few rustles of morning papers and quick looks about to see what was the matter, all was again silent.

I had consumed most everything within reach when I felt Bruni pull my arm toward her. She leaned over and whispered very softly in my ear, "We need to talk, but not now and not here." She let me go and picked up her knife and fork. She went through various cutting motions while once again eating very little.

After a few more minutes, Stanley came round with more coffee.

Malcolm dared to break the quiet. He said in a normal voice, which sounded remarkably loud, "Was it just me, or did something happen in the middle of last night? I mean, really."

The room grew completely still. I looked about. Johnny froze while his eyes slid rapidly from side to side. Bruni turned even paler. The baron remained hidden behind his paper while Elsa slowly focused her attention in Malcolm's direction. She smiled strangely, like she had just been caught watching something naughty on television. John and Anne put down their papers at the same time, while I noticed Stanley was very interested in the ceiling. Nobody said a word.

"Come on!" continued Malcolm. "I can tell something happened. You all look like you've been struck dumb. Out with it."

Everyone at the table, other than Johnny and me, began speaking at once.

"Hold on," Malcolm growled. "One at a time! First things first. Stanley, if it's at all possible, I would like a little hair of the dog."

Before Stanley could comply, John Senior said, "Since we seem to have passed over breakfast, why don't we move to the library and discuss it there. And, Stanley, a pitcher might be in order."

Stanley gave a "Very good, sir," while the rest of us made our way through the double doors to the drawing room. I was about to grab another piece of toast, but Bruni took my arm. She seemed a little shaky, so I quickly decided to leave it be, but with some reluctance. The happy memory of those little triangles with no crust would enter my mind at odd moments over the years and remind me of home. I pulled my attention off them and moved it onto Bruni, who was clinging to me.

I inquired politely as we made our way to the library if she was okay, but she simply nodded. Johnny walked beside us. He had a strange half smile on his face. I had seen that look before. It was our innocent look. We had practiced for hours and hours until we had the look just right. Obviously, he knew exactly what had happened last night. He was now trying to deflect suspicion away from himself to the best of his ability. Growing up in a hyperperceptive household meant overuse of the look could mark it as a tell, so we put it on only under dire circumstances. Whatever had we done? I wondered idly if it was possible to be held responsible for something one couldn't remember doing. I could have asked Bruni on the legal view, but we had arrived at the library. Besides, I wasn't sure she was in good enough shape to answer.

I loved this room. It always felt cozy and safe. This morning, in spite of the fineness of the weather, the curtains were closed and a fire burned in the grate. The room was a welcome sanctuary for those who had consumed too much the night before. We all took seats in a rough circle. Johnny was on my left and Bruni on my right.

Mr. Dodge said, "Malcolm, since you started this, why don't you begin."

"Well, ah…very well. The dinner was superb, and the wine, one of the best drops I can remember. I retired somewhat early for me, but I was looking forward to a good night's sleep, having traveled all of yesterday. Around two or three, I awoke. I don't know what precipitated that exactly. I felt a sense of unease. Something was not right. I lay there, my senses alert, when I heard what I thought was heavy breathing. Since I was the only one in the room and it was dark, I was disconcerted. So much so, I decided to remain where I was. I heard voices and then silence, followed by another voice that had a peculiar raspy quality, but I could not make sense of what it said. Then silence again, followed by a muffled thud. I tried to get back to sleep, but that was hopeless. I was wide awake. I put on my robe and opened the door to go downstairs for a nightcap. To my surprise, there was a dark man sitting in a chair at the end of the hall. He told me curtly to get back in my room. I had no idea what to make of it, but I did as I was told. Does anyone know who that was? I'm sure he wasn't a figment of my imagination."

At that point, Stanley wheeled in a cart with several tall glasses filled with ice, a large pitcher of Bloody Marys, and a small pitcher of consommé next to a bottle of vodka. "Hair of the dog, as requested: Bloody Marys and Bull Shots. Baroness, what may I offer you?"

Once we had all been served and Stanley was leaving, Mr. Dodge asked, "Stanley, do you happen to know why there was a gentleman sitting outside in the hallway last night?"

"It was Raymond, the chauffeur, sir. For protection."

"I see. Thank you, Stanley."

Stanley ghosted out.

"Do you always post a man outside in the hall at night?" asked the baron.

"Off and on, particularly when we have important guests such as yourselves in the house," replied Mr. Dodge.

"Very good. No hanky-panky." The baron chuckled.

Johnny and I looked at each other. Stanley was not taking any chances, which was a comforting thought.

"So, did you go back to sleep?" asked the baron of Malcolm.

"Well, I read for a bit, and then I must have slipped off. It was a strange night and seems to have been for others as well, am I not correct?"

"I slept like a baby," said the baron. "How about you, Elsa?"

Elsa smiled and purred, "I had a most provocative dream. I was taken from behind by a beast. I never saw my penetrator."

There were various sounds at this revelation. Johnny choked, and Bruni gave a quick intake of breath. The baron roared with laughter. Anne laughed as well and said, "Oh, Elsa, you're just impossible." John Senior smiled and shook his head. Apparently, this type of comment was typical of Elsa and expected by those who knew her well.

"A beast?" blurted Malcolm, who was not among that select group and had turned rather pink.

"Okay," she said with her marvelous German accent, "a demon then. It was singularly fulfilling. I love sleeping in this house!"

At the word *demon*, I choked on my Bloody Mary as a host of images that had been missing from my memory of the night before came flooding back. Johnny and Bruni slapped me on the back. I coughed some more to cover my shock at my new awareness and croaked, "Bit of pepper…caught in my throat."

I took my time recovering. No wonder Johnny looked the way he did. We seemed to have experienced a containment issue. Before I could begin to process this new insight and its implications, the baron asked me, "So, how about you? How was your night?"

"I had one of the best sleeps I can remember." A statement that was actually true.

"And before that?"

"An extraordinary evening. Truly memorable."

At that moment, I recalled there was more, much more. On that realization, I put on my best innocent face.

"Anyone else?"

John Senior and Anne looked at each other and held hands. Anne ventured to say, "John and I had a most…enjoyable evening. We did wake up in the night for no apparent reason. However, we eventually went back to sleep."

Elsa gave them both a long look and then turned to Bruni, "And how about you, Brunhilde?"

Bruni colored but said in an even voice, "I don't recall having woken in the middle of the night, but my dreams were troubled. I rarely remember them, but these were particularly vivid. I had several, which is unusual for me. I don't give much credence to dreams in general, so I'll leave it at that. I would feel uncomfortable relating them, but the fact that they occurred with such a life of their own was distinctly different from the norm."

Malcolm nodded. "Thank you. And you, Johnny?"

"Well, I didn't get much sleep last night, which in itself is unusual, so I suppose I would have to conclude it was a strange night all around. On another note, I would like to say that this

Bloody Mary puts a better spin on things. How about we all toast to a new day and a fresh start?"

We hoisted our glasses in response.

Mr. Dodge concluded by saying, "Yes, and it's a beautiful day outside. Take advantage of it, if you can. Lunch is at one. In the meanwhile, Anne and I have some household duties to attend to, so you'll have to excuse us. Why don't we all meet in the drawing room at twelve thirty? By the way, my mother, Mrs. Leland, should arrive sometime this afternoon, along with my half-sister, Bonnie. Hugo, what do you plan to do this morning?"

"I have some calls to make and some business matters to go over with Elsa and Brunhilde," he said, looking at his wife and daughter and then back at his host. "Can we make ourselves at home here? I will have to get my briefcase."

"Of course. You won't be disturbed, but if you should need anything, the bell is to the left of the fireplace. Stanley will attend to you. How about you, Malcolm?"

"I will catch a few more winks upstairs lest my traveling catch up with me tonight, if you don't mind."

"Fair enough. Boys?"

Boys was a moniker I felt certain we would never outgrow when we were together in this house. Johnny answered for both of us. "We will be attending to Robert by taking him on a long walk."

"That's it then."

We went our separate ways.

33

"Well," said Johnny. "I thought that went rather well."

Johnny and I were once again walking Robert. It was a convenient chore that allowed us to converse in private while making sure that Robert remained reasonably well behaved. The morning was splendid, with not a cloud in sight. We felt uplifted after the dark matters of the night before. Johnny was also delighted that there was no reason to suspect him in having a hand in the peculiar dreams of our guests and that his worst fears of murder and mayhem had not come to pass. We were approaching the woods to the south of the house when Johnny said, "So you *do* remember what happened last night."

"I think so. It came flooding back to me when Elsa said the word *demon*. What I do recall is more sensations and feelings than specific details."

"Why don't you tell me what you can remember, and I'll fill in any blanks."

"Fair enough. I remember quite clearly our presummoning

workup. Afterward, we sat down on the couch. You were on my left, with Robert sitting between us. The only light present was from the candles. We started to recite the verses. Nothing happened at first, and I was pretty sure nothing would. As we progressed through the reading, however, I thought that I might have been a bit premature in my assessment. Something had begun. I could feel it, and I began to get nervous. I felt out of sorts. Our location had somehow changed. We were still there in the house on the couch, but outside, the world had shifted, and time was running strangely. It was not the past or the future but a different time altogether. I don't know. I really started to freak out at that point.

"The sensations were so different from what I expected, and from what I had ever experienced. I think we paused at that point and looked at each other. As we did so, I looked past you into my room. The door was open, and I could see out the window. It was dark, but the sky had a hazy glow, like when the moon is near full. I saw tree branches outside my window, which was impossible. There are no trees close to the house. That disoriented me even more. The rest of what I remember is sketchier still, I'm afraid. I think I asked if we could stop, but it was too late for that. Something else was there in the room with us. I felt it rather than saw it. Frankly, I didn't dare look up. I kept my gaze down to read out the verses. I could have imagined it. I figured we had to get through them since there were several paragraphs that seemed important, like the 'no bodily harm' clause and a few others. I was barely hanging on. Once I had made it through those, I felt a bit of relief, and we had a drink of water. I looked around to see outside, but the door to my room was closed. This jolted me because I was sure it had been open.

"Nothing seemed stable anymore. I think you asked your question then and received a bizarre answer that the 'Eye of the Moon' was closed. I thought that was so typical. How could we have possibly believed we would get a straight answer from a demon, of all things? After that, the situation deteriorated rapidly. Perhaps we asked another question about the answer and that voided our contract? It's possible, I suppose. Another bargain was made, I think. What exactly, I don't know.

"The next thing I recall was looking into other people's heads. I had a vision of Bruni. We were naked in each other's arms in her bed. I visited Elsa. Her head was filled with erotic fantasies. I saw the baron, but he was unreadable, as was Stanley. I felt the love of your parents for each other. I sensed the loneliness of Malcolm Ault.

"There were other impressions, but I quickly became confused as to whose they were because they were coming at me faster and more vividly. In the back of my mind, I kept thinking that the exit clause was needed fast. Perhaps I tried to read it. I don't know. After a time, I sort of succumbed to the onslaught of images I was receiving by passing out. I can recall nothing else until I woke up. That's pretty much it. If I didn't know better, I would say I had consumed some serious hallucinogenic, but to my knowledge, I had not. How does that stack up against what you experienced?"

"We agree on several points, but before I comment, let me process what you said for a bit. I need to think."

As we walked in silence, I watched Robert. He was thrilled to be outdoors and off the leash. He raced ahead of us toward the woods and into the underbrush. I followed his progress by the tip of his tail above the greenery as he foraged at the edge of the lawn. I saw no change in him in spite of last night's doings. I wasn't so sure that was the case with me. I felt different. Slower, somehow, yet calmer. I had always been so paranoid and jumpy. Now, I seemed to be more willing to let the world come to me rather than always reaching for it. What had happened to me last night?

Johnny interrupted my musings. "Well, I think you got most of the salient points right. But I owe you an apology, a really big one.

I'm not sure what the outcome will be once you've heard what I have to say. Nonetheless, I promised myself that I would tell you. I also promised the entity we summoned. It's part of the agreement I made, but I'll get to that in due course."

Here he stopped walking and turned to look at the house, avoiding having to look at me.

"There's a part of me that always takes things too far. It's in my nature...I love living at the edge. I feel so alive out there, but doing so comes at a price. Not everyone likes to live like that, and I take anyone who's nearby along, whether they like it or not, usually by not telling them that they've jumped off a cliff with me. The costs of my decisions and choices are often at other's expense. Perhaps that's why I have so few real friends. The truth is I'm just not trustworthy, and I'm not honest."

"Johnny..."

He turned to face me.

"Percy, it's important you hear this — all of this — before you respond. I am not one to bare my soul, but there comes a time, and that time is now. I really do need to reevaluate my life. I promised myself, and now you as well, that I'll try to be less underhanded. I hate myself whenever I do it, and I do it a lot. Saying I'm sorry does nothing for me anymore, yet here I am doing it again. I have to stop, and I'm going to.

"The truth is I've always been at the center of my world. My life revolves around me. I've liked it that way, but after last night, I realized I've had it all wrong. In reality, I count for little. There are things out there that are much greater than me and far more significant than I once thought. I must either accept that and change or remain the superficial, self-centered person that I am. I've chosen the former.

"You're probably wondering what could possibly have led me to this juncture, so let me tell you what really happened last night.

251

I'll leave my analysis to the end. All I ask is that you hear me out in full. Promise me you'll listen until I finish?"

"Of course," I said. What else could I say to that? Obviously, I would not like what he had to relate, but then again, maybe I would. I was willing to hear it. I, too, was in a different place.

"Here goes.

"To start, I need to fill you in on some things I haven't told you. By chance, I discovered some notes written by Alice that were tucked between the pages of the odd-shaped book I borrowed from downstairs. They outlined some additional details as to how to contact and summon spirits — like a best practices outline. She recommended the use of a powerful object — particularly the jeweled bracelet — to focus her attention. She emphasized the direction to face, the lighting, and that sort of thing, quite specifically, so it was no coincidence that I created the setup the way I did. Also, she outlined what she experienced during a summoning and that her breakthrough came when she started using a supplement made from parts of the *Brugmansia* plant. The drug helped her achieve a greater awareness, and most importantly, it allowed her to become visible to those entities she wished to summon. She would prepare a tincture that she would take prior to her sessions. It was kept in a small jade box in the hidden library. She recommended the dosage of two drops in one and half ounces of liquid, aged single malt being the preferred medium. I hope you will forgive me, but I added that amount to your shot glass just before we began. I did not partake, partly because I was a chicken. I admit that. But also to make sure that if things got out of hand, there was someone there not only to act as a control but to take action, if needed. I was justified in this, but that doesn't excuse my irresponsibility and flagrant disregard for your choice in the matter. I hope you will forgive me. I really went too far."

Here he paused and looked me over to see how I was taking all this. I thought I took it rather well. What he said explained several things. There was no question that I had stepped into another world last night. At another time, I would have been completely beside myself and probably punched him. But I was not the same person I was yesterday. I saw at once the struggle that raged within him. His genius. His love of danger. His complete disregard for others. It was his weakness but also his strength. I saw him driven by his own uncertainty into his often frantic efforts to succeed. The greater the odds against him, the more alluring the paths became. I understood. I also realized it was not my forgiveness he sought, but his own.

I gripped his arm for a moment to let him know that there was no need to ask for what would always be there. Such was our friendship.

He gave a great sigh, and there were tears in his eyes.

"I probably don't deserve you, but I think the rest will be easier to relate. Thank you. Let me go on.

"We got right to it after we had worked out what to say. I really was curious to see what would happen. We rattled off the first several verses. I didn't notice much at first, but there were subtle changes. The book seemed warmer. I put my arm around Robert in case he got antsy, but nothing fazed him. He stayed still as stone. His ears pricked up at one point, and I felt there was something in front of us. You and I looked at each other. You looked like you were ready to jump out of your skin and said you wanted to stop, and at that point, so did I, but we were already off the deep end and had to soldier on. I wasn't sure if your fear was the result of the drug, or what was actually happening. You really did look a fright, and that began to concern me. I realized then that I might have made a huge mistake.

"There is another thing you should know. I took the liberty of adding a few additional clauses to our contract."

Again he looked me over carefully to see how this sat with me.

I was now quite curious. I shrugged. My judgmental side seemed to be on vacation. Robert continued to run about, leaving us farther behind. I motioned that we should walk. Johnny was usually more comfortable walking. He spoke. I listened as we wandered along the edge of the woods.

"Alice in her notes wrote something I thought rather profound. She noted that the gods get lonely. They need to be acknowledged and their existence confirmed. It need not be adoration. She cited the Hindu practice of Darshan, the 'auspicious sight,' or 'to see with reverence and devotion.' The gods need an audience is how I interpreted it. Practicing Darshan properly means the observer develops an affection for the entity, and in turn, the entity develops an affection for the observer; thus, a relationship is established. The 'properly' part is the ceremony or ritual. It is a kind of introduction, where both parties see each other and begin to know the other. Merit is bestowed on both parties. It was quite an insight, I thought, and established for me the theory, the matrix, that underlay our summoning."

Johnny tended to get technical when he had something personal and important to confess. He would get to the point eventually. I waited. It wouldn't be long.

"We approached our late-night meeting in terms of a contract. Contracts involve an exchange of a valuable or consideration for another. I puzzled over what it was we could provide in exchange for the presence of the demon and the answer to the question. Stanley exchanged his explicit knowledge and his implied protection for our explicit promise. It was sealed, and our relationship has become contractual in nature. This established a level of trust between us that I doubt we could have achieved with him any other way. The promise allowed him to tell us what he's kept to himself and told no one else.

"Using Alice's insight, the valuable I thought to give to the demon was this Darshan, the merit that comes from seeing him and acknowledging him. As Alice pointed out, this is a valuable commodity in the spirit world. I structured an additional clause that promised this acknowledgment by offering your Darshan. The idea was that the demon would get a glimpse of you and you would get a glimpse of him. You would, of course, have to become visible, and that meant using the tincture. What wasn't clear to me when I wrote that clause was that the way one becomes visible to such an entity is by opening your mind. In exchange, the entity — in this case, a demon — opens his to yours. Because I had not taken the tincture, you gave a lot more Darshan than anticipated and received a great deal more from the demon in return. At least, that's how I figure it, and it explains what followed to a large degree.

"Once we got through the contractual bit, we made a toast. You mentioned that you thought the drink was water, but actually it was more single malt with an additional drop of tincture in yours. Alice's notes cautioned that three was the maximum allowed. At this point, I was not exactly sure what was going on in the summoning. Something was happening to you, and Robert was aware of something in the room of a spiritual nature, because he gets all stiff when that happens. I decided to ask my question about Alice and awaited a reply. You were the one who answered, which surprised me. I wrote it down. 'The Eye of the Moon was closed.' Are you with me so far?"

"Yes, although I can't say I know what that means."

"I don't either. Well, now comes the bad part."

"The bad part?"

"Give me a minute."

He lit a cigarette and smoked a few puffs in silence. He had talked easily before, not so now. He struggled to get the words out.

"It was my fault, of course. If only I had just shut up, but no — I wanted to be the hero and be the one to discover the answer. I stupidly asked another question, breaking our promise to ask only one, and that's when you began to hiss. I must admit — if you thought you were freaked out, I lost it at that point. Robert leaped off the couch and into his bed. I can't blame him. I've never been more frightened in my life. I thought I crapped my pants. I did, in fact, I discovered later. All my attention was on what was happening. You grabbed my arm in a grip of steel and said one word: 'Broken!' You repeated it over and over, with your voice getting wilder and louder. Malcolm said he heard a voice with a raspy quality. Well, he was getting it one floor below. I was right next to you. I didn't know what to do. You got up and went around the table to the figurine. You grabbed it and held it to your chest. You looked at me with a look I'd never seen. It was the demon speaking through you.

"It said, 'For me, for him.'

"You for the figurine seemed like a deal to me, so I screamed, 'Yes. For you, for him.'

"But it paused then. 'He got more, much more, something extra. You pay more. Your word.'

"'My word?' I asked.

"'Your word.'

"'Okay, you have my word.'

"'Tell him, find him out, and keep him. Your word?'

"'My word.'

"'Seal it!'"

Johnny looked away and smoked some more. His hand holding the cigarette was shaking.

"You walked around the table, and you kissed me right on the mouth. 'Done,' you said. Right after that, you collapsed. The figurine crashed to the floor beside you and broke into several pieces. The jewel must have hit the table when you fell, because it sheared in two. You were just lying there. You looked dead. I was beyond freaked out. I panicked completely.

"I ran down the stairs and into Raymond. He must have just

gotten Malcolm back into his room. He asked me where the fuck I was going.

"I said, 'I'm going to get Stanley. Get the fuck out of my way.' You know Raymond. The more profanity the better."

Johnny laughed. I hadn't heard him laugh in some time.

"He asked me if I needed help. I thought about it as I looked at him and said, 'Maybe later. In fact, I'm pretty sure I will. Keep it in mind.'"

"He shrugged. 'I'm around.'

"I went over to the servants' wing, and as I got to his door, Stanley opened it. He was in his bathrobe. He asked what had happened. I said you had collapsed, and I didn't know what to do. That guy can move, I tell you. We made it up the stairs in record time. He examined you and said that Alice used to look the same after one of her sessions. He put you to bed and assured me you would feel great in the morning. He told me to get some sleep and that the three of us would talk after lunch.

"That's what really happened last night."

34

After his confession, Johnny took Robert to Stanley's office, while I continued to process what he had said. Bruni must have seen me as I walked back to the house. She met me as I opened one of the french doors that led to the drawing room and asked if I might take a walk with her. I agreed. A breeze kicked up as we stepped out the front door. She brushed her hair from her eyes as we walked up the driveway to the private road that led west toward the Hudson and, east, toward the main public road. There was at least an hour before we had to meet in the drawing room before lunch. We turned left toward the river.

After we had gotten well away from the house, she asked, "Do you have any idea what I dreamed about last night?"

"You and me?"

"You're right, of course. Do you have an explanation for that?"

"None that comes easily."

"But you have one."

"A possibility only, and I'm not sure I understand it. Frankly, I felt turned upside down by you last night, and I don't know what to do about that, either. I'm surprised we're even talking right now."

"You're mad at me."

"Yes, but mad is not the word. Confused and little betrayed, if you must know."

"Malcolm announced that he'd seen my husband. That's what did it, didn't it?"

"It did. Would you care to enlighten me?"

"I would, only it's complicated."

"Then explain it."

"Very well. I'm in a state of flux in my marriage. It's over but not ended. The dream I had last night has made me more confused than ever, and that is on *you*, I think. Would you like to know why?"

"Yes."

She stopped walking and looked at me. Her eyes were so blue — I couldn't look away. I didn't want to.

"Before I tell you, I want to clear something up. I admit I was not forthcoming, but did you really expect me to blurt out that I was married right from the start? Would you have handled it any differently had you been me?"

"No, I would've done the same. It was your bad luck and Ault's bad timing, although I did ask you about your marriage."

"Did you really ask me?"

"No, you're right again. I didn't have the nerve to ask you straight out, although I wanted to."

I was surprised by my answer. I spoke the truth. Revealing how I really felt was not something I did routinely, if at all. At that moment, all I knew was that it was very important that I be honest. Explaining what actually happened last night was another matter. There were levels of truth, but I had made a different start than I had before.

Bruni nodded her head slowly as she looked at me. "You

surprise me. Now you know why I didn't want to say anything. I didn't have the nerve either, although I wanted to tell you as well."

There was truth in what she said. I sensed it. We had begun.

A gust picked up, and we had to turn away from looking at each other.

She took my arm as we walked along the black road that disappeared beneath the trees. She continued. "There is something I wish to say."

"By all means, and thank you for explaining about your marriage." I felt better.

"You're not out of the woods yet, and frankly, neither am I. You have some explaining to do, but I'm willing to let you tell me in your own time. Talking truth is hard. It comes in layers. Someone once told me that you can't get to the heart of things without first cutting through the skin. I'm not open as a rule. Being a lawyer I suppose does that, but I want to tell you a personal story about me anyway, if I can."

"I'd like that."

"A number of years ago, I fell in love in a dream. It was passionate, and it consumed me. I woke up completely hooked on this guy. I saw him in person a few days later. I suppose I expected to take up where the dream left off, but his dreams, if any, must have been very different. When I threw myself at him, he freaked out. I knew at once I'd made a terrible mistake. The moment was extremely awkward. I backpedaled, but the damage was done. He avoided me after that. A long time later, he apologized for his reaction. I think he regretted not taking me up on my offer, but by then the very thought of us together made me cringe. It still does."

She smiled at the thought and said more seriously, "I don't trust dreams in general, and I doubt dreaming of someone induces a similar dream in the person we dream about." She looked at me.

"I would tend to agree. I had a similar experience. I dreamed about this girl I knew and woke up in love with her. The girl in question responded to my overtures, but whether because of my dream, my advances, or my looks, I was never sure. I didn't have the nerve to ask her if she'd had the same or a similar dream. I suspect she hadn't. The relationship didn't last. I was fickle and easily distracted at the time."

"Are you generally fickle?"

"I suppose I am, but then, I don't find myself in many situations where that might be an issue."

"Did you dream of me last night?" she asked, looking straight ahead.

"I was in your bed. I just don't know if I was dreaming that. It's hard to explain."

She stopped walking and looked at me again. Her eyes were so blue. "It was realer than a dream, wasn't it?"

"It was, but I never saw Raymond — the man in the hallway — and he didn't see me, so it couldn't have been real; yet it seemed so."

"I knew it. That's why I had to talk to you. I needed your…I needed confirmation."

On impulse, I pulled her toward me and kissed her. We melted together. After a time, we separated, slightly out of breath. She said finally, "You kissed me the same way in the dream."

"So did you."

She stepped in closer and played with the collar of my shirt and said softly, "It was more than a dream. I don't know what to do."

"What do you wish to do?"

"I'm not sure. It's not that simple." She stepped back from me. "You know, you've changed. And I don't understand that either."

"From the dream?"

"No, that part seems familiar. I mean, from yesterday. You're all of a sudden less uptight, more open, and more certain of yourself — more in control. I like it, but that's a problem for me. I don't want to like anyone right now, but I can't seem to help myself."

She stepped away and looked back along the road. "I was the one who started this thing between us. I like to play games with people — men, in particular. I enjoy unsettling them. I liked unsettling you. It was easy, and it was fun, but now the tables appear to be…turned."

"And that bothers you?"

"I can't find my footing, and I can't explain it. One moment I'm in control. The next, I wake up completely besotted. You are so completely under my skin, I hurt. I can barely think of anything else except you. I almost lost it and started screaming at breakfast. This doesn't happen to me. I don't fall in love at the drop of a hat, particularly when I don't want to or because it's convenient. I woke up and started shaking just thinking about that dream. What happened to me? What have you done to me? How?" She looked at me, perplexed. There were tears in her eyes, which she quickly hid by holding me.

One part of me was thrilled to have this beautiful woman in my arms. I wanted to say, "There, there. It'll be all right." And continue to hope it would be. But there was another unfamiliar part I was becoming aware of since last night that processed things differently and counseled caution. At some point, it noted, I would have to explain. I could fool myself into thinking that I didn't understand what had happened to her last night, but that was false. I had wanted her from the moment I saw her. Something made that dream come true: a demon. How could I possibly disclose that without a firmer foundation between us?

Bruni was also not like other women I had known. Bruni was like a tiger — an exquisite one, but still a tiger. There was a dark and predatory side to her. I knew this. My knowledge was intuitive but no less true. She was vulnerable now, but that would change. It was one thing to willingly surrender to another. Having one's normal defenses stripped away without consent was something else entirely. When she understood what happened, which she would eventually, there would be hell to pay — and pay I would. And willingly, if I was honest. I wondered as well if my circumstances were much different from hers?

I continued to hold her and stroke her hair. I understood her distress. I had once fallen in love so hard, I hurt physically. The girl had been delightful. For me, I loved her at first sight, but passion that intense was neither pleasant nor wholesome. All I thought about was her. I was insanely happy, extraordinarily so, but with that feeling came jealousy, possessiveness, and a peevish desire for her attention. If she failed to look at me or spoke with another man, I felt betrayed. Crimes of passion were spawned from such feelings.

It would take real skill to manage Bruni's feelings and emotions so that the passion she felt now wouldn't turn to hatred of the same intensity. Once she righted herself, I thought it might be possible to build a more stable structure, but I did not give it much hope. Passion can turn sour in an instant. The truth was I didn't feel the same intensity. I barely remembered last night, while obviously she did in detail. I thought it just as well. If I did, I knew instinctively that we would be consumed by a fire that would scorch all those around us, including each other.

She pushed me away. "I'm sorry. I'm not like this. I'm really not. Let's walk. We'll be late."

"Not so fast. Wait." I turned her face toward me. "We seem to have skipped several steps."

She looked me in the eyes and said, "You don't love me."

"I barely know you, and you barely know me."

"You don't deny it? Oh God. I've done it again, haven't I? I swore I'd never fall in love with someone who didn't love me, and I have. Shit!"

She pulled away and stormed off. I could have caught her, but then I decided to let her go. What would happen, would happen. She was angry with me but furious at herself for assuming I felt the same. We would talk again. We had shared a truth between us that we had shared with no one else. Its feeble flame seemed dull against the raging backdrop of her passion, but it was there burning nonetheless.

I followed her back to the house. By the time I reached the top of the driveway, she was opening the front door. I heard it slam from where I was. It was hard to imagine a door of that size slamming, but she had managed it. Logic and passion do not speak the same language.

Whether I finessed it or not, the situation with Bruni was bound to get stormy. Storms were in her nature, but I had another more pressing thought that nagged at the back of my mind: what exactly might I expect from her mother? It was a question I could barely comprehend, let alone answer. Bruni was a tiger, but a young one in comparison to the adult female of the species. Bruni might rip me to shreds, but Elsa would eat me alive. I needed to get through lunch, and then Johnny and I needed to consult with Stanley most urgently.

35

I made my way upstairs to change. We were due to meet downstairs shortly. Johnny was reading a report as I entered the common area.

He looked up. He was dressed for lunch and had on his questioning look, which meant he was curious as to how I was doing.

"There you are," he said. "I heard you come back — or at least I heard Bruni's return. I think she shook the entire house."

"Yes, she had a moment of pique." I sank into one of the leather chairs. They were remarkably comfortable.

"Relationship over?"

"Not exactly — simply a new phase. Apparently, I visited her in her dreams. It was passionate. She woke up besotted and nearly went ballistic at breakfast. We went for a walk, and she realized after we spoke that I did not feel for her with the same intensity. She bolted and nearly broke the front door. There are also additional complications: Elsa. I visited her last night as well."

"Good God! I was wondering about that. By the way, I must ask you before we continue, how are *we* doing?"

"*We* are fine. Not to worry. You're the only friend I really have, so you're stuck with me."

"I hoped as much. Once again, I offer my sincerest apologies."

"It's behind us. Let's speak no more of it. You're forgiven. What we need to do rather quickly is get our wits around the future. We really do need to consult with Stanley. There are several questions I have: First, what happened last night to me mentally, and what are the implications going forward? I've most definitely changed. There's a part of me now that seems to perceive things in a way I've never experienced. I get insights. It's like a form of intuition. I don't mean to sound crazy, but there it is."

"Is it a bad thing?"

"Neither good nor bad. It simply is. It manages to cut through my mental clutter and make observations. It's quite detached — cold, almost. I can't describe it more clearly, only to say that I instinctively trust it. It's pretty smart."

"I'm cheered, if it helps you. At least something positive came out of last night. You said you had several questions."

"Yes, besides the Elsa business, the last two are about that troubling little bargain you made and that figurine."

"The last is easily answered. I gathered up all the fragments and stuffed them in a shoe box that lies at the bottom of my closet. I have no idea what to do with them. I suppose that is best left to Stanley to advise. As to what happened to you, I can hazard a best guess, and that is that you and the demon rubbed off on each other. He got part of you, and you got part of him. Last night, you and he traipsed about. As to what that means exactly, we'll just have to see. I also have no idea if it's a permanent condition. I should think your late-night wanderings as an incubus were a one-time deal. Your intuitive part is likely more permanent. The more you use it, the more likely it is to unite with you going forward. If it's not a bother, it might be quite an asset. How do you feel?"

"Good, actually. Calmer and more certain. The Bruni situation is a good example. I am much more grounded and less influenced by her manipulations. I see them as such. It doesn't change the fact that I like her. I like her very much, but she may rethink how she feels. I've changed from a lap dog to a Robert, and that's not for everyone. She's married, by the way, but winding down. My inner voice says they have a very physical relationship but can't live together without fighting tooth and nail."

"So, what do you intend to do?"

"I would rather have her as a friend than an enemy, and something more, if possible. She's nice to look at and very smart. We're locked together in some way. We just have to sort out the details, and that might take some time."

"Message from your intuitive part?"

"I think so. Whether it's a wish, or a truth, I don't know. I have to become more familiar with that part of me to know for certain."

"No chance of a snappy little fling on my part, then?"

"Probably not. Were you thinking about it?"

"After dinner last night, I did indeed. While you were rubbing elbows with her mother, she and I had quite the little chat. You were a featured topic. She pumped me for as much information as I was willing to give, which was more than you would have liked, I'm sure. Just the same, she is remarkably sensual, and she got my juices flowing. But after thinking over our little escapade late last night, I've decided to retire from the field. It's my penance."

"Penance?"

"You heard it right. I endangered you and did you harm."

"Don't be so sure. Sometimes what we think are our worst misdeeds turn out to be the opposite, and what we hold up as our shining best is anything but, given time. You may do your penance if you wish, but I don't require it. Really, I don't."

"So, I'm free to woo the fair maiden?" said Johnny with a happy smile.

"I wouldn't go that far."

"Just pulling your leg. She and I would never work. Great sex, I think, but our personalities would clash, and over it would be. On a cautionary note, it will take extraordinary skill to keep her. I think she's like Alice in that way. Kindred spirits."

Johnny had moments of extraordinary perspicacity. I had to agree with him.

"At this point, it will take real skill to simply salvage a friendship, but enough of that; what about the bargain you made last night?"

"I'm at a loss. Frankly, it's not something I want to deal with but something I must. I leave that to Stanley to interpret, as well as your opinion. If my rubbing-off theory is correct, you probably have a good idea of what it means."

"I've thought about it. The good news is it's vague, and there was no time limit stipulated. 'Him' could be anyone."

"Or you. Let's table the subject until we sit down with Stanley. Right now, I feel like Hercules. I now have a task, a labor, although rather less defined. I will just have to do the best I can."

"Cheer up. You're not alone in this. I'll carry your club and be right behind you, goading you on. It will be quite a reversal of roles. I'm rather looking forward to it."

"Very funny. Although that also crossed my mind, but to put the ball back in your court and off my little diversions, this Elsa thing really concerns me. If Bruni's bad, the baroness is far worse. She'll have you squirming and pressed up against a wall in no time at all."

"That's if she knew it was me, which I doubt she does — unless mother and daughter compare notes."

"Hadn't thought of that. You really know how to complicate matters. Those two seem quite close, so have a care. You must promise me one thing. Don't be alone with that woman. Even if nothing happens, should the baron ever get a whiff of it, the sins of the father will most surely be visited unto you. There are too many parallels, and he has a brutish, calculating nature. Vengeance will enter his mind like a worm. I shudder to think what he might do. I am most earnest in this."

"You're more than correct. I'll watch my step."

"Very well. Now, we best get a move on."

I changed and put on a jacket. It was time for lunch, and the assembling for meals ruled our days and nights.

3 6

Johnny and I beat the crowd to the drawing room. I mixed two vodka tonics with additional splashes of gin and ginger ale as we waited.

"Cheers," Johnny said when I finished. John Senior and Anne walked in, followed by the baron and baroness. We moved over by the french doors to make room for them at the bar. John Senior finished mixing drinks for himself and his guests as Malcolm and Bruni finally made their appearance. Neither Bruni nor Elsa paid me any particular attention. Johnny and I drank and chatted until we were joined by the tall man who said, "I trust you had a relaxing morning. I certainly did."

"Excellent. That's the way it should be," said Johnny. "By the way, I've been meaning to ask you. How well do you know the von Hofmanstals?"

"I shouldn't say that I know them well. I'm more familiar with Hugo. He and I met at a shoot in Scotland years ago and have collaborated on a few projects since then — strictly business. I am less familiar with the baroness. She's quite something, isn't she?"

"That she is," said Johnny, smiling. "How about Bruni?"

"I have met her off and on too. Usually in France, at the odd party, but that is the extent of my relationship with the family. I take it you are on more familiar terms?"

"Yes, my parents have met up with them on numerous occasions in Europe somewhere or at their castle. This is the first time we've been able to reciprocate."

"I see. Well, this visit will give me a chance to know them better. I'm looking forward to it."

During the conversation, I watched the tall man's eyes flick toward the baroness. He had to make an effort not to stare. She looked stunning in a pale-green button-down silk blouse that was open and transparent enough to draw the eye. I suppose his height did give him glimpses that were unavailable to those of shorter stature. Bruni was more conservative in a pale-gray sweater. Both of them wore skirts and high heels. They were an attractive pair. Of that there was no question.

Stanley announced that lunch was ready. We finished our drinks and moved to the dining room. Bruni ignored me.

I was seated between Elsa and Johnny, with Elsa on my right, next to Anne. The baron was seated next to John Senior in his usual place. Bruni was beside him. Malcolm sat next to her and opposite Elsa. He had to turn his head away so as not to appear completely voyeuristic. Elsa was fully aware of his discomfiture and enjoyed every minute. She turned to me with a smile on her face.

"So, *Liebchen*, I'm so glad we have another chance to talk. How are things going with my daughter?'

"Stormy."

"Yes, I heard her come in. I think everybody did."

I switched to German. "She told me she's married."

"It is true, but there are all kinds of marriages. Her husband is an extraordinary man, but he is not flexible, and neither is she.

271

They are like two snow leopards. They are forced to live solitary lives except when mating. Sometimes, even that cannot be tolerated."

"I suspected something like that."

"Their break is a recent development. I shouldn't be telling you these things, but it is pertinent information, yes?"

"Quite pertinent."

"There is a divorce in progress. It is a prickly subject, but lucky for you, I'm the very opposite of prickly..."

She was interrupted by Stanley, who poured us each a cold Sancerre. I looked around the table. Bruni and Johnny were listening to John Senior and the baron discuss some aspect of central bank policy options, while Malcolm spoke with Anne about England. It was unlikely that the others heard what we were talking about.

Once Stanley had poured our wine, we clinked glasses and drank. It was wonderfully refreshing.

Elsa continued. "My husband and I have strong personalities, but we are also mutually supportive. We are ultimately pragmatists. When we started together, we had a choice to make. We could either follow separate paths and meet for brief spaces of time or form a real partnership, where we were rarely separated and our thoughts were open to each other. Of course we have our private times, but it takes neither of us very long to recharge ourselves and find our way back again. Together, we form a team that has few weaknesses and many strengths. Apart, our power is weakened. Both of us, in the parlance of economics, desire to maximize our preferences, but individually, our behaviors show diminishing marginal rates of substitution, when it comes to others. My daughter and I are not altogether different, although she has yet to understand that. Do you follow what I'm saying?"

"I think so. The sustained connection between you and the baron is far more important and beneficial than being alone. Bruni is the same in that way, although she has not come to that realization yet."

Elsa touched my cheek. She beamed like a small star as she said, "Not just a pretty face, after all, and here is our soup."

The soup was a butternut squash puree with a touch of heat and salt to give a zing. Sprinkled on top were a dozen tiny croutons. Dagmar's creation was a sophisticated blend of flavors whose balance was a culinary masterpiece.

I picked up my spoon and savored the first taste as I simultaneously digested what Elsa had related and implied. Elsa needed alone time, and so did Bruni, but the benefits of a connected long-term relationship always triumphed. Bruni had yet to experience the upside of such a marriage, and as her mother stated, such a relationship was what she ultimately needed. Perhaps it was a hint.

I asked my intuitive part. It replied that it was more than a hint. Her daughter was very much on Elsa's mind.

Johnny had mentioned that this new part might be an asset. It was, but I realized I could abdicate my own judgement quite easily in favor of its prescient calculating detachment. I had the choice to reject this addition or accept it. I considered both choices but decided that neither was the answer. What I needed was an assimilation of myself and it, not altogether different from what Elsa and Hugo had achieved. By working with this new addition as a team, I realized I might be willing to risk more and worry less. Difficulties and threats could become advantages and opportunities, rather than the evils I thought they were. It was what I knew I needed to do to transform myself.

I put down my spoon. I had barely tasted the soup. Luckily, there was still some left. I picked my spoon up again and savored what remained. I had a new fault. It was so easy to slip into my mind and play with my new friend, thereby shutting out the rich world around me.

"Elsa?"

"Yes, *Liebchen*."

"You studied economics?"

"I hold advanced degrees in mathematics and economics, as well as accounting."

"So you're not just a pretty face either."

She laughed. "Not at all. It keeps me amused and curious. I'm always underestimated. Hugo and I have a great time. Rivals and allies put all their attention on him while ignoring me completely. I become part of the furniture, and when he leaves, they have no idea I'm still there. They say things they normally wouldn't, if he were present."

"How could they not notice you?"

"I have tricks that can make me look so plain and uninteresting that if I came up to you, you wouldn't recognize me."

"That I would have to see to believe."

She leaned over in my direction and grabbed the last little crouton that was in my soup bowl with her fingers. She used her right arm to prevent her blouse from touching her bowl in a way that was suspiciously revealing.

The performance was impressive but not directed at me. I looked over at Malcolm. He was acting strangely. His breath was ragged and beads of sweat had formed on his forehead. I thought he might even launch himself across the table, but Stanley got to him first and whispered something in his ear. Malcolm's ardor subsided, and in a few seconds, he was calm and collected. I would have to ask Stanley what he said. I needed his advice in any event. The man had a skillset that was clearly in a class by itself. Stanley nodded in our direction before turning around and opening another bottle of wine.

"Yummy?" I asked the baroness.

"Totally delicious. If I could figure out a way to steal this cook, I would."

"You are a thoroughly wicked woman."

"In so many ways, you have no idea."

I shook my head and smiled broadly as I held up my glass, "Elsa, it's a pleasure to have met you. I wouldn't have missed it for the world."

"And me too."

We touched glasses, and she said, "So, what would you like to discuss? Galois theory, perhaps, or Laffer curves?"

"Neither — tell me something. I take it Anne and John are unaware of Bruni's marriage or pending divorce?"

Switching back to German, she said in a low voice, "Correct, and we'd rather wait until it's all finished before we tell them. Some things happen for which there are no preparations. Not even Hugo and I found out about the marriage until after she had eloped. Hugo was beside himself. He felt that she had betrayed him by going behind his back when there was no need. I was baffled and heartbroken, but Brunhilde is not easily cowed or silenced, as you well know. She's also correct in many of her decisions, when it comes to laws, structures, and relationships between parties. She made us sit down and listen calmly and rationally. This took some time, but she made us do it in spite of ourselves. She stated her case. In the end, what was done could not be undone only endured. Although I quite agreed with her logic, she completely missed the point. One must connect with one's partner mentally, emotionally, and sexually, or there will be tears. Marriage must invigorate and sustain, or it is no marriage. Hugo and I take great pains to keep the sparks flying, but there must be a real spark to begin with, yes? That is hard to know going in but easy to see on the exit. I'm only too happy to see the last of that marriage."

Elsa sipped some wine and then put a smile on her face as she turned to me and said, "I can't believe I told you all this, but I suspect I had to tell someone. I ask that you keep it to yourself."

"Johnny knows, but I see no reason to announce the fact. Malcolm knows too."

"He does?"

"He mentioned that he saw her husband in Cannes when he first arrived. I'm sure Bruni got to him before he made it public knowledge."

"I see."

Elsa looked over at Malcolm with a look quite different than previously. It was not a look he would have savored had he seen it. He was busy talking to Bruni. She turned in my direction, and our eyes met. She didn't look away, and I didn't either.

"How do you feel about my revelations?" Elsa asked.

"They make sense, and I wish her happiness in whatever she does."

"Yes. I quite agree. She deserves it."

Elsa really was concerned about her daughter.

Our next course of crab cakes with a sharp sauce followed, accompanied by a light salad. Another demonstration of perfection. During this time, Elsa and I chatted about places in Europe we had both visited. Anne joined us. Both ladies were charming and attentive. I enjoyed myself and reveled in their company.

When we had finished, Mrs. Dodge asked if we might go through. We rose, and Elsa stood close to me.

"I can't tell you how much I've enjoyed meeting you. Dinner last night was lovely and so was this afternoon. I look forward to our next chat." Once again she moved close to me to kiss me softly on both cheeks. Our hips touched in the most tantalizing fashion before she moved away. Whether this was deliberate, I could not say. I suspected it was simply Elsa being who she was.

It was time to talk to Stanley.

3 7

An hour passed before Johnny and I were able to disengage ourselves from our social duties to meet with Stanley. Once again Johnny played the Robert card to hasten our exit. The mere thought of Robert throwing a tantrum tended to unhinge the entire household, staff included. Given scant attention by Johnny caused Robert to grow sullen, if not vindictive.

Stanley motioned to us as Johnny and I entered the kitchen. I went over to Dagmar first and gave her many compliments. Before I was dragged away into Stanley's office, Dagmar said, "Come and see me later, if you can. I would so much like to talk."

I was more than happy to oblige.

If Alice had been a seer, Dagmar was a witch. Her tools were the mundane herbs of the garden and food for the table, but in her hands, they cast a spell that permeated the whole experience that was Rhinebeck. Growing up, I would often visit her and simply watch as she moved about her kitchen. For a child whose parents were hardly ever there, her presence and her kindnesses, which included the odd snack, offered a safe harbor. She was a constant supporter as I tried to navigate a future that required an excellence of myself that was often sadly lacking, a fact that weighed on my mind even at an early age. In her kitchen, her art took shape with a calming regularity that I was content to observe and experience. Supreme competence was possible. I could see it. I believed in it. I had hope that one day I might be able to emulate such skills in my own way.

Stanley had a similar level of mastery but in a different context. Johnny and I entered his office. He offered us a tumbler of his fine whiskey, which we gratefully accepted. Robert scrambled out from under the desk, lay down next to his master's chair, and promptly went back to sleep.

Once we were settled, I said to Stanley, "I understand you were instrumental in helping me last night, and for that, I thank you. I was unconscious, so I don't know exactly what you did, but I did wake up in my bed, rather than on the floor. It is most appreciated."

Stanley nodded. "Once I knew you had consumed some of the tincture, I was on familiar ground. I cannot count the number of times I put her ladyship to bed in a similar state, which is why I was confident that you would awake refreshed and restored."

"Which I too experienced, but with a peculiar absence of memory until later. Did that happen to her as well?"

"After a particularly powerful experience, it did. She kept detailed notes on many of her sessions. They are in a box in the hidden library. It would be a project to read them, but you are welcome to continue where I left off. The ones I have read are indicated by a check mark in the upper right-hand corner.

"You haven't read them all?" I asked.

"No."

"Why did you stop?"

"They were difficult to read. Painful, in fact." Stanley paused.

He looked away from us and out the window. "I so admired and respected her, but over time much of what she wrote became the ramblings of someone I considered not of sound mind. It was too much. With each one, my image of her grew more tarnished and more ghastly. I blamed myself for her addiction. The signs were there to see, but I chose to indulge her rather than put a stop to it. I decided I must live with that, and I have. What I couldn't live with was my growing sense of pity and disdain for her, and in no small measure for myself."

He took a sip of his drink and looked at us again.

"The truth is I chose to stop reading them. It was too soon after her death when I started that project. Since that time, I have better reconciled the two images in my mind. The woman who was brave, beautiful, and too good for this world, and the other one: a woman driven mad by dark visions and all-consuming nightmares. Nonetheless, I have never managed to find the time to restart the project. Perhaps I never will. I would be grateful if you both took it up."

Johnny looked at me. "I think that is something we should pursue. Which reminds me, I haven't had a chance to peruse the diary either. We must get to that tonight no matter what."

I had forgotten about the diary. Johnny and I had another late night ahead of us.

"No rest for the wicked," I said.

"None at all," said Johnny. "By the way, Stanley, I'm glad you were familiar with the effects of the tincture, because I'm not sure what I would have done without your assistance and calm."

Stanley smiled. "It's all part of the service. No extra charge. Now our time is limited. Why don't we begin by you both relating to me what happened last night as best you can?"

Johnny gave a succinct account of the summoning, including finding Alice's notes, his decision to use of the *Brugmansia* tincture, the bargain he made, and the shattering of the figurine.

279

When he was finished, Stanley nodded and asked that I relate what happened, which I did. Stanley leaned back in his chair and looked at us.

"Thank you for giving me this information. That was a night to remember, or not, as the case may be. I have several questions, and I am sure you have some as well. To start, I am pleased to know that the figurine finally turned up. I have been worried about it for years. When did you discover it?

"Robert found it hidden among the boxes when we first arrived and looked through the cellar," Johnny answered.

"I see. It must have somehow slipped through. Objects like that have a life and mind of their own. That was a dangerous thing to use. Her ladyship remarked that the figurine was probably the most powerful object she had ever held in her hands. Where is it now?"

"The remains are in a shoe box in my closet," continued Johnny.

"I would move them to the repository, but they can remain where they are for now. Whether its power shattered, I'm not sure. Perhaps whatever you encountered absorbed it. If that was the case, I should think that was more than enough to compensate for the additional question, but..." Stanley looked at me. "Whatever it was seemed to think that you received something as well. It demanded additional compensation to offset what it lost. Such have a reputation for being good at assessing the fairness of a bargain, provided they come out ahead to some extent."

"That is something I have a question about," I said. "Since last night, I have acquired an intuitive part that is quite astute and perceptive. It talks to me and gives me insights. For lack of a better question, what does it mean?"

"It could mean almost anything, depending on how you use what you received. Just exercise good sense and don't necessarily take what you get as gospel. One has to remember the source. Understand its strengths and weaknesses. But remember: you received a gift. To not accept it can be just as dangerous. After all, Johnny had to strike a bargain for you. Value and use it accordingly. I would, of course, be interested in what you discover. On a related topic: the bargain…but before we get there, let's back up a few steps. We are making a presumption that something other than a drug-induced hallucination took place. It's easy to jump to conclusions, so I wish to know what you think occurred? In essence, did you meet your demon, Johnny, or not?"

"That's the crux of the matter, isn't it? Nothing magically appeared, which was what I wanted. Nonetheless, something happened. Whether it was the result of the tincture, I don't know. A few of our guests coincidentally had some peculiar dreams. Is it proof? No. The real issue for me is that I made a promise to someone or something last night, only I'm not sure what I promised. It is decidedly ambiguous. To add to my unease, last night was terrifying in ways I had not imagined possible, which makes me view the promise as significant and potentially threatening. Stanley, what do you think?"

"Before we examine the specifics, as a general principle, a promise is a promise. If what you experienced was fantasy, then who received the promise? No other parties being present, I would say the promise was to each other. If what you experienced was not hallucination, then it was to a third party and all that entails. Regardless of the actual identity, you made a promise."

"I suppose so," said Johnny. "I'm stuck with having made it."

"You are, but I would not dwell solely on the consequences. Rather, let's review the information you received. You asked if her ladyship was murdered and the response was 'The Eye of the Moon was closed.' *Eye of the Moon* is a significant moniker that I have not heard in a long time. It could refer to her ladyship, since you were asking about her, but it could just as well refer more formally to Wadjet, the patron goddess of one of the great oracles of the ancient world located at Buto, in lower Egypt. She was known as the Green One and was often depicted as a cobra. She performed a protective function. If we think in terms of her ladyship, the phrase *was closed* is also ambiguous. Someone closing her eyes could mean someone killed her or she killed herself. If the eye refers to that of the goddess, she might have been asleep and saw nothing or she was simply unable to protect her ladyship. In keeping with such responses, the interpretation can be viewed in any number of different ways.

"The second part was 'Tell him, find him out, and keep him.' Again, *him* was not defined.

"I have found more than once that such utterances, if they are true, require a future context rather than that of the present state of affairs to make sense."

"In other words," said Johnny, "a whole lot of nothing, but then again maybe not. I suppose that's typical."

Stanley looked at Johnny. He seemed more tired than I had seen him. "It is," he said. "Sometimes one just has to live long enough to find out. The words will likely make more sense given time. In the meanwhile, I would suggest reviewing the notes and the diary. I would like to know myself what they say, but I do not have the heart to do so. At the very least, your experiment has livened up a potentially boring weekend with a little matter of life and death."

"Did you just make a joke?" asked Johnny. "Stanley, you're slipping. You're letting your human side show."

"Well, one must maintain a sense of humor. Sometimes that's all we can do."

"Speaking of humor," I said, "whatever did you say to Malcolm at lunch?"

"Ah yes. Malcolm Ault is a hypochondriac. Half his suitcase is filled with remedies. I discreetly mentioned to him that the baroness had a particularly stubborn skin condition of an intimate nature. He cooled off rather quickly. I make it a point to be familiar with the habits of our guests so that I might serve them better and give them a memorable visit."

As he said that, we heard the crunch of gravel from the driveway.

Johnny said, "That must be Maw and her minion. Memories are made of such things."

Any possible chance of boredom evaporated in an instant.

3 8

The chauffer stood by the limousine's door as the entire household hastily gathered outside in the driveway in welcome. She was, after all, Mrs. Leland, John Senior's mother and Johnny's grandmother. Even the von Hofmanstals and Malcolm Ault were in attendance. I had to hand it to her — she loved an entrance.

To Johnny and his family, she was known simply as Maw, a nickname she had acquired well before my time. Because I was not family, and because the word conjured up the image of a large mouth filled with teeth, I called her Mrs. Leland.

In other circles, those made up of various board members of several large multinationals, she was referred to in more disparaging terms. She was dubbed the Crone. She struck fear in some, irritation in most, and apoplexy in the remainder. Her reputation on the street was legendary, bolstered by a steady stream of rumor and innuendo, of which Johnny and I had heard many.

One concerned a singularly vitriolic board meeting that left a member dead. Some say from an aneurism brought on by an excess of exasperation. Others say on account of him choking on his own tongue and that death was the result of overreaching and subsequent asphyxiation. Whichever was true, the poor man rose up suddenly from his seat midsentence, turned purple, and after a series of hideous convulsions died on the carpet in front of the boardroom's double doors. While others looked on in shock, the Crone stepped over him without so much as a downward glance as she left the proceedings — her majority secured with the death of the dissenting member. Whether that story was apocryphal or not, all agreed that as a boardroom brawler, she had few equals. She gave no quarter, showed no mercy, and held her own counsel.

If she played with ferocity in the business world, she played with equal verve and passion in familial matters. Family was business after all.

Through marital death and adept administration, Maw had amassed a fortune and corresponding economic power that rivaled that of a small country. Much of this was hidden from public view by a complex labyrinth of trusts and legal entities, the total value of which was a closely guarded secret known only to one person.

Who would ultimately take the reins of this extraordinary fortune when she passed was an open question that was much debated, even on the corners of Broad and Wall. The two most eligible candidates were her son, John Senior, and his half-sister, Bonnie Leland. Banks, accounting firms, investment houses, and all who wished to partake in trickle-down economics allied behind one of the two contestants. It was winner-take-all, and whosoever backed the victor would be amply rewarded.

But the Crone was full of surprises. If neither contestant lived up to her expectations, she was quite content to pass the baton to a third, a large foundation of her own making. The foundation existed as a shell for now, but that could be changed with the stroke of a pen, a possibility that was brought to bear if the contestants failed to compete with the appropriate effort.

Financial stocks took a beating the day this rumor was leaked, and the decline continued for several more until a highly placed but anonymous source asserted that, as a whole, the existing financial system was sufficiently robust to handle such an eventuality.

Order restored, all affected settled down to await the outcome. They were still waiting.

In the meanwhile, John Senior and his half-sister maneuvered, schemed, and plotted. John Senior had the lead in financial acumen, but Bonnie had managed to get close to her mother by being her constant companion. She had her mother's ear, which neutralized John Senior's apparent edge. She had taken full advantage of this position. In a recent coup de main, she had managed to secure from her mother the promise in writing that should she inherit, she would have the Fifth Avenue apartment and the Dodge family would have to vacate immediately. This move had not gone unnoticed by the Dodge household and had yet to be answered by Mr. Dodge. All awaited a response, but so far nothing. Johnny and I speculated that perhaps this little get-together might have something to do with that. The fact that Bonnie was officially invited to Rhinebeck was unusual enough to cause us to pay attention.

Once everyone had assembled, the chauffeur, after receiving instructions from inside, opened the door. First came Bonnie, elegantly dressed in a dark shirt and skirt. She sported needle-sharp black patent-leather high heels. On her right hand was a diamond the size of a small egg. She pushed the chauffer away, so she could hand out her mother personally. Her opening gambit displayed her privileged position while hopefully gaining her mother's approval by offering assistance.

Of this, I was not so sure. Maw demanded obedience while

despising those who were overly fawning and obsequious. The boundary between the two was a constantly moving target that was not easily discovered until after the fact.

Maw slapped her hand away and barked something at her that was unintelligible. Bonnie leaped back as if struck and contorted her face into a grim smile to cover her shock. Gambit declined. Her eyes flicked to her half-brother, who showed no response to her setback.

At last, Maw was out. She stood before us, arms akimbo, cloaked in a full-length mink coat open at the front, revealing a light-blue denim work shirt and khaki pants. She wore roper boots of dull brown that were shiny at the front and sides from picking up stirrups. Her weathered face looked us over. Her gray hair was caught up in a ponytail held by an ordinary plastic hair clip. She gave the assembly a nod and said to Stanley, "I'd like some tea in the drawing room."

Without another word, she marched toward the house as the door was quickly opened to let her pass. There was no infirmity that I could see for a woman who was close to eighty.

Bonnie reached into the car to grab her mother's purse and her own, while the rank and file made our way inside. Harry and the chauffeur unloaded piles of luggage. I was last to the front door. As I watched from the steps, Bonnie managed to snag her heel on something in the driveway. It broke with a snap. She wobbled and almost fell. She looked down at the offending shoe and started cursing. She took it off and hurled it away. She took off the other, and it followed. In stockinged feet, she limped rapidly toward the entrance, muttering to herself. The gravel had sharp edges, making her progress painful. I went down to ask if she required any assistance, but she looked at me like I was something the cat had coughed up and hissed, "Get out of my fucking way." She limped up the stairs and into the house. It was a rough start. I had Mr. Dodge ahead on points, but it was early yet.

39

I followed the group into the drawing room. There were ten of us — actually, nine. Bonnie was trying to find another pair of shoes. I last saw her chasing Simon up the stairs to get at one of her bags. In the meanwhile, introductions were being made. Maw was seated in a chair with John Senior standing behind her with Anne and Johnny beside him. She had just been introduced to the baron, who gave a bow from the waist. Maw gave him a nod, enough to let him know that in spite of his title, her reputation and her wealth gave her a slight edge, but not so little as to mean he was not without standing. The baron introduced his family. Maw was charmed. Malcolm Ault gave a bow as well. Because of his height, he seemed unnaturally servile, but what else could he do? Maw gave a neutral nod, and then it was my turn.

"So," she said, "We meet again. It's been some time. You and Johnny are all grown up and still friends, I see. I suppose I had something to do with that."

"Yes, you did. It's good to see you."

She gave me one of her looks. Her gray eyes were now watery with age, but they missed little. It was rumored she had the gift of sight. I, for one, believed it.

"We'll talk later. You and I have some things to discuss."

I was dismissed.

"Where's my tea?" she called out, as Stanley appeared with the tray.

"Stanley, you devil. I was about to start yelling, but there you are just in time."

"My pleasure, ma'am."

She turned to her son. "I'd take him over Bonnie any day. Now, Johnny, where's that dog of yours I've heard so much about?"

Johnny looked about and moved toward the dining room. "I'll get him."

As he left, there was a jiggling of the main doors between the drawing room and the foyer, as if someone was having trouble with the handles. Stanley opened it smoothly, just as Bonnie was about to use her shoulder to try and force it. She stumbled into the room shoulder first, tripped, and fell headlong onto the carpet. Stanley got her up quickly, but she was quite wobbly as he supported her.

"It's your heel, ma'am," said Stanley in a neutral tone. She looked down, and sure enough, one of the heels looked crooked.

"Fuck," said Bonnie. "What is it about this place and heels?"

"If you give it to me, I'm sure we'll be able to repair it. I also took the liberty of recovering the pair from the driveway. They will be fixed as well."

Maw cackled and then spoke to her coldly. "Stop acting like a buffoon. It's embarrassing."

Bonnie, once again in stockinged feet and several inches shorter, sniffed at the rebuke and announced loudly, "Well, everyone, since I haven't had the courtesy of an introduction, I am Bonnie Leland, Mrs. Leland's daughter."

At that moment, Robert trotted jauntily into the room, as if he was up for Best in Show. Instinctively, he marched up to Maw, who clapped her hands with delight. Johnny was right behind him. The baron retreated to a corner to be as far away as possible, while Bonnie moved to the bar, upstaged once again. She fixed herself a stiff one and knocked it back in one gulp.

I wandered over to the window as Maw and Robert looked each other over and approved of what they saw. Animals felt good in her presence. She soothed them, commanded them, and they obeyed. Robert sat down in front of her, content to be fawned over and petted. Bonnie looked on with icy hate. She noticed me looking at her and scowled in my direction. We knew each other but rarely spoke even when in the same room. I avoided her if I could.

She was a younger version of her mother but without the commanding strength of personality. Maw had many defects, but she had a presence, shrewdness, and directness that was appealing. Bonnie simply had the faults. She was peevish, vindictive, manipulative, and above all, insecure. It was this insecurity that drove her to cut others down at every opportunity, while trying to make herself more formidable and imposing. I felt for her in spite of my dislike. Being Maw's shadow and constant companion could not be easy, but Bonnie was driven by a higher purpose. She was willing to sacrifice her present for the chance of becoming one of the most powerful women in the world in the future. She made sure she was indispensable and therefore deserving of the majority of the inheritance. No task was too degrading, humiliating, or underhanded, if she moved closer to accomplishing her goal.

My intuitive self noted that the more self-sacrifice and debasement she submitted to, the more she blamed her half-brother for having forced her into that compromising position. The humiliations she endured stripped her of her dignity and left her filled with a self-loathing that she projected onto others. She hid a cunning intelligence, motivated by an unrelenting thirst for revenge, retribution, and greed — an ugly but nonetheless powerful combination. She had a plan. I agreed. My intuitive self also noted that because I disliked her intensely, Bonnie and I might have much more in common than I had considered. Not a nice analysis but probably accurate. I would need to look at that more closely. As a final point, it posited that Maw was smart enough to know that once she declared in favor of her daughter, the mother's days were numbered. My intuitive part had a cynical side.

"Woolgathering?" It was Bruni. We hadn't spoken since she stormed off in a huff.

"Observing."

"That daughter of hers is a bit of a loose cannon. She's been in touch with my father. They're up to something. Thought you'd like to know."

"Thank you for telling me. There is a game afoot. I just don't know what it is."

"Perhaps it would be worth finding out. By the way, I apologize for my outburst. I'm not usually like that."

"Apology accepted. Perhaps we should start again."

"I would like that very much."

"I would too."

The informal get-together was breaking up. Maw wanted to rest before dinner. Drinks were at six, black-tie.

"See you for drinks," I said, "and thank you. I hate when people are mad at me."

"I doubt they could remain so for long. See you later. We'll talk some more."

John Senior and the baron made for the library, while the ladies retreated upstairs to get ready. Johnny came over to me.

"Well, that went splendidly," said Johnny. "That Robert can be a real ladies' man. He had ole Maw wrapped around his paw in seconds. He put Bonnie in her place too, which really pissed her off. Round one definitely goes to the home team, but we have work to do. How about we start our next research project?"

"Yes, we must. For a quiet stay in the country, we seem to be extraordinarily busy."

"It's our lot in life. No dithering. There's not a moment to lose."

One thing for sure, Johnny was still Johnny. He went from one project to the next with all possible speed. I followed him and Robert up the stairs for what seemed like the umpteenth time.

40

J ohnny pulled out the Alice's diary from its leather case and
handed it to me.

"You start reading. I'm heading downstairs to the
repository. I'll return the strange book and the shoe box in
exchange for Alice's session notes. I'll be right back."

He and Robert disappeared down the stairs as I opened the
diary. The pages were written in a clear hand, which meant I
would have minimal difficulty deciphering what she wrote, but I
doubted I would have time to read it all now. The diary began just
after she decided to take up her search for the people and discover
a means to combat her recurring nightmares. It ended several
weeks before her death. She began:

To those that come after:

If you are reading this, I am dead.

Will I be watching you, reading over your shoulder? Perhaps I will
only be a thought kept alive for three generations until the last person

who has seen me and spoken with me is gone, at which point I will have
vanished completely from living memory, and I will be no more.

Take comfort in knowing that in death, I have the answers.

Today, I have none. I am alive and have only questions and my
boundless curiosity to keep me company. A new day and new vistas
await me. I tingle with anticipation.

She was horrible with dates. She either didn't like them or never remembered to write them down. The diary was laid out in a sequence of places and events. I decided to focus on two elements: passages about those who might have interacted with her adversely, such as Lord Bromley, and unusual patterns as I came across them, such as codes or anything out of the ordinary. I noted she often wrote whole sections in hieroglyphics or hieratic without any further translation. At other times, she wrote in the demotic script of the later period. I could not translate these. For now, I would have to assume they were immaterial.

I was halfway through scanning the diary when Johnny and Robert returned.

"Anything?" asked Johnny.

"Too early to tell. You know, she never dated a thing. She just wrote the location, like Karnak Temple Complex, Luxor, followed by her observations. In the Karnak entry, which is a fairly typical example, there is a section that includes pages of hieroglyphs that she copied from the temple's walls, another in English on the Precinct of Mut, notes on the drunken Sekhmet festival, and then details on the excavation in progress, which are pretty dry and technical."

"Drunken Sekhmet festival? I like the sound of that."

"According to this, the goddess Sekhmet was slaughtering humanity until Ra, who was the initiator of the massacre to begin with, felt pity and wanted Sekmet to stop. She couldn't, or wouldn't. The ever-resourceful Ra came up with a bright idea: get the goddess drunk on tons of red beer, which she would mistake for human blood. This he did. She drank and drank. She got so wasted, she gave up any thoughts of carnage by passing out. Problem solved. The deed was commemorated annually in a festival that was attended by the temple's priestesses and the local population, who reenacted the affair by getting so drunk, they couldn't walk either."

"You've got to love those ancient Egyptians."

"The next day must have been hellish. I would be interested in the population figures nine months later, but they're not mentioned."

"You would be. Anyway, keep going. We have another hour before we have to make our way downstairs."

Johnny began to go through the notes from the box while I went back to my reading.

Alice jotted lines about parties in London and research projects at the British Museum.

She reported on the shaman practices of South America and how she was impressed with the use of native plants to open doors to the spirit world.

I have finally come across a means to explore the world of the people. The use of exotic plants will facilitate my interaction with those I seek. It is possible at last.

She described plants, practices, and preparations in detail, noting the effects of each, *Brugmansia* and its preparation being her preferred method for making contact.

Lord Bromley was mentioned several times.

I saw him in London from a distance. Rumors surround him like a fog. He was engaged, and then he wasn't...

He has been buying up various copies and originals of Egyptian papyri, including Books of the Dead. Coincidence, or is there a connection?

Stanley had covered most of what she reported regarding Arthur Blaine and leaving him in the jungle.

Malcolm Ault was mentioned several times as attending various parties.

Johnny and I were mentioned as well. She described us as "way too bright for their ages, but oh so cute." Johnny would love that.

My parents were mentioned, along with the baron, but only in social contexts.

After an hour, Johnny interrupted my reading: "How goes it?"

"Interesting but not exactly enlightening. Excavations are described in great detail. So far nothing really eye-opening, other than Alice refers to M. quite often toward the end. I wager she might be a woman. The first name has not been revealed."

"The famous recipient of the letter that was never delivered. Did M. have anything to do with her death, I wonder?"

"Unknown for now. Ault seems to be a steady presence in her narrative. Maybe you should ask him what he knows about her?"

"It's a shot in the dark, but I'll give it a try."

"How are your session notes coming?"

"I've read a few, but I see what Stanley means. It's heavy going. In a nutshell, she hoped for answers from the spirit world, but the search proved more frustrating than she'd imagined. Her main difficulty was that she could recall only a small portion of the sessions the next morning, and if the dose was too large, she couldn't remember a thing. She tried taking notes during them, but they were either illegible or made no sense at all. Occasionally, she succeeded in making a connection. I noted one in particular. Here's what she wrote:

"'They, whoever they might be, are not the ones I have met before. They see no reason to answer my questions to my satisfaction. They showed me things: places, people, children mostly, but there is no link that I can grasp between the images and the answers that I seek. The dead, if that is what they are, have obviously different concerns than mine. I can't make them understand. Perhaps, they cannot make <u>me</u> understand. I am frustrated and perplexed, yet I feel I am close, closer at least than I was before.'"

"Creepy."

"Yes, I wonder if we're following a journey into madness, like Stanley said?"

"It's possible, but there might be moments of clarity buried in one of them."

"I hope so, but that's as far as either of us can go for now. It's time to get dressed for dinner."

"Right you are."

41

We made it downstairs in plenty of time. I had borrowed one of Johnny's tuxedos, which fit reasonably well. We deposited Robert in Stanley's office and passed through the kitchen, which was in a flurry of activity. Johnny and I quickly retreated to the drawing room. The drapes were shut against the night. Cristal champagne was available in buckets of ice. I have never been one to pass up a glass. I poured Johnny one too.

"Cheers, my friend," I said. We sipped.

"Amazing stuff. Nothing quite like it," commented Johnny. "Now, we await the rest of the assembly."

We didn't have to wait long. Malcolm Ault, also in black-tie, came down with Bruni. She wore a sensational low-cut, midnight-blue, full-length evening gown, probably Dior. The color complemented the paleness of her skin, the blueness of her eyes, and the shiny blackness of her hair. A large indigo star sapphire hung from a platinum chain around her neck. It rested just above her cleavage. I managed to tear my eyes away as I poured them both champagne. Malcolm thanked me as Johnny dragged him over to the window to grill him about Alice. Bruni stood beside me.

"Nice rock," I said as she took a sip.

"Thank you. You like it?"

"Immensely."

"You can touch it, if you want."

"Tempting, but remember, we're starting over."

"We are, which is why you're allowed."

I reached out. Some things are just irresistible. The star seemed almost luminescent within the blueness of the stone.

"Very nice. You can wear that any time."

"I'm glad you approve. Some news for you. Both Miss Leland and her mother received envelopes by courier this afternoon."

"Do you think they are important?"

"I do. The games are about to begin, and we have a ringside seat."

She took my arm. "Let's go over and look at the painting."

We moved over to stand in front of the Constable.

"You have more news?" I said.

"Perhaps. Do you recall Dodge Capital doing a capital raise a couple of years ago?"

"I remember reading something about that. It was a debt issue, I think, underwritten by a New York bank."

"That's correct. That loan was recently sold to a single client, who apparently paid through the nose."

"That's interesting."

"Coincidentally, I reviewed the bank's offer last week, before I passed it on to my father. We are always looking for deals, and that particular bank shopped it to us on an all-or-none basis, since the offering was small by most corporate lending standards. I called back the next day to see if it was still available, but I was told it had already been taken down at a considerable premium."

"I thought that one of the reasons people went to that bank for financing was to prevent that sort of thing."

"Yes, but there are provisions usually in the fine print that allow them to sell their loans, provided they still service them. As a general practice, they don't."

"Why that loan?"

"I don't know, but there's more. It's callable under certain circumstances."

"Such as?"

"Immediate payment can be demanded if Dodge's Assets Under Management fall below a certain level. Secondly, there is a date coming up next month that allows the bank to review the loan. If the bank still owned it, there would be no concern. In private hands, it's another matter. The new owner, according to the loan documents, could quite possibly demand immediate payment, having asserted they reviewed the loan and want out. Having to pay earlier than expected might put a considerable liquidity squeeze on Dodge Capital. The firm could fight the demand in court and probably win; however, that might prove problematic. The legal battle would create publicity, and clients get nervous when that kind of thing happens. They might want to move assets first and ask questions later. If enough of them do so, the Assets Under Management provision would become active regardless, calling the loan for sure."

"Who picked it up?"

"I don't know, but it was definitely shopped and bought."

"Sounds like someone's up to something."

"There's more...Perhaps at dinner, depending on the seating, we could discuss it?"

"Good idea. I'd like that, and in case I didn't mention it, you *do* look stunning tonight."

"I'm glad you approve."

Anne and John Senior had just entered along with the baron

and Elsa. Both ladies looked elegant in black evening gowns. Anne wore a Cassini. Elsa sported her diamonds and enough cleavage to probably have Malcolm thinking twice about her supposed skin condition. I looked over at him and Johnny. The tall man glanced in Elsa's direction. Bruni was still beside me.

I asked her, "How well do you know Malcolm Ault?"

"Not that well. He's attended a fair number of parties I've been to and seems to know most everyone."

"He seems a bit of an odd bird."

"He has his quirks, but he's pretty harmless, as far as I know."

We were interrupted by the entrance of Maw and Bonnie. Maw always wore black when it came to evening wear, and tonight was no exception. A fine necklace of large emeralds and diamonds encircled her neck. She leaned on an ebony cane with a silver head of a dog with bared teeth. In contrast to this afternoon, she looked a bit worn. My guess was that the change was connected with the courier's package Bruni had mentioned.

If Maw seemed a bit subdued, Bonnie was in high spirits in spite of wearing a knee-length dress of plain beige to a black-tie dinner. Her choice of shoes must have influenced her decision. She had gone through two black pairs this afternoon, and Stanley would not have had a chance to see to the repairs before dinner, even with several additional staff. In spite of her doubtful dress choice, she oscillated from elation to suppressed irritation. Her laugh boomed across the room as she grabbed a glass of champagne. Her face looked determined as she concentrated on the speaker, in this case the baron. After a few moments, her eyes moved about as if watching for something that might catch her unaware. She was guzzling champagne, one glass after the other. Maw chatted with others and occasionally looked over at her daughter with embarrassed frustration. If Bonnie felt confident, then her plans must be progressing, and that could only mean ill for the Dodge family.

With all the guests gathered, the additional help circulated trays of Beluga caviar on points of white toast. Others poured more Cristal. Bruni and I ate several before we moved over to where Johnny and the tall man were standing.

"I understand there is to be an announcement," said Malcolm.

"An announcement?" all three of us asked at once.

"Don't know what it's about, but Miss Leland will have the floor is all I know."

. "That can't be good," said Johnny. "We'd better drink up while we can." Johnny moved off to speak with his parents about this development. He had a peculiar look on his face.

I turned to get a refill and almost bumped into the baron.

"Allow me," I said. I filled his glass and poured the rest of the bottle into my own. "Miss Leland seems to be in a strange mood," I commented to the baron.

"Yes, she is, but then, she's been at work for quite some time. Her plans are almost at fruition, I would imagine."

"You are aware of them?"

"I'm aware of many things."

"Would you care to enlighten me?"

"No" was all he said before he moved away.

"He still doesn't like you," said Bruni.

"No, I don't suppose he does. I try to make an effort, nonetheless. He won't let it go, whatever it is."

"Sometimes the past won't let you, no matter how much you try. How about some more champagne?"

"Absolutely. I get the feeling we're going to need several glasses before the night is done."

"I think so too, and thank you, by the way."

"For what?"

"For making the effort with my father and giving me a second chance."

"Bruni, you can have as many as you want."

"Thank you, Percy. I do hope we sit together this evening."

We ate caviar, chatted, and drank more champagne, happy to be together. Before we could wander over to Johnny and see what he was able to find out about the announcement, Stanley announced that dinner was served. We moved to the dining room to take our places at the table.

42

_____

Table seating was assigned as usual. John Senior and Anne took their places at the ends of the table. The baron was to John Senior's left and Maw to his right. Johnny helped her get seated and took his place between his grandmother and Bruni to his right. I was next down the line. I pulled out Bruni's chair. Her dress rustled as she sat down and scooted in. Any tension between us had magically dissipated since we had decided to start over, and what remained for me was a surprising happiness in her company. I was quite sure she felt the same. She was intelligent, personable, and tonight, with the possible exception of her mother, the most beautiful woman I had ever met. She smiled at me in thanks as I sat down.

"Someone heard our prayers," she whispered once I was seated. "We're sitting next to each other."

"They did, indeed." I answered.

Across the table from me, and seated next to Anne, was Elsa. She gave me a dazzling smile. I gave her a wink. To Elsa's right was the tall man. He looked a touch nervous, which I felt was justified, knowing Elsa's love for making mischief. He fiddled with his tie. Between Malcolm and the baron sat Bonnie. She looked only slightly miffed. I was not sure whether this was because she was not seated at the head of the table or because Maw was across from her and temporarily out of her clutches. She had tried to make a fuss when she had found out her seating assignment, but the baron had smoothly pulled out her chair before she could fly off the handle once again. He was a baron after all, and she couldn't very well say no. She fluttered at his attention. I had to hand it to him. He had a certain something that was hard to put into words. I imagined Napoleon had had it too.

The first course was a tuna tartare over Asian pear slices with a wasabi sauce. Champagne glasses were filled, and the table grew silent as the guests savored the first course. Dagmar aimed to impress from the start, which she did. With the beginning course completed, conversation resumed.

Bruni whispered to me, "My God, that was good. Wherever did our hosts find her?"

"It was Stanley. He lured her with his Scottish charm. His offer of marriage I'm sure helped. I heard that her previous employer became an ascetic shortly thereafter. Nothing could match her cuisine, so he settled for abstinence instead."

"I could begin to think with that. How long has she been here?"

"Since Johnny and I were knee-high. We never knew how good we had it until the day we went away to boarding school. She seems to have improved with age."

Bonnie's laugh brayed irritatingly across the table in response to something the baron said.

"With several courses to go, let's hope she paces herself," Bruni whispered.

"I doubt it. She has her announcement to think about, and Dutch courage may be what she needs."

"Guesses?"

"Nothing good for our hosts…"

I was interrupted by Bonnie standing up and knocking a glass with the edge of her spoon. She swayed slightly.

"I want to make my 'nouncement…now!"

The table grew quiet.

Before she could go on, Maw interrupted her, "Don't be so rude. Sit down until after dinner."

"I can be rude because I can, and because I can, I will — so stuff it. I've been under your thumb far too long. I won't endure another minute. Take a back seat. I'm finally in charge." She sneered at her mother and then turned to the head of the table.

"Hear that, brother dear? I got the whole enchilaaaada. I'm taking you to the cleaners. This house, your business, your life: they're mine. I've lived for this moment. It's so delicious. Speaking of delicious, you'll throw in the cook too, or you'll get nothin'… Nothiiiing! Come to think of it, why let you have a cent? I'll just take it all. Who cares? I don't, so put *that* in your pipe and smoke it!"

She belched, sat down, and reached for her champagne glass.

The table was silent.

John Senior looked at his half-sister and said, "Really? How nice. Aren't you perhaps being a bit premature?"

"Premature?" Bonnie giggled. "Premature? Nope." The *p* made an odd popping sound as she said it. "It's a done deal. Me and my pal here," she said, patting the baron's shoulder. "Read 'em and weep."

She smiled triumphantly. Her eyes rolled back in her head and flickered a few times, and then she slipped beneath the table. Stanley, Simon, and one of the maids were on her in an instant. Stanley got up and went over to Maw and said something while a limp Bonnie was maneuvered from beneath the table and out of the dining room. Her feet dragged behind her. One shoe fell off halfway to the door. Stanley followed the procession, picked up the wayward pump, and closed the doors.

There was a stunned silence.

"Well," said Johnny to the table, "more for the rest of us."

Everyone started talking at once.

I heard Elsa comment to Anne, "You know, I just love it here. Everything is so spontaneous and unexpected. I can't wait to see what happens next."

She didn't have long to wait. There was a fumbling at the door from the drawing room, and Bonnie was back. The door opened, slammed shut, and then opened again as Bonnie tried to pry her way back into the dining room while the help attempted to drag her back. I saw her head for a moment. Her eyes were wild, and she was breathing heavily. She was trying to say something, but nothing was coming out. The help renewed their struggle, and the door slammed shut once again.

Elsa clapped her hands. "See what I mean?"

I looked past Bruni at Johnny. Johnny was smiling to himself and sipping his champagne. He was getting a little too free with that tincture he had found. I was quite certain of it. I'd have to talk to him about that.

43

There were a few moments of quiet before a muffled wail rose from the next room that could have come from something caged. The cry started low and rose to a pitch I was not sure I had ever heard before. It ceased abruptly, and there was silence once again. The door to the drawing room remained shut and unmoving.

The company sighed. The second course, I was fairly certain, would be delayed until Stanley and the rest of his crew returned from dealing with Bonnie. In the meantime, we waited.

I watched the baron shake his head at a question by John Senior while Maw tut-tutted to Johnny. Anne looked at her husband at the other end of the table and sipped her champagne, while Malcolm clenched and unclenched his napkin.

I watched him lean ever so slowly toward Elsa. She was playing games by speaking in a lower and lower voice, requiring him to lean toward her to catch what she was saying. He was bent sideways from the waist like the leaning tower of Pisa, presenting her with his left ear while looking straight ahead. I was fairly certain he didn't dare look at her directly for fear that he might be caught glimpsing at more than just her face.

Bruni watched him too and whispered to me, "Mother can be so wicked. She'll bite his ear. You watch."

"Really?"

"Once at a dinner party, I saw her do the same thing. Her partner wouldn't look at her and leaned over farther and farther, until she suddenly nibbled his ear. The poor man lost it. He stood up, knocked over his chair, and fled the table, never to return. I am quite sure he thought my father would skewer him before we had finished dessert. Papa does have a fearsome reputation. Mother thought it was hilarious."

"You have quite the family."

"Tell me about it. What about yours?"

"Not much to tell. I've seen them only on occasion since I can remember."

"I met your parents once some years ago at a dinner party in Paris. They seemed quite dazzling — larger than life."

"To me as well. I don't know them, really. They're usually going off to other places. Have been for years."

"Does that make you sad?"

"In a way, but there are compensations. The Dodges have been very good to me, but to answer your question truthfully: yes, the subject makes me sad."

Bruni touched my hand for a moment. "I'm sorry I brought it up."

"Don't be. I'm used to it by now, or fairly used to it. Let's talk of other things."

"Of course. I said I had more news."

"Yes, you did."

"I learned Miss Leland has been busy trying to have her mother ruled incompetent by the courts. She isn't, of course, but there are several members among the many boards of directors she sits on who feel the daughter might be more pliable and open to their ideas. There has been an effort to solicit several doctors' reports to that effect."

"It might work, but Mrs. Leland could simply counter that with reports of her own, unless Bonnie was able to convince her mother to relinquish control and stick to her dogs and horses. Judging from the performance tonight, Bonnie must think she has that well in hand."

"I think so too. Blackmail of some sort is my suspicion, but what exactly I have no idea."

"We all have skeletons hanging about. Mrs. Leland is probably no exception. You seem to know a fair amount about her."

"I did some checking on both of them after the offer disappeared so fast."

"You have suspicions?"

"I do. It seemed contrived to me, like someone put the offer up because they had to, but the sale had already been prearranged."

"Someone has been busy."

We were interrupted by the arrival of Stanley and his team. Stanley quietly briefed Mr. Dodge and Maw. The table as a whole leaned in their direction, but Stanley had mastered the art of communicating in a voice so low that we heard nothing. He straightened up and, accompanied by his helpers, marched back into the kitchen. Anne gave her husband an inquiring look, which John answered with a shake of his head, indicating there was nothing to worry about.

After a few moments, the team reappeared, bearing soup. Tonight's was a simple consommé with brunoised seasonal vegetables. Wineglasses were filled, and once again silence reigned.

Course followed course in rapid succession among the glitter of candlelight on silver. Sole for the fish, and beef tenderloin for the main course, interspersed with salads and small slivers of fruit.

Dessert was Dagmar's signature pound cake with vanilla ice cream.

Anne announced that it was time to pass through to the next room, and dinner came to an end. Bruni whispered to me as we walked out, "Catch me before you retire. I'd like to slip outside and see the night. The moon will be up."

We separated, and I stepped closer to Johnny as the men made their way to the library.

I asked quietly, so only he could hear, "How did you manage to slip her that tincture?"

He smiled. "You noticed."

"Of course. Her expression told me. Stanley, I am sure, guessed."

"More than guessed. He suggested it."

I stopped short and turned him to face me. "You're kidding."

"Truth be told, I'm not sure what I gave her. I went over to find out about the announcement from the folks, when he slipped me a small bottle. Four drops, is what he said, no more, no less. I doctored Bonnie's drink and managed to hand it to her. The rest was easy. She was swilling the champagne and drank it all in one go."

"What do you think it was?"

"Not a clue, but I must admit, when it comes to that woman, I heartily agreed with whatever he had in mind. He bought us some time, I think. I mean to see him in a bit and get more information just to make sure."

"Bruni gave me some as well." I recounted what she had told me.

"Makes sense. I wonder what Bonnie has on Maw. It must be pretty big. Unless, of course, Maw is toying with her to see how far she'll go."

"That crossed my mind too. She's crafty. Your father was pretty calm."

"He rarely shows his thoughts, as you know. Remember our poker lessons?"

"Don't remind me."

John Senior over the years had taken great pleasure in fleecing us out of our allowances on a regular basis, particularly over Christmas holidays, when we were flush with tens and twenties. He called it "tuition."

"Did you get anything out of the tall one?" I asked.

"M. is a woman: Marianne Thoreau. She and Alice were close, but Marianne disappeared shortly before her death. She has been seen occasionally in the company of Lord B., if that tells you something."

"Betrayed, do you think?"

"Not enough information. Let's smoke a cigar and drink some good liquor. Things are too weird not to. I need a break."

"Amen."

We joined the others in the library.

44

"She can't hold her liquor," the baron was saying as we entered. "I dislike men who can't and sloppy women even more."

John Senior and Hugo were standing by the bar. Johnny and I sidled up beside them. Johnny handed me a snifter, while I grabbed a couple of cigars for us. We went through the ritual of lighting them, so they were burning nicely. Smoke billowed about the room as we all sat down. Malcolm remained standing, drinking a neat single malt.

With no ladies present, Bonnie was the topic of conversation. Malcolm directed a question at his host. "What was Miss Leland's rant and meltdown all about, if I might ask?"

"Upheaval, disruption, and disappointment. If one can't be happy with what one has, how can one expect to be happy by having still more?" answered John Senior, blowing smoke at the ceiling.

Malcolm looked puzzled. "She seemed serious. You're not worried?"

"Should I be?"

"I don't know much about it, but that woman seems unstable. I would hate to think of her taking the helm of even a dinghy, let alone a fortune."

"No one knows exactly what she's up to," said Mr. Dodge. "but I understand you introduced her to Lord Bromley rather recently."

Malcolm colored slightly. The baron gave him a piercing stare as a sneer flashed across his face. Johnny and I shifted our attention to the tall man. He looked like he had been caught red-handed doing something inappropriate. He waved his glass about. "Well…there was no harm in it. She asked nicely, so I set it up." Malcolm felt the baron's contempt and colored still more. "Don't look at me that way. You have far more to do with what is going on here than I do, and you know it. If you won't say it, I most certainly will."

"Rumors and innuendo, nothing more. I'm used to it." The baron puffed at his cigar, looked at the end to see how it was burning and then back at the tall man, as if daring him to continue.

John Senior added, "Lord Bromley can be a bad influence. Let's chalk it up to that. Events must play themselves out, and right now, nothing is certain. I simply stated a fact I was aware of. There was no accusation or aspersion implied."

"Well, thank you for that. I would hate to think that you might blame me for what Miss Leland is up to. I assure you I have nothing to do with it." He looked pointedly at the baron and then back at his host. "The dinner was marvelous, but I'm tired. What with all the excitement, I'm going to turn in. Good night." He nodded to each of us, placed his half-finished drink on the mantle, and slipped out the door.

"He seemed a bit defensive," said the baron. "But why ruin an otherwise superb dinner with such speculations? Shall we head back to the ladies, John?"

"Yes, let's."

He and John Senior rose together. Johnny said we'd be along in a minute. Once they were out of the room, Johnny refreshed his drink and sat back down.

After a pause, he said, "That last exchange was disturbing. Father didn't seem a bit concerned when Malcolm pretty much accused Hugo of being complicit in whatever it is Bonnie has planned. I know he plays a close game, but no reaction whatsoever? I hope he knows what he's doing."

"I'm sure he does. Perhaps your father believes in keeping his friends close and his enemies even more so. Your father knows far more than he lets on. If he isn't worried, why should we be?"

"You're right, of course, but then, we'd never know, would we? I suppose we'll just have to let events play out, as he said. I'm troubled, though. Changes are coming. Even Maw worries me. One day she'll be gone, and I don't know what the consequences of that will be for any of us." Johnny paused and then said carefully, "She mentioned she wished to have a word with you at some point. That might be a marvelous opportunity to try and find out what's up with her, because something is."

"I agree. I suppose I could try, but I wouldn't bet on my being overly successful."

"Listen to you. I at least expected an argument. You're doing okay?" He gave me one of his looks.

I laughed. "I'm doing just fine, all things considered. Maw, much to my relief, doesn't traumatize me as much as she used to. She's plenty scary, but in a good way, I think. You know where you stand with her. Still, I wouldn't expect much from my attempt."

Johnny thought about that while holding his drink in two hands.

"I think she might surprise you. She likes the direct approach, and you have the advantage of being an insider, but you are outsider at the same time. She's hard to reach, but it may serve her purpose to speak her mind to you."

"Intuition?"

"I suppose so."

"I'm game, whatever it is." I was feeling good.

"Most excellent."

Johnny sat back. His eyes twinkled with amusement.

I considered what he had said. My intuitive part, which had been quiet for most of the night, pointed out that those who were strong often appeared weak, while those who were weak appeared the opposite. It was likely correct. Maw was still in the game, but Johnny was probably right as well. She and I needed to talk.

"On another subject," said Johnny, interrupting my musings. "How is the Bruni thing going?"

"Rather well, actually. We're on comfortable terms."

"What does that mean?"

"She talks; I listen. I talk; she listens. It's good. I like it."

"I'm glad that's settled down. I was getting a little worried about that too. Girlfriend problems can get pervasive and usually at the wrong time. I should get to know her better, simply as a matter of course."

"You should. She's worth the effort."

"Well, I'm relieved. I suppose we should be getting to the other room, but I must speak to Stanley. Why don't you go in and mingle, while I talk to him? Robert needs to be fetched as well, and lest you have forgotten, we have work to do upstairs."

We put out our cigars and went our separate ways, me to the drawing room and Johnny to the kitchen.

45

I entered the drawing room and looked about. Maw was absent. She must have retired early. The remaining ladies had just risen from their seats. Elsa took her husband's hand and said they were off to bed. John and Anne decided to follow as well. They offered their good nights to Bruni and me and left.

"It's just us," I said.

"It is. What about Johnny?"

"He's in the back with Robert and Stanley."

"Would you care to take me outside for some fresh air?"

"Of course. Out the front or the back?" I asked.

"Out that way." She pointed toward the south lawn.

I opened the drapes, unlocked one of the french doors, and stepped with her into the night.

The moon was full and directly overhead. I had expected darkness, but instead the world lay spread out before us in a blazing tonal print of blacks and blues. The milky sheet that was the lawn stretched to shadowed trunks and silvered leaves in the distance. The cloudless sky of midnight blue had a grayish sheen near the horizon but darkened to blue-black as it rose to a moon too bright to look at. Nothing stirred, not a breath of wind, a leaf on a tree, or a blade of grass. The earth was without sound and without motion. Not a thing, living or dead, disturbed the stillness. We stood side by side barely touching, speechless, transfixed, and dazzled before an alien landscape of enchantment.

"What is this place?" Bruni whispered.

I glanced at her. She seemed mystified as she gazed about. Her bare skin blazed with moonlight. The sapphire above the shadow between her breasts gleamed, the star inside it searing bright and luminescent.

I dared not speak for fear of breaking whatever spell lay upon the land. We were in another time and place, and for just a moment, in a lifetime of moments, we were being given a glimpse of a perfection so exquisite, it hurt to take it in. I knew that nothing I had seen, or would ever experience in the future, would be its equal.

How long we stood side by side outside of space and time, I don't know. It might have been minutes. It could have been an hour. Time, if it existed at all during that period, held to an ancient, unfamiliar rhythm. There were no stars. Haze above the trees marked the boundary of the world. What lay beyond was mystery.

Bruni reached for my hand. I held it. We were speechless.

"There you are," said Johnny, with Robert on the leash.

We turned toward him, and in an instant we were back, having never left.

"Extraordinary night," continued Johnny. "Robert wanted to come outside, and I'm so glad he insisted. It's quiet as the dead but splendid in its peace. The old ones walk the earth tonight. I don't know why I said that, but that's the kind of night it is. Are you ready to go in?"

"Yes," we said. Bruni looked about as if to orient herself. I noticed the stars were there again. Where had they been?

Once inside, I locked the door and closed the drapes. Bruni said she was off to bed. She came up beside me and said quietly, "Thank you for this evening. Thank you so very much."

After she left, Johnny asked, "She looked a little shell-shocked."

"Tonight the house decided to display a different kind of magic. She experienced it herself, firsthand. Your mention of the ancient gods was wonderfully appropriate. I have no idea what happened, but something most definitely did. I felt it, and she did too. A drink before we get to work upstairs?"

"Sure. Why not? Eager to get back to our research, are we? That's a change. I think you're becoming more like me."

I fixed us both some single malt over ice before I answered.

"Hardly, but we're running out of time, and deadlines weigh heavily on my mind, as you well know."

"That's why I mention them over and over."

"Very clever. How about you tell me how it went with Stanley?"

Johnny and I lit cigarettes and settled on the sofa. Robert lay down in front of the fire, which had burned down to coals. He was asleep in seconds.

"I saw Stanley in his office. I told him that outside of the Bonnie incident, I thought the dinner went very well. I also complimented him on his quick handling of her sliding beneath the table. He said it was nothing out of the ordinary. He had had the foresight to brief his staff because she might come unglued. They knew exactly what to do, and she was packed away into her bed quickly and efficiently in no time.

"He assured me she would not be up and about until tomorrow afternoon, which will be a blessing. As to why he had her put on ice, he told me, 'She was disturbing that which resides here' — his exact words. I couldn't have agreed more. He mentioned that both Bonnie and Maw received documents. What they were exactly he wouldn't, or couldn't, say. What drug I slipped her, he didn't elaborate on either, just that the amount of alcohol she consumed made its effects more pronounced and erratic. She'll be fine by the big dinner tomorrow night. Other than that, he wondered about our progress on the diary and the notes. I told him we were making headway but that nothing of import had surfaced yet."

"I can't believe you guys got away with it," I said. "Bonnie will have a hangover of epic proportions. Well deserved, I think. Congratulations." I raised my glass.

"Cheers," Johnny said. "By the way, just to add to what you said earlier, you and Bruni appeared out of nowhere when I was walking Robert. You surprised the hell out of me. Thought you'd like to know."

"Perhaps we were very still."

"Perhaps you were."

We drank the rest of our scotch and collected Robert, who stretched his rear legs out, shook himself mightily, and followed us up the stairs.

46

We had been working for what seemed like hours. I was mentally fried. If I looked at one more indecipherable passage of hieroglyphics, I would go mad. I got up and walked around the room, looking at old, familiar book titles in words that I could at least understand poking out from the shelves that lined the common room.

"I don't think I can take much more of this, at least not tonight," I said.

"Sure you can," said Johnny, not even bothering to look up.

He was in auto mode, which meant he was reading something of interest but wanted to give me the impression he was listening. I tested this assumption by saying, "The part about the murder was particularly boring."

"Yes, I'm sure it was."

He continued reading for a full two seconds before he asked, "What was that?"

"Just seeing if you were listening. You weren't."

"I was but only partly. There were no murders in what you read. You were just testing me. I know your games."

"Very clever, but so far nothing of interest on my end. It's like reading a travelogue, written partly in English and partly in some unfamiliar language. I can't read another word, but I bet you're on to something. I'm distracting you, aren't I?"

"You are, so sit down for a few and let me finish. I need to read this carefully."

I sat. Robert was asleep again. Occasionally, he would make odd sounds and his legs would twitch, but other than that, it was dead quiet. I closed my eyes.

"I wouldn't do that, if I were you," said Johnny.

I opened them and lit another cigarette instead. The ashtray was getting surprisingly full. Johnny and I had pulled many an all-nighter over the years. One of us would fade, and the other would prod until some semblance of wakefulness returned. We would reverse roles, back and forth, until the sun came up. I was determined to get some sleep tonight, but old stimuli die hard. I sighed. I was awake again.

"Okay," said Johnny, "I've got something."

"Finally."

"Not so fast. Such hard-won moments must be savored. Patience is a virtue after all."

Johnny was looking beatific and thoroughly pleased with himself. Typically, he would keep me in suspense for as long as possible before finally telling me what he had discovered.

"Are you going to tell me or what?"

He smiled. "This was far more difficult than you can imagine, so prepare to be impressed. First, Aunt Alice really did go off the deep end. Stanley was quite right, but interspersed among some rather alarming passages, and some that are completely off the wall, is a story. I'll read it to you with the extraneous bits left out, for which you should thank me."

"I thank you."

"You're welcome. Dates and time, as you pointed out, seemed to be immaterial to her way of thinking, so I did the best I could in deciphering a sequence that makes sense. I'm not sure I got it right, to tell you the truth, but at least it's somewhat logical. I'm going to read the relevant bits out. Ready?"

"Absolutely. Fire away."

Johnny started to read.

"'I must make a change. Tonight I am going to double my intake of the tincture, a dangerous move, but I have little choice. The dreams are stronger and getting more frequent, and I wake these days out of breath, claustrophobic, and exhausted...

"'Oh, happy day, I made a connection last night, and I'm hopeful again. One moment I was sitting alone on the couch; the next I felt a presence beside me. I wondered if I was being paranoid, a not unexpected companion considering how much I took. The presence spoke to me in a childlike voice. I remember quite clearly as I am writing this that I could not turn my head. It told me to be still. The child, if it even was a child, told me that it was aware of my situation and had decided to help me. It said, "I must atone, a life for a life." I asked if I should kill myself, and the answer was "No, you must experience another kind of death: climbing the vine of souls." I asked what that was, but there was no answer. After a time, I could move again, so I grabbed my papers and wrote it all down. When I awoke this morning, I found that I had filled an entire pad with gibberish, but amongst the pages I found legible words, and then the whole passage in clear block-print capitals...

"'I have been so frustrated lately. Several times over the last few months, I knew I had experienced something important, only to recall little of any use the next day. No more wondering. I now have a trail to follow which is something I have not had before. I ought to be delighted, but I'm not. Instead, I'm anxious and more than a little afraid. I'm on my own in this. There is no one to guide me...

"'I remember now where I heard the words: the vine of souls. I was fleeing through the jungles of Ecuador, after I abandoned Arthur to his fate, when I came across a village. I spoke with a woman there who took me to their shaman. Between my guide's knowledge of indigenous languages and my broken Spanish, we were able to converse. I asked questions about our best route to safety. He told me and our conversation drifted to his practices and the uses of *Brugmansia*, my potent little friend and savior. The fact that I was a woman did not seem to bother him. He spoke to me quite candidly about the plant. He explained in detail several different ways to prepare it. Once again, I heard about the many dangers and its powerful effects. One particularly potent method was to combine it with two other plants, one of which was called the vine of souls. This was not for the faint of heart and used only as a last resort. It required several days of fasting to prepare the body before it was ingested. He then showed me a ceramic piece in the shape of a small teapot, but it was not used for that purpose. One blew through the spout, creating a peculiar sound made up of two notes, which when played together, created yet a third, a beat frequency that thrummed. He demonstrated it for me. The sound induced a peculiar sensation in my body and seemed to resonate inside my skull. I saw stars. Together with the draft, I imagined the effect would be quite shocking and traumatic. He offered to guide me through the ritual as he said I had a darkness that followed me. I knew this to be true, but I explained to him as best I could that I was being hunted and chased by a physical darkness in the form of bad men. I dared not let them catch me in the jungle. It would be a bitter and fatal meeting, which must not happen. I thanked him for his offer, but I couldn't afford the days of preparation that the ritual entailed. The men might cross the river at any time. He nodded and thought in silence. In the end, he gave me samples of the plants, which I later identified as *Psychotria virdis* and *Banisteriopsis caapi*. I traded most everything I carried, other than the idol, for one of the pipes. The next morning, my guide and I set out again...Perhaps I should have stayed, but being alive was better than cured and dead, or at least that is what I thought at the time. Today the choice is not so clear...

"'When I arrived at something resembling civilization, I searched my pack, but there was no pipe, only the idol at the bottom looking up at me from a bed of plants. The little pot had been there that morning. Where had it gone? Had someone taken it? Had I dropped it? I even entertained the idea that the idol had eaten it, but of course, the thought was absurd...Reviewing the incident with distant hindsight, perhaps it was not so absurd after all...So much of what I thought I knew has been turned on its head...

"'I need help. My mind has fractured. It has splintered in peculiar ways, some good, some not good at all. I am not quite right. I know this. Strange things, inexplicable things, have happened to me. They really have. Where could the pipe have gone? Who took it? Someone did. My paranoia, my terrible little sister, is growing. It is becoming more obvious...even to me. I can't stop it. I trust no one. I am alone, and I need that pipe now — that and the plants. I must make preparations...

"'I remember how surprised I was when I finally reached relative safety unharmed. I was flushed with a sense of triumph. I had defied impossible odds and survived. The only thing darkening my success was losing that pipe. I had a strong premonition that I would feel its loss most keenly in the future. I was right. That time is upon me. What am I to do? The idol I packaged so carefully and sent has not arrived, so I can't ask it what happened, nor can I make it give it back! It's driving me crazy...'"

Johnny paused for a moment in the narrative. "With me so far?"

"Fascinating and troubling," I answered. "I get the sense from what she wrote that she was close to the edge physically and mentally, like a runner at the end of a marathon who is paying the price for starting out too quickly. She did mention a pipe in her diary in the section about Ecuador and Arthur, but I thought it was just the kind one smoked. I should reread that portion to see if I missed something, given this context. The diary is very sparse in personal details compared to this."

"I think the diary was more scholarly in nature," said Johnny. "In the notes, she gave herself free rein, almost too much. I had to sift through numerous tangents to get even this amount of clarity. There is more. It's a sad read, but she never gave up."

"Do you think that, in the end, the dark parts of her mind overwhelmed her?"

"Hard to say. When I'm done reading, I'll give you my thoughts. The story is not over, as you'll see. There is even some information on the mysterious Marianne Thoreau."

Johnny continued:

"'I do love her. She is so rare. She says little and wants less, but she loves me, I think. She is jealous. I hate that. I can do nothing unless I explain everything. I tell her I am a solitary creature. I need time with myself...alone. Being with another is not for me. I'm done with that. Can she not understand? Have I not made myself clear? I need her nonetheless. She takes my mind off my mind. She has connections too. She can get me access to what I need. It must be pre-Columbian and authentic. Too many are just ancient imitations of the real thing. I will know its worth when I hear the sound it makes. I must search...In the meanwhile, I have cut my sessions to zero. I need to regain my strength. I am too strung out. I sound like an addict. Am I? I don't know. I'm not doing this for kicks. I do it because I have no alternative...

"'I suppose I'm a bigger fool. She knows him. Is she in league with him? I wonder. Does it matter? He has the real deal, the real thing. It's so typical. Our paths are linked, his and mine. Whatever am I to do? Perhaps there is a way. I will pay whatever the cost. He knows that too. Money is easy; it's what else he wants that worries me. I also wonder if this has all been planned out. She got to me so smoothly, so professionally. It boggles my mind that someone could take such pains to exact their vengeance, but I should talk. Revenge can be quite satisfying. I loved every minute of it. He must have too — another thing we have in common. I am such a fool...

"'I have a deal I think. It is a fine bait, but I sense a hook. I need Stanley. He will know what to do. He always does. Bless him...'"

Johnny paused again. "There may be pages missing. Stanley obviously played a part, and so did Lord Bromley, but what exactly happened, the notes don't say. She got the pipe she needed, that's all I know, which you'll hear about in a moment. We'll have to visit Stan tomorrow to get the details."

"Good idea. I do admire that he was always there for her."

"You trust him now?"

"No. He has parts that are hidden that may bite us — lest we forget, but I respect him immensely. I even like him, in spite of all my reasons not to."

"Well, that's a change. Let me read you the last bit. It sounds like an acid trip to me, maybe worse, but it tells us why she was so hooked on obtaining a particular Book of the Dead.

"'I have all I need. I cannot do it here. I need someone to supervise me as well — not Stanley. I would feel too degraded, and I hold his esteem too highly. He would do it in a heartbeat, but he would see a side of me I would be too embarrassed to reveal. This is a heroic undertaking in both its meanings. I will be purged. M. will have to look after me. It's a risk I have to take. Do I trust her? I must. Am I strong enough? I hope. I have prepared everything. The Carlyle has many secrets and to them will be added one more, my own. Now I must fast...

"'It's done. I am alive, not well at all, but alive. I have hope, and that is something. I'll take what has been given and be thankful...

"'We checked into the Carlyle. I took a suite for several days, in fact, the whole floor. I did not want to be disturbed or disturb others — a distinct possibility. I also knew it might take quite some time for the effects to wear off. I brought my own linens and cleaning supplies. I had warm food brought up, but it was not food that I needed. It was the warmers for the chaffing dishes, their little blue flames. I mixed the ingredients, followed the procedures I remembered, and prepared the dose. M. and I opened all the windows while the mixture was brewing, giggling at the thought of the management knocking on the door and expressing their concern that guests were becoming violently sick from a smell emanating from this suite that defied any civilized description. I was happy I had the presence of mind to take the entire floor. Once the mixture was prepared, I knew it was time to commit myself fully to the undertaking and cast aside my doubts. I had to drink a cup, at least. The concoction smelled positively awful and tasted even worse. I was so shocked by its foulness that I was able to drink the first few gulps without a problem. The last three-quarters was heavy-going. It tasted like fermented prunes mixed with soil of an organic and excremental nature. I was barely able to keep it down. I slumped on the couch, gagging and swallowing convulsively. I wondered vaguely if I could call a halt, but it was too late for that. I had drunk the potion, and the concoction was staying down. There was no turning back. M. blew the pipe, and everything happened at once. I felt a heat like I have never felt heat. I felt a cold like I never felt cold before. It spread through my body like evil blood. My mind detached. I saw pyramids floating in the sky. They drifted about me, or I drifted about them. There were geometric shapes everywhere, electric and filled with sound. I could not feel my hands. I could not feel my feet. I was numb; then I sensed water. I was near a river. I could hear the sound of water rushing by. Beside me was a dwarf. He was small and obscene looking. He swore at me, spat at me, and threatened me with long dirty nails that appeared sharp as razors. He scared me. I backed away, but he came closer. His eyes were filled with hatred. I can say quite truthfully, I have never been so frightened. There was no escape from him. He threw me down and stood on my chest. He jumped up and down. I hurt so badly, I could not breathe. He kept yelling and jumping. I couldn't understand what he was saying. I died. I'm sure of it. Eventually, I felt nothing. My body was dead. I was outside in the sky, looking at the city. I rose higher. There were many cities connected by strips of silver. I ran along them. I was a black panther. I was the huntress. I was Bast, not the tame goddess she became, but the warrior, eater of men. But then I knew this was not so. In front of me was Wadjet-Bast, the Eye of the Moon. The real one. She was huge, many times my size. I was overwhelmed. That moment was the closest I have ever come to turning insane. The goddess saved me. She calmed my soul and held me gently. She whispered in my ear the information about the path I now needed to follow. I had to travel one more time to this place to release myself from the curse I carried. She showed it to me. It was a red-black rock I wore around my neck. I had to leave it here with her but only after I had followed a precise ritual that was laid out in a specific Book of the Dead to allow me to pass safely into the afterlife. Whether I could return from there, she could not say. She showed me what the papyrus looked like, so I would recognize it when I was back in my world. "Find the scroll," the goddess said. I wept with relief, and then my body exploded, my real one. I was staring over the back of the couch, throwing up like I have never thrown up before. M. put my arm over her shoulder and dragged me to the bathroom. I stayed in there for a day, at least. The dwarf kept me company. He sat on the sink. I cursed at it. It cursed at me. After hours of cursing at each other, we started laughing. I couldn't stop. I laughed so hard, I was in excruciating agony. I curled into a ball on the bathroom floor. I counted the little white tiles that surrounded me, all of them, many times. I slept. I awoke. I had no idea how long I had been out. I felt drained and foul but alive. I remembered everything, every detail…I knew what I had to do…I needed to repeat this whole process at home, probably alone, but first I must find the scroll I need. I don't want to go down that road, but I must…He has it. Of course he does. I know it.'

"That's all I have, I'm afraid," Johnny said to me. "I don't know whether she passed away before she took that last trip or not. There are no notes describing it. Maybe they exist; maybe they don't. Perhaps the night she died was that last one, and it killed her."

"Quite possibly," I said. "I think we should discuss it with Stanley."

"I think so. We're getting closer to wrapping our wits around what happened, and that is progress."

"You mentioned before you started that you had some thoughts."

"I have a few. Firstly, the dwarf thing is strange. Perhaps she mistook Marianne for the dwarf, which would mean she was probably close to death and needed to be resuscitated. If that was the case, a second round might have been too much for her system, particularly if she had no one to watch over her. Secondly, she mentioned having to do the ritual at home. Perhaps she didn't trust Marianne after all."

"That occurred to me as well," I said. "In addition, Stanley rarely tells a lie, but he can omit details as he deems appropriate. He says he found her after her breakfast tray had been sitting for some time, which is likely true. What happened the night before was not really mentioned, was it?"

"I don't recall if he mentioned anything about the previous night. Your suspicious mind again?"

"I suppose, but it bears thinking about. I'm certain that Stanley would have done everything in his power to prevent her death, but with Lord Bromley somehow involved, that may not have been possible. The man had it in for her, and she knew it. Perhaps he did so indirectly, like giving her a false map or one that was correct except for a missing part?"

"I had a similar thought," said Johnny. "She also mentioned the Eye of the Moon, referencing the goddess. Perhaps, the goddess couldn't help Alice in the way that Alice wanted? Right now, it's all speculation. We should go over it tomorrow. Let's get some sleep while we can. Breakfast will be here before you know it, and tomorrow is 'gird your loins' day. Best be prepared."

With that, we said good night, and I went to my room to sleep as much as possible. We would need our wits about us tomorrow, and so would everyone else.

4 7

I awoke to Johnny pounding on my door. He always pounded
on my door first thing in the morning. Such was life.

"Get up. We're going to be late. Come on!"

I quickly showered, shaved, and dressed. I raced after Johnny
and Robert, taking the stairs two at a time. We skidded into the
dining room just as everyone was taking their seats. Johnny took
Robert to the kitchen.

Our places were the same as yesterday morning. There was a
seat next to Bruni, who looked radiant and happy, and Elsa, who
was lost in her first cup of coffee. I sat down. Elsa rarely spoke at
breakfast. She simply smiled whenever she was asked a question.
She gave me one as I sat down. I always appreciate quiet first thing
in the morning. We were similar in that way. The baron, too,
preferred minimal conversation. He was hidden behind the
Financial Times. Occasionally, he closed his paper, holding it in one
hand to have a sip of coffee. He would look around to see if he was
missing anything, and then the paper would snap open as he

closed off the rest of the world. Our host and hostess also read papers, but theirs were neatly folded into quarters and lay on the table beside them. Johnny sat down next to Maw and beamed at everyone. "Good morning, all," he said. We all murmured our acknowledgments. The mood was definitely lighter than the day before. Maw looked rested and ready for action. She got up before first light to see to the horses and dogs when she was at her home. It was probably late in the day for her. The tall man kept to himself. The only one missing was Bonnie, which was a relief.

Bruni whispered to me, "Sleep well?"

"Yes, what sleep there was."

"Up late?"

"Research."

"How studious. I thought this was supposed to be a holiday."

"It's my wickedness catching up with me."

"You must elaborate on that."

"Later, and only after a great deal more coffee."

"I'll hold you to it."

Breakfast came and went. When we were all getting up, Maw looked at me and said, "Let's walk."

It wasn't a request. I excused myself to Bruni and Elsa. Johnny gave me an encouraging look as Maw set off. I followed. My hope of a quiet settling into the day dimmed as Maw struck a brisk pace. When we had put some distance between us and the house, she slowed and got right to it.

"I'm not happy with you. Skulking off to California to lick your wounds in forensic accounting rather than dealing with the real issues is unacceptable. A rider who won't remount after a fall is broken. Horses can be violent and dangerous. They kill each other just like we do. As a rider, you must learn to dominate them. Domination is not physical — it's mental."

She whipped around and put her face inches from mine. There

was no forewarning. Her eyes bored into me. Her volume never changed, but her rage and intensity hit me like a punch in the face.

"Where the fuck are your balls? I want to know where they went, and what you're going to do to grow a pair right the fuck now."

I was struck dumb as a block of wood. It was either that or start gibbering.

"Don't gape. You haven't the time for it. I'm going to walk to the river and back. I want answers when I return. Think carefully. Forensic accounting, my ass. You're incredibly naïve and incompetent at that. Blindness isn't a disease. It's a willful state of being brain-dead."

She spat on the ground, turned her back on me, and headed west.

I watched her as she walked away. I felt unmanned, gutted like one of her former husbands, out of my body, and close to tears, all at the same time. My hands shook as I lit a cigarette. What had gotten into her? I was tempted to wallow in self-pity, but my intuitive part intervened. It posited that, firstly, if she thought I was a complete zero, she would not have talked to me in the first place. Secondly, she wanted me to look at something that I had failed to observe and was to her completely transparent. She was a successful businessperson. I was not. I needed to look from her point of view.

I didn't want to. I would have much preferred self-absorption and convincing myself she was a washed-up, demented old hag, but she had seen through to the heart of the matter: I had run away.

To Maw, this was an abomination. Maw would have fought tooth and nail. Convinced of her inherent rightness from an early age, she looked outside herself for the source of any conflict and eventually found it. To her mind, difficulties were not random challenges but deliberate barriers strewn in her path, contrived by enemies, and carried out against her personally. She lived by a simple maxim: make your enemies suffer, kill them when you can, but above all, never surrender…ever.

Given this mind-set, my intuitive part interjected, Johnny and I were likely conspired against. As a forensic accountant, even though I became one after the fact, I never once attempted to find out who was on the other side of the trades that sank us: a personal failing of some magnitude. To Maw, this was more than just incompetence. Submitting to fate without even a whimper indicated a profound lack of spirit. QED, I had no balls.

The question in her mind, I supposed, was whether I was a broken piece or a potential resource. She wanted to know the answer, and as I looked up, she was striding purposefully toward me to find out.

"Well?" was all she said.

My intuitive part counseled a pause and complete honesty if I had a hope of salvaging any form of a relationship with her.

"I ran, it's true. The thought that Johnny and I were conspired against never crossed my mind. I never even considered it until now, hence your conclusion of a naïveté that borders on incompetence. I am not altogether incompetent. For me, it's easier to blame myself than blame others. For some, it is the other way around. I need to strike a balance between the two. I thank you for your observations. I am not a horse, but that doesn't mean I can't be taught. I'm not broken in spirit. I have courage in my own way, so what job do you have in mind for me?"

"Well, well. You're not as thick as a post, I'll grant you. The courage part remains to be seen. I have two files for you to look at. Give me your analysis, the sooner the better, and then we'll see whether you have balls or not.

"Let's return to the house."

We walked. I had to hand it to her. She was a master. She could rip into you one moment to correct a shortcoming and encourage the next. She demanded and received maximum performance from those around her. I wondered at the severity of the lesson that was in store for Bonnie. Maw was Maw after all. Messing with her was like messing with nature — a bad idea.

48

When we returned, Maw disappeared up the stairs and came back down with two file folders.

"See what you make of these. I would get to it as soon as you can. Find me when you're done and bring the files with you. You can make notes, but I want them when you're finished."

Maw went out the front door while I climbed up to the common room. Johnny was there, reading the diary.

"How did it go?" asked Johnny, looking up.

"Touch and go. She ripped me a new one, but I survived reasonably intact. In the end, she gave me a job, which is something. She also hinted that our business partnership's demise was deliberate, instigated by parties yet unknown — although I suspect the identity and the evidence is in one of these two files. In a nutshell, she was less than pleased that I skipped off to the coast without a fight, and I am seriously underdeveloped in the testicle department. She said that far more bluntly and with an intensity that shocked me. I don't think I've ever been talked to in quite that way. It was a first."

"Ouch. Welcome to the club. She made off with my gonads ages ago. My little plan to find out what's up with her is obviously tabled."

"Completely. That I'm still in one piece is no minor miracle, although I suspect that the answer to your question is in one of these folders as well. There was no mention of confidentiality, so I have no qualms in showing you the files. I suspect she knows we'll collaborate. I also think this'll require some serious analysis and brain power. I'm to report back with recommendations."

"You need my genius." Johnny was always thrilled to show off his stuff.

"Always and, in this case, most definitely. It's 'gird your loins' day after all. I could go for a quick hair of the dog, but let's grapple with these first. Which file do you want?"

"The left, of course, always the left. And by the way, I had a chat with Stan, which I will fill you in on later. It was interesting, but this takes priority. Our future may depend on what we come up with."

"It probably does. The left it is. We'll trade later. You can make notes, but Maw insisted that they be gathered up and given to her. No traces."

"I'm lovin' it, and I haven't even started." Johnny reached for his yellow pad.

I sat down opposite and began to go through the folder.

It was made up entirely of Xerox copies.

The first document was a threat analysis regarding our little partnership. It was initiated by an investment house I had never heard of named Boskins and Harold and carried out by the investigations section of a legal firm by the name of Curtis, Provost, and List. I'd never heard of them either. The assessment included a letter from none other than our old friend, the horrible little man that Stanley had reminded me of — the one with the dead eyes. I had judged him more harshly than I should have, because he had recommended that within six months, 50 percent of his client's assets currently held at B & H be transferred out and managed instead by our partnership. The sum was in the eight-figure range — an extraordinary windfall had it taken place. The assessment concluded that Johnny and I posed a clear and substantial threat to B & H and that actions to mitigate the danger be undertaken immediately.

Next in the file was a follow-up letter written shortly after the assessment from the same investigations unit. The letter warned that Johnny and I were in the position to poach a substantial number of high-net-worth B & H clients due to their reliance on the advice of the now-not-so-horrible little man. The potential damage to B & H was estimated to be substantial and serious enough to question its viability going forward. They urgently recommended that actions be taken with the highest priority and speed.

The next document was an internal memo from a managing director to the CEO of the clearinghouse that had executed our trades and, coincidentally, those of B & H. The memo was marked *Sensitive* and *Confidential*. It outlined a request by B & H as to the feasibility of allowing the firm to front-run our trades — that is, delivering to B & H information on our buys and sells before they were executed. This would allow B & H to put on the same trades, but at better prices, or do the opposite, whichever B & H ordered. The originator recommended the minimum annual fee that B & H had to pay their firm to justify such an action, as well as procedures to keep said action confidential. He reiterated that B & H had to guarantee the proposed fee amount or no deal.

Next was a letter of authorization to the same managing director to execute the trading strategy per the phone conversation of the day before and stating that the fee arrangements had been approved by B & H management. Attached was a copy of another letter, dated the same day, asking for written verification that the means to monitor and execute the trading strategy as previously agreed upon was in place and ready to be activated. Further, once an affirmative reply was received, half the agreed-upon annual fee required would be wired to the clearinghouse immediately. Both were signed by Philip D. Sterling, assistant general counsel for Brunhilde von Hofmanstal, general counsel.

The last document was a series of trade executions processed by the clearinghouse. Clipped to it was an analysis by an accounting firm that concluded that B & H had taken advantage of the illiquidity of the bean contracts that Johnny and I were trading and had generated sell orders in sufficient volume to create a limit down situation that essentially locked us out of the market. Without question, B & H was behind the initial cascade that set in motion the several days of decline that caused the large unsustainable losses we endured.

I read the file again in detail.

I have no idea how Maw obtained this information, but if the data was true, and there was no reason to doubt its veracity, Johnny and I had been deliberately torpedoed and run out of town. I should have felt better knowing I was not totally to blame, but the information made me feel far worse on a multitude of levels.

The first was that the information exposed what I had thought was an honorable and just profession for what it truly was: a rigged casino where the big players used whatever means necessary, both legal and illegal, to do away with smaller competitors that might impact their profits. Although markets were larger than any one entity, there were times when size mattered and substantial damage could be done to individuals on the other side of a given trade. We were a case in point. I doubted I had the necessary ruthlessness to operate successfully in such a world.

On another level, my own naïveté surprised even me. How could I have missed this? For all my vaunted paranoia and seeing plots at every turn, I had failed to even suspect we were deliberately conspired against. That deficiency reflected a personal blindness of extraordinary proportions. I obviously saw only what I wanted to see.

Throughout my life, holding myself personally accountable and blaming my personal shortcomings had been easy, but ultimately, they were my reasons to fail — my most well-thought-out excuses. Holding others accountable, I realized, required courage, nerve, and a willingness to look outside myself that I didn't have right now. I knew I had to change, but I wondered what I would become? Like the ones I had just read about? Like Maw?

These were questions I decided to table for now. I could barely deal with the realization, let alone do something about it.

Lastly, Bruni was part of the scheme — and probably the baron as well. I felt betrayed, but that seemed secondary to the wound I felt in my heart. I had no idea what to do with that either.

"That bad, is it?" asked Johnny quietly, looking up.

"Worse." I dropped the file on the table.

"Well, that makes two of us. I was hoping your file might be a tad better, but obviously not. Trade?"

"I'm not sure you'll like what you get in return."

I took the file from Johnny. It was thicker than the other one.

49

I sat back and opened the folder. Once again, there were no
originals.

The first document was a copy of what looked like a
telephone transcript. Whether the call was taped internally or the
result of a wiretap was not indicated. The date and time were both
redacted.

> *BVH: This is the baron.*
>
> *Caller: Bonnie Leland here. I have a request to make of you that is to*
> *our mutual benefit.*
>
> *BVH: Do I know you?*
>
> *Caller: Not personally. My mother is Mary Leland. The Mary*
> *Leland.*
>
> *BVH: What can I do for you, Miss Leland?*
>
> *Caller: I would like to meet in person. I will be in New York next*
> *Tuesday.*
>
> *BVH: I'm busy next Tuesday.*
>
> *Caller: I'm sure you are. What I wish to discuss with you is*

confidential and very much in your monetary interest. All I ask is to be heard.

BVH: I told you I'm fully scheduled that day, but why not come by my office? Perhaps I can fit you in, if you're prepared to wait.

Caller: I prefer to meet at an outside location away from prying eyes.

BVH: Why the secrecy?

Caller: I don't...My mother...She has ways of getting information, and if there is one thing I've learned, it is the value of discretion. You do know my mother and her reputation?

BVH: I am aware of who she is, but why should I get between you and your mother? This is obviously a family matter.

Caller: It is, hence the need to be discrete. She doesn't have to know a thing, and as I said, it will be to our mutual benefit.

BVH: You keep repeating that. I mean no disrespect, but I don't see how it concerns me.

Caller: You are aware of the firm Boskins and Harold? Here's some news: my mother is aware of it too, and so am I. How much is two hours of your time worth?

BVH: I see. To answer your second question: a great deal.

Caller: Do you have a figure in mind?

BVH: I do.

Caller: Double it. I'll see you for lunch on Tuesday. I'll pick you up in front of your office at noon.

BVH: It will be a very expensive lunch.

Caller: If you only knew how expensive, but not to me. You may even decide to pick up the tab yourself.

BVH: I wouldn't bet on it. Bring your checkbook.

Caller: I never leave home without it. See you Tuesday.

The next document was a lengthy legal analysis put together by the Wall Street legal firm of Pringle, Palmer, Sullivan, and Duffy regarding board members of listed companies and their fitness to serve. It outlined the relevant case law and stated unequivocally that any criminal or regulatory investigation of a board member, regardless of its merit, could and would be grounds for a member's forced resignation. It supported these findings by citing notable real-world examples and concluded that the potential downside risk to a business's reputation was the deciding factor in forced resignations and in fitness to serve issues in general.

Next was a handwritten letter from Bonnie:

Mother,

I am exploring the possibility of coming forward with new evidence to open (or reopen) a certain investigation, but I have moral considerations on going forward. Do I go with family reputation and loyalty, or am I obligated to put what I know before authorities? It is a question that weighs heavily on my mind. I have even gone so far as to seek religious counseling to resolve the matter but am still in a quandary as to what to do. I am sure I will make up my mind eventually.

On another matter and no way connected to the above, I would like to outline a few things on my wish list. I believe you must write down your desires if you want them to manifest. You might try this as well. I have found the practice most helpful. Here are a few of mine:

1. I want full control and ownership of all blocks of voting stock you currently have in all listed and unlisted entities.

2. My half-brother is to get the absolute minimum cash bequest to prevent a legal challenge to your will. We could go over it together. (The maximum I would accept for him is a few million, although if legal counsel can give me reason to consider a different amount, substantiated by precedent, I would take that into consideration.)

3. I want the New York Fifth Avenue apartment put in my name, and I wish to occupy it as soon as possible. Current residents would have to vacate. You should inform them — rather you than me.

4. The Rhinebeck house is to be deeded over to me as collateral for the outstanding loans made to Dodge Capital that I now own or else I will call them at the earliest opportunity. You can inform them of this as well when you let them know about the New York apartment.

I may come up with others, but these should suffice for now.

What do you think? Perhaps you can advise me? My next attempt at the resolution to my moral dilemma will be to take some time away for quiet meditation and reflection.

Your loving daughter,

— BON

Lastly was a lengthy impact study of the financial, legal, and political consequences of Mrs. Leland relinquishing control in favor of her daughter. This was done by a Mr. Charles A. Dunn, CPA, CFA, attorney at law, and was confidential to Mrs. Mary Leland. A cover letter was attached that started with the usual "Pursuant to your request, the following summary is provided with supporting documentation..."

The study detailed the impact of generational transitions on family-controlled businesses up to and including Fortune 500 companies. It pointed out that although there were many successful transitions, those that included family discord were the exception. In every instance, the company in question imploded significantly across all metrics, regardless of size or scope of business. Primarily, this was due to incessant in-fighting that distracted management from adhering to earlier successful practices. The paper further highlighted that in the absence of significant grooming and apprenticeship from an early age, transitions to a new generation of owners often resulted in the eventual loss of family control, in favor of independent management followed by retrenchments in family net worth. The study concluded that due to the absence of training, apprenticeship, and demonstrated performance ability, the passing of control to her daughter would in all probability follow a similar trajectory. The analysis added that with the high likelihood of a contested turnover and taking into consideration the extensive nature of the holdings involved, the move might have far-reaching adverse repercussions. The paper recommended a succession plan with clearly outlined rules of qualification and performance, as the best preventative measure against such an outcome. If this was the direction Mrs. Leland wished to go, apprenticeship should start immediately once the qualifications and performance criteria were determined or a more suitable candidate, or candidates, chosen.

I put down the file. Johnny had already finished his and was smoking a cigarette, lost in thought.

"Well?" I asked.

Johnny got up and began to wander about the room.

"Let's summarize what we have so far: we have two files and several situations, four obvious from the data and one that is unstated but rather immediate. Let's start with the obvious," said Johnny as he ticked them off on his fingers.

"Number one is the deliberate sinking of our partnership. Two is Bonnie's hint of blackmail to force Maw to relinquish control. Three is Bonnie's threat to call in the outstanding debt of Dodge Capital to get her hands on the deed to Rhinebeck. And four is the transition conundrum.

"The fifth, which is unstated, involves Maw's motives for giving us this information in the first place. My guess is that she wants to know what we, and you in particular, are going to do about the fact that our demise was engineered. My tentative conclusion is that she's considering using you, or both of us, as successors to bypass the potential conflict between her immediate children, without having to relinquish familial control to an outside party. Now, for the moment, this solution is way down the list of possibilities, but if she likes what she hears and ultimately sees, the idea could gather some credibility. It's typical of Maw. She'll have several plans in play. This is merely one of them, but we should tailor our response with that in mind."

"It's an interesting take on her motives," I said, "and makes some sense, although I don't give the idea much of a chance, even if you're correct. I think she wants me to walk downstairs and blow away the baron or Bruni to demonstrate my courage. I won't do it, and I won't allow you to either. Frankly, I've no idea what to do about any of this."

"I understand. The Bruni thing is quite distressing, I agree," said Johnny, looking at me carefully. He knew that was the crux of the matter. "But you can't very well hand the files back to Maw and say, 'Thank you for the information. I'll get back to you when I think of something.'"

"True enough, although I must admit, that's exactly what I want to do."

Johnny sighed. "Look. Think of this as a test. It *is* a test, so let's treat it like one. Let's make it all hypothetical, like one of our brainstorming sessions. We came up with more than one brilliant idea, if you'll recall. I do happen to have some good whiskey tucked away in my dresser, and we do have a couple of glasses in the bathroom, which I'll even wash before we use them. You really must get into the spirit of the thing. Really, it'll be fun. You'll see."

"I suppose so," I said with some reluctance. "I hope you have something in mind because I sure don't. I'm completely blank."

"Not to worry. I've just the remedy."

Johnny whisked himself off to his room. He knew me too well. Bruni's involvement really bothered me, and until I had it out with her, I knew I would never get my head in the game. Now was the time for me to deal with it.

"I'll be right back," I yelled and slipped out the door.

50

I found her in the drawing room chatting with Elsa and Anne.
"Please excuse me, but may I borrow Bruni for a few minutes?"

Anne and Elsa agreed as Bruni stood up, smoothed her skirt, and told the others she would be back in a bit.

"What's up?" she asked as we stepped out the front door and into the morning sunlight. A light breeze carried the scent of lawn grass. It was still a gorgeous day, despite my mood. The easy companionship that had started last night was still there, but I knew she was aware that something was on my mind.

"Last night was truly magical," I said as we stepped off the driveway onto the grass and strolled in the direction of the tennis court.

Bruni stopped, and I did too. She looked me in the eyes. Away from her, I could forget the power of her beauty, but face-to-face, she dazzled me once again. Her eyes sparkled as breezes played with her hair. "It was perfect," she said, "but that's not why you got me out here."

My hurt seemed so acute and justified upstairs with Johnny, but looking at her, it seemed less significant. I wanted to prolong the peace between us, but then again, I couldn't very well ignore what I had read.

"The direct route is best," she reminded me softly.

"Yes, but that doesn't make what I have to say any easier." I paused again and then continued with just the facts as I knew them: "I read a report on Harold and Boskins. It involved you as legal counsel and a series of trades Johnny and I made. You authorized the actions that caused our partnership to go under."

She sighed and looked away.

"It's true, isn't it? I asked.

She stepped back from me and looked toward the distant line of trees. "I'm in an awkward position. As an attorney, there are things I can't talk about or even comment on. There's also a nondisclosure agreement. I have to stand mute. I know it's difficult, but trust me, if you can," she said, looking at my face to see my reaction.

"Part of me wants to very much, but there's also a part of me that feels betrayed and hurt more than I can say."

She nodded and looked away again.

The more I thought about the wrongness that was done to Johnny and me, the more my upset felt justified. I recalled the shock of the rebuke I had received from Maw and her pointing out that I had failed to stand up for myself. I felt like yelling and screaming, but my intuitive part intervened before I could let myself get out of hand. It told me to stop acting like an idiot. Bruni probably felt as bad as I did, if not worse, given the circumstances. Even if the facts were true, I didn't know the context, let alone why. Like any other corporate attorney, she had implemented what was decided by others. It wasn't personal. As she had pointed out, we had never met. Rage can look like courage, but fundamentally, they're not the same. What I needed was information, not histrionics. More importantly, I had to start living my life on my own terms. My intuitive part pointed out, somewhat sarcastically, that this was a far more useful definition of courage than loudly asserting my status as a victim.

I considered its analysis and had to agree. I had to let it go — at least for now. I took a breath and let the volume of my emotions dissipate. When they had reached a more subdued level, I asked, "Be that as it may, is there anything you can say about what happened that might be helpful?"

She turned toward me again.

"On that subject, nothing. I understand you may feel I've been dishonest toward you by not revealing what I know, but as I said, there are constraints. There will likely be other matters I cannot speak about. The fact is our lives became intertwined well before we met. We each have an image we present to the world. Relationships are built by allowing each other glimpses of who we truly are, and often it is not who we wish we were. It takes time. Just understand that today I do not mean you harm. In fact, quite the opposite. Can we continue under those conditions?"

"Can you?"

"I must, if we're to be friends. And you?"

"I can try. Two days ago, I would have said no way, but much has changed since then. I know you better, at least I think I do, and I'd like to know more. So, yes, I'm going to have to live with the possibility of more surprises."

"That's a relief to hear. For my part, I'll try to be as candid as possible. All I ask is that you talk to me." She paused and came closer. "I knew you were upset the moment you entered the room."

"I was. I came downstairs determined to have it out with you. Now, all that seems far less important. What was done happened long ago. That can't be changed. I'll just have to make the best of it. Besides, I doubt I can remain upset with you for very long either. I guess I'll have to live with that too. All I ask is that you don't take advantage of it…at least not too much."

She took my arm. "I'll keep that in mind."

We walked some more.

"Shall we sit on the steps?" I asked as we approached the drop off to the tennis court.

She nodded, and we sat down. The light slanted down onto the court and lit the leaves of the trees that sprang up just beyond the grass verge that ran around the fence. I wondered if Alice, or even Lord Bromley, had played tennis here.

"Have you ever met any of Alice's former husbands in your travels?"

She didn't answer right away, so I turned to look at her. Her cheeks had turned a slight shade of pink.

"You have."

"Yes."

"Tell me."

"I suppose it's only fair. I met Lord Bromley. He's the reason I became so interested in Johnny's aunt, by the way."

"Really? Now, you definitely have my attention."

"Yes, well, that's the problem. It wasn't my best moment. Besides, it's personal, and I don't do personal very well — particularly if it doesn't show me in a flattering way."

"I can understand that, but someone once told me the direct route is best, so you might as well tell me the story."

She laughed. "Yes, someone did, didn't they?" She paused again, looked down at her feet, and then wrapped her arms around her knees. "Okay, Lord Bromley…I was introduced to him at a party in London long before I became an attorney. I didn't think anything of him at first. He was an older man, although he was still strikingly handsome. He had very pale skin and jet-black eyes. He was well dressed — urbane is how I would describe him. He also struck me as a lady's man in spite of his age. He was with two much younger women when we met, who seemed to idolize him. A year later at a fancy-dress ball, he asked me for a dance. His manners were extremely smooth. I found myself agreeing before I could think. The next day, my mother, who saw us together, told me to have a care. I ignored her. I was, after all, no longer a teenager and had achieved some measure of maturity. It was my time, and I was on vacation in London. I love formal parties. I got myself invited to many. I liked the glitter, and I liked ballroom dancing. Lord Bromley was always there, and I found myself dancing with him more and more. He was a very good dancer, which was one reason, but more importantly, he fascinated me.

"He had a way about him that resonated with something hidden inside me. He also had a bad reputation. The business with Johnny's aunt was only one of many rumors that followed him around like a dark shadow. That didn't seem to bother the hosts who held such things. He was always invited, and in spite of his unsavory character, I was drawn to him. He asked me out. I refused. He kept asking. Eventually, I accepted, but the day before, who should storm into my hotel room but my mother. She had gotten wind of our meeting. How, I don't know. Had she not put her foot down, things might have turned out badly. I was young, true, but not that young. The truth was I was ill-prepared against any of his onslaughts. That man has a way with a woman. If he has the desire for her, there's little she can do. I experienced his magnetism, and I was spellbound. I'm sure that's what happened to Johnny's aunt, Alice. We're kindred spirits in that way."

"You're drawn to bad men with dark souls. I wouldn't have expected that."

Bruni blushed and held tightly to her knees. For just a moment, I caught a glimpse of what she must have looked like back then.

"I am pulled in that direction, it's true. It's one of my...secrets.

The only one who knows other than yourself is my mother. After the near miss with Lord Bromley — and it really was a near miss, even though it had barely gotten started — she sat me down, and we had one of the frankest conversations I can remember. She understood me in ways I had not expected and knew more about the inner me than I did. She married my father after all, and that should tell you something. We actually became exceptionally good friends after that and have been ever since."

"I'm happy it turned out well. Weren't you a little young for him?"

"Of course I was, but it's an ancient story, almost a cliché. Young, inexperienced woman is seduced by older, more experienced man. It happens all the time."

"I guess it does. Lucky for you, I am not so ancient and don't have a dark side."

She scoffed at me. "Oh, but you do. You're just too afraid to show it."

I looked at her quite stunned. "You must be joking."

"I'm not...not at all. It's there. I am well aware of it. It calls to me, and I find myself responding." She rested her head on her knees and gazed at me in a different way than before. Her hair hid much of her face, but her brilliant blue eyes looked back steadily. I felt myself turn slightly red.

"Well, let's put that to one side for the moment," I said rather quickly. "You mentioned being interested in Alice."

"You won't get off that easily, but we'll move on for now. I've been interested in Alice ever since that time. Mother also said she was tough as nails, which coming from her was quite a compliment. That alone would have made me curious. Mother rarely speaks of other women in complimentary terms. It's how she is. She likes the men to herself. No competitors for their attention. Alice was an exception.

"Although I don't know that much, I do know that there was bad blood between Alice and Lord Bromley that only intensified over time. After the divorce, she got involved in drugs and the occult — a bad combination. She died. It was rumored that he killed her indirectly. I was very young at the time, but Papa and Mother talked about it for years afterward. It occasionally comes up even now. It's why I wanted to see her bedroom. I'm sure you know more than I, but what I do find intriguing is that Malcolm Ault is still about. He's another of those men who seems to always be invited but are present when strange things take place. According to Papa, Ault and Lord Bromley are quite close."

"Do you think Ault had something to do with Alice's death?"

"I highly doubt it, but I'm sure he knows more than he lets on. So now that you know one of my biggest secrets, I suppose we better be getting back."

We got up and brushed ourselves off.

"So, who gave it to you?" she asked as she took my arm.

"The report?"

"Yes, the report."

"Strange as it sounds, I think I must stand mute."

"Very clever." She gave me a dig in the ribs. "You don't have to tell me. It was in the envelope Mrs. Leland received."

"I'm silent as the grave," I said.

"Charming."

We walked along, content to be in each other's company. I felt better, and although I had resolved nothing, my head was now clear enough to sit down with Johnny. It was a relief.

After a few minutes, Bruni said, "You should know I no longer work for Boskins and Harold and haven't for years. I left them shortly after that incident."

"Was that the reason?"

"One of many."

"Well, I'm happy to hear that, and speaking of dark souls, what about your husband? Is he a dark soul as well?"

"No," she said stopping me and standing close. "He was a mistake. One that will be shortly rectified."

She turned, took my arm again, and moved me along before I could respond.

51

"How did it go?" asked Johnny as Robert and I entered the common room. Robert had been moping about in the entrance hall, so I'd brought him along.

"It went well. I feel better and able to focus, which was the point. I had words with Bruni, of course, and I brought you your beast. I think he was looking for you."

"I figured as much on both counts." Johnny petted Robert, who forgave his master's neglect only after Johnny finally grabbed his head and kissed the top of it. Mollified, he plopped himself in his basket.

"She couldn't comment on the B & H thing since she was their attorney, but I figured she didn't know who we were at the time and was simply carrying out the plans of those higher up. I'm over the initial shock. That we were deliberately sideswiped is obvious in hindsight, and I suppose not seeing it shows a defect in my character, but what else is new? I'm moving on."

"I quite agree, although it would be nice to know who pulled the trigger."

"I suspect it was the baron. He and I are going to have to have a serious talk about a number of things. I've added that to the top of the list."

"Well, good for you. That takes care of one of the items I've written here. I've not been idle while you were absent, and by the way, there is a perfectly good slug of single malt in front of you, should you want some fortification. While you drink it, I have worked up a little action plan you can present to Maw, which I would like to run by you."

"By all means." I picked up the glass of whiskey that was on the table and sat down on the couch. "You did wash the glass?"

"As best I could, given our limited facilities."

"You simply rinsed it out with some running water."

"That's what I mean by limited facilities."

"I suppose it won't kill me."

"It better not. There's lots to be done here, and don't wrinkle your nose at it. That's a mighty fine drop, compliments of Stanley's personal stash."

"In that case, bottoms up." It was wonderfully satisfying. "So, what's the plan?"

"Regarding the sinking of our partnership, we need more information. You already talked to Bruni, and you have a mind to speak with the baron. Excellent. That's as far as we can go for now, but at least it shows that you are not letting it rest.

"About the blackmail. Two can play at that game. Maw can tell Bonnie to do her worst, and for every board seat lost, the entire block of stock of that company will be transferred to John Senior. Maw can always say she has too many board seats anyway. Even if Maw is in some way culpable, Bonnie will have to think twice about carrying on, given she will lose far more than Maw will.

"Bonnie calling in the Dodge Capital debt: again, go ahead. There's nothing to prevent Maw, if she so wishes, from refinancing the Dodge loan on a personal basis.

"The ownership transition. I think the Dunn analysis is correct. Bonnie would need to make herself qualified. This is not impossible by any means. One way is to start her working at each of the companies and get herself familiar with them from the ground up. It would be good for her, and if she shows promise, so much the better. The problem with putting my father in charge means a contested transition. A possible solution is to divide the estate in two, with the other getting to choose which portion, and in the event of any contesting or disagreement, the foundation becomes an option for Maw, and neither party gets a thing.

"As to why she dropped this in our laps in the first place, I still think she wanted to let us know what happened more than anything else, but she can at the same time see if we are possible candidates by whether or not we use the knowledge in some way. Does she want to see us exact revenge? It's a possibility, but with little hard evidence to hand as to who exactly was behind it, acting on the data would be premature and reckless — not something you would want in a manager. Anyway, that's where it's at so far."

"Good suggestions, but it's all very neat."

"You think it's too neat?"

"Yes, I do. It solves all the problems, and that's its defect. Maw is Maw. She's lived this long without our help. I'm sure she can continue just fine. Remember that sweet old lady who always wore black and was referred to us by one of our competitors?"

"Who could forget her? She had a ton of cash sitting in the bank and had us working on proposal after proposal for weeks. It was a monstrous waste of time."

"Exactly. She loved the attention and 'what do I do with all this money' problem far more than any solution. It's probably what kept her alive. I think it's the same here. Maw's just stirring the pot. If we go anywhere near this thing, we'll be in the same situation. It will amuse her to no end, but for my part, I'd rather pass."

"So, what will you say to her?"

"What I think. I'll thank her for the information and the opportunity, of course, but this is definitely hers to solve."

"Really!" said Johnny. He paused to consider this approach. "You know, I like it. Good for you. It's quite bold. Nonetheless, Maw may not react very well. That other lady was not pleased with us when I told her not to come calling anymore."

"That's an understatement. She stormed out and tried to slam the sliding door to the conference room — twice, in fact — and all it did was make a feeble click, which really set her off. She even wanted to lodge a regulatory complaint. I think that was the only botched sale that we ever celebrated."

"It was, and well worth it. We sidestepped a major headache. By the way, I stopped by to talk to Stanley, but he was up to his ears in preparations for lunch and tonight's anniversary celebration. He told us to pop round at the end of the evening."

"Fair enough. Now, it's time I have that chat with Maw." I gathered up the folders and notes.

"Good luck," said Johnny. Robert raised his head for a moment, saw Johnny was still there, and flopped back to sleep.

"Thanks. I'll need it. See you in a bit."

I doubted Maw would be pleased, but I was done with being led around by the nose. No more — not for love or money.

52

As I was walking down the second-floor hallway, Maw was coming up the stairs.

She motioned for me to follow her into her bedroom suite. She walked over to two chairs set around a small table in front of the open window. The sound of Harry cutting the south lawn carried in with the breeze. Maw sat down in one chair and nodded for me to sit in the other.

I handed her back the files.

"Well?" she asked as she placed them on the table between us.

"Based on the information you provided, I know Johnny and I were targeted. I suppose I should be outraged, but I'm not. There were lessons to be learned, and I learned them. I'm moving on."

"So, you'll do nothing," she said coldly.

"No action is also an action. The information is incomplete. The how is answered, but the who and why are not."

She stared at me for a long moment. "Suppose I supply them — what then?"

"Then I'll have to verify it and assess what to do. If the person responsible is more powerful than I am, which is very likely the case, I'll have to take the time to plan accordingly."

"Humph" was all she said. She looked away and stared out the window. Her grim expression said she was not pleased with me. My answer probably reconfirmed for her once again that ruling was a lonely business, made more so by the obtuseness and general recalcitrance of those around her.

Her cruel and unforgiving expression made me ask on impulse, "Why *did* you do it?"

She looked back at me and said flatly, "You're guessing."

I had expected a denial, but there was none. "Am I?"

"Until you know the answer, we have nothing to discuss."

"It was a test."

"Go on," she said, her pale eyes fixed on me like those of a snake.

Before I answered, I reflected on what Johnny had said about bypassing her immediate heirs. He was probably correct, as he often was. Only we had failed the test long ago, when we dissolved our partnership. It had been Maw who had engineered the debacle from the start. It was obvious when I took into account her capabilities as a businesswoman, the resources she commanded, and her belief in her absolute right to interfere with and control the lives of those around her. I said, hoping to restore some of her goodwill, "We may have failed, but more is learned through failure than success. Until one encounters defeat and knows how to advance in spite of it, one doesn't understand the difference."

She snorted at my answer. "Poppycock...You have your nerve implying I had something to do with it, but why should I care what you think? You're nothing but an insolent little prick."

Her caustic words sent waves of panic once again crashing through me. Had I just made another grievous error? I floundered and was about to apologize profusely, when my intuitive part interrupted. It counseled that I say nothing and ride it out. Even if my conjecture was completely off the mark, a fact she had yet to deny, my conclusion was a compliment, not an insult. By recognizing and acknowledging her capability to carry out such a plan, I had empowered her. Besides, it added in its sarcastic way, if I was wrong, it was likely the baron who was responsible. I had learned something through the process of elimination.

I stared back at her. Maw rose up from her chair and said coldly, looking down at me, "I don't know why I wasted my time giving you that information. You're not worth my notice, my interest, or even my breath. You're not even of my blood."

It might have been this last remark, her overall contempt, or perhaps my lack of sleep, but I'd had enough. I stood as well and faced her, eye to eye.

"I could say the same about you. You never wanted my analysis. It was just a smoke screen. What was the point of letting us know that we had been set up? Johnny and I had already failed your little test years ago. The only thing you could hope to achieve by your disclosure was that I would somehow blow a fuse, blame the baron, and attack him vigorously. No wonder you're here. He's got a hold over you, hasn't he?" I threw that out there. I had no idea if it was true. I said it solely based on anger.

Maw paled noticeably. "How dare you raise your voice to me?" she croaked.

"I dare, and I've only just begun. You have the gall to come to me about your legacy? You want a legacy? I'll show you a legacy. Look around! What do you see? Familial conflict brought about by greed, fear, and sustained hatreds — all born, bred, and cultivated by you. That's your legacy. You want to talk about blood? You can have it. Welcome to your life's work. It's a train wreck, and it's been years in the making. You want me to stop? I'll stop right now because we're done."

With that, I whirled and stormed toward the door.

I had my hand on the knob and was about to rip the door from its hinges, when she called out pleadingly, "Wait...please? There is something I must tell you."

I froze and turned, my hand still on the door. She looked older and worn out. The change from moments ago stopped me. My curiosity struggled with the reactions she had provoked. The woman had a gift for discovering and bringing to the surface my deepest conflicts.

I had experienced such elation when Maw had asked for my advice earlier that morning. I had finally felt a measure of acceptance, but I had misinterpreted her actions. She'd had no such intention. I was not a member of the family and never would be. The finality of this understanding, and the contempt she had for me hurt me more than I could possibly express.

I had always known intellectually I was not a Dodge. I had known it for years, but my heart had not. It had always harbored a faint glimmer of hope that somehow I might be accepted as a full-fledged member of the family. It would sing over and over, "Blood is not everything," whenever the debate over the nature of my relationship to them began in my head. As of today, it would sing no more, and I felt its pain. I had no family here, and that was the end of it.

I desperately wanted to get away and recover if I could, but my intellect also knew that the Dodge clan was as close to the concept of a family as I would ever know, and Maw was a part of it. I had craved their acceptance from an early age, and I had reason to. I lived in fear. A misstep might find me out on the street, where bad things could happen and death claim me before my time. To my immature mind, I had little real protection. My parents moved to unknown rhythms in another universe separate from the one I inhabited. They never knew my torment. Of course, my adopted household would have never thrown me out, but the possibility haunted me no matter what I did.

Maw had come to my rescue and seemed an ally when I was in

desperate need of one. By treating Johnny and me as equals, she had cemented my most important friendship. My gratitude for this single act and Johnny's acceptance of me was a source of comfort from the terror of abandonment that would occasionally consume me in fits of tears and trembling that would last for days at a time.

Maw was not the only one. Alice was the other deity in my life I gave thanks to. Both women appeared connected with the divine in ways I was unable to articulate. Within the boundaries of their different gifts, I formed for myself a kind of sanctuary. Maw was the sun and represented the protection of animals and the very young. Alice was the moon and guarded my nights. She was able to intercede with the ghosts that wandered through my dreams and imagination. The relief both had provided without their knowing, or even their intentions to do so, kept me rational and drew me back from the dark places I sometimes visited. Their presence in my life, and Johnny's too, all of them, had provided the nurture and structure I required so desperately until I was able to stand on my own. I could never repay that debt. I let go of the door and walked back over to the chair.

"Say what you wish to say," I said without any emotion, my defenses once again in place. I knew as I sat back down that I would need them. Maw gave nothing away for free, and the cost to those close to her was always the same: the exposure and disparagement of their most hidden and painful fears and imperfections.

53

"Thank you." Maw said once I had seated myself. Her color had returned, and she had recovered her composure. I wondered if her little display of weakness was just an act. After all, I was sitting down in front of her, which was what she wanted.

She raised her chin and asked, "I suppose you're proud of yourself?"

"I could ask you the same."

She glared at me and said, "You're insolent. It's a bad habit and unbecoming."

"From your point of view; from mine, it's called having to suffer in silence as one listens to one's betters, or some such nonsense."

She snorted. "Very clever, but it takes more than cleverness to get on. Knowledge and information are necessary. Had I not showed you the file, would you have worked it out?"

"It would have eluded me."

"Which proves my point: knowledge and information are vital, but before I begin, I would like to put an end to our previous discussion. Asking for your opinion about the files a few minutes ago was a means to an end, no more."

She paused, waiting for me to interject some comment, but I said nothing.

"Very good. Shall we move on?"

"Not yet. I think an apology is in order." It would not absolve her actions, but it would be a step in the right direction.

"I never apologize, and I won't start now. Each of us does what we must, and given the same circumstances, I doubt anything would change. Apologies sound nice, but they are merely social lubrication, nothing more. I had my reasons for doing what I did. Maybe I would have liked things to have turned out differently, but I doubt it. To apologize is to belittle the action and the rationale behind it, no matter how reprehensible the act might be. One always has a reason for what one does, even if it is instinctive. Apologies only serve to hide the truth from ourselves. Don't look for an apology from me, because you're not going to get one. I don't expect you feel like apologizing to me for your outbursts. In this, we are equal. Now, can we continue with a civil tongue or not?"

I nodded.

"I wish to tell you a story. You may choose to believe it or not. You may choose to react to it or not. That is up to you. For my part, I will tell you what I know to be factual. Memories change over the years, so what I remember may be inaccurate. It probably is, but I don't really care. The memory has served me well, and that's all that matters. Are you willing to listen and not interrupt until I'm finished?"

I nodded again.

"Say it."

"Why should I?"

"Even a lizard can nod its head up and down. It means nothing. I want to make sure we understand each other."

"Very well. I will listen and not interrupt, but if I have questions when you're finished, I expect to be able to ask them and get answers."

"It depends on the question. I won't be interrogated. You may ask, but I may not answer."

"Then I will listen but make no guarantee I won't interrupt." I was being recalcitrant. I knew this, but I was just not in the mood, and having Maw compromise, even if only an inch, kept her from running me over completely.

"Very well. It will have to do. Before I begin, I will say this and hope it is plain enough: I dislike you. To be even more frank, I have always disliked you. It may be unfair, but there it is. For some time, you were happily absent. It was a gift. You have returned, and I feel the same. Am I being clear?"

"Quite; in this we are also equal."

"I suppose I must put up with your rudeness. I have things to say, so I will choose to overlook it...for now."

We had always had an uneasy relationship, but the depth and extent of her animosity surprised me. I had had a taste of it this morning. Had I not held her in such high regard, I might have perceived it more clearly, but I had not. It was one more error in judgment among many.

She continued. "In truth, my dislike for you is misplaced. I know this. You are an innocent, and I have tried to compensate for it to some degree in our interactions. But I am old and don't have the time or the inclination to mollycoddle. Still, I have my personal reasons to dislike you. That won't change, but should you harbor any ideas about mending any breach between us or getting into my good graces, I promise you: that too will never happen. You can tell that to Johnny as well. He will probably try to dissuade me, but it won't work. You can also tell him that by being connected to you in any way, and I emphasize the word *any*, he will get nothing — not a penny. He's a clever boy. At one time, I did intend to bypass my children. I may still, but it depends on him. Let's see which way he jumps first, shall we? I will be most interested."

She actually smiled at the thought and then said, "I will speak to Johnny separately, but those are Johnny's terms. I have others, but they do not concern you."

I rose and asked, "Are we done? I have things to do."

I did not trust myself to stay in the same room with her. Much more, and it would end badly. Maw had no need for weapons. Her words were knives, and she used her cunning malice like a mace.

Maw mirrored my move and stood. "No, we're not. And as you pointed out previously, I'm just getting started, but it won't take long. It's about your parents. Will that be of interest?"

I sat back down.

She smiled sweetly as she sat as well. "I thought as much. I have your complete attention at last. Oh, happy day."

It took a force of will, but I decided to listen. She was easy to hate, and that had been the undoing of many. I would not succumb to it. I was sure she had left the worst for last.

"The time we have now and the information I will give you are the only things I will ever gift to you, and even this has taken a supreme effort on my part.

"You wanted to know the how, the who, and the why of the demise of your little business. It was me. I wanted to destroy you and drive you away. It was personal, and I make no apologies for it. Of course that alone is not enough of an answer for you, but it can stand on its own nonetheless. I made the decision. I am responsible. That may seem extreme and overly dramatic, but there's more to it, and that is what I wish to impart. I warn you in advance: this story will not answer all the questions it will generate, but it will have to do. I won't answer a single one of yours, I've decided."

She looked out the window. It was enough for me take a breath. My parents? This could not be good. I badly wanted a cigarette, but there were no ashtrays. She looked back at me and continued.

"Bonnie and John were not my only children. There was a third. Her name was Sarah. She was a beautiful girl, intelligent, and full of life. I watched over her as she grew up. I tried to make sure she made the best decisions. I sent her away to boarding school so that she might become better educated, get into a good college, and eventually come back to me, so I might apprentice her. She was from the very beginning the one I wanted to take over and manage my affairs. We were so alike. She had courage, discipline, and determination. The other two never came close. What I didn't plan for was her falling in love with a man who had everything to gain, while she had everything to lose. She kept it secret, but I found out about it. How could I not? She had been accepted at Vassar and was set to begin in the fall. When she came home, she was floating on air. I had seen that look. I had observed it in the mirror at one time or another. She was in love.

"I asked who she was seeing, but she refused to tell me. It took me some time, but I found out nonetheless. I had him investigated. My instincts were correct, and I was extremely disappointed with her choice. I confronted her with my discovery. The young man was a loser, and I told her that in no uncertain terms. I forbade her to see him again. We fought. Things were said between us — hard things, nasty things. We were two of a kind, you see, so you could imagine how extremely cutting and heated the argument became. Eventually, she could take no more and ran from the room.

"To this day, I don't know how it happened. We were in her bedroom on the second floor. It opened onto a hallway that had a railing that extended along the opposite side before it connected to the circular staircase that led to the main floor. She must have tripped. They're called balusters. I didn't know that at the time. They prevented her from going over, but they were set sufficiently wide apart so that a head could squeeze through. Hers did. They said it was a freak accident. She died from asphyxiation, the result of a crushed larynx. I could not get her head out. I tried. Oh, how I tried, but the balusters held her like the teeth of a bear trap."

She paused and took a breath. Whatever feelings she had for her dead daughter flashed across her face for an instant before it was replaced with the resolve to soldier on.

"It was a bad time," she said. "Initially, I blamed myself, but that was a fool's errand. It would never bring her back, and I had good reason to act the way I did. I was not to blame. Even if I was, the result was still the same. She was dead. One can mourn, and I did, but comes a time, you must get back to it.

"Management is my work. It's what I do. One can debate, one can argue the pros and cons, but ultimately, it's all about decisions. There can be no self-doubt, only the choice and then the action. Doubting is like a cancer. Once it starts, everything is affected. I held council with myself. It was the argument that led to the disaster, and the source of the argument was the young man. He was the reason. You may argue that my thinking was specious and arbitrary. It was…but all decisions are arbitrary — particularly the big ones. Uncertainty makes them so. One never has complete information. The best decisions and actions strengthen one's power, and the organizations concerned. One can be right for all the wrong reasons. It makes no difference. I made the choice, and the results speak for themselves. I decided the young man was responsible. That was the decision, and it strengthened me. I was able to carry on, when before it had been impossible. The young man was your father. It's no big revelation. You will have guessed that already, but there are things you haven't.

"Your father and I met officially only once. The day you and I met. Never before and never after. That does not mean we haven't interacted. I am happy to say I drove him from this country and into a somewhat impecunious and unhappy exile. You find yourself in front of me today because my son went behind my back and agreed to take you in as a favor to his friend. I was most displeased, but in the end, we negotiated an armistice of sorts. You would remain in the house, and I would leave your parents alone, provided they remained abroad and steered clear of this family. I have kept my end of the bargain for the most part. It is my wish to extend the same to you…Will you accept it?"

"Accept what, exactly?"

"You disappear back to where you came from, never to be seen here again, never to communicate with this family, and never to answer if you are contacted. In return, I will leave you and your family alone and untroubled. The alternative is I will make it my business to run every last one of you into the ground, even if it costs me a fortune. Make no mistake, I have a fortune to spend, and the resources available to make your lives a hell on Earth. You questioned my legacy. That can be my legacy. It will amuse me, and I like to be amused. You have my offer. Think well on it. I expect an answer tonight."

I kept my peace. I would not be railroaded into an answer until I had thought it through.

"How can I be sure you'll keep your end? I believe you said you had kept your end of the bargain for the most part, which implies you meddled nonetheless. I'll expect you to make adequate and convincing representations as to how you intend to fulfill your part. We'll talk again."

"I make no such promises."

"Then neither shall I."

"We shall see."

"That we shall," I said as I left her and made my way to the aerie upstairs. Stanley's family reserve and some time to think were in order. Once again I considered her name, Maw, as being entirely appropriate. I would make her gag. I just had to figure out how.

54

"She actually said that? Good God, and I'm related to her," Johnny said.

I had asked for a glass of Stanley's reserve as soon as I entered the room. Johnny supplied it in a flash, and I proceeded to tell him about the conversation in full. When I had finished, Johnny thought about what I had said and concluded, "There are several points. The sins of the father are visited upon us once again. I don't mean that as a disparagement, but it explains a great deal. You and she always had a bit of a strained relationship. The reason for it never entered my mind. I thought it was normal. Maw treats everyone like that, even the parents. She is bad-tempered by nature, but the depth of her dislike for you is truly in a class by itself, and now we know the reason why. That Sarah situation must have really knocked her for a loop. That she even existed was kept from you and me for years. How did we find out about it in the first place?"

"It was that French nanny. Death by misadventure was her obsession, if you recall, and she thought we could add to her storehouse of trivia on the subject. She was familiar with the facts and the peculiarity of Sarah's death, but no more. We knew nothing, so she proceeded to tell us all about it, much to our fascination and delight. As it stands, I doubt even your parents know the full story. If they do, I'm certain it was not from Maw. Until the nanny let the cat out of the bag and you attempted to verify the more gruesome bits by asking the parents about it one afternoon, they were quite happy to keep us in ignorance. The disclosure was a memorable event for all concerned. The nanny was sent packing shortly thereafter."

"I don't think that was the reason. How quickly you forget," said Johnny.

Johnny and I would often bring up odd incidents in our history together and recount them. It was an important ritual that cemented our friendship. We would argue the finer points. Such banter often distracted us when we were confronted with large and possibly insurmountable problems.

Johnny continued. "It was after you got your head stuck in the banister trying to figure out how it happened that sealed it. You cried and whimpered the entire time while the building super used a saw to cut you free with everyone in the house standing around watching. I was blamed as an accessory, of course, which was most unfair, but things really came to a head when you were asked how and why you put yourself in that position."

"You're quite right. I forgot," I said. "That was rather awkward, and then I foolishly assumed it was a rhetorical question. How was I to explain it? Your dad got quite upset when I said nothing. He thought I was defying him. I finally blurted out that we were experimenting, and the whole idea of a reenactment of the event came out in a rush. He said it was the stupidest thing he'd ever seen or heard. He grumbled about it for weeks, even after the repairs were completed. Underneath the surface, I think it really freaked out your parents. The parallels and coincidences, knowing the complete story, must have been very odd."

"Yes," added Johnny, "and the nanny was sent packing as a result. She left in tears, the victim of her own curiosity. I also recall that the results of our little experiment were strangely inconclusive, which may have troubled them also. Frankly, I've wondered about the whole thing ever since, but it could have been the particular type of baluster in Maw's house."

"I wondered about that, too. You don't suppose…"

"No way. The truth is often very peculiar. You can't make that sort of thing up. Still, it is a strange way to go. Back to the matter at hand," Johnny continued. "Why you ended up on our doorstep and why our partnership vaporized can finally be laid to rest. That is the good news, which leads us to the bad, as well as the final and most alarming point: Maw's offer or, more accurately, her ultimatum. For my part, I would like to make one thing absolutely clear: grandmother or not, riches or not, Maw can go to hell as far as our friendship is concerned. It means the world to me, and I hope to you as well, so don't do anything noble or foolish. I won't abide it." Johnny gave me one of his looks.

"I won't. I feel the same way, but hear me for a moment. There are issues we need to think about. Simply telling Maw to stuff it may not be good enough. In fact, I'm sure it won't be. What if Maw decides to get to you through your parents? There is that bond issue floating around that could threaten Dodge Capital, for starters. She could also let Bonnie loose and tell her to do her worst. That would mean the Fifth Avenue apartment would go away as well. I'm sure there's a great deal more. I'm not saying we acquiesce. We won't, and I'm very happy you agree. I'm just saying we need a countermove. Pawns can threaten queens and take them, but it must be set up well in advance. We don't have the time. We need to bring more force to bear now, not later."

"The parents?" asked Johnny.

"They'll need to be made aware of the situation, but I would rather not just yet. It's a special day for them. Why ruin it? I think I should talk to the baron. It would not be my favorite thing to do, by any means, but when I spat out that I thought the baron had a hold on her, Maw flinched slightly. There may be something there. There are also other matters I need to discuss with him."

"Brunhilde being one, I'm sure. I agree, but I recommend a slightly more indirect approach. Talk to Elsa first. Let her set it up, if she thinks it has a chance. I would also inform Bruni, so your actions are not misinterpreted. You and Elsa traipsing through the tall grass having some tête-à-tête might give her the wrong impression and add to an already tumultuous state of affairs, which neither of us need right now. Bruni might also give you more of an insight as to how to go about it. She works for her father after all. There is also Stanley. That man has a gift for intrigue that we should consult. In the meantime, it's nearing lunch. We'll have to get ready, and while we're at it, there are several things that are still on the old to-do list. Are you ready?" Johnny picked up his pad.

He was organized and methodical. I had to give him credit. I sighed. Around Johnny, work in some form or other rarely ceased. "Go ahead."

"I've penciled in Stanley late this evening. We need to grill Malcolm Ault about Alice. I think I'll do that, although we might manage it together, if we have the opportunity before lunch. You need to talk to Bruni, then Elsa, and finally Hugo. That will occupy your attention for some time. After which, we'll need to coordinate. In addition, there are the wild cards. Sleeping Beauty I'm sure is up and about, and let's not forget old Maw. She'll be sniffing around to see how her little ultimatum is sitting. I would suggest avoiding her, if you can, but if you can't, try to remain calm. Deep breathing works for me, followed shortly by strong drink. Actually, less might be better, and for sure no dark spirits.

They make you testy, and right now we need a plan, not a premature confrontation. What do you think so far?"

"Well, you did say it was 'gird your loins' day, so I agree. We've planned; now let's gird."

We dressed for lunch. Robert woke up and was waiting impatiently, looking from Johnny to the door and back again, eager to go downstairs. I was a little less so, but I had to do what I had to do.

55

W e were not the first down. Malcolm was pouring champagne for Bruni. It was Dom Perignon. In keeping with family tradition, Cristal was served only in the evening. Johnny and I had tried to argue our preference, but our requests to higher authorities had always been denied. Some things never change.

We congregated around the bar as Malcolm made a show of pouring so that there was a minimum of bubbles and a maximum of liquid. He must have had a great deal of practice, because he did it with surprising skill and speed. Once I had my glass, Johnny made a sign for me to speak with Bruni while he tackled "Mal." I heard him tell Johnny that those close to him called him by that name. Johnny quipped, "Well, then you can call me Johnny." They laughed and moved toward the french doors.

Bruni smiled at me.

She was like a ray of sunlight. She wore the same gray ensemble she had worn when I first met her. I gave thanks she did not have a change of dress for every occasion. I couldn't possibly deal with that amount of luggage if we ever went on vacation. I was jumping ahead of myself as usual, but the future always burns brighter than the present when there are difficulties.

"Been busy?" she asked, looking at me over the lip of her flute.

"Never a dull. I need some advice. I'd like to speak to your father, but I'm not sure the best way to go about it."

"You certainly move fast, I must say, and here I was thinking I was the only one." Her eyes twinkled, but I wasn't sure she was entirely joking.

"Very funny. How about we step outside?"

"We seem to be doing a lot of that. People might get ideas."

"I'm afraid that ship has sailed."

"It has, and we're on it. Lead on."

Bruni and I, with glasses in hand, excused ourselves as we squeezed past Mal and Johnny on our way to the south lawn. They looked like old pals. The breeze still blew, but the day was turning overcast. There would be weather by tonight.

Bruni looked into the distance. "There was a red sky this morning. You know the saying?" she said, turning to me.

"Sailors take warning."

"Exactly."

"You were up early."

"I was. I was thinking."

"About?"

"My life. My world has shifted. I welcome it, of course, but then again, I don't. As a lawyer, I always want to know the answer before I ask a question, but there are many times that's not possible. You and I are such a question. After last night and our talk this morning, I've made some decisions. You know one of them. Another is I want a more formal understanding between us. I'm going to make you an offer. You may or may not be ready for such a thing, but for my own sanity, it's necessary. I can't do this any other way. I really can't."

"What do you have in mind?" I asked.

"I will tell you, but you should hear this first."

She looked away again.

"I may look composed and sure of myself, but I'm not. I often need reassurance. This morning, I lay in bed and looked at the future regarding you and me. To simply see each other after this weekend will require a great deal of effort from both of us. We live thousands of miles apart. There are my father's objections to overcome. There are our businesses. Work has a priority all its own. It always does, and inertia will do the rest. I could list others, but it would just upset me more."

She turned back to me.

"It was all quite overwhelming in the clear light of day, but last night I made the decision to have a life — a real one, a happy one. I think you could be part of it, which is why I thought about our future. The depth of my feelings was also a surprise. Feelings and emotions are not always the best foundations on which to plan a future. I realized that some form of agreement was needed between us. I have formulated one. It may sound a bit stilted and formal, but I want to be clear above all. Are you ready to hear it?"

"Go for it."

"Very well. The offer is either accepted or rejected. There is a time limit. The offer expires when we walk through the door behind us. Silence is not to be inferred as acceptance. How am I doing so far?"

"Fine, but shouldn't I get an attorney?"

"I think you have one already, so listen up. This is important." She laughed, but I could tell she really was serious.

"Okay, I'm listening. Continue."

"My offer is my commitment to you to do whatever it takes to create a relationship between us.

"In return, I want your promise to do the same. Additionally, our relationship becomes senior to all other commitments. If there are conflicts of interest from the past, or in the future, then we agree to disclose them to each other as soon as possible and resolve them by mutual agreement.

"If you reject my offer, then we continue as friends, of course, but with anything more off the table from this time forward. It's one or the other."

"An ultimatum?" I asked.

"No, it's an offer, but from some points of view, it could be interpreted the other way. You may consider it so, if you wish. The offer still stands."

"Fair enough. Yours is the second ultimatum I've received today, and it's barely noon. The first was on a different subject entirely. I like yours. I accept."

I didn't need to think about it. It was sensible and appropriate, given the rocky landscape in front of us, but I was stacking up the promises. There was the one to Stanley, the commitment to Johnny, the promise to myself to live my life on my own terms. What could possibly go wrong? Knowing my past, a great deal, but there was one thing about Bruni's request that resonated and gave me some measure of comfort: I would not be alone, and that was something. It might even be everything.

"Good. So, promise me."

"I promise I will do whatever is necessary to make things work between us. Our relationship will be the senior commitment, and any conflicts of interest will be disclosed and resolved by mutual decision."

"Thank you, and I promise to do the same. Now, let's move away from the door, so we can seal it properly without a lot of prying eyes."

We moved to the side and put down our glasses. I held her in my arms and kissed her.

She sighed. "It's done. I feel better. There are no guarantees, but our odds have improved. There is a rightness about us. I felt it last night and this morning, and I feel it now."

"I feel it too."

Bruni reached down and picked up our glasses. She handed me one and said, "Now, tell me about the other ultimatum and what you wanted to say to my father. We'll have to go back in very soon, so give me the abridged version."

"Something Mrs. Leland said." I told Bruni succinctly about the ultimatum and that I wanted to ask her father for advice about how to turn the tables on Maw.

I had expected a reaction, but there was none. Bruni was all business. She could switch from personal to professional at a moment's notice. "Did she give a reason?" she asked.

"She blames my father for the death of her daughter, Sarah, although he had nothing to do with it. Mrs. Leland holds him responsible, and I'm guilty by association. Johnny and I either comply or suffer the consequences."

"I'm unfamiliar with that particular episode in their family history. Your father has obviously made more than one enemy, Papa included. I hope this tendency is not genetic for both our sakes." She smiled. "Getting past my father's prejudices to even ask for advice will not be easy. I have thought about that in relation to you and me, and the answer is the same. A direct approach won't work. You'll need to discuss all this with my mother, but let me smooth it first. She has far more information than me, and can manage him far better as well on both issues. Should I arrange that?"

"By all means."

She smiled at me and took my arm as we made our way inside. We had crossed a bridge.

"Then I will. Thank you for accepting," she said. "That meant the world to me."

"That was quick," said Johnny.

Bruni and I looked at each other.

"Excellent," I said, "that means we have more time for champagne before lunch."

John and Anne entered the drawing room, followed by Elsa and the baron. I reached for another bottle of Dom and some glasses. I felt I needed a little celebration.

56

I opened another bottle. John Senior and I poured champagne for everyone. Bruni went off to talk to her mother.

We were waiting on Maw and Bonnie. After the second round, John was about to ring for Stanley to hurry them up, when they both arrived. Maw wore the same jeans and denim shirt as this morning. Bonnie had on jeans and a button-down Western shirt of dazzling white. I doubted anyone would ask them to change into something more formal. It would only lead to more conflict, and there had been enough of that last night. Bonnie made her way rapidly to the bar, poured herself some champagne, and stared impatiently at her glass, willing the bubbles to subside. She attempted to drink it, bubbles and all, but from her expression, the result was unsatisfactory. She saw me watching her and scowled.

Stanley opened the doors to the dining room and announced that lunch was served.

Bonnie commented to no one in particular, "I'm not going anywhere without a decent drink."

She hunted under the bar until she found a bottle of Wild Turkey. She poured the leftover champagne into a cooler and filled her champagne glass to the brim with bourbon. She downed it in a series of massive gulps and sighed.

"That's better," she mumbled to herself. "Lunch it is, then. I seem to have missed breakfast, and I'm famished. Why are you looking at me?" she said, noticing I hadn't moved.

"I'm waiting for you," I answered.

"Well, I don't like it."

"I mean no disrespect. I thought I would be polite and let you go first. You are a lady after all."

Somewhat pacified by my answer, she said, "True. I'll go first." With that, we entered the dining room. There were two places left. Bonnie and I were seated next to each other. John and Anne were at the ends, with Maw seated next to John Senior and with Johnny next to her. I pulled out Bonnie's chair, which was next to Johnny, and then seated myself. Opposite me was Elsa, who smiled. Malcolm sat between Bruni and Elsa, while the baron was in his usual place on John Senior's left. Elsa wore a conservative button-down shirt and a skirt. Malcolm had little to fear from her as to what might be visible. I was curious to know what Johnny had discovered. Bruni gave me a wink. I smiled back and said hello to Anne. Bonnie fidgeted beside me. I turned to her.

"I don't think we've ever sat next to each other."

"Enjoy it while you can. I doubt it'll happen again."

"A once-in-a-lifetime opportunity then. I should take advantage of it. Can I ask you a question?

"Can you?"

"I suppose I can, but will you allow me?"

"I suppose this once."

From what I had seen, Bonnie used barbed comments and prickly replies as a form of protection. I recognized that behavior. I had done the same for years, but I had used evasive answers and vacuous comments instead. Neither of us liked personal attention and had become skilled in the art of deflection. My intuitive part had posited we were more alike than I had considered. I was curious.

"Are you good at what you do?" I asked.

"What kind of stupid question is that?"

"A peculiar one, I admit, but important. Some people have inborn talent. Others become good at something through constant practice and feedback. Some are driven by the force of their determination, others by their environment. You wouldn't be at this table unless you were pretty good at getting on. So, which are you?"

"Don't you want to know what I've planned instead?"

"Would it help?"

"No."

"There you go. Some people want recognition. Others prefer the shadows. Which one are you?"

"It's a trick question. I won't answer that. I'm bad whatever I say."

"Some people want to be in the shadows but are forced out of them. Some want recognition but never get it. Is either person really bad?"

"Now you're trying to find out my motivation. That's a dead end. You'll never know."

"Then what's the point of talking? Am I an enemy or a friend? You don't know that either, and neither do I."

Bonnie stopped toying with her wineglass and looked at me. "So, which are you?"

"I could be one or the other, and so could you. My side is my own for now."

"I don't need you."

"No, you don't, but it works both ways, doesn't it?"

"Humph." She sounded like her mother. "You're not a Dodge, but you're still in their camp."

"I don't think so. Ask your mother."

She stared at me and decided I was bluffing. "Okay, I will."

Bonnie leaned behind Johnny and tapped Maw on her shoulder. Irritated at the interruption, Maw stopped talking to her son and leaned back to speak with Bonnie. Johnny scooted forward to give her room.

"What?" Maw snapped.

"Is he part of the Dodges?" asked Bonnie.

"Is who part of the Dodges?"

"Him." Bonnie pointed at me with her thumb.

"Him? Good heavens, no. Now, do you mind? You're interrupting." Maw went back to her conversation.

Still sitting forward, Johnny gave me a quick look. He was wondering what I was up to. He shook his head slowly in warning.

Bonnie returned, cutting off my view of Johnny, and said, "You're not."

"Told you."

"Humph," she said again. "Well, that's different. I thought you were."

"So did I, once."

"Fancy that. I had no idea. That's quite surprising. I'm impressed."

"How come?"

"I'd never considered you not part of them. Are you taken, by the way?"

"Taken?"

"Do you have a girlfriend?"

Now it was my turn to be surprised. "Yes," I blurted.

"Tough luck."

"It happens."

"Hold that thought," whispered Bonnie.

We were interrupted by a chilled Montrachet and the first course. Lunch was in full swing. Display plates of light blue and gold were replaced by thin translucent ones of bone china, on which were placed matching bowls containing chilled cucumber soup. It was one of Anne's favorites, and since it was our hosts' anniversary day, every course was one of either of their preferred dishes.

Bonnie's change of attitude surprised me. Her mother's confirmation that I was not a Dodge seemed to have transformed her.

Bonnie whispered to me, "I could have done with a larger bowl. That was damn good." She then asked, "What do you do?"

"Forensic accounting."

"Right up my alley. I've done some of that. I've a degree in accounting. We're going to get along fine."

"I didn't know that. Frankly, I hardly know anything about you."

"It's a simple story. You're a neutral, so I can tell you. I was the third wheel of the family. Sarah and John…Well, Sarah actually, she was the favorite until she died. You know about that, right?"

I nodded.

"I was quite content living in the background, but her death started the process of changing everything in my life. She was a bitch and a half, but that's another tale altogether. I was much younger than the other two. To answer your question, I preferred the shadows. That's why I liked accounting — particularly, analyzing company reports away from people. I even helped design a Fortran accounting software program, as well as wrote a paper on cash flows and future market returns, but there was the matter of a suitable heir. My half-brother did his own thing, and Mom was not overly appreciative of his efforts to be independent, so I was yanked out from underneath my rock and placed center stage as an alternate, to make him toe the line."

Bonnie gulped the last of her wine, but she had hardly put it down when it was refilled. She picked up the glass.

"This is a Montrachet and a good one. I can tell. Where was I? Oh yes, it pissed me off royally. More than I care to say, which I suppose I just did. I blame them, all of them, but I shouldn't be telling you any of this. I drink too much, and it loosens my tongue. It's the wine. They say *en vino veritas*. I took an inordinate amount of Latin and ancient Greek. Accounting was not my first choice. I wanted to be an ancient-language scholar. Go figure. I even translated an edition of Precopius's *Secret Histories*. If you ever think family life can be dull, check out Theodora and Justinian. That's an eye-opener. It'll curl your hair. They also say, 'In wine, there is wisdom,' but that's not the entire quote, you know. It also says, 'In beer, there is freedom; in water, there is bacteria.' Ben Franklin said it. He must have had stomach trouble. Aphorism can be quite contradictory, but I digress. Tell me your story instead, while I recover my wits."

I was tempted to tell her to slow down, but I'm sure she'd been told that many times by others. I was sure it didn't help then. I doubted it would help now. I told her my story instead.

"Mine is also fairly straightforward. I grew up with Johnny, studied economics. Got a CFA and partnered with him. Your mom blew us out of the water, so I went off to California and into forensic accounting. Johnny invited me to this get-together, so here I am."

"Yeah, I heard about Mom blowing you out of the water. Mom *really* doesn't like you."

"Tell me about it."

"Been there many times. It's tough. She can be a vindictive bitch, if ever there was one. I don't envy you being on the receiving end."

She turned toward me and leaned closer. Maybe it was the wine. Maybe it was because I had never really looked at her before. All I ever remembered about her were her mannerisms, her sometimes bizarre behavior, and her seemingly innate clumsiness. She appeared almost simpleminded, but I realized I was very much mistaken. She could act as well as her mother but played a different part. She was not beautiful, but she was not unattractive. I had never noticed that before, either. Her eyes were a washed-out blue like her mother's. Her mousy blond hair was actually cut very well, but she didn't wear it to her advantage. Pulled back, she would definitely up her image. Dressed in black with high heels made of steel, she'd be quite something.

"It was your folks that did it."

"My folks?"

"Yep, your dad, specifically. Family secrets. We all have secret histories. I should tell you yours. You might learn a thing or two."

Before she could say more, we were interrupted by the next course.

It was cold deshelled Maine lobster with claws, served on platters for each guest, accompanied by chilled white asparagus, lemon, and potato salad set around a silver bowl of remoulade.

"Lobster!" cried Bonnie. "Now we're talking. I missed breakfast, but this makes up for it. I don't suppose they serve seconds. Do you know if they do?"

"I'm sure arrangements can be made. Ask Stanley," I offered.

Bonnie motioned for him to come over. His face impassive, Stanley bent down to hear her. Bonnie whispered, "Do you think you could fix me up with another lobster tail? You have one hell of a cook back there, and I'm a fan. Thanks."

Stanley ghosted away and returned with another tail as well as a corresponding amount of remoulade in a little bowl.

Bonnie was thrilled. If she harbored any animosity toward Stanley for dragging her away last night, it didn't show.

"Thanks a bunch. You're the best."

Bonnie dug in. Having consumed one lobster, she started on the other.

"Okay, she said, "You interested?"

"About?"

"Your history. Haven't you been listening? Don't fade on me now, Percy. Sit closer, so I don't have to shout, and drink some more of this Montrachet with me. I love saying that word. It rolls nicely off the tongue. Okay, hopefully this is news. If you've heard it, say so, and we'll move on to other things."

Bonnie spoke and ate.

"Here goes. People don't notice me. Well, that's not true. They do notice me, but for all the wrong reasons. I appear clumsy. I think I found it so useful, I actually became that way, like scrunching up your face and having it freeze on you. I definitely wasn't clumsy growing up. I was stealthy as a cat and silent as a mouse. As the third wheel, whatever I said or did made no difference. I was simply left alone. It was the best of times. Being a nonentity, I liked to know how the other half lived, so to speak, so I listened all I could — beneath tables, behind couches, under beds. I imagined myself as a spy. I even took notes in a code I made up.

"Anyway, Sarah hooked up with your dad. They got pretty serious. He would sneak in the back way and up to her room. Sarah usually locked her door when she wasn't there, but I'd break in anyway, read her diary, and check out her makeup. One night, the two almost caught me. Luckily, I heard them coming. Rather than brazen it out, I slid under her bed. Sarah relocked the door when they were inside, not noticing it was unlocked to begin with. Let's put it this way: they were distracted. It was a long night for me. They were doing it for sure. I don't mean to be offensive, but you know it when you hear it. I fell asleep after a while and woke up just before dawn when someone dropped a shoe by my ear. They made their way downstairs, and I was able to escape. After that, I kept tabs on them. Mom was oblivious. They grew complacent — not a wise move around her. One day, the penny dropped, and Mom put it all together. When she realized what was going on right under her nose all along, she blew a gasket big time. I mean, she lost it completely and confronted Sarah."

Bonnie lowered her voice.

"There was one hell of a row. I don't know who threw the first punch, but one of them did. I was listening next door, and I knew the sound. After that, what had been a shouting match spun into a free-for-all. Anything not tied down was thrown at each other. Furniture got busted up. They fought as if it was life or death, and it was. Sarah ended up in the banister, but" — here Bonnie lowered her voice even more, and I had to lean even closer to her — "it could have just as easily been Mom asphyxiated between those balustrades. They both went completely nuts. Mom had no way out but to end it. It was preemptive self-defense. She had no choice. The police were called eventually, but only after everything had been cleaned up, cosmetics applied in copious amounts, and a story worked out. I told anyone who asked that I hadn't heard a thing because I was asleep the entire time. I never changed my story. That kind of knowledge can seriously reduce your life expectancy. After that incident, I kept even more in the background, but I had my ears and eyes open. Your dad demanded answers, and Mom wasn't giving any. There were some very acrimonious exchanges. Nasty stuff. He threatened to go to the press and make a big stink out of it, but his attempt was doomed from the start.

"Disproportional asset piles tell the outcome before it even starts. If you're trading blows one for one, and giving as good as you get, the one with the bigger pile always wins. Mom had a much bigger pile. It's the way of the world. Once your dad saw it was a lost cause and gave it up, Mom went after him in earnest. She was out for blood. She hired private investigators and ran a scorched-earth campaign that had him running to Europe. There he met your mother, and you came along. For some reason, their having a kid seemed to incense her even more. He had no choice and pulled off what I thought was a pretty clever move. He dumped you at my half-brother's. They'd been friends a long time. It was John's acceptance of you into his household that eventually precipitated a truce, but it inadvertently pulled me out of the shadows. I don't hold it against you. You had no say in any of it.

"Truce or no truce, your parents were still very bitter. They pulled a fast one on Mom when she tried to do some deals in Europe. They made sure those went south. As it stands, Europe is off-limits to Mom, and the US is off-limits to them, but I think that's just for show. Each of them is biding time, while they harass each other by making the odd foray into enemy territory. How does that square with what you know?"

"It fills in many blanks and answers some questions. I appreciate you telling me. Thank you."

"Don't mention it, but you and I both know the Sarah thing doesn't quite add up the way it should, right?"

"Yes, there's something that sticks a little."

"Tell me why you think so."

"It's hard to imagine what would drive them to such extremes."

"Exactly. There was a surfeit of passion. That's a good name for a book, by the way, but you hit it on the head. That's what I thought, and that leads me to my pet theory of investigations. I call it the three-level hypothesis. You want to hear it? It applies to what we're discussing."

"Lay it on me." Again we were interrupted. This time by desert. It was fresh fruit and cheese.

Bonnie picked up a grape and marveled at it. "Look at this grape. Now that is a grape. Where did they find such a thing? It's a work of art, and we're eating it. Okay, my theory. It will help you in your forensic accounting. Ready?"

"Go for it."

"There are histories that you read or are reported to you as fact, like a witness statement. That is an example of the first layer. It passes for truth, but any researcher or good investigator knows it's probably a smokescreen. The fact is most people lie, and the first layer is mostly lies. It's riddled with half-truths and omissions, sad but true. Beneath the first layer lies another narrative that's hidden — the secret narrative. It is mostly true, and I emphasize mostly. That's the second layer. It's what any investigation wants to find out in the first place. You with me so far?"

"You bet."

"There is a layer below that, the third layer, and it's here where even good investigators get fooled. They get satisfied with what they've found at the second layer. They fail to dig any deeper because they don't believe in a third layer. I got news. There's always a third layer. It's where the perps conceal what they're really up to. It's at the third level you inevitably find what I call the hidden contextual fact. It's the one piece of information that supplies the context and makes everything in an investigation snap together like a well-machined puzzle. What I'm telling you right now took me years to figure out. If you forget everything I said, remember this: the key contextual fact always exists, and you aren't done until you have it. Pretty cool, huh?"

"Very cool."

"With that in mind, would you like to hear the results of my third-layer investigation into your family history?"

"I would indeed."

"Sure you would, but first a toast, because nothing looks the same once you know it. Grab your glass."

I grabbed my glass and raised it.

"To the third layer," she said, "and may we always keep looking until we find it. Cheers."

We drank. I had no idea where we were going, but I was enjoying the ride. She seemed pretty blasted, but then again, when it came to Bonnie, or her mother, you could not always be sure. She was making remarkable sense and was mentally far more astute than any at the table thought. In my opinion, she was grossly underestimated.

Bonnie drained her glass and continued. "You know the thing that puzzled me all along about Sarah's death? The volume. It didn't make sense. The level of hatred was way off the charts. I mean, it was institutional-type crazy. I couldn't figure it out, so I did some checking, and then more checking. I reread my notes. I talked to people, lots of people. After a time, I was rewarded for my efforts. So, are you ready?"

"Ready."

"Your dad and my mom had an affair before he and Sarah met. You may think that's bogus if you look at Mom today, but we always make the mistake of looking at some old fogey and forgetting that they would have turned your head a full 360 degrees had you met them years earlier. Mom looked damn good back then. She did indeed; combine that with her experience and a naïve young man full of testosterone, and it's a shoe-in. It was very physical and lasted the better part of a year. Now, given that piece of the puzzle, everything begins to make some sense, doesn't it?"

"It works."

"You bet it works. It's fact. Sarah knew nothing about their affair until the night she died. Mother was blind to her former lover's betrayal with her own daughter until she confronted Sarah that same night. I figure your dad met Sarah and must have liked what he saw, because the affair with mom ended shortly thereafter. Having dumped my mother, he began an even more clandestine liaison with her daughter until it exploded. Few things other than jealousy can cause that much passion. It was the missing piece of the puzzle. That's what really happened, but you didn't hear it from me, for obvious reasons."

"You're quite the detective. Is there a fourth layer?"

"Smart cookie. There is, but you don't want to go there, my friend. The fourth layer contains what you don't ever want to know. It's where the rabbit hole starts. You can stand at the abyss and look down, but that's all. There's madness down there. It's where the demons live. Just some friendly advice."

"Explain."

"Take the occult. Not to say there isn't truth down there, even great truths, but few survive the search. My step-sister, Alice, is a case in point. It breaks people's minds. Best to stick to the third level. Trust me on this."

It seemed to me that Bonnie had not only done her homework but had a first-rate mind.

"You're quite something, Bonnie Leland."

"I have my moments. It's been a pleasure talking to you, by the way. You're a good listener, just like me. But please do me a favor: don't take sides — stay neutral. I'd appreciate it. Believe me, you owe the Dodge crew nothing. They never shelled out a dime for you. Every year you were with the Dodges, your parents were the ones paying for your schools, vacations — everything you can name. The Dodges were never out a penny, and they made sure of it. An accountant tallied it all up, and guess what? Your lot picked up the tab for him too. No surprise there."

It must have showed in my face because she said, "Look, I didn't mean to lay that on you and upset you. It was never my intention. I thought you knew, but stupid me, of course you didn't. Nobody would've mentioned anything about that. Why take the shine off something when you don't have to? You probably think you owe them, and nobody told you different. You do, of course, but then, you don't. I'm sorry. It's rough. From me to you, that's the type of thing that just plain pisses me off."

Bonnie sipped her wine some more and shook her head.

What she had told me about my parents and the run-up to when I was born did not particularly bother me. My parents and I had always operated in different parallel universes of suitable remoteness that I did not take their behavior as a personal reflection. Bonnie's information made sense and explained a great deal more. But her offhand comment about who paid the bills had hit me like a two-by-four right upside the head. It stunned me. I didn't know what to say or how to react. As I sat there thinking, Anne stood up and announced that coffee would be served next door for the ladies, while the men were to be served in the library.

Bonnie and I didn't move.

As the others began to leave, I said, "That was a surprise. I hadn't even considered that."

"Don't take my word for it. Do your own homework. It's what we do. Us accountant types have to stick together. Besides, who else am I going to talk to?"

"I suppose you could always talk to the baron."

She looked around and noticed the rest of the guests had left. She stood up and I did too. Bonnie stretched hugely.

"I could, but that's like playing with the devil. You can get seriously burned. And one other thing for your ears only. Come here." Bonnie put her arms around me and flattened her body against mine, only partly for support. Her breath tickled as she whispered in my ear, "If you ever lose the girlfriend, look me up. I'm older, but that's been done before too. You might find it interesting. I certainly would."

With that, she pushed off and moved unsteadily in the direction of the drawing room. She raised a hand in farewell with her back to me and said, looking straight ahead, "Loved our talk, but I seriously need some coffee."

I left her to make her way as I passed through the drawing room, deep in thought. She was surpassing strange, but she had a wow factor about her. She hid it, but it was there, if you bothered to look. Someone was in real trouble if she was playing opposite. I didn't want to think about that. I parked it for later.

I let my feet carry me along while I thought about other things. I would have to reappraise my obligations. I owed, but then I didn't. I needed to find the correct balance and understand where I fit in. It came to me that perhaps I was actually free. I had carried a crushing weight of obligation to the Dodge family for what seemed like my entire life. An hour ago, I would never have imagined a world without it. With only a few words, everything had changed. My parents were not the deadbeats I had thought. I had never even asked them, but I hardly knew them because I had never made it my business to know them. What was I to do about that? I had not confirmed what Bonnie said, but I knew it was true. The Dodges had not paid a dime.

I was not aware of where I was going until I bumped into the door to Alice's apartment. I opened it and went inside. I sat down on the couch, where I had listened only a few nights before to Stanley talk about Alice. She was the one person I really did owe. I owed her my life. We needed to talk.

57

I sat on the couch and thought about her.

Growing up, I would talk to Alice. My grimmer thoughts would come at night, and she would listen to them. Sometimes she would sit on the bed. Other times in the chair by my desk. It was imaginary. I knew this, but on the boundary between waking and dreaming, it was hard to know one from the other, or which was more real. I took comfort in that she was always there and took the time to listen. She never spoke, which made me think it was always make-believe, but one night at Rhinebeck as I fell asleep upstairs, I think she really was present, because it was the only time she ever said anything.

I remembered her sitting at the foot of my bed. She said, "Little man, continue sleeping if you must, but listen if you can. You and I are alike, because we are of two worlds. We live in twilight. I will not speak to you again. Farewell." She touched my foot and left. I heard the door close and awoke. The room was dark and still. I was never sure whether I had dreamed it or lived it.

As I sat thinking, I recalled that moment. It must have been before she died if it was real, but I wasn't certain. The episode floated, sometimes before, sometimes after. I had no idea what she meant then, but I always remembered the words.

What she had said made more sense in light of today's revelations. I had been sitting there for several minutes and got up to go to the library, when Stanley looked in.

"Sorry," I said to him. "I must have tripped one of the alarms. I was just sitting in here thinking about Alice."

Stanley nodded. "I have done that often enough. You are troubled?"

"I suppose I am." I told him briefly about Maw's ultimatum, Sarah, and my parents.

"I see. Such is family life. On another matter, I have been meaning to speak to you privately in order to give you something. It's in the repository and will take but a moment."

Stanley opened the secret door and came back with an envelope in his hand.

"I have not been able to deliver this to you earlier because there were conditions. You had to be over twenty-five. It had to be delivered by my hand and with no others being aware you received it. That hasn't happened until now. I have discharged my duty. I suggest you make your way to the library now and read it later."

He handed it to me. I recognized the hand. It was from Alice. I put it in my breast pocket, my thoughts once again in a whirl. "This is quite unexpected."

"It is. And one other thing, per our promise of the other night. I am invoking it. You are to accept Mrs. Leland's ultimatum. I will inform Johnny of the same. I will take no questions. After you."

Stanley held the door.

5 8

I poured myself a large scotch over ice and sat down in a
comfortable chair next to Johnny. He was talking to
Malcolm, while the baron and John Senior were discussing
something that I could not make out. As I waited for Johnny to
finish, I sipped my drink and thought.

I considered my surprising reaction to Bonnie's news and to
my lack of one to the exploits of my father. It was like I was numb
in one area while hypersensitive in the other. I was quite sure a
psychiatrist would have a field day with those observations, but
that did not change anything particularly.

Invoking the promise was another matter. It had a material
effect on my decisions going forward. I could choose to ignore the
consequences based on my moral compass, but there was an
unknown element involved that might be laid at the door of
superstition on the one hand, or prudence on the other. I was
jumpy enough without involving the possibility of karmic
retribution. That Stanley had couched our pledge in a lot of
mumbo-jumbo, implying a higher and darker authority, prevented

me from simply ignoring the consequences of breaking my word. It was an effective ploy. Score one for Stanley. He was still a sneaky bastard in my book. He could be as cold as steel or extremely helpful, depending on an agenda that he alone was privy to.

There was also the letter from Alice. At least I assumed it was. I had to get away and read it, which was not an easy task given the social obligations stacked up before me. I decided that reading the letter was priority one. Talking to Johnny was priority two, and the rest would just have to follow when I could get to them.

I whispered to Johnny that I would meet him upstairs and made a hasty retreat.

I went out the front door and around the kitchen and the servants' quarters. The sky was gray with hints of darker things to come. Gusts rustled the leaves of the surrounding trees while the pines moaned and sighed. I passed in front of the garage until I found the spot I was looking for.

There was a stand of seven cypress trees to the east of the south lawn. When Johnny and I were small, we discovered that we could enter the stand from one end. Inside was a cathedral. The trees vaulted high above, and the air was filled with incense from the scent of pine. Hazy beams of sunlight would slant diagonally across the spongy floor in the late afternoon. It was a mystical place, hidden from outsiders and steeped in the ancient genetic memories of fairies, dwarves, and druids. Johnny and I lived and conversed with them for years, until we grew too tall to fit comfortably inside, at which point they continued on without us, silent as before.

Someone, probably Harry, had placed a bench behind the trees so that it was hidden from the house, and one could be alone and unobserved. I sat down and pulled out the letter.

It was from Alice after all. I knew her hand by now. She wrote:

My dearest Percy, my little blessing,

You will not be little when you read this. I would have loved to have seen you all grown up, but the amount of time I have left is uncertain. My body grows weak. Some have pointed to a life of excess. My doctors tell me that, but they are wrong. I have ventured too far down the paths I have chosen, and the methods I have used have taken their toll. There are limits, and I am approaching mine.

I write this while I can and have entrusted it to Stanley to deliver at the appropriate time. He is loath to do so for reasons you will understand, but I have overridden his objections by invoking my darker side, of which he is aware. You are reading this because he is the man he is. I hope he has forgiven me, but enough; it is done, and here we are.

I wish to relate to you two incidents that changed all of our lives.

The first occurred in Florence, some years ago.

I was passing through the city and had stopped at a small hotel for lunch. It is my custom to be inconspicuous when traveling abroad. I chose a table that was away from public view. A couple came in and sat down close by. It seemed they too wished some privacy, and for good reason, as I would learn. I was reading, as is my routine when I am alone at meals. They were speaking quietly, but there was an intensity that drew my attention, and then the man spoke more forcefully. There was no mistaking. The voice was that of my ex-husband, Lord Bromley. The girl's name was Mary. I learned over the course of the conversation that she was pregnant. Although he was categorically the father, Lord Bromley stated in no uncertain terms that he would not marry her. She asked him what she ought to do. His advice was incisive and abrupt: "You either get rid of it or you get Hugo to marry you right quick." She replied that they had yet to engage in sexual relations and the speaker knew that. He told her to find someone else then. Specifically, he said, "Anne will know of a likely candidate. She is very resourceful."

And there it was.

Over time I knew them all. Anne eventually married my half-brother, John, and Mary is, of course, your mother. We are good friends. I doubt there are many things more freakish and preternatural than that moment and its consequences, but such is life. Lord Bromley is your father. I cannot say it plainer. I will refer to him as such going forward in this letter.

Mary married quickly, and her secret was safe. Unfortunately, the couple had a great deal more to deal with.

It was I who counseled John that he offer to take the child and bring him up in his own household. He asked me why, of course, but I explained that I was aware of the unlucky couple's troubles and wished to help. I had even set aside a trust to cover all the child's future expenses. John could field no objections and, in fact, welcomed the opportunity. He and Anne had wanted a companion for Johnny in the form of a brother or sister, but Anne had been unable to conceive again due to complications during Johnny's birth. It was a gift that satisfied their most optimistic expectations, and so it came about that you and Johnny were brought up together.

John has surely wondered at my motives, but I have never disclosed the truth to anyone other than Stanley. He is a most penetrating observer, and one day he recognized my former husband in you. He confronted me with his observations, and such is our relationship, I told him everything. We had quite the exchange. It was the only time I seriously wondered if he would remain in my service. He was so put out by my revelation and your certain and continued presence going forward, that he told me he would be gone that night, but I too have my methods. I went down on my knees and grabbed his legs like the supplicants of old. I begged him not to leave me. I told him a simple truth. I loved him and would die if he left me. We had been through enough together for him to know the veracity of it. He almost leaped out of his skin when I did this, but I can be damn quick. I held him in a grip of steel. He had no choice but to acquiesce. It was the only time I have ever used that weapon, and I won't again. It was cruel, but women are cruel — much crueler than men when provoked. When I had extracted his most solemn promise to remain with me, I let him go and begged his *forgiveness. He said he could deny me nothing but would like an explanation. I will now give you the same.*

I was never able to have a child at any time. I knew this when I married Lord Bromley. I was remiss in that I never told him from the beginning. I should have. Many things would have been different. I had had an operation when I was young. One of the collateral effects was that my ovaries were removed to prevent any further recurrence. It was both a blessing and a curse. I would not have lived the life I have had I been able to conceive, but it left a hole. This has weighed on me off and on, but your presence in my life has helped me fill it, and I thank you for that.

I loved your father at the beginning. I truly did. He was perfect for me. We should have loved forever.

He was flawed when I married him. I knew this. I was not blind, but we all choose to overlook what we must. Good and bad exist in everyone. I knew what I was doing and accepted him for what he was. Your father has a cruel streak, different than mine. It is capricious. Why do you think Loki was a man? It is worth considering in relation to yourself going forward, but more on that later.

I will tell you about the second incident.

It was on our honeymoon. Your father loved horses. He probably does still. He never wore a hard hat. He said it was for wimps and cowards. Foolish man! While out riding one fine morning, he had a wreck. He was brought to me unconscious by a pair of grooms accompanied by the mutual friend who had invited us. It was in Shropshire, and although the doctor was called promptly, it was several hours before he was able to arrive and examine him. Eventually, your father regained consciousness but not before the doctor had pulled me aside and cautioned me on the severity of the injury. He told me to expect a change in personality or, at the very least, a change in behavior similar to those who have suffered a stroke. There was damage and likely clotting in the brain, but the facilities he had available to treat the injury were inadequate. My husband needed to be transported to a hospital as soon as possible. It was most urgent.

Once your father was conscious, I tried to persuade him to seek additional care, but he refused. We had a schedule to keep, and he said he would recover with no ill effects. True to his prediction, the next day he was completely recovered and himself. And so it seemed, until we journeyed to Italy. It was there that the delayed reaction finally caught up with him.

I will elaborate no further than to say I suffered terribly from the changes that overtook him. Our marriage dissolved as my heart bled tears and my willingness to continue leaked away with their drops. Toward the end, we fought incessantly, and one night at Rhinebeck in a fit of rage, I finally told him that I had been barren all my life, and that I was glad of it because that way I could make sure his line died with him.

Nothing I have ever said before or since has affected someone like those words. I saw to my horror that in his heart he loved me desperately in spite of the mental sickness that had consumed him. Until we met, he had never known the emotion fully, but with my cruel deliberate words, I killed what little remained, as surely as if I had plunged a knife into his chest. I too died that night. In our folly, and in mine most of all, we had managed to kill our most precious possession. I think we both went mad then. In fact, I'm sure of it. He, because I had killed his capacity to love, and me for the same reason. He never forgave me for that, and I never forgave him for what followed. I will spare you the specifics. If you must know, speak to Stanley. He will tell you, or he will not.

Sometime later, after we divorced, I nearly shot your father dead. It was in the jungles of Ecuador. What stayed my hand was the echo of the love we shared, and for that I give thanks. Had I done so, you would not have been born, and my life would have been that much more barren.

I have never chosen to display my feelings toward you, not because they don't exist, but because it was how Stanley and I agreed to continue going forward. Both of us have chosen not to act. I to not express my affection and he to not express the opposite. He hates your father, not just for what he did to me, but for what he was unable to do himself: to protect me from harm. To me, you are a living memory of a brief but sparkling happiness, but to him, you are a constant reminder of his powerlessness and his failure to keep me safe. I am sorry beyond measure for his anguish. He deserves better. He is the best of men.

I have two more things to tell you.

If life has given us gifts, what do we owe for having squandered them? To whom do we owe exactly, and what will the payment be?

The Furies, the Erinyes, as the Greeks called them, were never particularly kind. Their most severe torment was madness. Many may forget them, but that doesn't mean they're dead. They live. I've seen them. This is a warning to you for what is to follow. It is not a threat, but I would be irresponsible if I did not tell you of the consequences.

I have placed the Rhinebeck house in one trust and provisions for its upkeep in another. My half-brother is the trustee for both but with an as yet named beneficiary. That beneficiary is you, if you wish to accept it. The assignments are enclosed.

You will be responsible for the house and all its contents both physical and otherwise, including the libraries and artifacts. It is a heavy burden. Failure to care for the intangible interests that reside here carries heavy penalties and unknown consequences. Consider this carefully before you accept. What might be a gift may not be.

Lastly, Dear One, hear me, for this I consider to be most important:

I do not know if it is true that the improprieties of the fathers are visited upon the children and upon the children's children. Exodus says this, but the Bible and I were never close. It was the fall that broke your father. In those sunny days before it, he and I loved and held each other in a higher place. I prevented him from traveling down the dark paths of his past, while he did the same for me. It was supposed to be forever, but it wasn't. Untethered, we degenerated back to our baser selves. This was our sin.

You have the capacity for great things, but you also carry the potential for your father's excesses. I am anxious for you. Perhaps this is only the natural concern of one generation looking at the next. Time will tell whether you have the strength and ability to do better. I think you are capable and pray this is so, but you may wish to consider this advice:

Surround yourself with good people. Find someone strong to love, who will love you back. Make it last as long as you can. These words I know to be true. It worked for me for a time, until powers greater than my own intervened. Short as my brief period of celestial happiness was, it has sustained me through the rest of my days and nights.

I wish I had known Stanley sooner. It is my only regret.

I also wish I had been able to have a child, but then, maybe I did.

Love always,

— ALICE

PS I told you tonight that you and I are of two worlds and that we live in twilight. We travel the edge of light and dark. You know the truth, but understand you now have several names. Choose the one you wish. Become the one you want. May the ancient ones continue to bless you and keep you. Rely on them, for they rely on you. You are what my heart wanted most but was unable to conceive.

A.

59

I was quite stunned. The letter slipped from my grasp, and the pages swirled about, scattered by the wind. I scrambled off the bench in a panic. I gathered them up as fast as I could and stuffed the pages back in the envelope. I put it in my breast pocket.

After that scare, I could do nothing. I understood intellectually and analytically all that I had read and heard, but it was like a great pile of laundry that had to be sorted and folded. It was all in a jumble. I had to go through it piece by piece, but the implications and my potential choices kept wrestling with each other. My intuitive part was quietly amused. I was not. It suggested I do nothing until I had a plan and that what I needed was some time to sort it out. Easy for it to say, but time was a commodity that analytically I knew was in short supply. What was I to do? To which it replied: exactly the point. There was no arguing with it.

I considered Alice's suggestions instead.

There was Bruni, and there was Johnny. They were good people. I could talk to them. That was a good idea, but in the end, what I did would be up to me, and that was the crux of the matter. I felt I must act in some form or fashion, but I understood everything and nothing. Dividing lines of loyalty that had once appeared obvious were now vague. No one was who they seemed. It was easy to become paranoid and do something stupid. And then there was Rhinebeck itself. There was far more to it than its grounds and buildings. It was frightening in ways I knew I had yet to understand. Doing nothing seemed like a better and better choice. My thoughts went around and around nonstop.

Finally, I yelled, "Shut up!"

"There you are," said Johnny, coming around the cypress trees. "I looked for you upstairs, but Robert decided it was time for some air and led me here. Haven't been to this spot in ages. Good choice. Are you all right? You look a bit wild."

He had changed into his English farmer outfit, consisting of an olive-green three-quarter-length oilcloth jacket and green Wellington boots with yellow soles. I needed a friend, and he was my best friend. I wondered what he would say about Alice's revelations and the Stanley matter. Stanley and I would either come to terms or it would get very messy. The thought of Rhinebeck without Stanley was not a happy one, and what would Johnny think about Alice gifting me the estate in the first place?

"Knock, knock," said Johnny. "Anybody home? Don't tell me. Bruni left you for another man."

I took a breath and settled down. "No, she did not. I was going a bit crazy. First, it's good to see you. Second, I'm a bit out of sorts in all manner of ways. This seems to be an ongoing but, hopefully, nonterminal condition. Rumor has it that the day will end, but it may not. If it doesn't, then I would say it wouldn't be any more peculiar than the last several hours. You don't happen to have a flask and some smokes on you?"

"That bad? Well, lucky for you, the doctor is in, and I have both. We have quite a bit of catching up to do, and this is a good place for it. We loved this spot, remember? I'll let young Robert off the leash, and he can do what he wants for now. You're white as a sheet, by the way. No, I take it back, you're more ashen than white, but it's the greenish hue that troubles me. Are you sick?"

"No, just stressed beyond measure."

"You and me both. Stanley invoked that promise, which shocked the hell out of me for a start, but perhaps we'll go over that in a bit. Right now, we are both in need of some serious medication. Allow me."

Johnny whipped out a flask of surprising size from one pocket and a pack of cigarettes from the other. "One cup, I'm afraid," said Johnny. "We'll have to share. Here." He poured from the flask and passed me the cup almost filled to the brim. "Drink up."

I gulped it down and passed it back. I thought of Bonnie and our similarities. I wondered if Bonnie felt this way all the time. Perhaps I too would be going down the rabbit hole and drinking myself into a constant state of fumbling indifference. My mind just would not stop.

"Johnny, do me a favor. Slap me across the face, not too softly but not too hard."

Johnny clobbered me and afterward poured himself a drink from the flask. "Better?" he asked.

My ears were ringing. "Jesus," I yelled. "I said not too hard. But...that's better. In fact, really good. Thank you. I needed that. I really did."

"That's what friends are for. Now tell Doctor Johnny all about your troubles."

"I barely know where to begin, so I'll just start at the end and work backward. Read this, and when you finish, don't say a thing. Just don't. Okay?"

Johnny put down his cup and read. He kept his face impassive as he read the letter and went back once or twice to read earlier parts and then looked up. He looked me right in the eye and hissed, "You…you, bastard!"

My heart sank.

"You're a real genuine bastard. You know that?" He couldn't keep a straight face any longer and burst out laughing.

"Really? Is that all you have to say?" My heart recovered, and I started to laugh. His laughter and good spirits were infectious. After a point, what else was there?

"My friend, my friend," said Johnny gripping my shoulder. "There is only one solution for your troubles."

"Tell me."

"Drink heavily and many times a day. I'll write you a prescription. But seriously, this may be news to you, but I suspected your sullied lineage for quite a while. I just never mentioned it. I know you too well, and it would have only driven you crazy. You do shave every day, yes? It never crossed your mind? Really? Come on."

"Never a once."

"You're blind as a bat."

"That fact has been mentioned before. Do you think other people know?"

"Maybe, but does it really matter? I admit, to Stanley it does, but to Mother and Father? It would not matter a stitch. They must know, of course. Mary and my mom were thick as thieves, and she would have told my father absolutely for certain. They tell each other everything. But think about it; this does have some interesting ramifications. Maw, for instance. And the baron? It seems they've been barking up the wrong tree all along, but then, your supposed father and your real one have a passing similarity. With a different haircut and a few other things, you could be the spitting image of a younger version of Lord Bromley. This has some interesting possibilities. It would take some thought, mind you, but there's a plan in there somewhere. It'll come to me eventually."

"Johnny, this doesn't bother you? I mean, I'm the son of Lord Bromley, arch enemy and spawn of Satan."

"You well may be, but I figure we're both headed in the same general direction. With the burning fires our likely home, I'm thrilled to know the management. Better seating, I hear. Seriously, what do you think this changes? Who you are? How could it? It might mean you make different choices going forward, but really, what's changed? Nothing and everything, it's true, but it's mostly in your head. You think way too much. I've always said so. We're like brothers and always will be. Nothing you can do or say can change that, so settle down. Have another drink, a smoke, and chill while I expound."

Johnny held up the letter and shook it.

"This is all news — hot news. It makes so much sense. Finally, I understand. But the best part is congratulations! We get to keep the place, no matter what. That is really terrific. There is that Stanley thing, of course. You're absolutely right. He really doesn't like you."

"You know, I've heard that so many times today."

"Well, he's one, for sure. The others just think they don't like you. But back to Stanley. He tricked us, but two can play at that game. Look, we're both on the case. When have we not figured out a brilliant plan? I just need my notepad and a pencil. We got this. Really."

"Johnny, I don't know what to say."

"Well, don't. Now, you mentioned that we are working backward. What else?"

"I found myself in Alice's apartment after getting an earful from Bonnie. By the way, that woman has been seriously underestimated. She's no half-wit — not by a long shot. I must have triggered one of the alarms, because Stanley popped in, gave me this letter, and then dropped the promise on me. He said I was to accept Maw's ultimatum, and then he refused to take questions or comments."

"Yes, he informed me of the same after I left the library. This letter gives us some background as to the reason for it. I'm not sure if he was privy to the beneficiary thing, but I suspect he read the letter shortly after it was given into his keeping. I haven't worked a countermove as yet, but I'll put my mind to it. You mentioned Bonnie. How did that go?"

I told him about our conversation in full.

"What is it about you and women? It's like you have some kind of pheromone thing going on. I've never seen the like. Does this happen to you all the time?"

"It seems it's strictly an East Coast phenomenon. I can't explain it."

"It's probably genetic, but back to the matters at hand. That Sarah bombshell is another mindblower. It seems both our families have dark secrets. It's an arrow for the quiver to be used carefully, but I'm sure you know that. I have some thoughts, but let's leave that for now. Next?"

I told him about Bruni.

"Are more congratulations in order?"

"No. It hasn't come to that. Far from it, but we have a future of sorts. It needs work."

"She is lovely, and I'm happy for you. But I have a question. Does she eventually become Lady Bromley, or does she go with baroness? I have no idea how that all works."

"If she's an American citizen, it's neither. You're leaping too far ahead as usual, but it's one of many bizarre points that I'm sure we'll become overly familiar with given time. You're now up to date on my world. What about yours?"

"I spoke with Malcolm. Interesting fellow. I asked him about

Alice. He knew her for years. She and Lord Bromley were at his father's estate on their honeymoon. He first met her there."

I interrupted, "Where the accident happened, do you think?"

"He didn't mention it, but you don't go to too many estates in Shropshire on your honeymoon. There's a thread there for sure. He did say that toward the end, Alice was doing poorly. She had lost weight. She held a party the week before she died. It was fancy dress and Alice did the whole Egyptian thing. He said she looked the part. He also mentioned someone came as Lord Bromley for a laugh. It was in very bad taste and affected her badly. They were asked to leave. Before I forget, it's interesting that your father has made no move to contact you. As far as I know, he has no other issue. It's another of those tidbits to be put aside but not forgotten. Back to Malcolm. He has had financial dealings with everyone here except Maw, I think. His hobby is racehorses, and he even owns an Aston Martin."

"One of those DB5s?" I asked.

"Yes, I'm afraid so."

"Damn. I do like those. Remember when your father gave each of us a toy version one Christmas as a joke? He was highly amused that he had given us the car of our dreams. We were too old for a toy and too young to afford the real thing. You managed to lose yours that very day."

"I'm quite sure it was yours that got lost. How quickly you forget."

"Johnny, I'm far more organized. You, not as much."

"Which was why you took mine, having lost yours yourself."

"Not true. Not true." I smiled. We had a ton of memories, Johnny and I. Each day had been an adventure, and we were in constant trouble of one sort or another. Nothing had changed on that score.

"Things won't be the same going forward," I said.

"No, they won't, but that's not a bad thing."

414

"No, I suppose not. I thank you for being my friend, by the way. You've really helped steady me. We'll have to handle Stanley's ultimatum. That makes three today for me. I'm pretty sure that's a record. Any more information on Malcolm?"

"No, but during lunch, Maw asked if I had spoken to you."

"What did you say?"

"I told her I didn't think it was table conversation."

"You're bad."

"I am."

The wind had freshened. "There's a storm coming. Do you think it's an omen?"

"Most certainly. You *do* remember the first rule of prophecy and prognostication?"

"All omens are good."

"Exactly, so take heart. We'll win in the end." Johnny looked around. "Have you seen that damned dog?"

"No, can't say I have."

"Damn." In a burst of energy, Johnny stood up. "Well, that does it. Anything more will have to wait. Come on. Stand up. Look alive. We have a dog to find and a plan to rule the world that we must conjure up before dinner. We're in the game and on the hunt. We're made for this, so let's step lively. Follow me. He must have gone this way."

Johnny strode off in search of the miscreant Robert. I stood up and followed. I did feel better. Johnny had his methods. He knew how to handle me, and I loved him for it.

60

Robert was in the company of Bruni and Elsa, who were walking on the far side of the lawn. He was trotting jauntily beside them as we approached.

"You've found him," said Johnny.

Elsa waved, and Bruni laughed. The younger von Hofmanstal said, "No, he found us. This is a timely meeting. Johnny, why don't you and I go back to the house, and let these two talk? Since you grew up together, you can tell me more of Percy's deepest and darkest secrets. Those suitable for blackmail are the ones I'm interested in. Come on."

They went off, arm in arm. Bruni looked so happy and alive. Elsa took my arm. We watched as Bruni and Johnny headed back, with Robert tagging along. He didn't need his leash around Bruni. I hoped Johnny might get some pointers from her, but I was quite certain the subject of dogs would not come up. Bruni's last comment gave me a twinge, but I relied on Johnny's judgment as to what to say and what not to. She would find out everything about me eventually, so how she found out was not a major concern. I sensed she was more than a little possessive and more than a little nosy as well.

"So, you two are an item, as they say." Elsa steered me back the way I had come.

"I suppose we are."

"Do you love her?"

"I think I do. It needs time to grow before it blossoms to its full."

"A considered answer. Men look at their feelings and poke at them to see if they are real. Women know what they know and are less reserved. She's a good girl, and my friend. For a mother and daughter to have such a relationship is a blessing. I love her and want no hurt or harm to come to her."

"Nor do I."

"She said you wanted to talk to me about speaking with her father, but she asked that I speak with you first. Hugo doesn't like you, and that will make things difficult on every front, but you know that. I can work on him on your behalf, but there are no guarantees."

"Is that something you would like to do?"

"It's what I must."

"I'd prefer it if this was something you desired rather than an obligation. The result might be the same, but the motivation is what concerns me."

"You want to know if I approve of you?"

"I suppose I do."

"I have reservations."

"What are they, if I may ask?"

"I will tell you, but you won't like it. For years I have made assessments and observations for Hugo about the principals involved in a transaction in order to weigh their strengths and weaknesses. I'll do the same for you."

"Tell me."

"Very well. You're immature in spite of your age and hold on to hurt like a child. You are tentative rather than decisive. You harbor secrets. Through omissions, you skirt the truth. You look for what could go wrong rather than what could go right. You are naturally pessimistic. You are easily led because you do not trust your judgment. You try to see only the best in yourself and others. This makes you blind to the baser motivations of those around you and in yourself. You are, thus, easily fooled. You have a deep anger that you wish to hide, but of which you are afraid, and which prevents you from acting for fear of unleashing it. You say what others want to hear rather than what you think because you want others to like you. You hide instead of embracing all that you are. I could continue."

"That is quite a litany of faults."

"There are others."

I thought to myself it was a grim list but not untrue. I was at a loss as to how to continue, but then, I'd asked for it. I'd examine what she'd said later. She was either very observant or I was very shallow and transparent. Perhaps both were true. I carried on speaking as best I could.

"You're quite right. I don't like it, and given those attributes, I understand your reservations. So you will speak to your husband for your daughter's sake, not for mine."

"It is so."

"Do I have any redeeming qualities?"

"Do you?"

"You and I know the answer to that. Although I cannot disagree with your assessment, they exist nonetheless. I am loyal, for one. I do look at the good qualities in people for another. For instance, I admire and thank you for your willingness to support your daughter in spite of your misgivings."

"I know her well enough to not try and dissuade her."

"Are you jealous of her?" The words slipped out before I had a chance to bite them back.

Elsa stopped, and I stopped with her. She looked at me.

"The beginning of love is the very best of times. It has no equal. I am jealous of you for that. I am jealous of her. Why shouldn't I be? You're both lucky that you have your youth. You don't look in the mirror every day and ask the person looking back how they grew so old, when you feel like a child inside. I can't have you, either, and that is also an unpleasant and insulting reminder."

"So, you think you've lost your mojo."

"What is a mojo?"

"Your magic charm — the magic that makes men swoon over you."

"Now you're making fun of me, which I suppose I deserve for throwing your worst faults in your face."

"Elsa, don't ever doubt my admiration. You had me at dinner the other night. I would hate to think what might have happened at another time."

"You would not have liked it?"

"It would have been a complication of extraordinary magnitude. Of course I would have liked it."

Elsa gave me a hug. "You bet you would have liked it."

"I'll continue to worship you from afar."

"Now you really are making fun of me."

"Yes and no. You're an extraordinary woman. I admire you and always will. I know this. I am thrilled to have you in my life. I really am."

She held me at arm's length and looked at me. "I thank you for that. You're either much more dangerous and cleverer than I thought or you are gifted with an uncanny ability to soothe and conciliate, which is rare. You will be good for Bruni. It will not be so easy with her father, but you have my blessing and goodwill. I have decided this." She took my arm and continued to walk. "You are special. I see what Bruni sees in you. We will get along."

"We will. Tell me, what is it that the baron has against me?"

"You look like him."

"Like whom?"

"Lord Bromley."

I stopped in my tracks. I wondered if everybody knew. "Whoa, Elsa. I thought it was Mary and the duel."

"That too."

"Perhaps you'd better explain."

We had made it back to the cypress trees. I led us over to the bench Johnny and I had just vacated. It seemed to be getting a lot of use. We sat. The wind had freshened. It was going to rain, but hopefully not before Elsa had explained her last comment.

"Hugo and Lord Bromley have had many dealings in business and antiquities. They're also collectors, and in this facet of their relationship, they are rivals.

"I'm not as captivated by the fascination for spirits and obscure magics as they are. For them, it's an obsession. For me, it's a business. I have gone along with my husband's inclinations because the objects have intrinsic value. One asset is very much like another, as far as I'm concerned. With these, liquidity is not an issue, and some are quite beautiful. Others are not, but they tend to be the most desirable. With men, it's always about power and influence. With women, it's all about practicality. We want value for our money. Hugo looks at the prestige and influence a piece can manifest, while I check the price tag. I support him in his quest for acquisitions by keeping economics very much in the foreground. Acquisition is one of the reasons why we were invited, and why we are here. Bruni is available to handle the finances. I don't mean to deflate your ego, but you're a side dish, not the main course."

Elsa reached over and patted my hand. "A very tasty one, I

might add. I think Bruni has made some correct decisions. One she told me about was her determination to settle her life and be happy. I've been concerned for her. Her life has lacked harmony, and now I think it might be possible to change that. Deep down, I'm pleased, and I want you to know that. But back to what I was talking about.

"When it comes to collections, the bigger and better one wins. Those objects most closely linked to death are the most prized of all. John's half-sister, Alice, was in possession of some extremely powerful pieces. They're on the market, and buyers have gathered to find out. Lord Bromley and Hugo are two of the largest and most fanatical collectors of such artifacts. Malcolm Ault is Lord Bromley's agent. He's a skilled buyer, even though he looks like a clown. I've been toying with him, and it has disconcerted him greatly, I'm happy to say. Mrs. Leland has also been known to dabble in these, but for reasons I don't know. She's also a bidder, I believe. We are gathered, and tonight is not only our host's anniversary but when the bids will be compared and perhaps a decision made — tomorrow at the latest. This all has relevance in regards to your introduction to Hugo.

"He was quite upset when he saw you. He takes his collection very seriously. It was as if his competition were right there before him. Coincidence is a very tricky business in their world. There *are* no coincidences. It's what they believe. Synchronicity is everything to them. It's very serious. It means other forces are at work…Was that a raindrop?"

"I believe it was, and there's another. We best get back," I said.

Elsa and I got up and began to walk toward the house.

"Now you understand better. As for that duel with your father," Elsa said as we arrived at the french doors, "it's a minor issue. There was no shame in it, and Hugo has every reason to appreciate its having taken place. He would never have enticed a goddess like me into marrying him without it. He has a brutal streak, which I consider quite delicious, but more importantly, as far as you're concerned, he's a strong man with principles, who possesses a sharp mind that can be reasoned with. We'll find a way. Thank you for our walk. I'll see you tonight, but one thing more: you'd better be sitting next to me at dinner. Synchronicity be damned. Just make sure of it. We'll talk some more as to how to handle him."

She gave me a kiss on both cheeks and strode into the drawing room.

It had just started to rain in earnest.

61

"So," said Johnny, "the fair maid's mother found you acceptable and gave you her blessing?"

Johnny was stretched out on the couch, with Robert asleep once again in his basket. Johnny had thrown his coat over him. His black eyes opened momentarily as I came in and then closed. He snuggled under the coat and disappeared from view completely.

"In the end she did, but there's more troubling news, I'm afraid."

"Why am I not surprised? Tell me."

"According to Elsa, I do look like a young Lord Bromley, and that shook the baron at our first meeting. Lord B. and the baron, as we know, are rivals in the acquisition of occult antiquities, and he was not pleased to see a younger version of the competition in the drawing room, which leads me to her most significant revelation: the full purpose of this weekend's little get-together. The anniversary is one part, but in addition, a blind auction is taking place simultaneously for several of Alice's treasures. The winning bids are to be announced tonight — or tomorrow, latest."

"Really?" Johnny sat up. "That's unexpected, but it fits. Who are the bidders? Did she say?"

I sat down in one of the chairs and told him what she said. "In the running are team Baron von H., with Elsa advising as to valuation and Bruni providing liquidity; Lord B., with Malcolm acting as his agent; and Maw, of all people. Bonnie is a wild card. She may or may not be in the running, but I see her as a possible surprise bidder as well. If she is, I think she hopes to sweep the whole lot and then sell them back to the others at a discount, provided certain favors are carried out. She's smart enough, and if the others aren't careful, she'll do just that. They'll have to arrange their bids accordingly."

"Malcolm didn't tell me any of that, which is typical. No wonder he's here. I suppose Father is the auctioneer, but then again, maybe not. Stanley and mother are possibilities. Whoever it is, someone is doing a capital raise for sure, and that troubles me."

"It is troubling. We're aware of some of the outstanding issues, but Stanley or your mom managing the auction? I'm not so sure about that."

"Mother is quite skilled in that area. Both our mothers spent some time in the antiques trade, in sales and in the more unsavory inner workings of auction houses. You'd be surprised at their knowledge. Stanley is Stanley, and could be acting as an agent in some way. Aunt Alice may have made other stipulations of which we are unaware."

"It's possible. Nothing would surprise me in the Stanley department. I didn't know that about our moms, but there is the matter of provenances for the items to be sold. Technically, I'm only the beneficiary, but there was a clause that allowed me to become trustee, provided I show proper qualifications, and more to the point, I have a final say as to the distribution of the physical house and its contents, if it should come to that. I haven't seen the trust instrument, but a sale of some of the physical assets means something has occurred that has forced the trustee to sell. It's not a happy thought."

"No, it isn't. It adds yet another wrinkle to a complex situation. The way I see it, I need to get more acquainted with the state of the family exchequer, and soon. It makes no sense unless we're in the throes of a major crisis. How exactly your status is to be made known is another complication. But the big issue for me is that Stanley must know about your part, and the parents must as well. It's not like them to be underhanded, so I don't quite buy it. A trustee has the power to sell, mind you, but it has to be in the interests of the trust and the beneficiary. I believe the letter stated that Aunt Alice had arranged for Rhinebeck's upkeep. Unless there have been some major developments that put the sustainability of the upkeep trust in jeopardy, I don't understand it. Of course, a big loss in the portfolio would do the trick."

"I do hope it had nothing to do with that trouble you had unwinding one of the legs of that gold trade?"

"Very funny. No, Father has not let me dabble in the family trusts, so I had nothing to do with it. Besides, this weekend was arranged months ago. What bothers me is that once again we're in the dark on several pertinent issues. On top of that, we have a time crunch. Just to remind you, it's white-tie tonight, which means we'd better start getting ready. I suggest we do so and think about all this. We are playing catch-up once again. I hate that."

"We are, and I hate it too. One other point I'd like to emphasize: Alice made it clear that by my acceptance of the estate, I would be responsible for not only the physical but the otherworldly elements of the house as well. They are to rely on me to protect their interests. She included a not-so-subtle warning that to fail to uphold that trust would have dire consequences — far worse, I'm sure, than anything Stanley could conjure up."

"I read that, but I took it to mean you could also count on their support, which means we have resources of some standing available to us, provided we can access them. And speaking of promises, Maw will want to know what we've decided — and Stanley too. It's just a question of how we go about it. Let's ponder while we dress. I think a little prayer to those higher authorities might be in order."

"Way ahead of you. I trust you have a white-tie outfit for me?"

"Indeed I do. It's in the closet."

Johnny went off to collect my outfit while I considered one other element. It was more than luck that I was invited this weekend. I had a part to play, but no one had informed me of my role or what my lines were. I would have to come up with them on the fly. I had to trust in my ability to know what to do when the time came. I had to speak with Bonnie again. She might be able to give me an insight. She was a wild card, and I was another. The one thing of which I was completely certain was that I was in need of some serious divine assistance.

There was a distant rumble of thunder. Robert stuck his head out and looked at me.

Perhaps it was a sign.

It would be a stormy night. I fervently hoped that Alice's trust had been well placed and that I could live up to it. I would do my very best. I had never met the more mysterious elements of the property, but I was aware of them. They seemed to be aware of me. It was that responsibility that weighed most heavily. Alice must have felt the same — and Stanley too, for that matter.

62

Johnny went off to settle Robert in Stanley's office while I tried to get more comfortable with my wing collar. I was in the drawing room, and there was Cristal available in an ice bucket. I would just have to drink a few glasses and hope for the best. Given enough, I would not be able to feel a thing. Johnny and I looked like we were part of a past century, but that was the dress code for tonight's festivities. The ladies must have been having fits, but maybe not. It was an occasion and a chance to look their best.

Bruni entered and took all my attention. She wore a silver satin gown with bare shoulders. She clutched the front of the dress to lift it. The glowing sapphire of the previous night sparkled just above her cleavage. Her hair was pulled back and held in place by a diamond clasp.

"Well?" she said and pirouetted in front of me. The thick fabric of the dress flared and hissed as she moved.

"Gorgeous and then some." It was true; she was stunning.

"Don't just stand there, others will come in moments."

I held her in my arms. "You really are extraordinarily beautiful." I kissed the place between her neck and shoulders. She sighed.

"I'm glad you appreciate it," she said, swirling away. "Mother thinks you're divine and approves — her reluctance banished. So, one down, one to go. Any more breaking news?"

"More than I can possibly say. I don't even know where to begin, but I think there is one thing you had better know right off the bat. I hesitate to tell you, but — "

At that moment, Malcolm lurched in. He looked about and saw Bruni.

"Oh, I say, Brunhilde. That is quite an outfit. I hope we sit together this evening."

"Why, thank you, Malcolm." Bruni liked the attention. I passed her a champagne glass. "It'll be luck of the draw, I'm afraid."

"Isn't that always the case?"

He moved to the champagne as Johnny slipped in by way of the dining room. "I wasn't supposed to come through that way. Stanley and crew have really done it up, I must say. Amazing spread. That storm is picking up. You can hear it much better in the kitchen."

"It's fitting," I said as I poured him champagne.

Within a few minutes, we were all collected. The men were dressed in their tails while the ladies looked like elegant birds of different species. Elsa wore a simple devastating gown in black and white that bared her shoulders and emphasized her slim figure while accentuating her cleavage. Diamonds of extraordinary size and brilliance circled her neck. She looked spectacular and knew it. The tall man beside me goggled at her, besotted once again. Maw wore black and was bedecked in gigantic emeralds that more than compensated for the plainness of her dress. Bonnie wore red — fire-engine red — and a diamond necklace. She had pulled back her hair and had skillfully applied makeup. She looked a different person. Gone was the awkwardness. She had completely made herself over. Anne wore a strapless gown of coral and black. A necklace of gold and diamonds encircled her neck. She was comfortable in formal wear and moved about the guests commenting on how wonderful they each looked. Stanley's crew came by with flutes of champagne on silver trays while others passed plates of hors d'oeuvres of caviar and smoked salmon. It may have been the champagne, but my impression was that the level of conversation had gone up in volume.

Bruni stood beside me and asked, "What were you about to tell me when Malcolm interrupted?"

"It's complicated," I said, "and not for everyone's ears. I'll have to tell you later, I'm afraid."

Bruni was disappointed, I could tell, but she understood that the current circumstances did not allow for intimate conversation.

She nodded. "I look forward to it. Perhaps later, when you help me with my dress."

With that shot, she went off to circulate. I distracted myself with more caviar. I didn't even want to think about what that meant.

I wandered over to Bonnie and commented, "Compliments to you. You look heavenly."

"You're not just saying that?"

"Not at all. Your new look suits you. It really does."

"If it means I see more of you, I'll keep it."

She gave me a wink and moved off to get more champagne.

Johnny came up and stood beside me. "I see changes taking place. Bonnie has upped her game."

"She has indeed."

"Are you still committed to our plan?"

"Yes, as much of a plan as we have. I was unable to tell Bruni. I doubt she will be pleased having been kept in the dark and having it sprung on her."

"Tough luck, but I'm sure a simple statement of facts would

have been insufficient. It is better this way, I assure you. I've had experience."

"Really?"

"Well, no. At least not on the scale you are about to embark on. You've managed to take that to a whole new level. I'd try and go easy on the spirits, but then again, a little extra might just settle you down."

I shook my head. We were in the hands of the gods. Johnny and I had formulated a plan, but we both felt it was sketchy, since it depended on taking advantage of circumstances. We gave it up in the end and decided to let events unfold while enjoying the feast. It had every indication of being a night to remember on a culinary basis alone.

After a suitable period for mingling, Stanley made an announcement. "Ladies and gentlemen, it is with great pleasure that we welcome you to a special anniversary dinner." He turned off the lights in the drawing room as the doors to the feast were opened. The theme was gold. Lit only by candlelight, the table settings shimmered in fine splendor amid the many matched glasses of different sizes and the cutlery laid out like a surgery at each place setting. Behind each covered chair was a gloved footman ready to seat each guest. The room was suffused in golden light.

There was a hush, followed by suitable comments. I found myself placed next to Elsa after all, who was seated to my left, with Anne at the head of the table to my right. Opposite me sat Bruni, who beamed as she placed her napkin in her lap. She loved the elegance and sumptuousness about her, and it showed in her face. To her right were Malcolm next to Bonnie, and then the baron next to John, at the other head of the table. Seated to John's right was his mother, with Johnny next to her, completing the circle.

The table seating was subtly different from the previous night.

Johnny was very much aware of Elsa sitting next to him, and Malcolm did not quite know what to do with Bruni or with Bonnie. He kept turning one way and then the other. I complimented Anne on the dinner arrangements and her dress.

During a lull, Elsa leaned over to me and whispered in my ear, "Have you had sex yet?"

"Elsa, you're being wicked again."

She giggled. "Just thought I'd ask."

"You just wanted to see if I'd turn red."

"That too, but one can discover an awful lot by being direct and watching the reaction."

"How's it going with the baron?" I said in an effort to steer the conversation onto safer ground.

"We do it all the time."

"Elsa…"

It was going to be that kind of evening. She loved to discomfit as much as she loved to sit at a brilliant table. Her insouciance was her way of showing her enjoyment, and judging from the opening salvo, she was delighted in every way.

Our first course arrived. Amuse-bouche of hamachi, salmon roe, and basil topped with a small flower on wafers. There was a tiny dab of wasabi. Anne and John liked sushi, and this was Dagmar's way of indulging their love of Japanese food in a European setting. The dish was paired with a glass of a Château Haut-Brion white. The wine was heavenly.

"Cheers, Elsa," I said when we were finished.

"Prost." She leaned right across me, bending low almost in my lap and asked Anne, "What price for the cook?"

Anne laughed. "She is priceless, I'm afraid."

Elsa sat back, happy. She had produced the desired effect. I looked at Bruni and rolled my eyes. She laughed and shook her head. Malcolm couldn't tear his eyes away from Elsa's torso. I looked around the table. Everyone was smiling and chatting, even Maw. Bonnie caught me looking at her and raised her glass. I did the same. I had the feeling she wouldn't take no for an answer. I had gone through a paucity of women for years. Work and my own issues had dominated my prior life. Money had been just as tight. Perhaps I never noticed, but since my arrival, I found myself attracting more attention than I wished. I'd always thought it was supposed to be the other way around. Perhaps it was a legacy. I could see it leading to no end of trouble.

The next course was a small bowl of cream of watercress soup served cold and garnished with a sprig atop a little dollop of crème fraîche. The courses were small considering there were seventeen different spoons, forks, and knives at each place setting. It was going to be a long night.

The fish course of sole amandine followed. The wine was not changed simply because there was little that could match it and because John and Anne were particularly partial to its taste. I couldn't fault them on that score. It worked for me as well as for the rest of the table.

Roast beef, John's favorite, came next along with the infamous Château Lafite. Thanks to Stanley, Johnny's and my theft slid by unnoticed.

Just before we started on the entree, John stood up and said after gathering our attention, "On behalf of Anne and myself, I would like to thank you all for coming and celebrating our anniversary at this beautiful table. There is so much I could say about the many years we have been together. Each shines on its own, better and better. The wine you will drink, of which we have only two bottles, has been with us all that time for the sole purpose of being opened tonight on this very special occasion. Please wait until we are all served, after which I will make a toast."

We waited dutifully until each had a glass poured by Stanley from a decanter. Stanley placed one empty bottle in front of John and the other at Anne's end, so they could read the notes they had written to each other long ago.

John Senior stood back up, swirled the wine, and held it up to the light. He gave it a taste. "It has lasted and aged as well as our marriage. Anne, to you, my beautiful wife. I thank you."

Anne stood and raised her glass to John. "John, to you, my husband. We are so lucky. Let us all drink."

We raised our glasses.

I looked around. Bruni and Elsa had tears in their eyes. The hard exterior of the baron had softened. He looked in Elsa's direction and nodded. Elsa nodded back. I looked at my glass in the light. The wine was a dark red, almost opaque, with a brownish hue. It had an unusual scent but tasted smooth, followed by a complex aftertaste that was surprisingly strange. It reminded me of something. I looked up to see Stanley watching me. I raised my glass in his direction. A small smile appeared on his face as he looked away.

There was a silence at the table as all our attention was held by the taste of the blood-red liquid, not the bright arterial red, but the darker one from veins that had spent their oxygen. A slow and grumbling cadence of thunder wafted through the thick curtains behind me. I saw Bruni shiver, and our eyes met. There was a flicker of fear, I thought. I wondered if she was afraid of thunder. I loved it, but lightning frightened me. Perhaps she felt the same.

The storm that had been building throughout the evening had entered the house, and the guests looked at one another for reassurance. Something threatening yet undefined was coming. No one had words to articulate the vague sense of unease and tension the future held as it stalked the present, revealing itself in syncopated flashes of foreboding. They felt it. I did too. The gods were assembling outside. I heard and felt them gathering behind me in that moment. It was nearly time, but my part I still did not know. It was as opaque as the wine. I remembered the strange liquid from the troubling little bottle of emerald green caged in ancient silver that Johnny and I had drunk to seal our oath in what seemed like ages ago. So much had changed. The wine had an eerie similarity. I looked about for Stanley, but he must have ghosted back to the kitchen.

63

Neither Johnny nor I were ever clear as to what led to Maw's outburst, but we both agreed it was toward the end of the evening, immediately after the vodka-infused raspberry sorbet.

The storm outside the walls had been building throughout the night. After a particularly violent reverberation, Maw learned forward and called down the table in a loud voice, "I want to know what you decided. You hear me? Answer me!" With that, all conversation ceased. Those at her end looked about, wondering who was being called out.

She glared down the table in my general direction, waiting for an answer. Johnny and Elsa wisely moved out of the line of fire. Maw was more than a little drunk. It was understandable. She had spent several hours consuming ten courses and drinking numerous glasses of vintage wines, including one of questionable origins. In truth, I think we were all teetering on the edge.

I did my best to defuse the confrontation, but not really. I had reached that state of inebriation myself where caution was overruled in favor of saying what I really thought. I took the high road but answered her with thinly veiled contempt, "We're here to honor our host and hostess's anniversary. Now is not the time, and here is not the place."

I had thrown down the gauntlet through my insolence, and Maw accepted the challenge. "I don't give a damn, you little shit. I gave you until the end of the night. Now answer me!"

I stood, and all eyes turned toward me. "I will answer your question, but for the benefit of those present, I will explain."

"No, you will not!" she yelled, rising from her seat as well.

Maw's rages were legendary, but only a few present had experienced them firsthand. Those who knew them cringed inwardly, while those uninitiated were stunned by her ferocious intensity and her capacity for violent intimidation that had remained hidden until now.

I continued. "We must be clear and precise as to what's at stake, and I demand there be witnesses present."

A clap of thunder punctuated my remark.

"You demand? You will do no such thing." Maw's voice had turned shrill, uncommonly loud, and jarring in a way unique to trainers of riders and horses.

"Very well. If you insist on my silence, then I will reject your ultimatum, whatever you think it is, with all that it entails right now, and you will have your answer." There was a clap of thunder so loud the table shook. No speech was possible for some moments as the rumble rolled on and on until it finally petered out. I added when it finally stopped, "Which is it going to be? Or were you just making the whole thing up to bully me with a lot of hot air?"

Heads swiveled in unison first in one direction and then the other as each of us spoke. I had gone too far, of course. There were sharp intakes of breath all around me, while Maw stood trembling visibly with her fists clenched in fury. I finished with a sneer as I sat down, "I thought so."

There were vague cries of outrage from everyone, but Maw's shriek cut them off before they were fully formed. "How dare you! You...you..." Realizing she was about to lose control completely and was already making a spectacle of herself, she pulled back from the edge with great effort. In a more even tone, she said, "It makes no difference. If you feel you need to bore the rest of us, go right ahead. You will answer for it in the end. That I promise you." She sat back down.

There was an audible sigh from everyone.

"Very well." I stood up again and addressed the gathering. "I apologize for this intrusion, but Mrs. Leland wishes to know my decision as to an ultimatum she gave me earlier today. She stated that it was her intention to bypass her immediate children and make Johnny the sole heir to her fortune on one condition: that I disappear back to wherever I had come from, never to communicate with anyone of the Dodge family and never to answer if contacted. In addition to the inheritance arrangements, she stated that if I failed to comply, she would make it her business to destroy my parents and me utterly, even if it cost her all that she possessed."

"You bitch!" It was Bonnie. She jumped up and screamed at her mother, "How dare you cut me out. After all I've done for you..."

What semblance there was left of a formal dinner party was about to spin irretrievably into a melee. To prevent that, I shouted out the first thing that popped into my head: "Stop! There's always the Sarah option."

It stopped her. It stopped everyone.

Into the silence that followed, John Senior asked quietly, "What has this to do with my dead sister?"

"Unfortunately, a great deal," I answered.

"Explain yourself, and I want no interruptions. None, do you hear? All of you!" Mr. Dodge rarely commanded, but there was a quality about him that demanded compliance, and he too had consumed a great deal of wine. He had little patience when sober, but given sufficient alcohol, he was just as intimidating as his mother when provoked. Johnny and I knew this well. He had often commented that our juvenile antics had brought out the worst in people with surprising regularity, him in particular. Intoxication only aggravated his displeasure. There was silence after he spoke, broken only by a grumble from the storm, but it too seemed to pause for breath.

I looked about. Bruni was pale. Her mouth was open, and I could see the tips of her perfect teeth. Malcolm was slumped in his chair but attentive. Bonnie looked curious, the baron impassive. John Senior had his face tilted up slightly, waiting, but boiling below the surface in resentment at the intrusion. Maw was looking down at her plate. Johnny was fiddling with a spoon while Elsa smiled in happy wonderment. Anne was not pleased. Stanley looked at a point on the opposite wall.

"Years ago, Sarah had an intimate affair with my father. Mrs. Leland found out about it and confronted her with the fact. The result was tragic. The exact details of that night are known only to a very few."

I looked at Maw. She had stopped gazing at her plate. Our eyes met. In that brief moment, she knew that I knew. I noted that Bonnie's eyes were a little wider than normal as I continued. "I am merely stating facts. My father did what he did, and to Mrs. Leland's mind, he was to blame, and therefore he should be punished. Through various means she forced him abroad, where he met my mother. I was born, and due to circumstances, I was brought up in this household. Mrs. Leland's dislike was extended to me, and in the effort to rid herself of my presence, she gave me that ultimatum and now desires an answer.

"For personal reasons" — I looked directly at Stanley — "I

choose to accept the ultimatum. Stanley, have I or have I not, fulfilled my obligation?"

"You have."

This last was met with puzzlement all around except for Johnny, who nodded and actually smiled. I half expected him to pull out his yellow pad and tick it off. We had completed step one.

"What was that all about?" John Senior snapped.

"A private matter between Stanley and me that is not particularly relevant here but which will have a bearing later on. Mrs. Leland, did you hear my answer?"

"I did, and I am happy with it. It will be good riddance. I can't stand the sight of you."

I looked around and noted that Bonnie was about to explode, when John Senior cut her off.

"There is something I don't understand. You mentioned the Sarah option. What is that exactly?"

"The Sarah option is a choice Mrs. Leland can exercise if she wishes. It's an alternative she's not aware she has. I will explain."

I looked at each of those present. Maw had paled. She knew that something was in the wind but did not dare press the issue for fear of what might be revealed. Elsa whipped her head in Maw's direction and then back at me. She could sense that a nuclear weapon had just been unveiled, but whether it would be detonated was still in question. She was ecstatic. Anne looked thoughtful. Stanley had a strange smile on his face. Bruni had turned professional. She showed nothing. The baron had not moved a muscle either, while Malcolm was frowning. He looked confused. Bonnie was interested and following right along. John Senior's patience was wearing thin, and his temper was barely in check. There were crosscurrents here he did not understand and that irritated him. Johnny sipped his wine.

"This weekend has been full of extraordinary surprises — for me in particular. Much of what I thought to be true was very different in reality. One person who impressed me, Mrs. Leland, was your daughter, Bonnie. She is far more qualified to run your businesses than you think. I do not presume to meddle in your affairs, but Johnny and I have discussed this extensively because it concerns both of us. We would like to put forward an idea. Bonnie becomes the sole heir in exchange for the following: The Fifth Avenue apartment is titled over to Mr. and Mrs. Dodge in a way acceptable to them. The bond issue, which is now in private hands" — I looked directly at Bonnie and the baron — "finds its way to Dodge Capital. It is to be titled over to the corporation, so in effect, it is redeemed. Further, a permanent truce is called between the Lelands and the Dodges. I do not presume to know the hearts and minds of our host and hostess, but it is my understanding that independence was always what they wished for and that this solution might be agreeable. I propose that this solution be substituted for Johnny becoming the sole heir. Mrs. Leland?"

"I would like time to consider it."

"I see. Perhaps I should elaborate on why it's called the Sarah option..."

Maw understood immediately and seized the opportunity provided, "No, no. I like it. It has merit. I approve, young man, but the other part still stands. You are gone."

"I quite agree."

"Then we have a deal and before witnesses," said Maw, satisfied with the arrangement.

There was a smattering of applause in relief. "Excellent," I said and quickly sat down.

John Senior looked thoughtful as he weighed the good and the bad of this arrangement. "I was unaware of this ultimatum," he said. "On the surface it seems acceptable, but I should have been told. I want no more squabbling, and I want no more interruptions this evening." Gradually his irritation subsided as he looked about.

Bonnie had tears in her eyes. Anne was relieved. The baron nodded, while Malcolm looked about as if he had just woken up. Bruni's gaze was admiring. I was thrilled to receive it, but knowing what was coming next, I wasn't sure it would be there for long. Johnny gave me a thumbs-up, indicating step two was complete. I noted that no one raised any objection to my exile, and that was more than a little troubling.

Elsa whispered to me, "Peace in our time? Skillful, yes, but I would like to hear about that interesting bit you left out."

"Let's put that aside for now. In truth, that peace accord was the easy part, it's the next phase that's rather tricky."

"There's more? I can't wait. This is so much better than the theater."

Elsa's reference to Chamberlain's 1938 Munich Agreement with Hitler just before the outbreak of World War II was uncannily close to the mark. Mine was just as much a false peace. Anne had risen and suggested we move through for coffee and after-dinner drinks when I interrupted.

"There is one other small matter before we go that I would like to bring up." Everyone turned to me again. I remained seated and said, "I believe there is an auction for certain items taking place this evening. I don't not mean to be rude, but I forbid it."

Thunder boomed. The storm had only temporarily abated and now made its presence known once more.

64

Everyone stared at me. Events that had only involved a few now concerned all.

"I don't see how you have that authority." It was the baron who spoke.

"Unfortunately, I do. I received a letter from Alice today."

"But she's dead," said the baron.

"She is, yet I received one nonetheless."

"Perhaps you should explain," John Senior said. "You seem to be doing a lot of that lately." There was a sarcasm and hardness to his words that I interpreted to mean that I was on very thin ice indeed, and I was.

It had never been my intention to hurt anyone, but I supposed even serial killers believed that, just before they started piling up the bodies.

I rested for a moment and drank some water. The storm had only been gathering itself, and during the brief pause before my reply, I heard the wind moaning to be let in behind the thick curtains. I would have gladly let it do the talking.

The solution that Johnny and I had hammered out upstairs and which had been delightfully accepted downstairs had one serious drawback. I was sacrificed in the process. Johnny and I had agreed from the start that was never going to happen, but we had been unable to figure out how to solve all the issues simultaneously. Instead, we decided to look at the solution as a series of negotiations. The first stage was to take care of the two ultimatums from Maw and Stanley. That part was now complete to their satisfaction.

The next stage was to renegotiate the defective part from a higher-power position. This looked good on paper, but when we ran the scenario from this point forward, everything ended up broken, no matter what we did. Johnny thought this might not be so bad, because we could take the broken pieces and ultimately fashion a better structure. I took the more pessimistic view that once broken, it would remain that way.

In the end, we recognized that we had to start someplace. If everything blew up, we would just have to put it all back together as best we could. Taking the initiative was the better course, so here we were.

I looked at Johnny, but his face was blank. Bruni looked troubled. I wished I had been able to tell her, but that moment had passed. It was just me — and whatever support I might receive from other forces at work. I wondered briefly if my reliance was misplaced, or at the least naïve. To any rational mind, it was madness. To which I would have happily agreed, but I was their voice and proxy.

After a brief moment to collect my thoughts, I said, "The letter I received was to be delivered only under specified circumstances. Those conditions were fulfilled today. Stanley was the intermediary, and you may verify that fact if you wish. In it were two pieces of information that are relevant.

"Firstly, I am not who you think I am. I am the son of Lord Bromley.

I let that sink in and looked around the table. Three faces registered no surprise, and from this I surmised that they had known all along. They were Anne's, John Senior's, and Malcolm Ault's. Malcolm Ault's inclusion was a surprise to me, but he was Lord Bromley's agent, so it was highly likely that he knew. Bruni's expression hurt the most. She looked utterly horrified and had placed both her hands in front of her mouth as if praying. I had to force myself to turn away. Maw and Bonnie looked shocked. The baron had his mouth open, and Elsa was calculating the implications but had come to no conclusion. I sensed she had put a distance between us. I was saddened by that.

I continued. "It was as much a surprise to me as to you all, but there it is. I cannot change it.

"The second piece of information was that the trusts set up to hold the title to Rhinebeck and all its contents, and I emphasize all, had an as yet named beneficiary. That beneficiary is me. I am not the trustee. That responsibility has been yours, John; however, there are provisions for my taking over in that capacity, and that has performance implications I needn't go into at this time."

John looked at me with a coldness I had never seen. I had insulted him because I had implied there would be legal consequences if there was any wrongdoing. I had done so deliberately, but I had also let everyone know where I stood and to what lengths I would go. Any movement of the treasures, covert or overt, would require my explicit approval.

Johnny and I had discussed the possibility that with the exception of himself, I would end up friendless by the time all was said and done. He had counseled that I accept this as a consequence and that I be absolutely ruthless. I was up against some of the best negotiators and manipulators in the world, and I would be eaten alive if I didn't play hardball from the start. He had also pointed out that it wouldn't matter how they felt initially because eventually they would change their minds. Absolutely no one would risk being uninvited after a weekend like this one. Of that, I wasn't so sure anymore.

I continued on. "In addition, Alice made explicit that I have a responsibility to the spiritual elements connected with the treasures. I would suffer the consequences if I failed to protect them. Although those consequences were unspecified, I'm inclined to think they would be severe. I apologize if I seem abrupt, uncaring, or demanding, but I have a duty in that regard that requires I be absolutely clear — the items are not for sale." I almost said, "While I am still alive," but withheld myself. I didn't want to give out any ideas. I was growing paranoid again, just when I thought I had made so much progress. Being in a precarious position always brought out this element in me, and now was no exception.

Elsa asked, "Alice hated Lord Bromley. Why would she do such a thing?"

I answered, "She had her reasons, not the least of which was that she loved him at the beginning and that my being here was a reminder of that happiness."

"Alice paid for all your upbringing as well," added John in a grim voice from the far end of table. "I have known about your lineage for some time. Anne informed me of that fact sometime after your arrival. She cautioned making an issue of it in order that you grow up in an environment devoid of unnecessary turbulence. Against my better judgment, I acquiesced. I apologize for that. The matter came to a head just before my sister's death.

"Alice and I sat down to discuss it, but she asserted that your lineage was not mine to disclose. She had the right to tell you, because she had paid for your upbringing. Alice promised me that she would inform you in her own way, and I once again agreed. After her death, the need to do so seemed less urgent.

"Anne and I both think we've handled it poorly. It's been the subject of several heated discussions, and is the only area where we've ever disagreed. Nonetheless, we each argued with your best interests at heart, in spite of the hurt we caused each other. We did the best we could, and if you use what little sense you have, you will see that was always the case.

"That being said, I was aware that a beneficiary had not been named, but I thought that may have been my sister's negligence, as was the case in most of her financial matters. I was mistaken. I would like to see the assignment for the record, but I'm willing to forgo that for now.

"However, to be clear, as you have so often repeated tonight, there are things for which I will never apologize, not now, not ever.

"That you might consider for a moment that I would simply give away a part of my sister's legacy on a whim or manipulate the assets for personal gain is an insult I cannot and will not tolerate. Do you hear me? To even imply that is insulting to me personally, and I won't stand for it. I will chalk up your newfound bravura to the power you now find in your possession.

"Nonetheless, there are facts that have compelled me to act in the way I have, and I will not discuss them here, in this room, or at this time. You have disappointed me in a way I can barely get my wits around. I speak for Anne as well in this matter. That you are obligated by your prior agreement to have nothing further to do with this family I find fitting and appropriate. I will hold you to it, and if you and Johnny think you can possibly come up with some scheme to circumvent that promise, I will make it my business to follow through in my mother's stead. Am I making myself clear?" His voice rose. "I will be even more specific. After tomorrow, I will have nothing more to do with you. Neither will my wife. Nor will my son. As to him, he might think carefully on the matter, because I will make it my business to disinherit him if he has anything more to do with you. You can remain in our company until tomorrow, during which time we will have a discussion as to the disposal of the trusts."

I had never noted the similarity between Maw and her son until now. He had her way of slicing one to ribbons. It was another surprise, but I had hurt him deeply. I knew that. The cessation of his affection and respect was devastating. He was a good man, and I loved him.

I cried, but no one ever saw my tears. There was a terrific blast and the french door windows blew out, and a wind of extraordinary violence extinguished all illumination and sent glasses and silverware crashing in the pitch darkness. There was only blackness and chaos. Screams were drowned out by the fury of the wind as the curtains streamed outward. I did not care. I was consumed by a sense of loss so profound it seemed to open like a dark chasm before me into which I plunged.

Time slowed to a crawl. My intuitive part, which had been silently observing for some time, posited in its peculiar detached way that I had experienced a low-pressure anomaly similar to a mini tornado, because the windows had blown outward. This was confirmed by the fact that my ears had popped with the pressure differential, and the direction the curtains had billowed. It also hoped that I was quite done, because I really was extraordinarily naïve, and there was much work to be done. Mr. Dodge was his mother's son in every way, and he knew exactly how the game was played. It was time I saw that and all that it implied. Power is assumed but rarely given up without a fight, and that was the essence of my situation. It also noted that I might want to skip Elsa — she was a survivor — and check on my girlfriend. A good rescue would do wonders for repairing that, or any relationship, for that matter.

It was infernally right, of course. I hated that facet of it, but it had indeed saved me from surrendering. I had been sideswiped again by my naïveté. I would fight back, but not now. Someone had come in with a flashlight from the kitchen. My thoughts had taken only moments. Right now, I needed to see to the physical needs of the guests as best I could.

65

The dining room looked like the wreck of a sinking liner that was settling on an even keel before its final plunge into oblivion. Flickering light picked up overturned candelabra, scattered glasses, spilled liquids, and overturned chairs. Jumbled cutlery was everywhere. Two or three of the footmen looked slightly injured from the glass. Almost everyone was on the floor except Malcolm, who was bending over the baron.

The wind now whipped the curtains inward, and the hiss of rain accompanied the dull rumble of thunder.

Stanley's voice boomed out. "Ladies and gentlemen, a triage area is being set up in the drawing room. Make your way there. Simon, medical supplies. Jane, I need lights now! You, with the torch, give it to me." Someone had come in with a flashlight, and Stanley seized it as he took charge.

I saw Bruni on her hands and knees nearby. I went to her and attempted to help her up. She looked ghastly in the bobbing light that Stanley was pointing here and there. "Don't touch me," she whispered angrily. "Don't touch me."

She got unsteadily to her feet and staggered toward the drawing room. It was what I feared, but I had no time for her upset. Anne was collapsed on the floor nearby. I moved quickly to her.

"Anne, are you hurt?"

"No, she said, "I'm actually just resting." It was an odd response, and I wondered if she was in shock. "I suppose I'm a bit stunned, but no matter. What a mess. Help me up." I did as she commanded. "We do need to talk, and very soon." She sighed, reached for my face with both hands, and held it. "He loves you, you know. It's why he's so upset. That and the drink, but we'll talk later. Now, I must see to my guests."

I escorted her toward the drawing room. All the electric lights were out, but there was a line of flashlights making their way from the kitchen in that direction. Anne was under her own power.

As I turned around, Bonnie grabbed me by the hand and dragged me behind the Chinese screen and into the pantry just before the kitchen. It was dark but not pitch-black.

She wrapped her arms around me and held me so tight I could barely breathe. She was very strong. "Jesus Christ, what a night." She pushed me away but still held me with her outstretched arms. I saw her only dimly. "You are a surprise! Yes, you are. That being said, you really drove a poor bargain on my behalf. You fucked yourself completely, and for that I thank you. We don't have time right now I know, but listen. I have exactly six things to tell you:

"One, I really am your friend for life; know that. Two, if you ever need a safe harbor, call me, day or night. Three, talk to me before you see my curmudgeon of a brother. I know where all the bodies are buried. Four, I'm trained as a nurse, so I want to check you out." Bonnie had a flashlight, which she had discovered in a pantry drawer. She blinded me for a moment as she turned it on and examined me.

"I had a lot of time on my hands as a spare wheel, so I put it to good use in emergency medicine. You don't look like you're in shock. That's the usual with this type of thing. Outside of a racing heart, you're fine. Wait one, for item number five."

The light went out. I heard and vaguely saw her pull up her dress waist high in the gloom.

"Five, I'm always prepared." She whipped out a flask that had been attached to her thigh with a garter. "Drink a shot of this, hombre. It will put you right. You just need to settle yourself."

I drank a swig. It seemed to help.

"Better? Good. Now stand still." She kissed me on the mouth. She knew how to kiss remarkably well. "Keep that in your file. Your girlfriend looks like she's about to do a runner. Lastly, point six, you're one hell of a man. Don't let them get to you." She took a swig herself. "I mean that. You got grit, and that's more than I can say for most of the assholes out there." She pulled up her dress and reattached her flask. "I'm off to triage. See you around. Stay sane."

With that, she disappeared toward the drawing room. I stood thinking for a moment, when I saw a light coming toward me from the kitchen.

"Ha! There you are. What? Does it take a disaster for you to come see me?" It was Dagmar with a candle. "Thank my stars it happened after the last course. How's it going out there?"

"A bit of a mess, but I don't think there are any casualties."

"Well, that's a blessing. So, you're the new master, just like she said. Her ladyship said it would be you and Stan in the end. He hated that part, but she spoke truth. I know it. She had the eye. Not all the time, mind, but you know it when you hear it. It'll take some work and a great deal of drink, but you'll both see she was right in the end. I'm making some tea for everyone. Join me. You won't be doing any good out there. You'll just be part of the confusion, and I have some words for you."

With that, she led me into the kitchen. Candles had been lit and just because the lights were out and the dining room was in shambles didn't mean that work had ceased. There were maids cleaning dishes and men drying, while others were putting them away in velvet-lined cases. This was Dagmar and Stanley's kingdom. It was a parallel world to the one I experienced on the other side of the pantry door. Both were mutually dependent. Without the other, neither could exist.

"So, what have you been up to these days? We've time," she said as she set a small service and two teacups on a side table that had two chairs. A larger service had already been set out and prepared for the drawing room. She poured me some tea and sat down to listen.

I told her about my life and drank the tea.

Although Dagmar and I rarely had extensive conversations, we were quite familiar with each other. In my early days, I would often sit on a stool and watch her as she worked. As Johnny and I grew older and the magnitude and frequency of our crimes increased, we were put to work polishing and cleaning. Those in authority were pleasantly surprised by the marked reduction in the number of our transgressions, and yet we became regulars in this area of the house by our own volition. Outlaws were always tolerated by those lower down the social ladder, and it was here that we had finally found a ready acceptance. More importantly, we were accorded status based solely on the merit of our work. Under the demanding tutelage of our laboring peers, we prospered, grew to embrace a job well done, and learned to give orders by learning to follow them in the first place.

It was an unintended blessing. Both Johnny and I held those in service and our time spent here in high regard. It was a sanctuary for us from the far more demanding and consequence-laden tasks of social interaction.

Dagmar simply listened to me. It was her gift, and it was this ability that was prized by those in the servants' quarters. The amount of information that was amassed and analyzed about their employers, along with their guests, was worthy of any intelligence service.

Dagmar sat at the center of a network of gossip, commentary, and service that exchanged information in small but continuous packets. She and Stanley were able to monitor the house's emotional pulse at regular intervals and respond as needed. From here, all movement was regulated and controlled.

Rhinebeck was, in sum, a living and breathing entity. The building was its body. Stanley and Dagmar, along with their helpers, formed the sinews, nerves, and systems that made it work, but Alice was the soul, and I would be its mind, given time. The others, those otherworldly creatures that never slept and moved about unseen, were the watchkeepers, with something else hidden, powerful, and mysterious at the center that energized the whole. Together they formed an organism that had a life of its own.

To be responsible for it all was both a joy and a burden. I told Dagmar this and all the recent developments. Those downstairs probably knew already, but I needed to regroup and revive from the thrashing I had just received. Telling her unburdened me so that I could be rejuvenated and made whole.

"Well, I've been receiving a blow-by-blow, and it seemed to me you received a bit more than you gave. Not to worry. It will all work out, you'll see. You are the master, and her ladyship meant for you to take it. She didn't say it would be easy. Transitions are usually bumpy, but you'll get the hang of it. You'll need to talk to Stan. I've told him the same. Both of you, no matter the hour, are to report here and then to the office, when all the commotion has died down. I've put aside a rare brew, some smokes, and some savories. I've told him, and I will tell you the same, I don't want to see either of your faces until you make your peace. I won't tolerate discord, and that's final. We've known each other long enough, and Stan more so, that I mean business. Her ladyship is gone, but she's still mistress here, even if only in spirit, and neither she nor I will be denied. I mean it. Now get along. I've said what I needed to say. I've got work to do."

I was dismissed.

She was not a particularly large woman, but she carried a great deal of weight. She always seemed larger than she was. I said thank you to her back. She was already in motion. That she had said that much to me was an indication of the depth of her feelings and determination.

66

I made my way from the kitchen through the dining room to the drawing room. Harry and another man were already at work boarding up the french doors until adequate repairs could be made, and several staff were at work cleaning up. The drawing room was candlelit and intact. Anne moved among the small groups of guests, while Bonnie worked on one of the staff, who had received cuts from the flying glass. The von Hofmanstals were talking together in low voices in one corner. Maw lay full-length on the couch with a compress on her head. John Senior was in conversation with the tall man. I picked out Johnny, who had parked himself out of the way, and motioned for him to follow me into the foyer. It was dark, but someone had put a candle on the table next to the bust. The ships of the line on the face of the casement clock tacked back and forth. It was raining, but the storm had lessened. The ticking was loud in comparison.

"Well?" I asked when I had closed the door behind us.

"Well, indeed. I think the whole thing went off rather well."

I shook my head in exasperation. "That's like saying the operation was a success but the patient died."

"You're being overly pessimistic and probably paranoid as well. I thought you gave that up."

"I did. At least until tonight."

"You must be firmer with yourself. Really, you must. Self-discipline works wonders. I could give you some pointers."

"Johnny!"

"Fine. I just wanted to confirm you weren't in one of your darker moods. You can get rather gloomy, and that won't do at this point in the game. Now, the way I see it, you forced Maw to accept an alternative deal. That has happened only once or twice in her lifetime. You should be proud. Not only that, Stanley agreed that we fulfilled his little attempt at coercion, so that's off the table, and also good. The treasures are going nowhere for now, and the news is out. All in all, that's a fine day's work."

"Okay, I can see that, but..."

"I'm not finished. That being said, there're few points we'll need to take up. I don't quite see how you can go into exile from here when you own the place. There are a few other items as well, which we'll need to go over. With that understanding, I want to make sure you're prepared to put in the necessary effort. You know the drill. There is no rest for us wicked folk. The good news is I have some ideas, but I'll hold off until later. Now, I noticed you disappeared for a while there."

"Bonnie pulled me away, and then I had words with Dagmar. Bonnie told me to see her before I talk to your dad. She offered to give me some ammunition. I'll take her up on it. Dagmar pretty much ordered me to sit down with Stanley tonight in his office and not to come out until we had settled our issues, once and for all. Alice apparently told her all this would happen, and that it would all sort out."

"Better and better. If Alice predicted it, and Dagmar concurs, not even Stanley will be able to wiggle out of that one. Excellent news. We need as few distractions as possible before the main event: the sit-down with my dad. It'll be a long night, but it'll be well worth it. We're in the home stretch, so take heart. Speaking of hearts, you might want to have a word with Bruni at some point. You were quite correct — "

We were interrupted by the baron, who opened and shut the door to the drawing room behind him.

"We should talk," he said, looking at me.

Johnny smiled and gave me an encouraging look before he slipped away.

"I think the library would be suitable. Bring the candle."

We made our way down the dark hallway. I was slower than the baron since I carried the candle and didn't want it to go out. The fire in the library was lit but had burned down to dim coals.

"Brandy?" He called out from the bar. He must have had eyes like a cat. I could barely see a thing, and I had the light.

"Please." I set the candle down on a table and sat down in one of the chairs. He came over, handed me a snifter, and sat down as well.

He sniffed his glass and drank a sip. "It's late, but I'm having a cigar."

After he went through the ritual of lighting, I asked, "You wished to speak to me. What's on your mind?"

"Several things. What's on yours?"

I did not wish to play games, but with some people everything was a negotiation. "I can start, provided you tell me what's on yours when I'm finished."

"That's acceptable."

"I think we got off on the wrong foot when we first met, perhaps because you thought I was someone else. It's understandable. I've been doing it for years. I'd like to start again, if possible.

"Second, there is the matter of the artifacts. At this time, based on the information I have, they are not for sale.

"Third, your daughter and I have decided to see each other.

"Fourth, you know my real father. I do not. I'm familiar with his reputation, but that may or may not be a true representation. I'd like to know more.

"Fifth, it has never been my intention to create discord. I dislike it, but there are times when there's no alternative. I find myself in that position, and it's uncomfortable.

"There arc others, but those will do. And you?"

He looked at his cigar.

"Tell me about your mother."

"I think you know more than I do."

"Tell me what you know."

"She had an affair with Lord Bromley while she was engaged to you. I was conceived. Anne arranged for my...the man I thought was my father and Mary to meet. There was the duel. You and my mother went your separate ways. Since I've been with the Dodges, I've seen her less and less and then only briefly. That's it in a nutshell."

He said nothing for a minute. He just smoked his cigar and looked at the coals of the fire. Finally, he said, "Consider this our first meeting. I wish to speak. You will listen. I'll answer most, if not all, the points you mentioned. Is that acceptable?"

"By all means."

The baron spoke with a slight accent.

"Uncertainty is what investors dislike and fear most. It implies that risks cannot be adequately quantified or identified. You're familiar with this. Forming new friendships is similar. The outcome is uncertain.

"Will the friendship prove worthwhile and sustainable, or will it end, such that one regrets having formed it in the first place? A friendship requires a substantial input of time to make it grow.

There's also the matter of trust. How much can be revealed? Can the potential friend keep what they know to themselves, or do they tell everyone they meet? Some friendships happen spontaneously. They progress without effort and with little choice in the matter. These can be the more dangerous, and the most hurtful when they fail.

"I can tell you, it's better to do without than to have a false friend. This applies in less senior relationships as well."

He stopped speaking and smoked his cigar. He spoke to the fire again.

"I have a few close friends. John is one. My wife is another. I have great trust in her. She tells me you would be worth the attempt. My daughter obviously feels similarly. I'm not so sure, but I am now slightly more inclined to do so. You told me what I wanted to know, even though it might have been viewed as unfavorable. It was an honest reply. I knew about the affair. Your real father and I discussed it when we first met. He told me straight out because he didn't want to build a relationship on falsehoods. It was a surprise at the time. Tonight, he surprised me again. That there was a child should have been revealed, but it wasn't. It puts the relationship in question and creates uncertainty. Is the son like the father, or is the father like the son?"

He paused again.

"We met some years ago, Bromley and me. I forget how. It might've been at a party. We liked each other instantly and met again. Shortly thereafter, we were driving along a country road beneath the castle. I drive very fast. A horse and rider burst from the brush on one side and bolted across to the other. Bromley reached across and controlled the wheel with one hand before I could react. It was masterfully done. We avoided the horse and rider on the left and a deep ditch on the right. A couple of centimeters either way and the outcome would have been a disaster rather than a moment of fear followed by laughter. I have often wondered about that moment. I doubt he could repeat it if given the chance. I doubt anyone could."

He looked at the tip of his cigar before continuing.

"We concentrate on those times when something has occurred, but it is when nothing happens that is often the more important. One is closest to the divine and never knows it. It is the absence of anything significant happening, you see. One rarely perceives what isn't there, only what is.

"How close I was to divinity, I only learned that evening. It left me speechless. The rider had been my daughter. She told me that she had failed to warm up the horse sufficiently but had decided to take it into the countryside anyway. The horse spooked at a bird when it went up before her and launched itself down a steep embankment. There was no stopping, only managing the descent; then there was the ditch, the road, and a wall on the far side. She was so proud that she was able to pull the horse together for the ditch, manage the two strides across the road, and then cleanly take the wall. She said they were almost hit by a car traveling at high speed. It was so close she heard the car strike the hair of the tail but couldn't turn to see it because the wall held all her attention.

"Life moved on. I didn't mention I was the driver at the time. I was too shocked to say a word. Hitting anything at that velocity would have been disastrous not only for the rider and horse but for us as well. My life — everyone's, in fact — would have been different had we collided. For a single instant in space and time, all of existence was balanced on the edge of a knife.

"That nothing happened made me question everything I knew. How often do such events occur and why? Jung wrote about coincidence but from the positive. I became aware of the negative. If it hadn't been for your father and his quick, decisive action, nothing would have mattered. I can never repay him. Luck follows him. I know this. He has a gift. Where other men find defeat, he discovers victory. After the marriage and divorce to John's half-sister, he prospered. She nearly killed him years later. He should have died, but he did not. Instead, he amassed even more capital through contacts he met on the journey. I once asked him the reason for his success.

"He told me that some men are smiled on kindly by the gods. He had that good fortune and made it a point to thank them. He became a collector of powerful objects for that purpose and suggested I do the same. He said I too was held in high regard but not in the way I thought. My life was defined by the things that didn't happen to me, and he was right. He was the positive, and I was the negative. He thought it was amusing, and that it explained how we came to find each other.

"Some friends turn out to be traitors. This is the most unforgiveable sin. Still, we made the choice to befriend them, didn't we? One only has oneself to blame, regardless of what the other did. I say this because friendship is a serious commitment.

"Your father later had an intimate affair with my daughter. She does not know I know. It was brief and torrid. Elsa put a stop to it. It would have destroyed our friendship eventually. It's not that there was anything to forgive in the act itself. Who, even at his age, is not enchanted by a woman?"

Here he paused. I gulped my brandy to cover my shock. I understood Bruni's reluctance to say anything about the extent of the affair. Now I had added to her burden by revealing that the man was my father. The baron never looked at me but continued speaking. Perhaps he thought I knew, but more likely he was simply answering my question. I had asked it and now had to accept the answer.

"There is a German expression: *Behüte mich Gott vor meinen Freunden, mit den Feinden will ich schon fertig werden.* 'God preserve me from my friends; I can deal with my enemies.' I confronted him. He apologized and begged forgiveness. I told him I would not, but I would tolerate it, provided he never did such a thing again. He agreed, and that was the end of it. I asked myself, did I forgive him? The answer is no. To forgive is to forget. Why be blind to the faults of others? To accept someone is to accept the good and the bad. Otherwise one is fooling oneself.

"You are here. You are his son. Was his affair with my daughter a foreshadow of the future, or are you a harmonic of the past? These are the questions you should be asking yourself in relation to Brunhilde, and they are important questions. The coincidence is remarkable.

"I am not my daughter. If we are to embark on the path to friendship, it is independent of that. What happens between you two I can only watch. I will not interfere unless it affects our relationship. Any child of mine, let alone one formed from Elsa and me, will be unique. It is not an easy task you have set for yourself. I wish her happiness. In the end, that is the best a parent can hope for. I wish you both happiness, if it is possible. It may not be. I cannot say one way or the other.

"I have answered your first and third points as well as some of the fourth. John Dodge and I go way back. We really did some incredibly stupid things together. It has been a wonderful gift to have such a companion.

"John is in a precarious position right now, but I'm not the one to tell you. I'm sure he will, in detail. My offer to purchase those items of his half-sister was my way of helping. I never met her. Elsa did. I suggested that he put such items as he could up for auction among a select group of bidders. I asked that he make Bromley aware of the auction as well. His and my bidding against each other would ultimately drive the prices up. It would be a help to John. When Mrs. Leland's daughter got together with me, I suggested she go for it all and outbid her mother. She was quite keen, because she could sell them to Mrs. Leland in exchange for control of her fortune. Her mother sleeps uneasily and has looked to unusual remedies. I doubt they'll work for her.

"I'm not betraying any confidences here. You know most already, and the rest you'll be told, so now is as good a time as then.

"Malcolm can be a fool, but he is not. He's angry that he's involved in a bidding war that I set up. He'll get over it. Bromley couldn't very well come himself, so he sent Ault. Ault knows he will be paying through the nose at this auction because it is set up that way. This means his benefactor's money will go to John rather than on the things Ault had in mind, which are more lucrative for him on a commission basis.

"How you choose to deal with this information is up to you. John is under as much pressure to protect the legacy as you are. His half-sister gave him a similar speech. You pointing it out that you are under the same burden didn't help. His options are limited, and this upsets him. He feels he has failed. John can get a bit dark, but then, so can I. It's a commonality that we watch for in each other. I told him to lighten up — at least I think that's the expression. You both will talk. Who knows what you will decide? I don't know the answer to that either.

"Where there is disagreement, there is disharmony. Sometimes there's no way to bridge the gap. We make false assumptions, which lead to wrong decisions. The discord you think you are creating may not be the discord you are making. You should consider that when you make your decision. One must often look deeper.

"You may have questions in your mind as to whether I had something to do with the failure of your partnership. I played no part in it. My daughter worked for the firm that was involved. She played no part directly. When I found out what had been done, I told her it was bad business, and I would not tolerate it. I hired her away, and that has been a benefit.

"I have answered your questions. I would like for you to answer one in return. What became of the idol and the jewel?"

"It was found on Wednesday and shattered shortly thereafter, when we tried to summon a demon."

"Did you succeed?"

"I'm not certain. Perhaps we did."

"Then I'd advise you to sell nothing. I must take Elsa to bed. We will talk again."

"What about my father?"

"What is there to say? I owe him my life. But is he my friend? No, he has a different status. He's more my brother. Unlike friends, we're wary of each other, yet we are drawn together as often brothers are. We see the good and the bad. We know each other's thoughts.

"Bromley has betrayed me more than once. He will do so again, but I cannot change who he is. *Betrayal* is a strong word, but where trust is concerned, that word applies. In the end, I have accepted your father for who he is. It's likely you will turn out similarly. He is the best and the worst. Once met, he cannot be forgotten. He has a power. Perhaps you do too. He has accepted and embraced his. I have done the same. You must as well, if you wish to succeed and survive in a good place. He once told me that the difference between powerful men and others less so is that powerful men embrace their faults. It is often these that prove decisive in the end. Those who don't are destined to waste their time and energy fighting themselves to become someone other than who they are. Greatness takes all we have. In the end, one can only be who one is. It's that uniqueness that makes all the difference. That's enough for one night. Let's return to the others. I'm tired."

With that, the interview was over. I picked up the candle and accompanied him back to the drawing room.

67

The lights in the hallway were on. Power had either been restored or the emergency generator was running. The drawing room was empty except for Anne and Elsa. They rose from the couch as we entered.

Elsa took the baron's hand in hers and said they were going to bed. Elsa wished me good night and gave Anne a kiss. The baron merely nodded to both of us.

"How did it go with Hugo?" Anne asked after they left.

"Good, I think. He's different than I expected. He's a thoughtful man."

"He can get pretty deep. We should be off to bed as well. I tried to speak with John before he went up, but he said that everything could wait until tomorrow. He will see you at eleven in the library. Don't worry. It'll all work out. It always does, somehow."

"I have more to do tonight, I'm afraid, but I'll at least escort you up the stairs."

"In a minute. I'm quite fine, but I thank you just the same. Are you worried?"

"Yes and no. The powers that exist here seem to have everything well in hand. At least I hope they do, because I don't, but that's not anything new."

"There's that, but I'd put more faith in a good night's sleep. Don't stay up too late. I knew this day would come, of course. It happened not in the way I imagined. I promised Alice I would do what I could to smooth it along. I've not been overly successful, I'm afraid. Change is hard. We get comfortable and set in our ways. You will talk to Stanley. I assume that's where you're going now? Alice told me she fretted over that meeting, but that is for you two to work out. Dagmar is prepared. She told me she had a broom ready to thrash you both if you acted like idiots. Walk me up the stairs."

After I made sure she made it, I went in search of Stanley.

Dagmar sat in the kitchen at the side table with a cup of tea waiting for me.

"He's in there. Good luck. I'll be here, even if it takes all night."

She gave me a hug and then maneuvered me into Stanley's office. He was sitting down with his back toward me, facing the window. I could see his face in the reflection, and he could see me. I sat in one of the chairs on the other side of his desk. In the past, I was always eager to break a silence. Tonight, I allowed it to go on. It may have been five minutes before he sighed and swiveled around to face me.

"So it was foretold, and so it is. I have often wondered about this meeting. It is our first with all the cards on the table. I have played it out in my head many times in many ways. What I would say. What you would say. I was sitting here just now thinking, watching you in the glass. Do you know what surprises me most?"

"No."

"The sterility of this moment. Reality is plain and unassuming. I expected to feel something, but I don't. In all those different mental rehearsals, I never once envisaged that I would feel nothing."

"Why should you? For me, you are who you always were. I am who I always was. I have a different name. That's all."

"She gave you the estate. Your status has changed."

"She did, but I have not accepted it yet."

Stanley leaned back and placed his fingers together.

"Why ever not?"

"I'm not altogether certain, but much depends on what happens in this room tonight."

"That is also unexpected — and perhaps illogical."

"I love this place, but if my taking ownership destroys it in the process, I wonder at the wisdom of doing so."

"Then why are you here?"

"Right now, or on a more existential basis?"

"Take the broader view."

"I'll answer, but I have a question first. Do you hate me?"

"You personally, not really. It's your father that I hate, and you by extension. I wonder at my having felt so strongly for so long. I cannot conjure the passion in the now, as I could then."

"What would you have me do?"

"Leaving might be better."

"Suppose I can't."

"Then I don't know."

"Would you leave?"

"I'm not sure. I'm older than when I threatened to leave her ladyship. I feel my age. It would be hard to start again, and I doubt I have the depth of feeling to carry it off. Dagmar loves it here, but she is younger. It would be hard for both of us."

"What happened to you, Stanley?"

"Whatever do you mean?"

"I always saw you as the one who held everything together,

preserving what needed to be preserved and holding us all to a higher standard."

"That's hard to know, because I don't rightly know myself. I suppose I'm tired."

"Would you be willing to work with me if I accepted the estate in spite of my being the son of Lord Bromley?"

"That is the question, isn't it? I doubt it. I'm set in my beliefs."

"Do you think there would be too great a disharmony between us?"

"I've held on to my hatred for Lord Bromley a long time. Reconciliation is impossible. There would be disharmony."

"Then we should look at a more fundamental concept. Why are you here?"

"Existentially or immediately?"

"Start with the broader view."

He smiled at that. "You're difficult not to like, but so was his lordship."

"I have my charm. Why don't you begin and I follow? Is it all right if I smoke?"

"Yes and yes. Her ladyship is the answer to that. You know my story."

I lit a cigarette. "Then that's a starting point. Johnny and I read all the material you gave us. He managed to put Alice's notes into a sequence that made sense. You know about her going to the Carlyle with Marianne Thoreaux?"

"Yes."

"At the end of it, she said she needed to repeat what she did there, but in this place, using a specific Book of the Dead. Are you aware of that?"

"Yes."

"Alice's health was failing at the time of her death. She was wrapping up her affairs. I suspect she knew she wouldn't survive. I will stop here because we're at a significant juncture. Several nights ago, you gave Johnny and me an option of hearing the rest of Alice's story in exchange for a promise. This moment is not dissimilar."

"A harmonic?" asked Stanley. He looked vaguely interested, but in his case, it was hard to tell.

"Possibly, but no less important. The choice we face must be made by both of us together. It is the reason I have yet to fully accept what she gave me. I see two paths before us. The first is simple. I give the assignment of the estate over to Mr. Dodge. It becomes his in full, and I move on. Mr. Dodge then sells what treasures he can for whatever he can get and replenishes the maintenance trust, so the house can continue. On the surface, it seems a workable solution, and it is within my power to grant. The estate survives. Nothing really changes, but from another view, everything does.

"This house has a life that exists on a separate and, I think, higher plane. The problem with the first path is that this spiritual element becomes secondary compared to the physical. What will be the cost of that decision? I think a light will go out. You asked me why I'm here, and I asked you the same. I don't know the answer specifically, but preserving the essence of this place might be close. The day we turn our backs on its transcendent elements will be tragic in a way I cannot put adequately into words. Do you agree?"

"I am aware of what you're saying, but I don't see an alternative. Are you willing to do what you say?"

"I'm not unwilling, but I see it ultimately as a failure. Just the same, a possible solution is better than none."

"I'm surprised you would consider it," said Stanley.

"And why is that?"

"I think of you as self-absorbed and selfish. Your father certainly was."

"Perhaps I am, but at least I have learned to look at a problem

469

from many different angles in an effort to find a solution that seems best. I take all stakeholders into account. Even then, there is no guarantee it will all work out. There is a second solution that might preserve that magic, although it does not immediately resolve the financial needs of the estate. At the least, it sets the importance of the spiritual element at the level it deserves. We'll have to rely on the possibility that a better solution will present itself. Provided we are able to reach a harmony between us, perhaps we might be able to work together and come up with something to preserve this place intact. It might not work, but we will at least have made the attempt. Does that make better sense?"

"You seem to think our differences are the key here."

"I do. Right now, you more or less hate me. I more or less distrust you. There is no peace between us. You are right from your point of view, and I am correct in mine. Suppose, hypothetically, you were compelled to stay on? Suppose I was too. What would this house become? A battleground? We would have wished we had taken path number one. I for one will not live under such conditions, magic or no magic. The first path, with its no-win outcome, will always be preferred, whatever happens, unless we're able to resolve our issues. Therefore, those issues are where we must begin. So far, no other ideas have been put forward other than selling the treasures. Maybe there is another way. Working together, it might be possible, but with our current attitudes, that's not likely to happen."

Stanley interrupted. "So, if I get this straight, there are two paths. The first is you leave and the status quo maintains. The second is we resolve our differences, and the first path is still available, but another also becomes possible. It becomes the better choice. I might agree with that. Still, I don't see how I'm going to change my mind about you. Once I've decided, I rarely change. More importantly, I don't see how the sale can be avoided."

"Neither do I, but stranger things have happened. Did you expect that I would simply walk away?"

"Frankly, no."

"Perhaps I'm a different person than who you think I am."

"It's possible. What did you have in mind for resolving our differences?"

"I've learned a few things this week. I admit I've never been the strongest advocate of honesty. I never really grasped the point. Being truthful, from my experience, has created just as many problems as solutions. I see it differently now. One lies well enough, and one even fools oneself. One can then be fooled by others. The world one perceives no longer is a true reflection of what is. I've been wrong in so many ways. I've made assumptions that were invalid, been blind with my eyes open, and generally had my head handed to me by professionals because I was filled with false perceptions. I've been compelled to change my views about many things, and it was discovering the truth that did that.

"Given that as a premise, I think we both may have it wrong. We see each other none too clearly. For a brief period, we should give each other the benefit of the doubt. I propose we be completely straight with each other. No bullshit. No lies. No half-truths. I have questions. You may have some also. We will answer each other as honestly and completely as we can. How could it hurt?"

"What if we still feel the same at the end?"

"We follow path one."

"You will do that?"

"I will. My gamble is that we won't need that solution."

"To me it seems I win either way."

"You do, but remember, if it comes down to the first path, you'll have to live here when I'm gone and so will Dagmar. I'm not sure what the consequences will be, but there will be some. Let's at least try. Are we in agreement?"

68

S tanley looked at me for a time before answering.
   "Do you know why negotiations are often carried out late at night?" he asked.

"Attrition?"

"Exactly. Slowly our barriers are eroded. It is a tactic I have observed in my employers. Eventually, we give up and compromises become possible. The only danger is our reaction the next morning, when we're filled with doubts and second thoughts as to the merit of the agreements reached the night before."

"I've experienced that firsthand," I told him. "It could happen, but this is not a one-night stand — all or nothing. I expect there'll be many more discussions and renegotiations. It's a process, not an event. All I desire is that we be willing to start and build a foundation for a better relationship. Nothing more."

"You're an optimist."

"Actually, I'm quite the opposite, but I'm aware of my pessimism and try to balance it. I have low expectations; therefore,

I'm not disappointed. We could set our sights lower. We could simply talk."

"We could, but you asked if I agree to at least try. It is a reasonable request, and I will acquiesce to it. You may wonder at my reluctance. Her ladyship said over and over to me that you and I would become good friends. She told Dagmar as well. She told Johnny's parents. They would tell me of their conversations with her on numerous occasions. Each time, I would wonder if it was simply her wish, rather than something set in the future. Dagmar is convinced her sight in this was genuine. She is often correct. If and when you marry, you will discover for yourself how often the other half is wiser than we are. Frankly, I find it disturbing. Perhaps it is the male tendency to want to be correct in all things — in which case, it is hubris. We can rail all we want, but at some point, we must resign ourselves to our fate of having to surrender to powers greater than our own. I could howl my protest, and have, many times. It would perhaps be better to simply agree at the beginning. It is something to consider, but where is at least the illusion of control and a small nod to our manhood? In the end, we must capitulate. I do so now."

Stanley looked down at his desk for a few moments and then looked up at me before continuing. "So...here we are. I think I know where this is headed. You want to know the specifics of her ladyship's death. It is perhaps the height of irony that it is the opposite of what you probably think. I will tell you, but I am not sure having the details will fully resolve the matter for either of us. That being said, confession is supposed to be good for the soul. Mine has been locked away for a long time. Someone should know. Perhaps that is why I offered to tell you and Johnny her story — to get to this moment. It might as well be you who hears it. The gods speak in peculiar ways."

He smiled and looked at me.

"The irony is thick. You are his son." He shook his head. "I can hardly believe it. Life indeed may be circular, but I digress." He looked right at me and said, "My sin is not that I killed her, in case that is what you are thinking, nor is it that I assisted in her suicide. Nor is it your father's. In the end, I could not do what she asked or, more accurately, begged me to do. I broke my oath. I could not kill her. It was beyond my capacity, and in that, I failed both of us utterly."

There was silence in the room for quite some time.

"Care for a drink?" he asked.

"I'd welcome one."

I did not comment on what he'd said. He would get around to the details in his own way. I had thought he might have killed her or had played a part. I always assumed the worst in people. Stanley more than others. The boundaries that might restrain many did not exist for him. I was not so cold and calculating, but we weren't so far apart, knowing my lineage. We had both protested as fate dragged us along. Surrender was the only answer for him and for me. I could feel the house singing. Everything that was supposed to happen of importance had just occurred.

I realized that I had finally reached maturity through my surrender and subsequent acceptance of who I was, including the bad that was my heritage. I would be who I was no more, no less. I now understood Stanley better. More importantly, we had bridged the abyss that had separated us through our mutual surrender to our respective destinies.

Stanley got up and poured a measure of his private reserve into two glasses of cut crystal and handed me one before he sat back down. The pattern of the glass was so sharp it almost hurt to hold. We continued as if nothing had happened, when we both knew otherwise.

"Cheers," he said. We drank. The whiskey was even better than I remembered. "You might want to try one of these." He offered me a plate of small snacks that Dagmar had made for our meeting.

I ate one and then another. "Thank you. They're out of this world. Dagmar has a way."

"She does. Are you ready?"

"Please."

"Her ladyship was keen to make another attempt, like she did at the Carlyle. We had few secrets. She told me what she was doing on a regular basis. One day toward the end, she asked for me and stated that she had been to see several doctors on Park Avenue. They all concurred. She had heart disease. How long she had left, they didn't know. A year was the most optimistic prognosis.

"Aware of her impending death, she escalated her involvement into the realm of the shamans. It was a frightening development. I was to take Marianne's place as her guide. She was not certain she would survive and made preparations. She wrote the letter I gave you earlier today. She left her day-to-day financial affairs in disarray for fear that if they were in order, it might appear that she had committed suicide. She justified this by telling me that certain insurance policies would be invalidated if suicide was ruled the cause of death. In doing that, she failed to consider the alternative interpretation, which was that she was murdered.

"She became obsessed with ensuring that her death should appear as anything other than done by her own hand, which of course led me to believe that that was what she intended. That she would have been able to survive the effects of the drugs and the violent results they would trigger in her body was simply not credible. I was to force it down her throat, using any means necessary. This she commanded me to do. The night she had determined as the most favorable eventually came to pass as all such singular events relentlessly come about. The hours slipped toward the hour, and then the minutes became the moment. For me, it was like an approaching execution. The week before, she had made me swear an oath. I confess to you it was with the same book and small chased green bottle that we drank from the other

475

night. You can understand the seriousness of it. I cringe just thinking about it.

"She had dressed in her Egyptian clothes, along with every talisman, artifact, and piece of ancient jewelry that she possessed. She had prepared the potion in her bathroom using a hot plate. It was late, and everyone else was asleep. She handed me a funnel and a large cup filled with the foul-smelling liquid before she lay down on the floor. She looked up at me and told me to pour the entire mixture down her throat. I was to use force if needed and not hold back.

"There is love between a man and a woman, a husband and wife. It is physical, intimate, and fulfilling. There is another love between a collector and a particular piece of art. One experiences in the object an ideal, something unworldly, something divine. Looking down at her at that moment, whatever illusion I had harbored for all those years shattered. I saw her fully for the first time. I saw an ordinary human being but one that nonetheless held my heart since we had first met. I shrank back. She must have realized that I could not go through with it. She grabbed my wrists with each hand to force me. A struggle ensued. She cursed me as her face turned purple...and in a second she was gone.

"I cannot tell you the relief I felt. I was overjoyed at my escape. I threw the mixture down the toilet and cleaned up where it had sloshed about. I ran to the next room and sat on the bed. I was aghast and elated. It was my elation that shamed me. It still does, but there were other consequences. No lightning struck me. I was not turned to stone, but in some ways, it would have been just as well. I changed. My heart became frozen, joy evaporated, and happiness was not to be found in the everyday things I had loved most. As you said — a light had gone out. I cursed my circumstances. Drink became easier. Accounts that had been so faithfully followed grew sloppy. A hole opened up, and it swallowed me. I may have slowly bankrupted this place. I don't know. It's now up to others to salvage what I cannot."

Tears dropped from his eyes. He said no more.

I said nothing. I couldn't. I had been in the dark place he found himself. Perhaps it was a type of curse after all. Alice must have struggled under the weight of something similar. I tried to reason how it was that I had managed to escape my own darkness. It was Johnny who had done that for me. For every black cloud I threw at him, he countered with an optimism that seemed to dispel the darkness. When our partnership died, I went off to California, but the memories of him kept me company. I was not Johnny. I could not reverse the downward path Stanley was on in an evening, but we had made a start. I would help him all I could. He was the best of men. I harbored only good will toward him.

"Stanley, I trust you. I didn't before, but I do now. We will see it through. All I can say is thank you for confiding in me. I will try and live up to that confidence. We have talked, and that is a start. To me, you're worth your weight in gold. Did you study all those books to see if there was a means to lift the curse?"

He nodded.

"If I might ask, what did you promise exactly?"

"That I would help her complete the ritual."

"Did you promise that it would be successful?"

"No. I assumed complete meant finished, and it wasn't."

"I'm sure you looked at this, but if she died in the middle of it, how are you responsible? The specificity and exactness of a curse, a spell, an oath, or even a legal document, are important. Perhaps you have assumed too wide an interpretation."

"There is the spirit of the law."

"There is, but that's why there are judges. Poor wording or improperly drawn-up contracts can create problems in the enforcement area, and there is no excuse for it. That's why we pay so much to have a good attorney."

"I have looked at that, of course, but you have a different take on it. There are no judges for this kind of thing."

"Perhaps it's because we judge ourselves, but I'm willing to argue the case in your favor until you are convinced. There is one other point. In Alice's notes, she mentioned that the Eye of the Moon made no guarantee that she would return once she passed into the afterlife, only that she would pass safely into it. Putting aside Sir Henry's dream, perhaps she was successful? We don't know the answer to that. Sometimes even the gods are loath to say the whole truth when it will disappoint. In any event, I will be your advocate. Would you be willing to work with me?"

Stanley looked at me. He pulled out a handkerchief and blew his nose. "I don't want charity."

"I was never under the impression this was a charity-type organization."

"I suppose not." He sighed. "We have talked. It is a start. I feel lighter. I never told anyone. I suppose there was never anyone to tell until now. I agree to hold everything in abeyance. No decision concerning my employment is the best I can offer."

"That's more than adequate. It will all work out. Get some sleep. I have a couple of visits to make before this night ends. No rest for the wicked. I'll send you my bill in the morning."

He smiled as we rose from our seats. "I might even pay it."

I held out my hand. He shook it willingly. It was a beginning.

69

Dagmar was waiting at the kitchen table. She stood up and looked us over. She seemed pleased with what she saw. "Well, I won't be needing the broom," she said. It stood ready, leaning against the table next to her chair. "Come on, Stan, we must sleep, and you had best do the same," she said, referring to me. "But I suspect you have farther to travel tonight."

My life was an open book, apparently. She put one arm through Stanley's and picked up the broom with the other. She guided him to the back hallway. I heard her whisper as the two receded toward the back stairs, "See? She was right. I told you it would all work out. He's a good lad, and so are you."

I did not hear his reply, but I thought I saw him pat her hand as I turned toward the dining room. I had Johnny and Bruni still to speak to. Johnny was probably asleep on the couch upstairs waiting for me. Late-night planning was a passion of his that I did not share, but he was so relentless on the subject that I took it for granted that he would still be there when I finished. The person I really had to speak to was Bruni. Not only was I uncertain of her state of mind but I was not exactly sure which room she was in. I had narrowed it down to one of two possibilities. I crept up the stairs and down the second-floor hallway. I tapped softly on one of the doors and waited. It opened, and Bonnie stuck her head out. She smiled sleepily when she saw me and pulled her hair from her face, showing a bare arm. She whispered, "Next door, cowboy. Good luck and thanks."

She smiled again and closed her door. She would let the hand play out. She was seriously smart. I sighed and moved on down the line. I tapped once again and waited. There was no answer. I tapped again and paced back and forth. Nothing. I didn't want to knock any louder and turned toward the hidden door that led upstairs, when I heard a click. The door opened, but no one peeked out. For a moment, I hesitated and wondered if I'd gotten it wrong once again, but I was resolved and entered. I closed the door quietly behind me.

"Bruni?" I asked in a whisper. It was pitch-black.

"What?" I recognized her voice. It was Bruni's room. I was in the right place.

"Can we talk?"

"No. It's very late, and a lady doesn't open her door in the dead of night to have a conversation. Now get over here."

It was a night full of surprises. Obviously I had a lot to learn about women in general, and Bruni in particular.

"I can't see a thing," I said, stumbling about.

"Your eyes will just have to grow accustomed."

"Somehow I don't think they ever will."

She chuckled. "Now that's the best thing I've heard all night. Let me help you."

I felt around for the bed. She took my arm and guided me toward it. As my eyes adjusted to the darkness, I realized she wasn't wearing a thing.

70

Bruni reached over me to the side table, holding the sheet in front of her and turned on the light. A pack of cigarettes lay there, and she lit two.

"Smoking in bed?" I commented.

"Absolutely. It's the best, and I'm wide awake. How about you?"

"Pretty awake, I'd say, and happy."

She sighed. "Me too. We're sexually compatible." She rolled toward me. "You have no idea how important that is to me. I had to put that to rest before we spoke about my behavior earlier tonight. I suppose that's manipulative, or at least calculating, but I had to know first."

"What if we hadn't been?"

She reached for an ashtray and held it for us. "It would have cast grave doubts on our future, at least for me, but thankfully, that's not the case." She hugged me. "Now, I have an apology and a confession to make. Not my favorite things to do, but I must. First, I'd like to apologize for my behavior downstairs and offer an explanation. You being the son of Lord Bromley both shocked and repelled me because the affair I had with him was not just platonic. You may have guessed that. Maybe not, but there it is."

She looked at me for a reaction.

"You father told me."

Bruni sat up. The sheet slipped from her shoulders. Her eyes widened as she looked at me, and I suppose mine did too.

"Good god," she said in German. "I had no idea he found out. He never mentioned it."

"Would it have helped?"

"I suppose not. *Mutti* told him, of course. I should have figured that."

"Welcome to my world. There are no secrets."

"Really?"

"Around here, the staff knows everything as well."

"Even about us?"

"Absolutely. There's probably a betting pool."

"I suppose that's to be expected."

She lay back down. "Sitting up I think was distracting you," she said.

"Most definitely."

"I'm glad to hear it. Did my father say anything else?"

"Yes, but not about you, other than that he wants you to be happy — both of us, for that matter. He was not overly optimistic, but he wasn't pessimistic either."

"That's how he is, but I'm glad he said that. It means he approves, and that's important. He did not approve of my first husband. Anyway, I should have been more transparent when I told you about the affair, but I wasn't. I was embarrassed. I hate to appear stupid and foolish, and I was both. It's hard to for me to reveal who I really am. When I realized the implications of you being Lord Bromley's son, the unnaturalness struck me as unsavory bordering on the perverse. That did not go down well as a point of personal reflection. I felt sick. If it hadn't been for the windows blowing out, I might have actually thrown up."

She shuddered and continued. "I could barely get my wits around it. Knowing I had to confess the extent of that relationship to you made it almost unbearable, but you found out anyway. Horrible truths have a way of surfacing when you least expect them. It was when I was sprawled on the floor and I saw your face looming above me that I realized how utterly horrid I must appear. I even thought for a moment you were him, and I fled. I've never really run away from anything, but I did tonight. I looked at myself through your eyes, and I was both shocked and ashamed at what I saw. I ran. I could barely control myself."

She stared off into the distance, lost in her thoughts. I reached out to her.

"The perversity of our circumstances was not lost on me," I said. "When I realized who my father was, I was both pleased and horrified. You don't know the relationship he had with Alice. It was abusive, cruel, and demonic. It started with love and ended in madness. I'll tell you about it one day.

"There is the saying: the apple does not fall far from the tree. I think there is some truth in that. Enough for me to know that the same capabilities and tendencies lie within me, dormant and unexpressed, but they are there nonetheless. Will they crawl to the surface? I cannot say. Your father strangely enough understood that. He wanted me to embrace those elements rather than suppress them — to channel them and not be willfully blind to them. Tonight, I asked myself if you would accept me, knowing what lies inside me? I didn't know the answer. I still don't. You said I have a dark side. I do, but it isn't dark. It's black."

She turned toward me and said seriously, "We're the same. It's why we're drawn inexorably toward each other. It's our weakness and our strength. You must understand — you'll never drag me down. I descend. Your blackness holds no fear for me. I will always be there with you, however dark it is."

She kissed me gently.

I looked into her electric-blue eyes and said, "Thank you. I feel blessed that you're here. Had your life not taken the path it has, we'd not be together. I am grateful for all that has happened to you and all that you've done. I mean that. Other than knowing you better, your past doesn't really concern me. When we made our promises to each other, I chose to become hopelessly biased in your favor. I will be so always." I kissed her.

"You don't care what I've done or what has been done to me?" she asked.

"No. You are who you are, and I like that well enough."

"Since you're biased, does that mean I can do no wrong?"

"Pretty much. You could hurt me, I suppose, but that's the risk I take. I have made the decision to love you no matter what happens. It's my surrender to you."

"That's a lovely thing to say. I like that." She kissed me. "Acceptance is hard for me. That incident with your father was one of many that appear out of nowhere from time to time. I want to be perfect. Intellectually, it is foolish, but my heart refuses to listen. It's stubborn, like me. Having at least one person love me in spite of all the mistakes I've made is a gift, and I thank you for that. On more immediate matters, you seem to be in a bit of a precarious situation. Do you know what to do? Would you allow me to help you?"

"Thank you for the offer, and I accept whatever help you might give me. I do have a question you can answer. If you make a promise as one person only to find you are somebody else, is the contract binding?"

"I take it you are referring to the promise you made to Mrs.

Leland. There was no attempt to deceive, and you were competent when you made it from a legal standpoint, so it stands. The contract could be voided by the other party, but not by you. Mutual promises can be valid contracts. Enforcement can be problematic, but reneging can lead to a loss of reputation. Your best bet would be to renegotiate. I hope that helps."

"It clarifies my position. A lot depends on my meeting with John Senior tomorrow. Stanley and I have made a start, and I'm very happy with that. Running this place without him would be out of the question."

"Will you live here, then? Will we live here?"

"You wish to?"

"Of course."

"Then we will. I have to pack up and tie up my affairs in California, but I'm quite sure I can transition back East. I have several clients in New York."

"I have a place in the city. There is room."

"Thank you. I think I'd like that."

"We'll work it out." She sat up again and stretched. Her body glowed in the soft light from the bedside lamp. I was spellbound. She asked, "So, you accept my faults?"

"Absolutely," I murmured.

"Faults imply that I have more than one."

"Very few faults, actually," I said carefully.

"How many? Be specific."

"Ahh…"

She put the ashtray aside and lay on top of me. "I gotcha with that one. Admit it."

"You did. I was distracted while on dangerous ground."

"Very dangerous ground. What plans did you have for the rest of the evening?"

"I'm flexible, but I promised Johnny…"

"Early-morning meetings are better. Trust me; I know. I'll set the alarm for six. How about we leave the light on this time?"

"Fine by me."

Johnny would have to wait.

71

The alarm brayed. Bruni turned it off, kissed me with abandon, and pushed me out of bed. It was six in the morning. I gathered up my clothes and opened the door carefully. All was quiet. I slipped across the hall, opened the hidden door, closed it behind me, and climbed the stairs. Johnny was sleeping on the couch. Robert lay on his back beside him with his paws in the air. His black beady eyes opened, and he sat up staring at me. He cocked his head to the side. Johnny stirred and asked groggily, "What time is it?"

"Five after six."

He opened his eyes. "You're not wearing any clothes."

"Easier than putting it all back on. I'm going to shower, and then I'll tell you about last night."

"From your appearance, I can guess."

"That too. I won't be long."

I showered, shaved, changed into comfortable clothes, hung up Johnny's borrowed tails, and felt like a million dollars. I passed

Johnny on his way to the bathroom and asked, "Care for some coffee? I can nip down and find some. I think."

"That would be heavenly. Black. Bring a thermos, if you can. You're full of vim and vigor bordering on the obscene, but do hurry. I think I need a transfusion."

I slipped down the back stairs to the kitchen. Coffee was on the stove. Several of the staff were up and about. Jane got me a thermos and two mugs. I almost ran over Dagmar as I headed for the back stairs.

She took one look at me and said, "Ha!" And then over her shoulder, she yelled, "Pay up, Stan."

"Yes, Dagmar, and a wonderful morning to you too. How big was the pool?"

"Big enough. That was a side bet. You and Stan must have had a good talk. He slept the soundest I've seen in years. It's a blessing. You leave this afternoon. Make sure you see me before you go. Now off with you. I've work to do."

The aroma of fresh coffee permeated the top floor as I filled the two mugs. Johnny stepped out, dressed and awake. Seeing the coffee on the table, he said, "If this is a demonstration of the establishment's new management practices, I heartily approve. Now tell me about last night."

I outlined what the baron had told me, my meeting with Stanley, and mentioned Bruni, but in a general way. He got the idea.

Johnny put down his mug and said, "Well, well, an outstanding night's work. We finally got to the bottom of the Alice story. I never thought I'd see the day. I could go on about that, but time presses. In addition, Stanley is now in your corner, and you're on a first-name basis with Hugo. Excellent. I'll keep all of this and Bruni's status in confidence, but a word to the wise. You're flashing like a neon light this morning. I won't spill the beans, but you most certainly will."

"I'm afraid that's out of the bag already, at least in the servants' wing. Dagmar was a winner for sure."

"There was a pool?"

"Apparently."

"Typical. How big was it?"

"No idea. Dagmar wouldn't say."

"Damn. I would have liked to have taken a piece of that action. Sometimes they have all the fun. Anyway, on to more sober things. While you were carousing, I was thinking. I made some notes."

Johnny picked up a yellow pad and a pencil.

"First order of business. You're not abdicating, and inheritance or no, our friendship stands inviolate. Agreed?"

"Absolutely."

"Point one carries."

Johnny ticked it off and said, "Point two was Stanley. I will mark that as complete. More to go, but it's possible he can now put pressure where needed. Just a thought, but keep it in mind as we marshal our forces."

"Yes."

"Point three was Brunhilde. That is complete as well. She is a legal brain. We may need her advice. I assume she is solidly in your camp?"

"Most definitely."

"Good. Those were last night's immediate problems. Now for today's agenda.

"I spoke to Mother last night. The meeting is at eleven. It'll be in two parts. The first will be just you and Pater. Obviously, the maintenance trust needs to be shored up, but by how much is unknown. Mother estimated a couple of million. The second part is to handle the bids for the treasures and arrange payment. You are correctly opposed to the sale, but that doesn't handle the financial hole in the maintenance trust. I have a couple of ideas for that. Are you ready?"

"Fire away."

"First, a wine auction at Christie's. We have quite a cellar down below. It would need an appraisal, but we have cornered the market on several vintages that have disappeared from the world's stage, so it's possible they will move on it. Even if it's a success, I doubt on its own it'll raise the amount needed. A few nice trades could make up the difference. I know what you're going to say, but as a stop-gap solution, it has quite a lot going for it."

"No, it's a good idea and worth exploring. Stanley will have a cow, but better a cow than no home at all. Just the same, I feel leery trading with my back up against a wall. That rarely ends well. You do recall our last adventure?"

"I thought you'd say that, but remember, it was Maw who sank us, which leads me to point two: I noted that we might explore the legal ramifications of that. A donation might make it all go away. Then again, holding her feet to the fire might just blow everything to kingdom come. Whichever way you cut it, somebody made a packet at our expense, and they owe. We just need to know who profited and collect."

While Johnny was talking, Robert got up, trotted to the door, and sat looking at it. There was a knock. Johnny and I looked at each other. Nobody ever came up here other than staff, and then only when we weren't around.

Johnny called, "Enter."

The door opened and in stepped Bonnie in jeans and a denim work shirt. She had applied makeup and pulled her hair back. The new Bonnie was much in evidence.

"Sorry to barge in, but I have a keen sense of smell, and your coffee drew me up here. I could use a cup, if you don't mind."

Both of us stood up and invited her to join us.

She sat on the couch. Johnny gave her his cup and offered to get a clean one as well as top off the thermos.

"That'll work. Take your time. Give us about twenty minutes."

Johnny said, "I'll walk Robert and return in thirty."

"Perfect," she said, taking a sip. "Just what I needed."

Bonnie looked around as Johnny with Robert in tow trotted off.

"I like it up here. It's nice."

"It's been home to Johnny and me for years."

"Lots of books. How did it go with the GF?"

"Quite well."

"Well, I'm happy for you. We could get into a world of trouble, you and I, but I won't pressure you. I'm taking that off the table for now. It would lead to complications. Besides, I'd rather have you as a friend. I trust you, and that's a rare commodity in my world. Can you live with that?

"I can, and I look forward to it. You made a big impression on me."

"I'm glad. We have a connection, and it's an important one. I also wanted to talk to you in private. The coffee was an excuse to do that, but I welcome it just the same."

She drank some more and said, "I spoke with my mom late last night. I wondered if she was inclined to back out on the deal, but I'm happy to say she's warmed to it."

"I'm thrilled to hear that. You're her best and, I think, only option. John Senior doesn't have the drive, or that X quality that you have. It was clear to me after we talked that you were the one. I have a question for you — a personal one."

"I'm listening."

"Do you think you and she will ever bridge the gap between you?"

"We're on the same wavelength, because that's what I want to talk to you about. Dealing with my mother can be a crapshoot. As I took her upstairs, I wondered what she really thought about her decision after she'd had some time to mull it over. Deciding that I would be the primary inheritor was a big move for her, and she was somewhat strong-armed into it. I got her upstairs, all tucked in, and sat down at the end of her bed. We had our first-ever real conversation. I told her I wanted to make peace with her. It takes at least two to fight, and I'd made a decision to let go of my end — provided she was willing to let go of hers. It was touch and go, but we actually succeeded. What convinced me that she'll carry through with the deal was our talking about Sarah and what I knew about that night. That I'd kept quiet about it all these years impressed her, but even more so was my certainty that she'd acted correctly. The facts are she had no choice. Mom's really tough, but not even she can carry the burden of killing her own child, even if in self-defense, without consequences. It has weighed on her like a stone, and I told her it was time to lay it down as best she could. We talked it over, and I think she finally understood some things she hadn't before. We sometimes pore over what we might have done differently. She did the same. She'd replayed that incident in her mind so many times that she didn't know what was true and what wasn't. It's hard to justify what you did when you're no longer sure of what really happened. The thought that she might have got it wrong terrified her — that and having to conceal it from everyone. I confirmed for her what actually happened. In addition, she was finally able to tell another person without fear of judgment. I never really saw her cry until last night — not once in all the years I've known her.

"I wanted to tell you that, but there are two other things. You need to have a talk with her yourself. Harsh words were spoken. Although she'll never apologize for them, the sting can come out of them. She mentioned indirectly that your other dad, the one you thought was your dad, was to blame but not to the extent she'd been thinking. With you being Lord Bromley's son, she realized her animosity toward you was pointless. I suspect that's how you plan to wiggle out of the promise you made. Am I right?"

"Yes, it is."

"I thought so. Nice play, but iffy, which leads me to the last bit. Her guilt about Sarah has gotten so bad, she's started seeing Sarah's ghost — at least that's what she said. She became convinced that she needed a talisman to protect herself. I wasn't about to try and convince her that she was imagining things. Who knows what she saw? I don't. But an expression of goodwill on your part might go a long way to bridging the divide between you two. It could be a rabbit's foot for all I care. Its value is in the power she thinks it has, not what you or I give it. Such a gesture might just dissolve the other side of that promise you made. Quid pro quo.

"Her reconciliation with you would also send a message to my half-brother that he's all alone. With Anne and Mom on your side of the fence, it might be enough to allow him to hop to the other side as well. Happy ending. It doesn't handle the money you need, but it smooths the way for the possibility. I'd help if I could, but I still owe for the bonds I have to give to John. I'm not grousing about that. It is the best trade I've ever made. I'm in the pilot seat — at least it looks that way — and we'll do business. I want you to be a part of that. What do you think?"

"It's a good idea. I like it, and well done for following up. I was correct in thinking you would make it work. Thank you, Bonnie."

"No. Thank you. Confidence is an interesting thing. I got it now. That it took a luncheon conversation between us to set the stage for all that has happened is a mindblower. I think I'll become more social. Tell Johnny thanks for the coffee, and I'll speak to him privately later this morning. He and I need to mend some fences as well. Adios."

Bonnie rose and went to the door and looked at all the books again. "Did you read most of these?"

"Yep."

"Me too."

With that, she left.

7 2

Johnny and Robert returned with an extra cup and a full thermos.

"Bonnie left? Well, more for us. What did she have to say?"

I told him and mentioned that she wanted to talk to him later, one-on-one. Johnny sipped his coffee and thought, while Robert flopped on the floor.

"Quid pro quo is an interesting concept," he said finally. "I have an idea. We could find an oddly shaped piece of stone, and you could present it to Maw as the lost pinky of Beelzebub. You could say it has been handed down generation to generation as a defense against the living dead, or some such. I mean, what does she know? It could work."

"It might, until it doesn't — then what?"

"We could sell her the rest of his digits one at a time on a payment plan or, better yet, the whole arm at a bulk discount. That would take care of any deficit for sure."

"Very funny, only we would be partaking in one of the oldest cons in existence. Yesterday I might have. Today not so much. I see her as just another tortured soul burdened by guilt."

"A very cantankerous soul and a bane to humanity's better interests, in my opinion, but I understand your feelings on the matter. We're close to some major resolutions. You don't want to rock the boat, but there's a part of me that relishes the opportunity to pay her back. She torpedoed our partnership with little regard for how we might have felt about the matter — or the damage she created." Johnny started to get angry. "Look — she deliberately harmed us. You lost a fortune. I lost a fortune. To her, a few million is not in that category, but to us, it was real money — not something theoretical or make-believe. We sweated bullets and countless hours to make it. She stepped on us like we were little people. We're not little people. It's time she knew that."

"Johnny, I don't think I've ever heard you so charged up. What gives?"

"I don't know exactly. It's been building slowly, but I've had it. I want to help you, but I can't. I've no dough of that magnitude in the bank. True, we could have blown all those profits the next month, but we would have been the ones blowing them. That's fair. You pay your money, you take your chances, but that's not what happened. We were robbed, plain and simple. That's unjust, illegal, covert, and undeserved. Maw owes, and she needs to pay up! That's the essence of it, and I'll be pissed at her until she does. Actually, I'm not just pissed — I'm mad as hell about it, and you should be too."

I looked at my friend. He really was peeved, and he was right. I thought of adding that I had let it go, and perhaps he should too, but his words resonated with something I had put aside. We had been deliberately taken to the cleaners, not because we were incompetent and stupid but because we weren't. The wrongness of it would always be there, no matter how much I tried to smooth it over.

"You're right. I suppose I buried my outrage, but it's there if I look. I apologize. I should have seen to this much earlier."

Johnny took a breath. "I think we had other things to worry about, but I'm happy you feel the same, and there's no time like the present to come up with a suitable plan."

Johnny's eyes burned with the light of the righteous. He looked at me steadily.

"I've seen that look before, Johnny Dodge, so just a word of caution: Emotions run deep. Yours right now are hotter than mine, but that doesn't mean I have none, which means there's no one minding the store. We need to act smartly. Maw has displayed a chink in her armor and an uncharacteristic weakness, or so it seems. We can take advantage of it, I think, but it requires cool heads."

"Let's not mistake eagerness for rashness," he said.

"I'm just saying what I'm saying is all. Our roles are somewhat reversed."

"In that case, you have a plan?"

"I have some thoughts."

"Lay 'em on me and don't stint," said Johnny.

"Let's start with what we know. We don't know whether Maw profited directly, but she was the instigator because she said she was. We talked about two million. That is in the ballpark of what I lost, perhaps a little on the low side. If we are going to seek restitution, we need to add another two at least for your portion, which brings the total to four."

"I like where this is going, but this puts things in a whole new category. Two is big. Four is huge."

"It's the facts. She should make restitution of at least that amount. If we lawyer up, it'll get very messy, and the collateral damage will be extensive. The cost in terms of time and money is also prohibitive. Does that make sense?"

"It does. It would take forever, and the lawyers would get at

496

least half. We could threaten, but she would reach the same conclusion we did. She'd call our bluff. Legal is out. What do we do?"

"We need to sell it instead, and you are the best person in sales I've ever met. I'll help, but really, this one's yours."

"You're correct, but I'm not happy with her, and that'll come through."

"I know, and that can work for you. You need to tell her why. You need to make her see that she needs to do something about it, or Sarah won't be the only ghost she sees. She wants peace? It's possible, but buying the odd trinket won't solve it. If she insists on going down that path, you can tell her to consider making an investment rather than an acquisition. She puts half the money into the maintenance trust and gives you the balance. Such an action will do something. I don't know what exactly, but it couldn't hurt and likely will do her some good. Improvise."

"Improvise? No pressure then."

"None, actually. A positive outcome is unlikely. It could work, but I'm looking in a different direction."

"You're going to tell me what that is?"

"No, because I don't know either, but there is one. I feel it. I have to let things play out and have a little faith."

"I hope so. I don't envy you your eleven o'clock, but I'm looking forward to talking to Maw. She owes, and I'll make her pay. If I wasn't family, she'd be in deep trouble."

"She never would've done it if you weren't family."

"That too. How twisted is that?"

"Twisted."

"Very twisted. There's the beginning of a sales presentation in there somewhere. I think I'm in the need of breakfast to help me think. How about we head down? If I pull this off, a serious thank-you will be in order."

"If you do, I'll put a little statue of you by the bust with your own little candle."

"Really?"

"No, but I'll let you keep your room."

"You're a bastard. You know that, don't you," said Johnny with a grin.

"That too, among other things. Let's go, and good hunting."

"I'm loaded for bear."

73

Breakfast was a subdued affair other than perhaps for Bruni and myself. She glowed beside me, radiating a happiness that was as fresh and full of promise as the morning that lay outside the curtains. The rest of the dining room was dark in comparison. The curtains were shut to hide the damage of last night's storm, but other than that, there was no indication that something untoward had happened.

John and Anne read the paper, as did the baron. Elsa looked at something far away as she sipped her coffee. I noted a raised eyebrow when she looked at her daughter as she sat down. Bruni's radiance didn't seem to bother Elsa, other than put a smile on her face before she went into her morning trance. Maw sat next to Johnny. He asked her a question in a whisper that I hoped was to arrange to speak with her. She seemed quite eager and nodded with some enthusiasm, although it might have been that he asked if she wished for him to pass the toast. I could not tell. He did pass the silver toast holder. Stanley and crew glided in and out. Bruni asked for seconds, which caused a mild stir. Other than that, the meal proceeded at a regular pace. Malcolm looked strangely pleased and gave me a wink for what reason I could not fathom. The meal passed with hardly a word spoken. I did yelp once when Bruni grabbed my leg.

The end of the meal was signaled when John Senior rose and walked out. He'd said not one word to anyone the entire time. I was not relishing my coming meeting, when Elsa slipped up beside me and whispered, "I'm very happy for you two." She kissed me on the cheek and patted my arm. She did the same to Bruni.

Bruni took me outside via the drawing room doors. The morning light was bright, the grass wet, and no cloud marred the sky's perfection.

She marveled at the day. "Mother gave us her unqualified blessing."

"I noticed that."

"We're embarked on an adventure. I'm excited and more alive than I've been in a long time."

"I'm happy for you. I feel the same. Even my meeting does not seem so foreboding with you here, but I'm concerned about it nonetheless. John looked singularly bleak."

"John is in a dark state."

I looked into the distance and noticed that Maw, Johnny, and Robert were headed in the direction of the river along the access road. Johnny was not letting any moss grow on his desire to have it out with Maw. I would have loved to listen in on that conversation. Maw was a genius in her field, but Johnny was as well. He was her descendant, and I believed that attributes often skipped generations. They were evenly matched, although I figured the odds favored Johnny, in that he had moral rightness on his side, and he had the look. When Johnny had it on, he was not to be trifled with. He could talk anyone into or out of anything.

"Are you thinking about your meeting?" asked Bruni as she

walked beside me holding on to my left arm with two hands. She had noticed that my attention had wandered.

"No, I was observing another." I pointed in Maw's direction.

Bruni looked up and briefly shielded her eyes from the sun with her hand. "Johnny and his grandmother?"

"Yes, and Johnny had the look this morning."

"What's the look?"

"Imagine a brilliant mind focused for a brief period on a single objective, willing to do whatever is necessary with no reservations whatsoever. Johnny raises himself to that status on rare occasions, but when he does, look out. He is right now doing the sales presentation of his life. He wants to close Mrs. Leland for a very large sum of money."

"I like that. Do you think he has a chance?"

"Better than fifty-fifty. I've watched him over the years. His genius is remarkable. All my life I've been in awe of his skill at persuasion. It's gotten us into and out of trouble more times than I can count. I'm a feeble flame in comparison. When he burns bright, he's like a small sun."

"You admire him."

"Tremendously. We had a parting of the ways a time back, but we've settled that. Mrs. Leland was the cause, and Johnny is determined to make her pay for that crime."

"You're lucky to have such a friend. I have very few. You make that list and so do my parents."

"You've more than I do. I have two. Johnny and you. I have hopes for three or four more."

"Who, may I ask?"

"Your parents. They are quite outstanding. Bonnie will be one and Stanley too. So, four more."

"My parents are worthy of that. Most children have trouble with their folks. I never had any, other than being headstrong on occasion and incurring their wrath, but those moments were few.

My childhood was not always happy, but overall, it was wonderful because of them. Bonnie I'm not so sure about. She makes me a little jealous."

"Really?"

"Speaking of looks. Women have them, and when it comes to you, I get upset if I see it on their faces. Bonnie had it."

"You needn't worry. Bonnie says that's off the table, and she means it. At the same time, she wants me involved in her business, which would be an opportunity. You'll be part of that. I'm likely on dangerous ground in saying that I think she has exceptional qualities. She'll be an ally to both of us, and a worthy one at that."

"You have a knack for stepping onto dangerous ground."

"I do, but you needn't worry."

"Even with your father's reputation?"

"Even with my father's reputation." I stopped her and held her. I took her face in my hands. "You are more than enough for me. I am a moth, and you are a flame."

"What about when I grow old?"

"Have you seen your mother lately?"

"You really do know how to put your foot in it, don't you?"

"I suppose I just did, but it proves my point. You'll always melt men's hearts and drive them mad for a very long time. Mine right along with them. I can't prevent that, but you are who you are."

"I suppose I'm assuaged, but you do need lessons in handling me. I suppose I'll have to teach you. I hope you're a good student."

"Very good."

Bruni turned and faced the house. "Which room will we live in?"

"Alice's."

"Are you sure?"

"Very. I asked her permission years and years ago one afternoon. I told her that I liked her apartment and asked her if I could live in it. She said yes, one day, and changed the subject."

"You think she was a seer?"

"I think she was. She had a gift. Stanley thinks so and so does Dagmar."

Bruni walked a few steps with me and said, "One of the reasons I asked about which room you would take has to do with Johnny's parents. Perhaps they think you'll kick them out?"

"They might think that, but I won't. They can have the master bedroom for the rest of their lives. I could not live in it. It would feel like I was trespassing in my own house."

"You're smarter than you look, and you're very good-looking."

I kissed her. "So are you. What can you advise me about the meeting, since you're probably pretty good in that department?"

"Know your agenda and keep to it is my first rule. Speak less and listen more is the second. Lastly, get it in writing before you leave, if it involves a decision or an agreement. That pretty much sums it up. Do you know what you want? That will determine your agenda. Others have theirs, which is why you have to listen for what is important to them. Once you know their key issues, the negotiation starts. Give away what's not important, like the bedroom. Hold on to what is necessary with determination. Use your head, not your heart."

"Clever and wise."

"I am. How about we go inside? You should change into something more formal, a business suit. Bring a briefcase. It intimidates."

74

The hall clock struck eleven as I came down the stairs. I had on a dark suit, crisp white shirt, and dark tie. My shoes were polished, and I held a briefcase in my left hand. Stanley was at the foot of the stairs waiting for me.

"Mr. Dodge is in the library. I will escort you there momentarily, but first I wanted to thank you for our dialogue last night. I feel alive for the first time in a long while. Hold still for a moment."

I stood. Stanley looked me over from top to bottom, came forward, and adjusted my tie by a few millimeters.

"You look presentable. I won't wish you luck because you won't need it. Dagmar and the rest of the staff, however, have decided it can't hurt and wish you prodigious portions. By the way, I've arranged to have a small concoction brought to you in fifteen or twenty minutes. I suggest you accept it. It'll only be for you. It will show your place in the new hierarchy, if nothing else."

"It's not one of those peculiar ones, is it?"

Stanley smiled. "That could be arranged, but it is special. Dagmar had a hand in it."

"Then I'll drink it for sure. Thank you, Stanley, for looking after me."

"With pleasure. This way."

I entered the library. John Senior sat at the french desk, which was away from the comfortable chairs in front of the fire. He was in a suit as well. He was holding a typed document and reading it through a pair of half-lens reading glasses with thin gold frames. He reminded me of my headmaster at grade school. We'd had a one-sided relationship that usually involved a great many pointed questions on his part and a great many vague answers on mine.

I sat in the thin, framed chair in front of the desk and put the briefcase beside me. I watched him read. After several minutes, he threw it down and looked at me over his glasses.

"You have nothing to say, I suppose?" he asked.

Five days ago, or what seemed to me to be at least a year, I would have started apologizing and ingratiating myself, but I had hardly slept, and as those close to me have noted, I am prone to an uncharacteristic sharpness of temper when sleep has been in short supply. I felt my temper rise but said nothing.

"Very well — here is the current state of the maintenance trust." He passed me a document of many pages. "I've taken the liberty of withdrawing some $1,750,000 from the account to repay the sum I have contributed to the estate personally over the years. The accountant verified that amount as correct. The balance remaining is some $43,000. Expenses run some $30,000 a month, including taxes, insurance, payroll, and upkeep, but do not include any sinking funds for larger items such as roofing, drainage, plumbing, and electrical. Funds for those purposes have been depleted to maintain day-to-day operations. The total amount needed to maintain that amount of monthly expense without spending principal is estimated at some 4.5 million, given the current state of interest rates and conservative investment. That figure does not include the need for a sinking fund. I doubt you could raise that amount, even if you sold the place."

I was seeing a darker side of John Senior. I hadn't seen it often, but often enough. Johnny and I had managed to antagonize him sufficiently on numerous occasions to know that he could be vindictive, harsh, and implacable. His judgments as to our transgressions were delivered in the same tone as he spoke to me now. I thought about the vast sum needed. It was overwhelming. I hoped that didn't show on my face. I took my time. I was quite sure the accounting was correct, but in my forensic work, I had learned that there were two classes of plunderers: those who nickeled-and-dimed and those who thought in much larger numbers. It was one or the other. They rarely did both.

I scanned the figures the accountant had provided. John had assuredly put money in. The amount was large in total, but given almost twenty years putting in $8,000 a month yielded close to that amount. From what I could see, the dimes and nickels were accounted for. This was a matter of large amounts.

"Do you have the accounting since Alice's death, including the starting balance, activity, and investment track record?"

John scowled, and an even larger document sailed across the table, hung for a moment, and then started to fall off the edge. I caught it neatly before it fell and prevented it from scattering over the floor. I looked at John. That was a typical intimidation tactic. There was nothing like having the opposition scramble about on their hands and knees picking up pieces of paper and attempting to put it back in order while speaking.

I looked it over briefly and said, "This paperwork looks fine at first glance. I'm amazed it's all available."

"I have kept it up-to-date on a monthly basis. My sister told me there might be a beneficiary. I felt it prudent to keep the accounting up. That eventuality proved correct."

I looked at John. He was not a thief. I had always found him remarkably straight up in all my previous dealings. If something had happened, he was the victim of circumstance rather than design.

Nonetheless, something had taken place. I was certain of it. If I looked objectively at what he presented to me, the anger, the intact paperwork, the fact that he seemed to see me as an enemy rather than a friend (or, at the least, someone who thought very highly of him) induced in me a nagging suspicion. My intuitive part chimed in: *He did something. Make no mistake. Find out what it is by finding out what he wants.* It was good advice.

"It seems a lost cause. What do you advise that I do?"

John breathed easier. "Well," he said, "large estates are hellish to run. They hemorrhage money at an astounding rate. Without the necessary funds to help it along, you'd eventually be forced to sell. It has no mortgage, which is a plus, but it's the upkeep that'll kill you. The numbers speak for themselves."

"What would you suggest?"

"I have had a document drawn up that reassigns the beneficiary status to me."

"May I see it?"

"Certainly."

It was the paper he had been reading when I first sat down. The amended assignment was prepared by Curtis, Provost, and List. I had seen that name before, in one of the documents Maw had shown me relating to the downfall of the partnership. It was the connection that made me ask, "You like this firm?"

"I use them regularly. I would even go so far as to recommend them, if you have the need."

"Thank you. I might. To be clear, you wish me to assign the beneficiary status over to you, as well as forgo becoming trustee because the estate is, for all intents and purposes, insolvent. Is that correct?"

"It is."

"What about the sale?"

"The sale would keep it limping along. It might clear a million or two tops, and that is being optimistic. There are a large number of objects, books, and items. The entire lot would be sold in its entirety."

"All of it?"

"I shouldn't see why not."

"Forgive me for saying so, but Alice wished those pieces to remain with the estate."

"Times change. They have value but contribute nothing to running the place. With those items liquidated, the house has a chance to survive in the family rather than being sold off to a developer or an institution. Besides, Alice is not here. Decisions must be made. It can't continue."

"Perhaps they contribute in some way."

"Don't start. Although I've seen the odd bit here and there, frankly, I think everyone other than myself has blown the importance of those items way out of proportion. I need the money to run this place, and that is a fact."

I paused and said, "I also see no inducement to do what you suggest."

"That's what I thought you'd say. You should be compensated. I must admit I was impressed by the bond deal you made. Dodge Capital is in much better shape now than ever before. I'll give you one million to rid yourself of the burden. Let's call it walk-away money."

"So that is your proposal, in a nutshell."

"It is."

"Does Anne know?" I said that on impulse.

"What the devil has that to do with it?"

"Nothing or maybe everything. I don't know. It was a just a question."

John Senior's anger was now very much in evidence. His face was red. He put his hands on the desk to keep them from shaking. At that moment, Stanley opened the door. He carried a small crystal glass of amber liquid on a silver salver. To the side of the glass was a folded piece of paper. He approached me without saying a word. I thanked him, picked up the glass with the note, and said, "That will be all, Stanley. I'll ring if I need anything." His back was to Mr. Dodge; he was almost grinning as he walked out. I sipped my drink and read the note.

It was from Johnny.

Success! Got two. Pater got the other half. Tread carefully. Good luck, J.

I looked at John and put the note in my breast pocket. He seemed to deflate when Stanley did not acknowledge his existence. The power he wielded here was his no longer, and he knew it.

I drank some more. I felt significantly better. It was alcoholic with hints of herbs and flavors I had not tasted before. Dagmar had outdone herself again. Time seemed to stand still. I had to understand what was going on here. I loved John. I could not understand why he was being so contrary. I needed to see the accounting activity at the time Johnny and my partnership exploded. My thoughts whirled about. Numbers appeared at random. John seemed a long way away. I was in a sloping forest of tall pines in Austria, perhaps. The path before me split in two. One fork led up. One led down. On the downward path I saw John. He was alone. Anne had died.

His shoulders were hunched with the weight of the world. He was a broken man who was forced to endure a long and unhappy life. I looked down the other, and he was himself. Anne was with him, although not present. He seemed happy, connected, and alive in a way I had not seen before. I saw that his life was shorter — very much shorter. Someone behind me whispered in my ear the words: *Choose carefully, and it will be as you say.* Whatever did that mean? I wondered.

"Are you all right?" asked John, his anger forgotten. He looked deeply concerned. "I'll ring for Stanley."

I crawled into the present from wherever I had gone. I croaked, "I'm fine, actually. It was too early for a drink, I think. Perhaps we could take a walk. I might feel better."

"Yes, yes, we can finish this later. Come, fresh air will do you good. Might even do me some good as well. You do not look well."

No one saw us leave out the front door. I was a little giddy. I had no idea what Dagmar had put in that drink, but it had a kick like a mule.

"How are you feeling?" asked John as we walked up the drive. He had my arm. It steadied me.

"Better, thank you."

"You gave me a fright. You had the oddest expression on your face. I've seen that look before, but only once. Funny, I had forgotten all about that moment until now. I was with my sister. She said she'd had a vision."

"I had one just now. It came out of nowhere and left just as abruptly."

"What was it, if I may I ask?"

"You really wish to know?"

"I do."

"It concerns you. I was in a forest and two paths lay before me. There were two of you. You were halfway along the trail on both. On one, you were a broken man with a long life. On the other, you were free from care, but your life was short. Anne was dead in one version and alive in the other. I didn't see her, but I knew that it was so. Something, or someone, told me to choose carefully which of you I would prefer, and it would be that way."

He looked white. Probably as pale as me.

I told him with feeling, "I want you happy, John. From the

bottom of my heart, I want you happy. You hold so high a place in my heart, you have no idea. I know what I would like, but it comes at a cost. I don't know how to give you everything you wish for. I wish to God I did."

I could say no more. It had taken all I had to say it. I had chosen, and the choice had sucked something out of me. I had no more left to give.

We had stopped some distance up the drive. There was a stillness in the air like the pause between exhale and inhale. Imperceptible, but in which lies the difference between the living and the dead. We looked at each other. I felt tears stream down my face. I was tired beyond measure.

John looked shaken. He took hold of both my arms. "Steady. Steady. We need to sit. I know a place."

He guided me toward the cypress trees some distance away and the bench that lay behind them. I'm not sure how I got there, but I did. We sat down, and he began.

"Alice said the same thing almost exactly. She wept for me. She said she would do anything to spare me, if only I would spare myself. I had no idea what she meant then; perhaps I do now a little more."

I understood full well. There are consequences in what we do, and there are times when all we can do is watch, tortured by the choices others make. I asked if it was all right if I smoked.

"I'll have one too, if you don't mind," he answered.

I gave him one and lit his cigarette and then mine.

"I don't usually smoke cigarettes." He inhaled and exhaled. "But I need something. The truth is, Percy, it's a mess. I've tried so hard. I really have. This house, the business, you, Johnny, Anne, Hugo, all of you — I've always tried to do my very best, but in the end, it wasn't good enough. That's something I live with every day. Every minute, if truth be told, other than on rare occasions. This weekend was such a time, at least until last night. It was so good to see you and Johnny. To watch you and Brunhilde get to know each other. It reminded me so much of Anne and me when we first met. Now that was a magic time. I ache just thinking about it. I would do anything for her, and I suppose that's what happened. She needed money. Of course, we all need money, but it's when you don't have it personally but are surrounded by it that troubles come creeping up beside you and whisper in your ear."

"Tell me. We'll work through it."

"I know you know. You don't know what exactly, but you know. It took you all of a few minutes, but then I should have expected that. There are no stupid people here other than myself.

"Anne and your mother worked in the auction and art trade before I met her. After we got married, they kept in touch. They were good friends. Mary would talk to her about her deals, and Anne would get electrified. The amounts involved were outrageous.

"Money is such a paradox. To make great sums requires taking on tremendous risk. To keep it requires the opposite: taking very few. Most people can barely do one or the other. The great fortunes, ours for sure, were built by paradoxical people who excelled at both. They could also muster the mental hardness and iron discipline needed to cut expenses to the bone and preserve what they had built. I suppose it's why wealthy families are so miserly with money in regards to their children. I did it with you and Johnny. My father did it with me. Profitable businesses are all about cutting costs. Children never see it that way, but habits formed early pay dividends later on, when it really counts.

"Anne did not come from big money and never knew that lesson. She knew how to risk but not when to stop. I was never really interested in art. I liked it, but it was never a business that excited me. The biggest gains are in finding unrecognized treasures hiding in plain sight, but they are rare. Forgeries can be even more profitable but require great care, particularly in establishing a provenance. Your mother is a careful woman. Whether she knew all along or only after, I don't know. When she needed extra money for a particular piece, Anne supplied it. Your mother sold many things and turned a profit on most, but she always ran short. It's in her nature. Money slips through her fingers like water. Her expenses are inevitably greater than her income. She had to find ways to make up the difference. Anne would often forgo her end of the profits because she didn't need them like Mary did, and this helped. This went on for years. Anne kept your mother and your stepfather afloat for the most part. Perhaps it was not enough.

"It was a Venetian mirror surrounded by blue glass and etched margin plates that proved their undoing. The stupid part is that it was worth only twenty to thirty thousand dollars if it had been an original, a moderate if not a small sum in that world. It was a fake, and Mary knew it. When Anne found out exactly is unclear. In the end, it didn't matter. What they should have done was go to the client and offer to take the piece back immediately or pay the difference. They did neither.

"The women had formed a partnership early on. They should have formed a corporation to limit their personal liability when the enterprise grew large enough to warrant it, but they didn't do that either.

"In the art world, reputation is a valuable commodity. Sell a fake, and it's ruined. Future sales dry up because no one trusts the seller, but it's in past sales where the trouble lies. Sell a thousand pieces and two will likely turn up as forgeries or be suspect even with expert knowledge and pristine motives. It's a risk. One has to limit the damage at once. If the rumor is allowed to get out, all the items the seller has sold will be scrutinized. Former buyers can use the rumor to redecorate. It's easy to get an expert to say that it's likely a forgery and return it for the price paid in order to get something else. The woman they had sold the mirror to had a house party, and an expert saw it for what it was. The woman had purchased many pieces from them over the years and saw this as an opportunity to refresh her several residences. Mary was personally liable, and so was Anne, since she too was a general partner. By the time the final bill was tallied, the expert hushed up, and the scandal buried, the liability had reached several million, and the bill had to be paid or risk the possibility of criminal prosecution. It was a big deal. Mary had little saved, so it was Anne who had to foot the bill, which put me in a precarious position. I had to decide to backstop them or let the cards fall where they may. When someone you love comes to you on hands and knees, what can you do? I did what I did, right or wrong. My love proved stronger than my principles.

"I took the needed funds from the business and the trust with every intention of paying them back. I figured that many of the pieces returned were originals and could be resold. I would be paid back almost in full when they were. Fundamentally, the plan was sound, but it failed nonetheless. Mary put all the returned pieces in storage to be used as inventory, but there was a flood, and water damage was not covered by their insurance. It was a disaster, a total loss. I did a bond offering. That temporarily covered the funds I used from Dodge Capital, but ultimately, I still had to pay the business back. That $1.75 million is the amount needed to put the accounting at Dodge in order. I took 2 million from the maintenance trust and borrowed 2 million more from my mother. Close to 6 million in all. I was lucky with my mother. She'd just completed a 4 million deal and had the funds still available. I still owe her. I am sorry it has come to this, but I couldn't do anything other than what I've done. Love and money are uneasy companions when one of them requires the services of the other."

John looked down at his feet. I nodded. It made sense.

I said, "It's true. I don't mean to add to your burden, John, but it's best to get it all on the table, so we can deal with it. The two that you borrowed from Maw were half of the profits realized from the series of trades that destroyed Johnny's and my trading partnership. Maw wanted to split us up and engineered a way for that to happen. I'm not sure if you're aware of that."

He thought for a moment before he spoke.

"When I came to her, that atrocity had already happened. She told me what she'd done. I was outraged, but I was not in a position to refuse, or even comment, since the funds were needed immediately. I hope you will forgive me."

"I do, but you will need to talk to Johnny. He's spitting mad over it. Your mother can be such an ass, but Johnny has recouped two of the four. I received this note from Johnny during our meeting."

I showed it to him.

"That's typical of my mother, I'm afraid. She has in effect called my loan. I wonder how my son got her to do that?"

"We'll find out soon enough. Perhaps we can make all this work. Dodge Capital is made whole with the 1.75 million. Take the funds out of the maintenance trust as you intended. It puts to rest one leg of the problem. I have 1 million of the 2 million that Johnny will collect from Maw. Johnny will likely chip in his one. I'll take that on as a personal debt, so that means we have 2 million for the maintenance trust. He will agree to it, I think. We just need another 2.5 million. We are just a few good trades away, as Johnny says. Has Anne and my mother's partnership been dissolved?"

"Yes. It was the first thing I had Anne do when she told me."

"I'm glad to hear it. Putting a stop to the bleeding is always the first step. I should let you know that I've decided to become the trustee, and I will sign off that all is in order. It may not be, but I accept the accounting as is. We know where we stand. You and Anne will have your room here until you pass from this earth. I will be in Alice's apartment."

515

John looked shocked. "Thank you. I don't know what to say. I do apologize again. I owe 2 million to the trust. I will pay 1 million immediately. The sum I would have paid you. I apologize for even offering it. I was caught in the undertow of my previous desperation. The other 1 million will take some time."

"Take all you need. Now we have three, and we only need another 1.5 million, but first let's decide to lay any friction between us to rest. Emotionally, it's too expensive."

"I will gladly do that, but if you don't mind my asking, isn't residing in Alice's apartment a little suspect?"

"I got her permission years ago, but I thought you didn't believe in that?"

"My words come back to haunt me. The truth is we all believe but only at certain times. At some moments, it's harder to embrace the idea than at others. Magic may or may not exist, but I would rather live in a world where it does, if you really hold me to it. It keeps our dreams alive. I'll help you all I can."

"And I'll accept it gladly. I think you're on the better path — at least, I hope."

"I think so too. I don't feel as beaten down or as shrunken as I felt even an hour ago. You have my thanks for allowing me to explain. You have no rancor?"

"How could I? It's not my place to judge, and it rarely helps in the long run."

"I also must apologize for my behavior last night. It was probably too much wine, but uncalled for nonetheless. What I said is best forgotten. I hope instead we'll grow closer over time."

"I'm sure we will. As Johnny is often telling me, avoid dark liquor. Let's chalk it up to that."

"It's settled then. And I'm glad for it."

"So am I. Personally, I can't thank you enough for all that you've done for me over the many years we've known each other. That can never be repaid."

We stood up. I hugged him before we went back in. It was time for round two.

As we walked toward the house, a weight had been released from me, but only partially. John looked whole again. I too had made my choice. I loved him and thought that one will do more for love than fear — in many cases, far too much. It was a lesson I hoped I would remember in the future. Love, it seemed, required far more aptitude than I had once thought. It could lead one into lands bereft of any hope and happiness for all the noblest and best of reasons, but like the filament of a bulb exposed to air, it can burn bright, but only briefly.

75

J ohn Senior and I walked through the front door. Stanley was there with two flutes of champagne on a silver tray. We each took one. It was Cristal. Finally, someone was seeing sense.

"Thank you, Stanley. Change is in the air, I see. Excellent choice."

"I know you prefer it."

Mr. Dodge took his glass and excused himself. He told me that he'd meet me in the library. He was off to get his checkbook.

As Mr. Dodge walked away, I said to Stanley, "Our meeting was a success, and by the way, what was in that drink you served me earlier?"

"You will have to ask Dagmar. I had nothing to do with it. She did want me to ask if you enjoyed it."

"Wonderful aroma and taste but with a decided kick at the end. I'm not exactly sure what would happen if it were served en masse, but it would be a noteworthy occasion that would probably make the morning edition. I will give her my thanks in person after lunch. In spite of its surprising effects, it helped shift the meeting onto a new and, I hope, better path, which I'm sure was her intention. We're still a tad short in the trust account, but much closer to keeping things humming along for the foreseeable future."

"Excellent. If I might make a suggestion?"

"Of course."

"Allow Mr. Ault to speak first. It will save a great deal of time."

"Really? Thank you, Stanley. I will."

"No trouble at all." Stanley fidgeted. I had never seen him fidget.

"Is there something else?"

"Yes, I hesitate to say this, but I am compelled to. Dagmar said to wrap it up soon — one by the hall clock at the latest. She's made an extra effort. Those were her words."

"I see."

Stanley fidgeted some more.

"You have more to say?"

"It was…I would normally never have said what I just said, but Dagmar made it part of a new agreement that I follow her suggestions. Her argument hinged on my tendency to hang on to a point of view contrary to hers when the evidence no longer supported it and the results ultimately proved she was right after all. I am sure it will all calm down given time. I am due for a comeback in that department. The Ault suggestion might do it for me. It would be most appreciated if you told Dagmar I pointed you in that direction."

"Of course I will."

"I should also warn you of one other development."

"What's that?"

"Miss von Hofmanstal and Dagmar have been talking together all morning. They're getting quite close. They're comparing notes, if you get my meaning."

"I see. Stanley, we'll just have to stick together."

"My thoughts precisely, sir. I'm glad we agree. Now, if you would follow me, the bidders are waiting for you in the library."

76

Stanley led me back to the library. Maw, Bonnie, Hugo, and Malcolm were present. John Senior stepped in shortly after I entered. Greetings were exchanged. Stanley poured whatever beverage the guests required. I whispered to John that Malcolm should have the floor and that he had worked a solution of some sort, at least according to Stanley. John Senior raised an eyebrow and said, "We should hear it then."

He called out in a louder voice, "Malcolm, you have an idea?"

"I do. I do." Malcolm unfolded himself from his chair like a giant stick insect and had everyone's attention. He announced, "I rang my principal very early this morning. I explained the situation here. He told me to offer the enclosed bid but with the following proviso. The treasures are to remain where they are and not to be moved, since they would remain in the family whether they were here or in the UK. Those were his exact words. Problem solved! Of course, it depends on the amount needed." This last was said more softly.

John said, "That's an excellent solution."

I thought about it. It was a good solution. At least my father acknowledged me. It was a first. I wasn't sure what that meant, but it was something. I parked the thought for later.

"Not so fast," interrupted Hugo. "Given time, I think I could say the same. What do you say to that, Malcolm?"

"Well, it's not up to me, is it?"

Hugo looked at me. "What's the sum needed?"

"One-point-five," I answered.

The baron looked at Malcolm and asked, "Bromley chipping in that much?"

"Well, not exactly."

"What is the maximum bid you are authorized to make?"

"I don't believe I can disclose that."

"Come on, Ault. Some commission is better than none, and yours is about to disappear."

The baron had hit Malcolm exactly where he lived. "I'm not… Well, I think my offer is very timely and creates a win for all concerned."

"But falls short," interrupted Hugo. "I say we split the amount. Seven fifty each."

Malcolm was seeing his commission whittled down, but at least it hadn't evaporated altogether. He shifted on his feet, thinking, and said finally, "I'm not sure I have the authority to authorize that."

"Get Bromley on the phone. I'll speak to him. A draw is not a win, but it's better than a loss. Besides, we each save some money. Elsa will be thrilled; Bromley will be too."

John Senior said, "By all means, but don't you think, Hugo, we're getting a little ahead of ourselves? The family part, I mean. The lady in question hasn't exactly agreed, and I believe there might be a divorce that has to be finalized?"

"You know about that? Surprises all around. Well, somebody had better get busy sorting that out." The baron looked at me. I looked at him. "Well, don't just sit there. There's a deal on the table. Time waits for no man. Strike while the iron is hot. Off you go." He sounded like Johnny.

"I suppose I'd better see to it then," I replied. "No pressure, eh?"

Hugo smiled. "You know the story about diamonds..."

"Don't you even start. Work your magic on my father, and I'll be back shortly. Whatever happened to simple?"

The baron laughed. It was the first time I'd ever heard it, and I wasn't sure I liked it. Having him as a father-in-law was going to be an interesting ride — provided Bruni agreed, of course. And that was the crux of the matter. My chances were good, but I also recalled that women are not always keen to agree to anything when an ulterior motive is involved.

Stanley opened the door for me and stepped out beside me.

"She's in the kitchen with Dagmar," he said as we strode along.

"Stanley, how is it you managed to be in the room this whole time? I never even noticed you there."

"I never left."

I said, with some annoyance, "Tell me something I don't know."

"Being completely motionless is a skill best learned early in my profession, if you want to know what's what."

"If you say so. Suggestions, Stanley?"

"None, sir."

"Thank you, Stanley."

"Very good, sir."

We passed the clock on the way to the kitchen. It was twelve fifteen. I had forty-five minutes.

Bruni had an apron on and was watching Dagmar make a sauce. They were chatting away like they had known each other for years. Dagmar saw me and said to Bruni, "There he is. Off with your apron. Remember what I said, and now off you go. I'll finish here. Timing is important, and we don't have a lot of it."

Bruni's eyes sparkled as she turned to me. "Dagmar is a living treasure."

"Yes, she is, and she and I will be having a little chat before too long. Won't we, Dagmar?"

"Oh yes, sir. That we will, but not now. Go! Go!"

We were shooed out.

"Sit or walk?" Bruni asked.

"Walk."

"Good idea. I've been standing around all morning. So, what happened? Tell me."

The hall clock ticked its steady cadence as Bruni and I stepped out the front door. A mist was forming in the direction of the river. It would envelop everything before too long. We walked up the drive. I told her about John and the current state of the finances.

"Almost there then — so, what about the bidders? Shouldn't you be inside working on it?"

"Some kinks are being ironed out that don't involve me directly. Are you and Dagmar hatching something?"

"Well, yes and no. She told me to speed things up in terms of you and me. She said she had her reasons. She can be remarkably forthcoming and opaque at the same time."

"They all can be. Trust me. It's a skill. What was your impression of her?"

"Very capable. A culinary master of the first order. She has a remarkable knowledge of obscure plants, herbs, and spices. She recommended I start drinking a special blend of her tea."

"Really? Interesting. She and I will definitely have a talk. Dagmar wasn't the only one to tell us to speed things up. Your father did as well."

"You're kidding!"

"Would you like his exact words?"

"Yes, I would."

"Time waits for no man, and I need to strike while the iron is hot."

"I can't believe he said that. Was there money involved?"

"That's the thing, but before I go there, I have a question. Do you get the impression that we're being herded? Perhaps there's a better word, but events, staff, parents, and friends are pushing us together. *Orchestrated* might be better."

"Very much so."

"How do you feel about that?"

"I'm loving it in some ways and am puzzled at the same time. It's like someone is trying to drop a very big hint."

"Exactly. The question is do we take it or not? If we take that orchestration out of the equation, how do you feel personally about us moving right along?"

"I think I know where this is going. I think I'm ready. I can't explain it, but there is rightness and wrongness in things. Us together is a rightness. I have made mistakes. Likely I will make more, but we are not a mistake. This I know."

"When will you be divorced?"

"Soon."

"Then marry me when it is done."

"I will."

"Really?"

"Really."

"That was simpler than I thought."

We held each other. Bruni whispered in my ear, "You had help. Dagmar was all over me like a rash, extolling your virtues. Finally, I said, 'I suppose you want me to marry him?' She answered, quick as a flash: 'Oh yes, it's going to happen whether you like it or not, so get on board. If he doesn't ask you, ask him.' She wasn't subtle. She was damn serious, and she emphasized it had to be soon. If she had started talking about the alignment of the planets, I wouldn't have been a bit surprised, but there was an intensity about her that was actually eerie, like she had an inside track on the future. I believed her. It was something to behold."

"I know what you're saying. She always talks about Alice being a seer, but I get the idea that it takes one to know one."

As we held each other, Bruni said, "I do expect a formal proposal, complete with something large and sparkly, but I can wait. You have to get back and make sure the deal goes through. I should tell you again, when my father starts talking like that, money is involved. Was it?"

"Yes. He's convincing my father to split the cost and keep the treasures here since they stay within the family. It was the family part that was uncertain. He pretty much threw me out of my own meeting to handle it. All I can say is I'm glad he did. Having your parents as in-laws will be interesting."

"Having your parents as in-laws will probably top that."

"You may be right. We'll have to see them at some point."

"Oh god! Let's not think of that right now."

"Let's not."

We returned to the house hand in hand.

7 7

"It's done then," said the baron. "This calls for a celebration on several levels. Well done, everyone — even you, Malcolm. A deal finalized and in the bag is one of life's little pleasures that keeps the heart pounding and dreams alive and kicking."

Hugo came up to me and said, "You will come to Austria." It wasn't a request. "This house is a beauty, but there's nothing like a castle to send the spirits soaring. You should see the torture chamber in the dungeon. Now that is impressive. I'll show it to you."

I was assuring him I would only be too happy, when Stanley announced that lunch was served and to step smartly. Everyone wanted to see the treasures, but that moment was deferred until after lunch. Stanley could be quite commanding when he wanted to be.

Maw had not said a word through the entire meeting. She came up to me as the others left and said, "Well, I don't believe we've been formally introduced. I am Mrs. Leland. You may call me Mary."

Seeing that this was her way of bridging the gap between us, I said, "Bromley — Percy Bromley. You can call me whatever you want."

She cackled as she said, "And I will too, now that we begin anew. Percy works for me. I wish to tell you a few things. Will you listen to me?"

"Of course."

"Everything seems to have worked out for you in spite of all contrary indications. Bonnie thinks the world of you, which surprised me. I've had to make a reassessment. You know what Napoleon asked before he passed a general the field marshal baton?"

"I believe he asked if the receiver was lucky."

"Exactly. If he answered no, Napoleon refused to give it. There is something to be said for those who are lucky, and you *are* lucky. It is an ineffable quality that defies categorization. Your luck seems to affect all those around you in some way as well. They become lucky too. You don't know that, but we here have had the collateral benefit. It's a great gift, but few who have great gifts really know what they are. Of course, they think they know, but they fall on their heads anyway. What they thought was their great gift was not the gift they truly had. I recognize great gifts — those a person truly has. That's what I do, and that's why I'm special. With it, I can create and hold great wealth, but that strangely is not my greatest gift. My greatest gift is with animals. They love me as I love them. They gladly do what I wish. We understand each other. You seem to have the same attribute with the people here. Mark my words, this is where you belong; make no mistake about that. When I leave this afternoon, I will be taking something special with me. Not just that I have a daughter I have never had before, but something else. You will learn about it from Johnny. It was a remarkable pitch, by the way. He's positively extraordinary when he chooses to be — such passion, such emotion, so convincing. It surprised the hell out of me, and I am not easily surprised. He has a great gift as well but lets it out only too rarely. It's his passion — when he lets it run free — in case you hadn't guessed. Everything falls before it, even the world if he wanted it. We did a deal, he and I. I got Robert the Bruce, and you both were made whole, at least partially. How he managed it, I barely know, but there it is. The dog will be good for me, and I will be good for him. Robert and I have an understanding, as you can see. He's a magical dog."

I looked down, and there he was, standing beside her, silent, looking up — watching.

Maw smiled down at Robert and asked, "Did you know he was in the meeting the whole time? You didn't even notice him, did you?"

That startled me. "Good heavens. I did not."

"He's perfect."

"I also suppose he's the only 2 million dog in existence."

"Let's not insult him," she said with a flash of her former self. "Four million, when you include the amount I gave my son."

"I see. He's quite the dog, I must admit. You do know Robert has a fetish for tennis balls and eating various intimate articles of clothing?"

"I would be very surprised if he didn't, but he'll be fine with me. I think I will call him Light Bulb Head, but only in private. He's quite handsome."

"Mrs....I mean, Mary, I may have said some things..."

"Pssst!" she said, raising her hand, cutting me off. "Don't ever back down. I enjoyed every minute of our confrontation. I know that's not what you want to hear. You expect us to trade apologies. Blah, blah, blah. I told you I never apologize. I enjoyed our match. I found it therapeutic. I know I'm not very nice to people and highly inappropriate, but the difference between me and everyone else is

I know I'm inappropriate and not very nice to people. I'm quite comfortable being the way I am. Animals love me perhaps for that reason. They always know their place and where they stand with me. It comforts them. They have nothing to fear."

"Shades of Artemis, I think."

"Perhaps, but I'm no virgin goddess. Just the same, we do have some similarities. Let me continue. I wish to extend my thanks regarding my daughter. Bonnie has learned how to be herself for all the world to see. She is coming into her own, and I think I have you to thank for bringing her truly to my attention. You have a good eye for talent. She will do very well. I have said what I wanted to say. Now, come on…Not you," she said to me, "the dog."

"Oh," I said to no one in particular. She and Robert had already walked off.

I made my way toward the dining room alone. It would take a while to process what she'd told me. She was an extraordinary woman. Johnny and I needed some words. I hoped I was sitting next to him at lunch.

7 8

I walked into the dining room. The place setting at the head of the table was empty. Bruni was at the opposite end where Anne would sit. Someone had decided that she was lady of the house. I realized then that the chair at the head of the table was for me. Johnny was to my right, and Bonnie was to my left. Next to her sat Maw, with Robert under her chair. Hugo and Elsa sat together next to Maw. Anne and John Senior with Malcolm were on the other side. Everyone was looking at me expectantly.

I looked at all their smiling faces. There was a happiness and satisfaction there I never thought to see among such a diverse group of gifted individuals. I knew I was expected to say something.

"I would like to extend my thanks to each and every one of you, personally and all together. Without your presence and without your many talents, the future of this house and all its fascinations would be in doubt. Today, that is replaced by a brighter future. Speaking for the estate, I do not know the consequences of your contributions, but I suspect that your lives will be supported in unaccountable and unlooked-for ways. That thought gives me great pleasure. From myself, I extend to you an open invitation to Rhinebeck. You will always be welcome here, no matter the day or the hour. Thank you from the bottom of my heart."

There was a brief applause. I saw in their looks that I had gotten it right. They began to talk among themselves. Bruni looked at me from far down the table. I knew she wished we could sit together. I did too. I blew her a kiss in consolation. Her eyes sparkled in acknowledgment, and she blew one to me in return.

Bonnie was talking to Maw, so I turned to Johnny and said, "Johnny, you were extraordinary today. I might just do that little shrine thing after all. Maw was most impressed, and frankly, so was I."

"A small shrine might be appropriate. It was an outstanding performance even by my standards, I admit, and by way of commemoration of that brilliant moment, I'm accompanying you to California."

"Really?"

"Yes, really. Don't look so surprised. You need to get back here, and my presence will make sure it happens that much sooner. I will ensure your energies are directed with the appropriate vigor. Besides, you owe me 1 million."

"I do. I should have asked you first."

"No need. It was a foregone conclusion in my mind and a happy one at that. We are still owed another two from Pater. I will collect my share from him. You actually owe me nothing."

"You are the best of possible friends."

"I am, but it is to Robert the Bruce that you should be giving thanks. He closed the deal with Maw."

"I've been meaning to ask you about that. You sold Robert."

"I did. It was inspired. Best trade I ever made. We made millions. Besides, Robert and Maw is a match ordained by heaven.

It came to me like a bolt from the blue, sizzling with portent. I almost fell over when it struck me."

"Won't you miss him?"

"Are you kidding? He ran me into the ground. I'll finally get some peace. When I told Maw I would throw in the dog, it was like the woods began to sing. Everything smoothed out. It was child's play after that. I may sound flippant about that inspired moment, but I felt seized by something much larger than myself. The gods spoke through me at that instant. It was most unsettling but effective. I doubt I'll be the same after that. I shudder just thinking about it."

"You are full of surprises, Johnny Dodge."

We were interrupted by the arrival of three superb cheese soufflés. No wonder Dagmar wanted us seated on time. She was leaving nothing to chance, and her soufflés were perfect as a result. They were accompanied by a simple cold salad with a heavenly dressing of garden herbs, olive oil, and vinegar. The wine was the customary Sancerre.

Lunch moved along at a pleasant pace. I looked around me once again to ensure I wasn't seeing things, but everyone was smiling. It was a blessing. In addition, I could count each of them as friends worth knowing, even Malcolm Ault. His gift, it seemed, was always being present when significant events transpired. He had a knack.

As the meal wound down, Bruni eventually stood and asked that everyone pass through for coffee. Stanley must have spoken with her, because she announced that he would be bringing some of the pieces around for their inspection and that the guests' transportation would arrive starting at three thirty.

She came up to me and asked, "How did I do?"

"You're a natural. You belong here."

"Nicely put. I know that I'll love living here. Dagmar asked me to tell you that she's available now. Stanley gave me her message.

On another subject, we'll be parting soon. When will we see each other again and be back here?"

"Friday, I think. Johnny is accompanying me to California to speed things along. I wish to be back by Thursday. Sooner if I can. We can drive up Friday for the weekend and make some plans."

"That would suit me very well. I have a lot to do, but that's normal. For now, I will see to the ladies. John will see to the men. Tell me what Dagmar says."

With that, she kissed me, and I made my way to the kitchen.

79

D agmar was sitting down at her table with a cup of tea.
There was a glass of Stanley's finest whiskey in front of
an empty chair.

"May I join you?" I asked.

"Please. Thank you for sitting down with me. May I begin?"

"By all means."

She waited until I was seated and then folded her hands in front of her.

"Consider this to be our first meeting in our respective roles. What concerns me is our future. The world outside is changing. I sometimes wonder if we will simply disappear behind the fog and mists that surround us, becoming invisible to others, or endure a darker fate. What the future holds in this regard is closed to me. What is more certain is that to preserve us will take great skill. Assuming power is one thing. Keeping it — another. You've made a good start, and that is hopeful. Leaders serve those they lead, or they won't for long. It's best to be aware of that from the outset because it is a burden you must carry. Fail and you fail us all. It's the simple truth. In the end, nothing succeeds like success. Fail and nothing will be forgiven. There will be consequences. You should be aware of that.

"We stand at a crossroads. There will be no turning back.

"That being said, the future is brighter than it was. Your wife-to-be is a treasure. She will bring new life here. Stanley will be your friend and steward. He is a scholar and the keeper of ritual and ceremony. It's the performance of our rituals that acknowledges and strengthens the power here. You may want to know more. Stanley can direct you.

"I love my work, and it's a blessing to be able to practice my art. I express the oldest language in the world. With it, I create, sustain, or end life. I wish it would be forever, but that is not up to me. We each serve in our respective ways. Mine is as an intermediary. Yours will be to protect and preserve. How long we have here depends on all of us, but mostly, it will depend on you. It is a hard task but not without compensations. Do you have any questions?"

"I have always sensed a power in this place. Can you tell me more about it?"

"I can, but I won't. My knowledge is not mine to give. You must make your own discovery. Now, to the business at hand. The moment has come. Have you made your decision?"

Her bright eyes held mine. More was happening here than I understood. I would be entering into an agreement whose covenants extended far below the surface and out into a world beyond anything I knew existed. To succeed, I would have to trust in my abilities and in something else that was unknown and undefined. Perhaps it was simply the future. I would either embrace its promise, or I would not. All I knew was that I could not hide anymore. I had to make a stand and trust myself, something I had never done before.

"Dagmar, I accept my responsibility to all that is here. I will do my utmost best. If you have anything to say, anything you need, don't hesitate to tell me. Advise me as you see fit."

"I will. You are alone in this, but then, you are not. You have chosen, and I am satisfied. Drink half the glass, and I will drink the rest."

I drank. It tasted like Stanley's whiskey, although I could not tell for certain. She looked at me bright-eyed with what may have been a twinkle in them. I put it down. Her gaze never wavered as she picked up the glass, knocked it back like she'd been doing it all her life, and slammed it down on the table with a report like a pistol shot.

"It's done then, for better or for worse. Now, when might we expect you back?"

"Friday."

"It will be as you say. Now come here, give us a big hug, and then see to your guests. I'm happy this day has finally come."

80

They were all outside. The luggage had been stowed in the five cars that lined the driveway. The staff were outside too — even Dagmar. Johnny told me that was a first since Alice was in residence. It was time to say farewell. The guests had been saying goodbyes among themselves. I stood apart, as was my place.

The first off was Malcolm.

"Malcolm, it's been a pleasure to meet you. Give my regards and my many thanks to my father."

He smiled and said, "I will, but I would suggest a visit to see him and thank him personally. I would do it sooner rather than later, if I may be so bold to say. All in all, a happy time. It ended well, and I played my part. It was a weekend I doubt will have an equal any time soon. I'm off. You have my number. Call me, and I will see to the arrangements."

Next were the von Hofmanstals in the same outfits they arrived in. The baron in his cleaned coat looked me over and said, "I expect to see you in Austria or probably New York fairly soon.

Once Bruni gets her act in order, which I expect to be very rapidly, we'll see to the necessary arrangements for a more permanent union. Now, I hope you won't stick out a hand for me to shake. That won't do." Instead, he wrapped his arms around me like a bear and squeezed the breath out of me. "That's more like it. You will love my castle. Goodbye. Godspeed."

Elsa followed and gave me a more sedate hug. "I'll miss you. If you plan on any weekend parties, I insist on being invited. I wouldn't miss them for the world. I do love this place." She said as she looked around, "You never know what will happen next." She gave me a kiss on both cheeks and squeezed my hands.

Bruni was next. We had already had a private goodbye that had left me reeling. She slid into my arms and said, "I'll miss you." She whispered softly, "I'll restrain myself in the interests of propriety. I'd never leave otherwise." In a normal voice she said, "Call me when you land. I'll expect you Wednesday. I'll show you my place. You'll like it, but I have a feeling we'll be here more often than not. Love you." She disappeared into the car. I watched it drive off.

Maw and Bonnie were next, along with Robert the Bruce. He was not on a leash. I think he felt that with his new elevated status, it was beneath his dignity. Perhaps it was. I admired and complimented him on his good fortune.

Bonnie gave me a big hug. "Don't be a stranger. I had a long talk with Johnny. We made some plans. He will brief you on your way to California. I wish to thank you once again. I am not sure what all happened here, but something did, and I'm the better for it. I suppose it's a process rather than an event." She kissed me on the lips with a wink. "Just to let you know what you're missing. Some things are too good to resist. I apologize. Stay frosty."

She got in the car.

Maw was next. "I suppose I will have to as well. Come here." She hugged me.

"Mary, I think that was a first."

"It was, but you deserve it. I'll invite you round — you and your lady. I have horses aplenty, and of course Light Bulb will be there too, but then, he's not for everyone. Bonnie said she has some thoughts that she discussed with Johnny. Listen to him. Safe travels."

She got into her car. I noticed she needed no help, and Bonnie didn't offer any. They had definitely redefined their relationship.

Anne and John Senior were next.

Anne came first. "So, you have come into your own. John told me about your conversation. We — actually, I, because I insisted that I do it personally — will do my best to return the sum you forgave us. I have resources. It won't take long. You should see your mother. I know a lot has changed, but you should. She's an amazing person. She gave birth to you, after all. I know I didn't, but I have always looked on you as if I did. I hope you will forgive me. I still have work to do on forgiving myself, but your forgiveness will mean a lot to me."

"Anne, if you wish forgiveness, then I forgive you, but you will never need it from me. I'll always see you as my mother, just as I see Johnny as my brother. It may not be true, but it's true enough. So let's not hear any more about it. You owe me nothing. Neither you nor John, as far as the trust is concerned. I mean that. Of course, the odd contribution would not be turned away if you should feel so inclined. I just know that owing money between relations creates uneasiness when there should be nothing but goodwill."

"You're correct, but I will do what I can. I accept the spirit behind what you are saying."

"Very well, and you'll always have your room here."

"John told me. I must go before I start blubbering. Kiss. Kiss."

John followed. I hugged him and said, "It's been wonderful seeing you."

He stepped back. "Likewise. I will rustle up all the funds and see to the paperwork. It will all be available for signature by Friday. Anne and I are away after that for two weeks, but we'll be back in town. I'd like to see you then, if that's all right?"

"Of course. I'd like it very much."

"We're off then." He hugged me once more for a long moment. "Thank you, just thank you."

He got into the car. Raymond, Mr. Dodge's chauffeur, closed the door. Before he got in, he said, "Congratulations, kid. You done good. By the way, it was me who moved the curtain in the apartment. Stanley told me to tell you in case you wondered. I was doing the rounds. Later."

He got in, fired up the limo, and the car moved off.

It was just Johnny and me left.

I went down the line. Stanley was first. He said with a smile, "I don't expect a hug."

"Not on your life. It might shift the world off its axis. By the way, I had an interesting chat with Dagmar. I forgot to mention your contribution. Frankly, it blew right out of my mind when I talked to her along with everything else, but I'll mention it now. I'll be back Friday."

"Very good, sir. Do mention that point to her. I will have the apartment serviceable by the time you return. Call me, and I will make any arrangements you need. I act as your concierge, among other things."

"I will. You will have to educate me on how all this works, but between the two of us, we'll figure it out. Thank you, Stanley, for everything."

"Satisfaction is what I strive for. Have a safe trip."

I went farther down the line and thanked each of the staff one by one. Harry's handshake was like squeezing sandpaper. Dagmar was last. I gave her a hug, propriety or not.

"Thank you, Dagmar."

"Thank you, sir. Be back soon."

"I will." I then told her about Stanley's help earlier. She beamed. "He's a clever lad. I'll keep it in mind. He won't be in purgatory forever."

Johnny and I waved and got into our car. I looked out the back window as it moved up the drive. The mist had thickened. The house seemed to shimmer in and out of focus and then was lost to view, swallowed in a gray cloud as if it had never existed. I wondered if it had in fact disappeared. For a moment, I thought I heard someone calling out for me to come back, but when I turned around, all I saw once again was the road behind me fading into the mist as the car swished forward. I could have been mistaken. Johnny was saying something instead.

"I have a few relevant points we ought to discuss."

"Oh yes?" I asked, but I was quite sure it wasn't Johnny that I had heard.

Years later, I wondered about that moment. What if I had heeded the call and turned back?

Would the future have been different?

THE END

ACKNOWLEDGMENTS

Getting a book published and out to the general public is not a solitary activity. I had a great deal of help and support along the way. I would like to thank Mary Jo Smith-Obolensky for inspiring me, Tom Hyman, who offered encouragement and suggestions as my editor, Nick Thacker for his cover and book design, Joanna Cook for her oversight, and lastly, the many readers, who gave me vital feedback that made the book much better than it was originally.

www.ivanobolensky.com